MAJA KRIEL

Rings in a Tree

KWELA BOOKS

ACKNOWLEDGEMENTS

With deep gratitude to Helena Kriel, Lexy Kriel and Ross Kriel for the sustaining years. And to my husband and helpmate David Zeffertt. I would like to express my indebtedness to Annemarie van Niekerk for her encouragement and impeccable judgment, and my appreciation to Annari van der Merwe and Kwela Books for making it all possible.

Copyright © 2004 Maja Kriel
C/o Kwela Books
40 Heerengracht, Cape Town 8001;
P.O. Box 6525, Roggebaai 8012
http://www.kwela.com

All rights reserved.
No part of this book may be reproduced or transmitted in any form or by any electronic or mechanical means, including photocopying and recording, or by any other information storage or retrieval system, without written permission from the publisher.

Cover design by Alexander Kononov
Typography by Nazli Jacobs
Set in Goudy
Printed and bound by Paarl Print,
Oosterland Street, Paarl, South Africa

First edition, first printing 2004
ISBN 0-7957-0190-X

For Evan

ONE
The Market Place

"CHAVALA, CHAVALA, COME OUT AND PLAY."

Every day it is the same. The children stand outside her window and call. She pulls off her yellow apron, embroidered with white flowers, clean that morning but not for long, throws open the door and runs out with her hair flying behind her. Then they all race through the dry potato field, chasing crows and kicking up the dust. They pick up fist-sized clods and throw them into the air, catch and crumble them into powder. The red dust hovers over the ground like smoke, and the perfect furrows, worked and ready for planting, are broken by their footprints. They kick off their boots and tear off their stockings, running, circling, screaming through the wide space, feeling earth between their toes and cool air on their naked legs. Chava runs fast, picking up her skirt to stop it from tripping her feet, and Wlad must catch her before she reaches the tree, or else she is Queen and the others must serve and spoil her for the rest of the day, call her "ma'am" and say "your humble servant". She is an imperious and exacting queen, and must be stopped. Wlad tackles her and she falls while he laughs at her pale legs showing under her skirt, hidden from the light all winter and coming out, now, white as mushrooms after rain. Then all the children compare arms and legs, falling and rolling about with laughter, especially at the sight of Dahlia, whose legs and arms are white all over, beginning to spot with freckles and tender as the skin in a baby's armpits.

All the children play together in the Polish village of Sharabka even though, in a way that she does not understand, Chava's family is not quite the same as the families who stay in the stone houses on the landlord's estate. There are only thirty little wooden cottages like the one in which she lives. The synagogue and market are one hour away by cart.

This is a happy day, the end of winter and the melting snows of spring. Mosquito larvae are twitching in the bog. Today is longer than yesterday, shorter than tomorrow and the first time the children have taken off their boots in the warming earth. And even while they are laughing at Dahlia's white legs, her skin is beginning to burn as red as her flaming hair and eyebrows and eyelashes and the downy fluff on her arms. They will play and laugh through the summer days and dream lightly into the twilight nights with the sun balancing on the lip of the earth. "Chavala! Chavala! Come out and play." Catching warm milk squirts from cows' udders and stealing fruit from the landlord's orchard. The one-roomed school closes when the older children help with the harvest. They cover their heads with scarves and straw hats, but their faces still ripen like the brown cherries on the trees.

Chava will not be confined to the dark wooden cottage or to playing quiet games with her sisters Faiga and Gittel on the smooth paving stones outside the front door. Her older sister, Faiga, spending hours twisting strands of hair around her finger to make it fall in springy corkscrews on her shoulders, and her younger sister, Gittel, lining a box with old socks for her cat. Those are things to do around a fire at night!

Chava only has eyes for the plain opening wide in front of her, with the single tree, the Queen Tree, making a pool of shade in the heat, and the pathways that lead up the hills calling her. She knows every twist and turn in the track and every bulge and curve along the ridge against the white-blue skies. She can see Sleeping Beauty with her hands folded across her chest for all time and covered with a white blanket in winter, and she can see frog and mushroom and camel's hump – a profile forever. She never tires of climbing those steep pathways, plodding up a foot at a time and running down breathless with great leaps. Once, as she thundered downhill, a snake slipped away from just under her feet and turned back to look at her with a gaping mouth and an evil eye. They watched each other in fear for a long time, eye fixed on dilated eye and afraid to move, until it slithered away into the bushes. Did it curse her with those eyes? And there are wolves that howl with hunger in winter and bats and owls and red foxes that steal chickens at night and frogs and newts that breed in the brack marshes of those hills, and once she saw a small buck with a bushy white tail.

She and her friends disappear with the cows early in the morning, driving them from behind with sticks and prodding the sharp bones on either side of their tails. The sticks make dull sounds as they bounce off the tightly drawn skin, and the cows skip ahead for a few paces and then lapse into the same slow rhythm again. The children move steadily across the plain, side-stepping rippled dung cakes and plunging through puddles, allowing the brown water to drench their clothes. Chava loves the feeling of heaviness around her ankles as the muddied skirt beats against her boots. When the mud dries into fine dust she will shake off her skirt and wear it again the next day. Her mother dresses her in rough brown cloth and brown socks, no longer even trying to control her nature, changing only the apron every day.

It takes them an hour to reach the rocky stream where there is water and thick grass mixed with little yellow flowers for the cows, and shade where the animals stand and chew and swallow and chew again all afternoon. The children spend the day searching for crabs and coloured stones, filling their pockets with pebbles and snail shells, washing their feet in the icy water and making little straw fires. Sometimes Wlad makes a pipe from a hollow bone, stuffing it with smoky grass. He breathes in slowly and breathes out with the pipe gripped between his teeth, then passes it to Chava who coughs and laughs with the first inhalation. They lie back against a stone, blowing smoke into patterns and watching the clouds melt and merge, making giant shadows that glide slowly across the plain.

"Teach me to whistle," says Chava. And then she cannot purse her lips to make the sound because her mouth is wide open with laughing and Wlad is prodding her ticklish ribs with his finger as she rolls in shrieking agony over and over the blue-green moss.

They lie quietly again, cushioned by leaves and eating the sweet white centres of the grass. It is all grass now, in summer; the pull of bovine tongues around it and the rhythmical grind of molars as cows move like slow dreadnoughts through flossy stamens or stand rump-high in grassy shafts that flick like tails or fly like flags. And ferns and reeds and clover and bulrushes that grow in colonies around stones in the stream and then explode into sneezy fluff or itchy powder. They know a dozen tricks with daisy chains, forget-me-nots and buttercups; forever grass and speckled meadows and green and gold all over.

They eat sour black bread with cheese and cucumbers and drink sweet water from the stream, feeding the crabs with crumbs to watch them scuttle sideways and nibble with trembling mandibles. The day is too short. They have just found a glory hole of coloured stones, emeralds and rubies and the smoothest granite with shards of gold. A queen's dowry, a pirate's ransom, but Chava only wants the plain white stone shaped into a perfect heart. The others are fighting for possession of a rare black opal with spangles of red and green when they hold it to the light and nuggets of purest crystal, diamonds, surely, of priceless value. But now they must go back. They know the time from the long shadows and when the cows lie down with billowing udders resting between their legs. The wind is coming up, making thin ripples across the stream and they begin to walk home, smelling of animal musk, grassy smoke and wild rosemary.

They always go back through the pine forest, collecting gum from the trees and pine nuts from ripened cones. If they stand very quietly the squirrels come out. Once Chava sees a small grey owl clinging like an outgrowth of fungus on a branch. The forest is a wild place which harbours feral cats and rabbits and white ermine in winter. A secret place for night-time troglodytes that live in hidden holes, and every stone conceals a cave. They do not talk when they walk among the trees because it is dark and silent, inhabited by elves and enchanted spirits. Their hearts beat as birdcalls break the silence. The first one to utter a word will be doomed to slavery in a wizard's castle. They always pass the stone convent and listen for the sounds of women's voices behind the wall. Once as they hid behind the trees they watched a young girl in ordinary clothes enter through the steel gates, and Dahlia swears she saw the smallest flicker of a white starched skirt as the railing swung open. Sometimes they see deliveries of bread and vegetables, but no one from the village has been inside the walls except a frost-bitten trapper who died there and the doctor who is sometimes called but never speaks about what he sees. Once he brought a little baby back to the village, but people said that it was thin and yellow and it died within a week and was buried outside consecrated ground. If they are there on the hour, they hear the bell ring through the forest, metallic and echoing like the sound of a dread prophecy, or a warning, or a death and the birds flutter out of the trees into the light, beating their wings against the branches. The children run away until they reach the other side where the spell is broken by the sun and they can talk and laugh again, pushing and teasing as they run back to the village with the cows dripping milk from their udders.

When Chava gets home she steps out of her skirt and pulls off her boots, leaving everything in a reeking heap next to the front door, to shake out and wear again tomorrow.

At night, as they sit near the stove, her mother opens out Chava's plaits to brush out the sticks and grass. One side first and then the other because her hair is thick and wavy. Chava feels a writhing impatience, suffocation in being captured by her mother – caught and forced into the slow ritual, her mother's pride – and when she has finished the rhythmic grooming, brushing out every little snag, the waves shine in the firelight. She spits on her fingers to rub two little curls from the loose ends next to Chava's ears.

"Just like a Kirghiz," she says as she draws her finger along Chava's nose and wide cheekbones.

Her mother knows that the other Jewish families gossip that Chava's rough nature and her closeness to the Christian children cannot be an accident. She was born nine months after the soldiers ransacked the village. She is not like her sister Faiga, who curls her long red hair and embroiders white tablecloths and napkins and then folds them carefully to store away, perfumed with lavender, in the deep wooden chest of her trousseau. Faiga has slowly decorated white sheets with chains of pink roses and made pillowcases to match, edged in the slightest lace. She is very quiet when she is sewing near the stove at night. She is always quiet, but her eyes are full of secrets. And Chava is not like Gittel, who hatches birds' eggs in her breast and carries orphaned chicks in her apron pocket. Gittel cries softly and wrings her hands when the cow gives birth, and walks in the house with the cat lying across her shoulders, its thick tail wrapped around her neck like a sable collar.

Chava is always restless indoors. At school there is something elastic and jumpy inside her which resists the authority of the alphabet and the strictness of making disciplined figures along straight lines. It is torture to sit still on those wooden benches. Faiga's writing is as measured as her embroidered roses and the pages of her books are as orderly as the folded sheets of her trousseau. But for Chava the stories printed on paper are dull compared to the potato field in summer, and skipping flat stones across the stream, and running screaming on the open plain with shining eyes, or in winter rubbing snow on her cheeks until they bleed.

High summer now, and the world has turned edible: branches are breaking with the weight of apples, and plums burst their skins, bleeding juice in an excess of growth. Strawberries and mushrooms erupt through the grass, and hedges and fields are spotted with raspberries and red currants. The storks have returned to their shaggy nests on the rooftops and migrating swallows feed on midges and mosquitoes that swarm like dense pockets of mist in the humid air. Every day the women work in the orchard from first light until sunset. Baskets are full, cherries are crushed under foot and the trees spill their fruit recklessly until they are bare. The labourers on the landlord's estate load the carts for market, eating and spitting out the small stones when the overseer's back is turned. Everyone is working and money changes hands. They steal moments of rest when the overseer is not looking and then quickly bend their backs over baskets when he turns around to watch. But an army of workers cannot meet the abundance of the trees.

"This summer we'll have money," Chava's mother says, watching her husband load the cart. "I have to repair the roof before winter, and Chava can't go on wearing Faiga's old clothes and the same brown skirt every day. And I owe the doctor some money for Gittel. Next time he won't come if we don't pay him soon. This summer we'll make money and spend it. A party, a dinner with stuffed goose and honey cake, music and presents, we'll all dance. There must be money for fun and spending."

Mordechai Schneider rubs his thumb along the skin of a cherry and bites into the plumpness to test the flavour. "I must take them early tomorrow." His lips are purple with pigment. "They are feeding them to the pigs, they are rotting on the ground, I have to sell twice as much to make the same money."

Always taking pleasure in his face, his wife looks at him, wondering how it felt to be under the skin of it: the moulded sockets of his eyes with the fine shadow in the fold, delicately lidded. He is looking up, stroking his beard, enjoying its thickness, the same denseness and chestnut colour as Chava's hair. He is her father, it is in her hair, despite the village gossip: the same ripple of highlights, the same coarse waves. Mrs Schneider looks into his eyes, green facets when the light strikes them; honest, gentle. He is sorry, pleading with his eyes. But stubbornly unchanging. Cruel! Sometimes she hates that face. Something like a muscle inside her goes limp. Her shoulders slump.

"Last summer we lost money because the crop was bad and I understood it. The year before we had hail. The year before that it was a warm winter and a late frost. But this summer we are losing money because the harvest is good. I don't understand. Not too much sun, not too much rain. Once in four years the cherries are magnificent. This is our year. But you will always have a reason. Must I accept this for a lifetime? We will never have money."

Once a month Chava goes with her father to market. The air is cool and dark in the morning and Chava wraps her best yellow scarf over her shoulders. She splashes her face with water and quickly smoothes her hair. This is a day for wearing a clean skirt and polished boots. She sits straight-backed and quiet next to her father in the cart. Everyone in Sharabka is still sleeping and only the chickens are awake and scratching for food. She thinks of Wlad lying in bed with soil wedged under his nails, while she is dressed, clean and ready for the world of buying and selling in Lodz. The sky is black but a vast light is scorching the edge of the earth, dimming the morning star which is fading into the retreating universe. Watching and watching to see its actual extinction. Squeezing her eyes to hold on to it. It is still there. Or is it just the memory of its existence in the sky? Now it is gone.

She loves being alone with her father on the flat road to Lodz, head and shoulders in the cool air and a blanket over her legs; moving along the road with the dull thud of the horse's hoofs like a drum beating, and then the joining up with other carts from small sand tracks, carrying farm produce to the same centre. Her mother says it is not a place for girls: men fight there and women swear and chickens are slaughtered and money is counted and recounted and always changing pockets. Not like at home, where money is something her mother talks and cries about like an illness, but she doesn't know the weight of it in her hand.

Chava knows they are nearly there when they see the pine trees on the horizon. They grow in a circle around the town to shield it from the winter winds which blow across the plain. Then the town arises suddenly, as though a giant hand has scooped all the trees and houses into one pile. It is a great place. The streets are cobbled with smooth stones and the houses have tiled roofs. Not like the bushy straw that covers her own cottage, constantly threatening to burn down from sparks which fly out of the chimney. But she loves watching the smoke rise from the fireplace, and slowly filter through the straw. And waiting for the storks to make twiggy nests there in spring and the sounds of their chicks mewing through the thatch as she lies in bed at night. The grassy smell when it rains, and its dark coolness in summer.

It is a wonderful thing to be a traveller on a road and to enter far-away places that are just waking up from the night. She has been sitting wide awake on the cart with her father for hours, while here in Lodz the women, still confused and dull, are opening the shutters for the first morning air or shuffling their feet slowly to the well for water. Why does it take people such a long time to wake up, yawning and coughing from the night? Her mother always looks grey and creased as though she has been working in her sleep. Chava just opens her eyes and stands up.

Schneider lets the reins go slack as the horse follows the other carts across a wooden bridge and into the open market square. The bridge shudders. Already dozens of wagons have taken up their positions according to their produce. Chava recognises the square like a familiar map with everything in its right place. They always enter through the clothing section, passing the same racks of men's suits and coats protected by canvas awnings or large umbrellas. She wonders if anyone ever sells anything. The same barrows are piled high with tangled scarves and petticoats. Wicker baskets stand on the ground with heaps of second-hand shoes or oddments of hand-made lace. Always the same women bent over and stirring the pot as though mixing large vats of stew.

Once she went with her father to buy a tweed cap, helping him to choose from six different baskets. She watched while he tried them on for size, pulling the peak down over his right eye and arching one eyebrow in front of the mirror. Stroking his beard, always stroking his beard. It helps him to make up his mind. He let her choose a scarf, yellow, her favourite colour, which she tied around her neck. Then they went to the photographer next door. Her father stood next to a cardboard palm tree and she stood on a stiff wooden chair next to him so that her head would nearly reach his shoulder. When the photo was printed it came out with chains of flowers around them and a bird flying over her head with a ribbon. She laughed at her father standing next to the palm tree, wearing his cap with a strange fixed stare. And Wlad laughed until he cried when she showed him the picture: the crooked smile on her face, one eye closed and the bird flying. A freak etched on paper for her whole life. He imitated the smile, nearly falling over with laughter, pulling his lips sideways with his fingers and closing one eye to torture her. Wlad has told her that when she smiles she has quite a pretty face. Is that picture what she really looks like?

Schneider drives past the double-storey houses surrounding the square like a wall, and guides his cart into the produce section. He takes up his usual place outside the saddle store. His cherries are crowded in by apples with stalks and leaves only torn off yesterday, watermelons spliced open like red meat, and baskets of blueberries. Wagon-loads of tomatoes are built into pyramids and radishes and spring onions are scrubbed and tied into fat bunches. Schneider buys two ice-cold ladles of sour milk for their breakfast and two twisted bagels studded with crystals of salt.

He always gives her a few coppers to buy sunflower seeds, which are weighed on a scale and wrapped into a small paper cone. She walks among the horses and carts splitting the salty shells open like a parrot and spitting out the chaff, she has a real talent, until the little cone is empty and the tip of her tongue is raw and swollen.

She is slowly making her way to the gypsy wagon near the river. Her father has told her not to go alone to the gypsies because they kidnap children. But she is not afraid. She stands back, watching the caravan from a distance. She can stand the whole morning watching them: their dark skins and black hair tied back with scarves, red or yellow like hers, the sound of steel against steel as the sharpened knives slide off the flint. A man shocks the crowd by drawing blood to show the sharpness of the cutting edge. Wlad has told her that a gypsy blacksmith made the fourth nail for the crucifixion of Christ. She wonders what makes them different from the milk-skinned Poles or the bearded Jews who fear the sight of blood and run away from it. What are the secrets of the ooze that drips from the purple cut on his arm? Is there something inside it that makes music and madness and knows the riddles of life? Or are all the mysteries hidden in his black eyes? She envies them their private language and the separateness of their lives in the steamy wagon-tent. She wants to be with them, learn the power of numbers, the prophecies of the pictures in the cards, know the secrets of people's lives from the lines in their hands, cast spells, make magic and have gold in her teeth and rings in her ears. To swallow fire and juggle knives. This is the knowledge she wants.

Sometimes the Tartars come to market selling skins and furs from the mountains. She loves their swaggering walk and the rancid smell of leather and lamb's fat that surrounds them. She watches them tear off pieces of dried salted meat with yellowing teeth and feed wedges of tomato into their mouths with the tip of their curved knives. She looks at her own face in the window glass and pulls back the skin of her eyes to make them slanted.

"Chavala, Chavala, come out and play."

She goes with the other children to the bridge near the market. They watch the gypsy women doing their washing in the stream and they help to water their horses. She walks along the muddy banks with the hem of her clean skirt trailing in the water and her polished boots sinking into the thick silt. She digs her fingers into the mud and rubs it roughly against the skin of her face, washing it off with the cold water until her face shines. She kneels down where the horses are drinking and puts her mouth in the water next to theirs, swallowing with panting gulps while her hair floats with the current in the stream. Then she is a Tartar and wraps her yellow scarf around her head making a turban and swaggers down the cobbled market street with the other children swaggering with her.

They all sit under a tree and share out their own special hoard of roasted chestnuts, hard-boiled eggs, gooseberries and poppy-seed cakes. Chava takes a small pocketknife to sharpen against a stone as she saw the gypsies do, then rubs her thumb against the blade to feel its edge. She performs for her audience; perhaps she is a Jew after all, as she cannot get herself to draw blood from her arm. She slices open the oval of the egg, skewers the yellow centre and puts the segment into her mouth, closing her teeth against the steel as she slowly withdraws the shaft. The other children watch with admiration and repeat the trick with slices of chestnut and piercing bright green gooseberries, without shedding a drop of juice. The knife is passed around the ceremonial circle like a ritual instrument until Ivan performs the feat with his eyes blindfolded. Gregory stands up – he can only do one trick: he dares them to walk on their hands while clicking their feet, and then Agata begs Sophia to teach her to do backbends and cartwheels.

The stream of traffic into the market is slowly beginning to reverse itself, with empty carts leaving for their villages and farms. Schneider is waiting for his daughter. It is Friday and he must be home before the first star comes out. He is feeling satisfied with himself, sold everything, and he has bought his wife a piece of black lace. Tonight she will set the table with silver candlesticks and an embroidered cloth and when he opens the door he will get the spicy smell of meat and potatoes and beans that have baked slowly in the oven all afternoon. Friday night, and there will be a special pleasantness and comfort in the house. The Book says the world changes from the profane to the sacred. That means all the fighting will be forgotten.

The cart is empty. Chava feels its lightness as it bounces on the road behind her. She is also excited about the piece of black lace they are taking home. She wants to throw open the door and see her mother's face. And she has some pretty coloured stones in her pocket to show Wlad. But as she sits in the cart with the horse's hoofs beating dully on the sandy road, her yellow scarf floating behind her, her mind is full of pictures of bright steel and sparks and dark blood on a gypsy's arm. She rubs her new stone, her best stone, shaped into a perfect heart. A secret stone or it loses its magic. She closes her eyes and rubs it for Mama and Papa and Faiga and Gittel and the cats and the cow. And she rubs it again for herself and for Wlad, holding it tightly in her hand under a darkening sky.

TWO
A World In A Corner

CHAVA AND GITTEL ARE ALREADY SLEEPING, BUT FAIGA IS ALWAYS THE LAST one to close her eyes, letting all the images of the day fill her mind; that poem: "But the sweet kiss of our meeting – I wait for it." The words saturate her senses like music, this Sabbath, with the window open and the light of the moon on her skin. A particular sweetness, this Friday night, when Papa spread the new black lace on Mother's shoulders. It was the first time she looked beautiful. A radiance on her face for a moment and everyone felt the rapture of it. Then she took off the lace and went back to work.

No matter how early they begin in the morning, they rush to have dinner ready before the sun goes down. "Ten minutes to candle-lighting time," calls Mordechai Schneider, like the timekeeper of a race. Then they run from room to room to be ready, always having to call Chava inside quickly to change her clothes, and shouting at Gittel to wash her hands after playing with the cats. A race against the clock. The bread is not ready and Chava is always late, always, and the cats are always under their feet as they run from place to place – and then – suddenly it is silent as Mama stands in front of the candles, opening her arms to draw the holiness of the night into herself, and prays. Sacred time. After that it is all slow and quiet. They bless the fruit of the vine and break the bread, still hot from the oven. Friday night, lazy and a little drunk as they sip the sweet wine and eat: carp or roast chicken and potatoes baked slowly in its own juices. The air is warm with the smell, fragrant and spicy, and the silver and glass on the table reflect the candlelight. Mama, leaning back against the chair, is wearing her black lace. When she is quiet the whole house is quiet and when she is shouting even the cats hide away. Friday is the only night that she leaves the table untidy, and she and Papa go to bed arm in arm. The pleasure of an untidy house with the litter of dinner left where it was discarded: breadcrumbs on the tablecloth, uneaten potatoes on the plate, a crust of bread on the floor. The luxury of leaving everything where it is, the surfeit of good food. Chava lies stretched out on the floor holding her stomach, she nearly fell off her chair because she had eaten too much, and Faiga is sitting on a cushion next to the fire, feeling Mama's black lace with her fingers. She drapes it over her head: "Like a Madonna," she says quietly. "Don't let Mama hear you," says Gittel, looking at the door.

The room is full of shifting shadows and waving lights. Once Chava saw a flickering devil that changed into a water-carrier, and Gittel saw, for an instant on the wall, a violinist that flickered into an upside-down cow. Gittel slumps forward with her head on the table, her eyes open but seeing nothing, and slowly the lids close. Chava tries to stand up, losing her balance, and then she and Gittel, supporting each other, totter to bed. Every person, they say, has an extra soul on the Sabbath and must rest.

Faiga loves the quiet time at night with sounds of breathing all around her and the heat of the fire burnt down to its last residual glow. Only the candle still flutters against the wall. A little draught blows through a space between the wooden slats, pushing the velvety flame to one side. It is a trembling presence in the room. Something in its nature aspires to the upright, wanting to correct its obliqueness and pull back to the centre where it burns pure blue and vertical. But the draught blows it over again where the fire spills out. What appetite is in that yellow fire that twists and wrestles with its hunger but comes back to its own blue heart again? And what inner defect makes it burn down voraciously through its core, hissing like a snake? She must take her eyes away from the fire or it will make her mad.

She leaves the room, trying to find the shape of known things around her. Slowly the outlines emerge in the bedroom – three beds and a chair next to each, a chest, a table and a small cupboard for their clothes. She knows every board of wood in this room: the crooked window-sill with paper stuffed into a gap, the knotted floorboards under the table which make one leg higher than the others and the pieces of folded paper stuck under the short ones, and the loose board in front of the doorway which creaks every time someone leaves or enters. She knows every sinew, curling hard and resistant with age: the grain in the wood on the opposite wall. Sometimes, as she lies in bed, it looks like ripples in the sand, and other times like a face puckered with pain; the tangle of fibres, a flaw, an injury, that has nowhere to grow but into its own dark centre. It traps her eyes with familiarity. Ordinary things seem altered and unstable in a world blacked out at night, inhabited by creatures dreaming of other lives.

She cannot breathe in the room that she must share with her sisters. Gittel's cats lick their paws through the night and pace the room silently. Sometimes they hunt fieldmice or wail on a wall until morning. Chava's boots under her bed smell of three generations of feet that have worn them and no air comes through the small window that was only intended for long cold nights. Nothing changes. The sameness rubs against her like a rasp.

She wants to run outside into the autumn night, to call him with her whole body like a prayer. He has never touched her except at school when he stood too near her table, bending low to examine her books, accidentally touching her hand. And why did he ask her, once, to stay late to help him? And the gentle teasing when she comes late for class, when anyone else would be punished. Surely it is true that when he reads Pushkin he looks at her more than the others: "Your beauty, your sufferings have vanished in the grave. But the sweet kiss of our meeting – I wait for it; you owe it to me." She watches him as he paces the aisles reading, and when he looks at her, the dark centres of his eyes grow wide.

There is something inside her, like the yellow flame, which has a nature of its own. It wrestles inside its own skin, always reaching for an object outside. But her feelings will not be snuffed out with a pinch.

"Come, Janusch. Come."

Chava takes off her shoes and shuffles into bed fully dressed, lying next to the window. It is the fire that makes her tired, the heat and smoke and ceaseless flickerings on the walls. Too much food on Friday night and the sweet wine that sedates her like a drug. If she has an extra soul tonight it will have to contend with indigestion, the fullness in her stomach and a giddy head.

Suddenly awake, she lies very still and listening to the night-hawk calling from the trees, a sharp descending wail: tche-u-u-u-tche-u-u-u. She can trace its flight from the cry, piercingly near her window on the pine tree and then further and further away like an echo from the wheatfield. Now lethal as it swoops onto the mice hiding in the haystacks. Once by clear moonlight she saw it drop at terrific speed onto its prey. Then it ascended into the darkness with outstretched wings like the angel of death, vanishing with a small thing held in its claws.

She is too tired to sleep and little cramps twist the muscles in her legs.

The lazy careless time for watching the wheat grow is over – all week she has been working. First the men move in a long arc across the field as though they are hunting foxes, their backs bent and summer flies stinging their skin. They cut into the living wheat with curved scythes and leave the yellow stuff limp and tangled on its side. Then the women follow behind raking the stalks into sheaves and exposing the stubble, ragged and angry underfoot. The breeding quail and grouse and brown hare take flight, and the cows move into the fields to graze the remnants. Everyone is working continuously, only stopping for bread and milk in the middle of the day, going on through long afternoons which turn into luminous evenings, and hoping for moonlight so they can continue into the night. They have left the wheat to ripen slowly under the baking sun. With every day it gets dryer and sweeter, but once it is cut the race is on to store it before it rains.

Deep summer falling into autumn and she is astonished at the fullness of the fields; the wheat swelling like the brooding deep as the wind breathes life into it. When the children run through it, it closes over their heads and you can only see them by the ripple through the tufts. She wades waist-high in it, her skirt knotted in its thickness and crickets leaping in the wake. A rich fatness covers the earth. Then when it is cut the world is lean and spare again, all lines and planes and angles, covered by a flat blue sky.

She feels quite proud of her strength in pitching the fork. She digs deep into the sheathes and lifts them with one sweep onto the cart. As the load gets higher she swings wider and wider with her arms, and the boy in the cart jumps on the wheat to push it down. Her neck is long and sinewy and her arms are growing hard under her blouse.

"Feel," she says as she rolls up her sleeve and flexes her muscles.

"We'll put you in harness to pull the wagon," says Wlad, "and retire the horse." Then she stuffs a bunch of wheat down his shirt and pushes him onto the ground.

"Apologise, apologise," she demands as she sits on him and pins him down on the scratchy stubble. Then she lies over him, covers him, and they are spread-eagled like a star.

At night her hair and her skirt are stuck with stalks like Faiga's pincushion. Her mother looks at her. Chava knows that look. She sees too much with her eyes, enlarged and dilated like an owl when she wears her glasses. Her eyes allow no secrets. Sometimes she even looks into Faiga's drawers. Is she going to say something or is she going to keep quiet, thinking her own thoughts, and carry on around the house?

"What is the matter with you, always outside? Don't you live in a house anymore? Your skin is as dark as a sailor's and look at your hair. You and your farm boy, like two animals living in the field. Why is your father working and why am I saving? Don't you want a better life than mine in this village?"

And now Chava is lying awake in her bed, listening to the night-hawk wail in the trees. How can she have a better life than working in the wheatfield with Wlad? Kneading her hands deep into his back to take away his stiffness from bending over the wheat, or feeling his skin under her fingers and pressing into the smooth curve along his spine, lying with him in the long autumn grass and finding quails' nests hidden deep in the stubble and giving the chicks to Gittel to feed and release into the trees. Mama is always speaking about her life as if she can make it, like making a dress, add a frill or take away a pocket; or as though it is a possession that can be pawned for something nicer.

She is suddenly afraid of the darkness and the things outside of the window that crawl and fly with the collusion of the night: the adder of the wheatfield and the black spider with a red hourglass on its belly that lives and lays eggs in the thatch. What will happen to her family in Sharabka? And what will happen to her? She often sees her mother with an anxious look on her face but Chava has never been worried about her life before. And Gittel? Small and pale, only eating buttermilk and beans and bread because she says that she will not eat the cow's meat: "I call them each by name and they come. And how can I eat the chickens that peck food from my hand? They know my face. And sometimes when we break the eggs there are streaks of blood in it." The bones in her legs are soft, bending outwards, and Mama saves the cream from the milk for her to drink.

Tonight for the first time in years Chava remembers the little baby who cried weakly during the night. They only named him to bury him in the small Jewish graveyard on the other side of the trees. And after that, she remembers, Mama went to bed for a long time. Even now she goes to bed for six days of every month, day after day, and her face becomes very white. And there is only Papa who goes out to work. Chava has heard them speak quietly about leaving Sharabka because it is safer to live in Warsaw with other Jews.

How could they desert the cow and the birds that wait for Gittel to feed them every morning and night? And abandon the house where she and Gittel and Faiga were born, where every mark on the wall has meaning and every object has its own place? Grandfather's army cap decorated with gold braid in the special drawer with photographs. The ball of string that Mama saves for roasting chickens. The little silver ballerina with a marquisette eye that stands on Mama's bedroom table. The model of the Ten Commandments that leans on the kitchen shelf next to the frying pan – always falling down and put back in the same place. Sometimes she feels as though the house has too much history: the empty space under the bench where the old dog used to lie, and the dark passage where she used to trip over him at night. She feels oppressed by it. Always to see the Ten Commandments on the kitchen shelf and to know the dull metallic sound when it falls. Sometimes she wants to smash it like Moses. But always picking it up.

How long must she lie in her bed in the dark? When will it be day, with children playing outside and the cow softly moaning to be milked? What will happen to Wlad? And what will happen to her sister standing at the window with her smooth white arms held around her body, rocking forward and back, silently praying into the night?

Gittel is breathing heavily in her corner of the room. Her back is supported with three cushions to keep her upright while she sleeps. She has become used to sleeping in that position and she is surprised when Chava says to her: "You were restless last night, moving and coughing in your sleep."

"But I was dreaming that the cow was eating lilac flowers, and when I woke up I was in the same position that I went to sleep in, and still holding my handkerchief in my right hand."

She lies with her legs in front of her, making a little nest for the cat who had kittens on her bed two weeks before. When she turns onto her side, the cat moves into the hollow made by her thighs and buttocks. The kittens mew feebly through the night, and the blanket is beginning to smell from the sticky fluids that came out with the birth.

"Take the cat off your bed," her mother begs her. "You'll get sick. It's disgusting."

But Gittel will not allow the little den to be moved. So Faiga and Chava have to sleep facing away from her bed, covering their noses with napkins smelling of lavender. And tonight the cat has brought a rat inside from the night, and lies licking and gnawing somewhere in the darkness of the room. Even Gittel cannot touch her when she is eating a rat.

Faiga goes back to her bed and lies with her eyes open for a long time. It is impossible to sleep in the late summer. The nights are hot and short and the sky pulses with Arctic lights.

Slowly they fall into a deep sleep in the room they have shared since early childhood, each occupying a world in a corner with a bed and a chair.

THREE
Looking Back

THE DAYS ARE LIKE THE SEASONS IN SHARABKA, FINELY POISED BETWEEN two poles: tilting towards the light or tilting towards the dark. Daytime is active and optimistic and the anxiety of the night melts away in a world warmed by the sun.

The morning current grips Chava and pulls her through the door. When she opens the gate the world appears in front of her, a wide place waiting for her imprint on its emptiness. She knows it is spring from the soft air on her skin and the screeching beetles in boggy holes that are suddenly quiet when she stands near them and then screech again when she has gone, and the small yellow flowers that grow through the grass. And the grass and the grass and the grass. She wants to lie in its softness and look up at the arching sky, translucent with its delicate daytime moon.

Then she strides out towards the plain, walking with strong legs, lifting her face to the cool air all around. As she walks past the safety of the Queen Tree she sees herself, a single figure walking alone across the wide surface of the uninhabited earth.

She tells herself that she is not allowed to desire anything or anyone that she has left behind, and like Lot's wife, she is forbidden to look back. Her whole life has been encircled by her footsteps, around and around like a track that leaves and returns to the same place. All memory is contained within the links of those steps, imprinted with her own special pattern that could never belong to anyone else. Why was Lot's wife cursed for looking back a last time to everything she loved?

When the tide is full and strong in her, spring tide, then Chava will walk far across the spongy plain without looking back, facing the horizon in front of her, her footsteps filling up with water from the wetness of the melting snow.

Once she and Wlad had climbed up the hill on the other side of the plain – the distant hill that looks like the saddle on a horse's back. She told Wlad that she was forbidden to stop or look back until she reached the top or she would be turned to stone. She fixed her eyes steadily ahead, but wanted to stop, to catch her breath and turn around to see where she had come from, how far away she had moved. They had gone on, snaking their way upwards on a long zigzag path, placing one muddy boot in front of the other, the zigzags getting steeper, until they came to the top where they could sit on the saddle and see the valley on the other side: the convent with the forest around it and the small cemetery. She could see the whole known world, everyone and everything in it, where they were going and where they had been. All at the same time: the men coming home for lunch and the smoke curling through the chimney from where the food was cooking, and the half-ploughed field behind them with the horse turned loose to graze. A map of their lives, past, present and future, and she could see it all, even the glint of the butcher's knife in the slaughtering yard while the chickens were still pecking in the soil. When she looked up she could see the high hill above them, the one that looked like a monster, half-man half-animal crouching on his hind legs like a lion. And over that the cloud hanging low and turgid like milk curdling around it, that could suddenly begin to churn like milk in a pot, boil over and over without stopping, and a terrible wind could begin to blow. Spring could be a fierce time if it was too early and too hot and the melting snows would suddenly ravage the hills and flood the little streams into uncontrollable torrents. Once a young man on a horse was swept away trying to cross a surging current. And they always had to watch that treacherous cloud on the monster's head. It was Sharabka's god of weather.

They had sat across the saddle of the hill eating bread and cheese, looking down on the fallow field of the next valley: the crows pecking in the crumbly soil and a small dog chasing them to the other side, letting them settle and chasing them again. They could hear the delayed, far-away clap of his bark. Wlad lay down, putting his head on her lap. Her fingers combed through his hair, stretching out the waves and feeling them recoil again under her fingers. The more she stretched them the tighter they sprang back. She bent down to his cheek and felt his breath against her face. They watched the crows circling in the air above the field, gliding down, scattering, drifting. And above them the cloud hung like a frilly collar around the monster's neck.

"What would happen, Wladimir, if you were behind me and I was forbidden to turn around and see you? I would only have the memory of you in the deep well of my mind. I would never again have the feeling of my fingers in your hair or your breath on my face. Why did your mother call you Wladimir? Did she want you to be a student in Warsaw?" And Chava took a piece of grass and tickled his ear until he scratched it and tickled his nose until he sneezed, tormenting him with the grass as they laughed and laughed.

When they faced the other way they could watch their own village, Sharabka, and the landlord's estate with the orchards and stables lying like a little settlement of dwarfs. She could blot it all out with the palm of her hand: the manor-house where each person had a bedroom that could sleep twenty people, and the reception rooms that could contain her whole house twice over – she had peeped through the windows once, without being seen. And all the small outhouses that served it, clustering around it at the back like an outgrowth of cells. Wlad was pointing to his own cottage near the gate. But his mother would be in the manor-house making bread or polishing pots. Sometimes she brought home pocketfuls of potatoes or turnips. Once she had hidden a bunch of raisins under her apron after a party, and she had been allowed to take some leftover soup meat and some buckwheat pancakes.

Everything looked harmless and quiet, with single figures in the road and cows eating dry stalks in the fields. She could see only the roof of her house behind the tree, but Mama would be in the kitchen wiping and cleaning, or sweeping the floor. It was always the last thing that Chava would hear in the night: the brushing of the straw broom on the floor. "No one can sweep it like I can," Mama would say, and after that no one was allowed to eat anything in the kitchen. "I don't want to see crumbs in the kitchen. Not even one." But sometimes Papa would go and eat something in the night and his sins would be discovered in the morning. Mama could reconstruct everything he did from the clues he left behind: a buttered knife on the table, a crust of bread on the floor, ants around a drop of jam. Mama would wipe it up muttering to herself. Perhaps Faiga would be in the bedroom writing in her book and then hiding it away. She always changed the hiding-place. Once Chava had seen it under the blanket, wanting to look inside. She had opened it with a beating heart, irresistibly, trying to make sense of the small print, as small as the stitches in Faiga's embroidered tablecloths. She saw something that made her gasp; a small drawing of the feared symbol and the naked, suffering figure impaled on it. She closed the book immediately, frightened of being caught and hearing Faiga's screams, and too ashamed to read Faiga's terrible secrets.

Looking down from the hill, Chava had thought about the whole family. Perhaps Gittel would be sitting near the fire knitting a blanket for the cat, small uneven squares with dropped stitches which she sewed into a quilt. She punished the cat for days when it brought birds, half-alive, into the house. "Poor one," she would whisper as she prayed and tried to warm the creature with her breath. Once she put her whole mouth over a bird's head to revive it, and it bit her lip and flew away. Sometimes she would say, "Vassily, you can't help it that you're a cat," looking into its green eyes with their needle centres, trying to understand and forgive its nature.

There was a neatness about this distant little colony at their feet. Watching from the hill, Chava thought it all too miniature to know suffering. Every cry would be a small one. Even the cemetery on the other side of the forest was a small irregular circle with tiny tombstones that looked like studs on a lady's shoes. Perhaps God ought to come close, with His feet on the ground and look carefully into the houses – everything felt different when you were nearer. She had never been to a cemetery before Grandfather died. She had been too young when they had buried the child – Papa's kaddishel – the son who should have said prayers at his father's burial. It was good and it was right. Instead it had been Papa saying them over the small coffin. Mama would not allow them to lay a tombstone on the grave until the time when he would have been older. She couldn't bear to think of a large stone pressing on the little body beneath it. There were times when Chava walked there to feel the quietness of the graves. No one would ever think of looking there for her, sitting on the grass and thinking about the people lying still and silent in the ground, released from the agony that had brought them there. Sometimes she thought it was a terrible thing to do to people whom you loved – leave them outside and alone in winter with the ground frozen hard.

No one had liked Grandfather because of his temper and selfishness. But she had understood his humiliation. It was deep and bitter and he hated his weak legs and reedy voice. "Listen to my voice! Like a castrated goat. And my eyes! Like two stones in my head." And after they buried him a bird pecked at Gittel's window for three days. "It's trying to come in," Gittel had said.

It had all been easier to understand, sitting far away on a hill and looking down on it like on a patterned carpet. God's carpet perhaps. But you could only know its sadness if you were close, near enough to hear the whispers of its life.

Everything had suddenly seemed fragile: the tiny village and everyone living in it. She wanted to run home without looking back at the monster hill behind her and the cloud which had risen around its head like an executioner's mask.

The tide had gone as far as it could go and was turning back to where all tides began. Chava wanted to run back to the house near the tree, to close the curtains and sit with the quietness of the cats. To rest with heavy lids and watch the fire – now a lump of bloody meat, now a fiery eye.

Home, where she can open her small book with David's psalms written in special decorated lettering. Every day to read them as a blessing for Gittel's breathing and Faiga's secrets, especially for Faiga who is unwell and not eating supper at night, and the cats and birds and Wlad and to feel still and quiet again. She loves the one that says:

> *Hear my prayer Lord*
> *And give ear to my cry*
> *To my tears be not silent,*
> *For a stranger am I with you*
> *A sojourner as all my fathers were.*

FOUR
Patterns In The Ash

THEN A TIME COMES FOR ALL SECRETS TO BE KNOWN. THEY MULTIPLY LIKE mushrooms and the spores thrive in the dark. Try and bury them but they will grow towards the light. If the secret is revealed after the person has died then you must think again of their whole life and think again about your own, remember them in another way, perhaps love them more, perhaps hate them until you can understand and forgive them. The labour is all yours: to plead for them and argue on their behalf. Perhaps you will hate yourself or blame yourself forever. How can the dead forgive you? If the person is alive, the secret flourishes in the dark, and then its discovery can be like a death, and in Chava's house it is as though Faiga has died.

The old fringed cloth still covers the pine eating-table. Every evening it is carefully folded and put to one side when the table is set for meals and then after supper it is unfolded again and spread over the table when the last plates have been cleared – the final punctuation point to the meal like the closing of the curtain in synagogue. Irrevocable.

"Can't we leave the dishes until tomorrow?" Faiga asks. "We'll stack them away neatly and no one will mind."

"But I mind," her mother says.

"We'll cover them carefully under a clean cloth, perfectly folded, corner to corner, and no one will know." There is some irony in her voice, but Mama does not hear it.

"But I'll know, and when I'm sleeping I'll still know. Those dishes will intrude into my dreams like a bad conscience."

So they sweep the floor, if only to stop Mama from talking, until the last crumb is caught. She searches all over with shrewd eyes enlarged by her spectacles into glassy moons until she finds a grain which she lifts with pincer fingers. They watch her. Even Papa waits. There will be no rest until she is satisfied and sits down.

Winter-time, with the winter arrangement of chairs around the fire. Mama sits in a chair and looks at the house. Everything in its place. At rest.

Strange, Chava thinks, how people still bring fire into their houses like cave creatures and allow it to burn. You bring the enemy inside and it becomes your friend. She brushes Faiga's hair, sometimes curling it fancy on top of her head, gripping the hairpins in her teeth. Faiga's eyes are gentle, blinking slowly from the soft touch of her hands. Gittel has fallen asleep on the bench under a shawl, her eyes hypnotised by watching the slow brushing. And Papa is writing numbers in his book: two sheep, four cows, ten bags of potatoes, a bag of nails, four boxes of cabbages. Adding up his profits and taking away his expenses until there is nearly nothing left. The remainder is what he gives Mama for the house. Chava has seen his lists. Little scraps lying around the house. Always his lists: ten chickens, five dozen eggs. Sometimes when he is sitting with his legs crossed at night, even when there is no paper and pen in hand, he traces figures with his finger on his knee, round and round, and then signs his name at the end, his finger repeating the pattern: Mordechai Schneider Mordechai Schneider Mordechai Schneider. His eyes are wide open and stretching wider but not seeing the fire or the chairs or tables or anyone sitting in the room.

"Why are you staring?" Mama asks. Her voice is suddenly too loud, like the slamming of a door. He looks up with vacant eyes and the magic of the letters is broken.

Even when everyone has gone to bed, Mama still sits in the room alone, looking and looking: the candlesticks, the pots hanging on the wall by their handles, the shine of copper in the firelight. Sometimes Papa makes her tea and pours in some schnapps, and brings a blanket to cover her legs. She sits for a long time and then stands up, looks around again, folding the shawl which Gittel left behind into perfect corners. She has taught her daughters to make perfect corners but she cannot teach Papa. He hates corners and rolls everything up into a ball. Mama picks up a rolled table napkin from the floor, twisted and wrung in one corner where Papa was winding it round and round his finger and staring with empty eyes, then she leaves the room, closing the door behind her. Irrevocable.

But today there are no plates or knives and forks and no food on the table. Neither yesterday nor the day before. There is no water boiling on the stove, and Chava is trying to bring the fire back to life by blowing at an ember. The clock ticks like a failing heart beating more by habit than desire; each beat hesitates, then falls; one wheel turns the other, its inner life visible behind the glass.

Three men and a woman sit on the bench against the wall and Papa looks out of the window at a group of children standing outside staring at the house. Mama sits near the fireplace making circles in the ash with her foot. The beat of the clock is unbearable.

Chava gets up suddenly and goes outside to fetch more wood. She claps her hands at the children, shouting, "Go away from the house!" Then she sees a hand drawing back a corner of the curtain in the neighbours' window. She covers her head with her shawl as she goes to the woodpile, and on her way back walks slowly past the neighbours' window, looking at the dark shapes standing behind the curtains. People they have known since childhood, now hidden and suspicious. Inside the house she arranges small pieces of kindling wood, blowing the embers into a flame, and then larger logs until the fire is burning. Mama begins to make rocking movements with her arms folded around her body, casting long swinging shadows against the wall.

Chava leaves the room, nauseous from the sudden heat and the room swaying with the shifting patterns on the wall. She hasn't eaten and her mouth is dry. She hates the mourners, arriving promptly and unsolicited at the front door when there is a sadness and otherwise never seen or heard. They have a talent for mourning, unerring decorum and grace: pale-faced and hushed in grief. Black becomes them. And their fat cakes sit on the pine table uneaten. Tragedy has put her on display, her sadness as transparent as the machinery of the clock. She is a spectacle in her own home. Their house is public. Any stranger may enter uninvited and stare. Who told them? She hates the conspiracy. Faiga is not dead.

She goes into the bedroom. The loose board rocks under her foot. Hateful thing. The sameness is an offence to her. Always the same dull sound. She sits quietly with Gittel for a long time without speaking. It is early afternoon but the cloud has kept the cottage in darkness all day. Now there is a yellow light that comes before snow.

"What is going to happen, Chava?"

"I don't know. Everything is very quiet. But those children won't go away and one of them has a stone in his hand. After what Faiga has done even the Jews will begin to avoid us. I'm becoming afraid to leave the house."

Chava looks around the room where she has lived all her life. Faiga's bed is there but all the sheets and blankets have been removed.

"The whole house has changed," Chava says, "like a body that has died: outwardly the same, but no longer human. Do you remember how Grandfather's face slowly stiffened into a snarl? I kept going in to look at him, seeing the transformation. A house is a living thing and feels everything that happens inside it. I'm sure when Mama sweeps the kitchen floor she is looking after its soul, and when Papa throws rubbish down he is hurting it.

Sometimes I play a game; I imagine I'm an old woman living in a foreign place and I'm telling stories to people about my home and remembering all the things I knew as a child. As I stand here now, surrounded by everything I know, I'm beginning to see it as a memory, like seeing Faiga's empty bed and remembering her body inside it. Today the house feels different. No longer alive, as though it is already a memory."

The draught rattles the twisted window-frame. A nagging sound that persists even though they try to block the gap with old stockings and candle-wax. The window will not succumb and the floorboards will rock underfoot until doomsday. How you can suddenly look at a house without feeling any love or affection for it any more! Chava stands up, unable to sit any longer.

"Listen to me, Gittel, and don't move. I'm going to look for Faiga and bring her home. Don't react to what I say. She doesn't know what she has done. What was she thinking, looking out of the window for hours, never speaking to anyone and keeping everything secret? This time she did something bad. There's only one place where she could be hiding and I have to find her."

Chava gets up and takes her coat and shawl from the wooden peg on the wall, overlapping them firmly around her body and buckling a belt tightly around her waist.

Gittel is whimpering. "I know where you're going, and I'm too scared to name it. I beg you, we'll lose you too. They'll capture you and keep you there. It's happened before. And if you take her away the village will turn against us violently, expel us and burn our houses. You've heard the stories from Mama about what happened before you were born. The burning and killing. We're only a few Jewish families here. We have to be careful. Have you ever seen a thatched house on fire? Faiga was always writing her diaries and thinking about God. What did she mean in her letter about being saved? Why was she lost? We can't change her. And tonight is Friday night. We are supposed to eat and have pleasure no matter what. You remember how we told stories about Grandfather that first Friday night after he died. And how we laughed about all the things that used to make us cross, until we cried. We must leave Faiga where she is. We'll all get used to it."

"Promise not to tell them until after I've gone. No one must know. This is our last Friday night in Sharabka and the house knows it. Tell them to pack whatever we can carry and leave the rest behind."

"What about the cats?"

"When I get back everything must be ready. We'll have to run. Pray for me."

She puts the shawl over her head, covering her nose and mouth and tying the ends behind her head. Her small knife is in her pocket with the bone handle in her hand, familiar and harmless in all the years of playing games. Is this another childish feat, an act of bravado to tell Wlad? She has kept the edge sharp by rubbing it smoothly against stone, a perfect edge. And tonight – she, Chava, might cut into flesh to save herself.

The snow grunts under her boots as she walks toward the potato field and then onto the open plain. Earth and sky are white on white with no features. A blind man's landscape that blights her eyes. She passes her tree, the Queen Tree, skeletal as old bones, crippled by the wind. It will take her more than an hour to reach the forest and it will be dark as a cave on her way back with only the faint outline of hills against the sky to guide her. Already her legs are aching from lifting them out of the soft snow, and her skirt – why are women so encumbered? – is already weighed down with ice beating against her boots.

Her body is beginning to steam under the thick coat like fresh bread in winter, but the wind burns her eyes. She has never been alone on the plain in winter and she remembers everything that has been said about it: the sky that suddenly delivers a blizzard that can bury a man alive, or an icy squall that whistles like a speeding train. She remembers the villagers rescuing a trapper, half dead; seeing them cut off his boots to save his feet, black and stinking, and seeing his lips gaping with sores.

She is frightened of the emptiness all around her, like the dark place under her bed that hides creatures at night. She wants to run home, but the way back is as fearful as the way ahead. The clouds hang lower, a spongy ceiling over her head, and the wind beats the snow into the air, blurring the horizon. The plain is gone, lost under drifts of white ash. She tries to calculate distance as she walks, like trying to measure the surface of water; nothing definable anywhere. She fixes her eyes on a point, an imaginary detail like looking at one grain of sand on a beach, and counts each step towards it. The snow compacts under her boots as she counts and the beat turns over in her mind like the sprockets of the old clock. Twenty beats and she is there. Each count takes her foot forward to press a grunt from the breathing snow. Count again, her eyes focused on a pinpoint of white like a blind spot, and the snow grunting like a pig.

Her legs ache and it is only the rhythm of her pace that makes her go on. She is moving slowly as she drags her feet out of the snow. At any moment her legs could stop, stand still where they are and go no further. Her will is too feeble to move them. The rhythm breaks and she tries to feel her feet again, numb with cold and palsy. Why resist the softness underfoot and the cloud embracing her into its folds? How consoling to be alone on the plain, away from obsequious mourners and grieving family. She remembers the villagers saying that people who die in the snow experience a great exhilaration. Here, every step claims a world free from suffering. How pristine, each flake. Sequins on a wedding dress and fine as confetti. Sugar crystals, sweet as candy. She relaxes her legs and lies in it. Surely death is blissful. The highest achievement, with every event of one's lifetime seen in transparent clarity. A gentle dissolution of body and mind. An infinite snowfield without sound or sensation.

Then she thinks she sees a shape in the distance. A shadow on the horizon. She stands up wanting to run, but holds herself to a steady pace for fear of exhausting herself and then collapsing on the return journey. The image is getting larger and beginning to separate into trees as she gets nearer. The pine forest, and a skein of smoke twisting upwards, greyer than the grey sky.

She pushes forward through high drifts, cracking the crust and smashing the loose powder below. She leans, panting, against a tree, breathing with a rasp in her lungs. She thinks of Faiga behind the old walls, left alone in a cell by the blue-eyed sisters, kneeling under the dreaded crucifix they had been too afraid to look at. They squinted sideways and looked down, terrified to see the suffering creature hanging with his body on the nails;

purple drops on a pallid skin, God's blood, and the fabric of the whole world bleeding. Mama prayed to be saved from the thundering Cossacks, flattening the wheatfields and burning their houses, their crossed swords everywhere, and now Faiga is holding one. Perhaps it is too late and she is crouching on her knees to this other God.

Chava has never seen the convent in winter, the pines standing in the snow like tombstones. She approaches the last row of trees, hiding like the small child who watched the girl waiting to be let in; the sound of metal haunted her sleep and the flick of starched white cotton – a snitch, a flash – filled her dreams.

And now she is standing there again, repeating the events of an old story. Her hand reaches out to pull the bell. The silence is an ache in her ears.

The sound bounces off stone walls, an injury to the absolute stillness. Snow slips off a branch. Run and hide behind the trees – but she stands there unable to move. There are people behind the walls, women who will take her inside, warm her hands and dry her clothes. They have saved injured animals in winter, they cannot turn her out to die. She will find Faiga and together they will help each other home.

A sudden rattle of keys, the click of a heavy lock and the gate slides open. Something tears and beats in her chest, breaking out through strangled noises in her throat. Starched cotton beats against leather and hands are holding her tight. Her mouth is dribbling and she cannot stop the twisting of her lips. She wants to be sick. A smell of mouldy stone, her legs dragging along the floor. She yields into the closeness of bodies around her, thankful for high walls against the snow. She cannot see, her eyes are blurred with tears. Uncontrollable noises block her throat. She thinks she is going to choke. Hands are working her, beating her back. She begins to breathe.

She lies on the bed. She is unable to feel her feet. A vague question circles her mind like a bird high in the sky . . .

She does not know how long she has been lying there. Slowly the room comes into focus. Small and dark, a bed against each wall with two crossed wooden sticks above it. Folded blankets and pillows wait on the beds for an occupant. A place for human life, safe from the harrowing plain. She lies quietly for a long time without moving, as though she has been ill. The slow return of blood to her feet.

She thought she was alone, but now she sees a girl sitting very still on the edge of her bed. A bell rings, the soft tap of feet and a rush of skirts. Chava has not heard human sound since she left home. Language is a voice inside her own head. Speech, a strange activity. What can she say? "Little friend . . ."

Silence absorbs the sound.

"Help me . . ."

Hollow in the stony room.

"I am looking for a girl with long red hair. She calls herself Francis."

The girl does not speak. Try again, this trick of making sounds with the mouth. "I've come to be with her, I can't bear to think of her alone . . ."

She must keep talking. Words will make something happen. Chatter like a monkey.

"I've come so that we can be together."

The silence must not be allowed to prevail.

"I can't bear to think of her alone. She always liked pretty things and nice dresses and to grow her hair long and shiny and we all used to sit together and eat until we were bursting, holding our stomachs and laughing. I must see her and talk."

Her breath is steaming in the cold room and her face is hot with tears. She looks at the girl: silent. Her hair is cut coarsely below her ears but the ragged ends are shivering. The back of her neck is young and the skin is irritated the way her sister's skin erupted in a rash when she was upset and now that Chava looks carefully through the wetness of her eyes she thinks that the colour of the hair is red. "Faiga?"

Chava is afraid to approach. She is looking at Faiga as though she has been ill. It has been three days since she left home but her whole form is altered. Her body looks out of proportion without the dense hair. Her head is smaller, and now Chava sees the real shape of her neck, short and squat. Her ears are too small and her breasts are too large. It is like the shock of seeing her own mother without the wig that Jewish women must wear, the rudeness of the head and her whole body looking thin.

Faiga turns around to show her face. Her skin is blotchy and the hair is torn down to the scalp. She looks bloated and gaunt at the same time, puffy around the eyes. She holds a wooden cross in her hands. Flagrant. She was always fascinated. Wanting to wear one: "Don't tell Mama . . ." as she took it out of her drawer, wearing it secretly, pretty around her neck with shiny coloured stones.

"Can you see how ugly I am? Ugly under all the pretending. Look at me."

"Why have you done this thing, Faiga?"

She puts her hand over her mouth. Carefully she begins to speak like someone trying to use a painful limb.

"Janusch promised. He said He would save me. That is what they say when a Jew goes over to Jesus. He told me that a soul suffers endless unimaginable suffering. More than the worst suffering of the body. And I became afraid of death and this terrible pain of the soul, worse than any agony the body can feel. To be cursed and never to see God's face. He made other promises. We would leave Sharabka secretly and live a different life. He called me his angel and read me poems: 'Tomorrow is a day of prayer and sorrow. My angel, wherever souls may dwell – my angel, do you see me?' Do you remember how he looked at me at school? Everyone knew. I was so excited. I stood at the window at night waiting for him. I didn't care if I left home, if I never saw the family again. But now he has left me and I have nowhere else to go. Last night I dreamed that a woman stared at me with burning eyes, pointed at me and threw me out into an empty place and I was falling through space without anything to stop me. I sat up, terrified, and then I began to rise off the bed and I had to hold myself down with everything spinning around me. Every night I have dreams that I am lost in dark places or surrounded by high mountains and black lakes, and now I only want to be saved from my dreams. When I think about that woman I know it was Mama. Even Papa thinks of me as dead. And look how you are looking at me, too appalled to touch me."

Chava puts her feet on the floor. Frightened of approaching this woman. She wraps her yellow shawl around the head to cover its shame. She cradles the head, strokes it, begins to rock the body forward and backward, stiff, strange, until slowly it begins to soften. She feels the touch of an arm. And they sit holding each other for a long time.

A long time. Friday night. Sabbath, a time of enchantment. She smoothes the splintered hair, kisses her face and they talk about home.

And it was evening and it was morning and they are still awake and together.

Then, on her knees, Chava begs the pale sisters to release her.

And that night the moon is a revealed planet shining its borrowed light over the snowy plain as Chava goes home alone.

FIVE
Windows

CHAVA IS STANDING AT THE WINDOW. THE WORLD IS A PICTURE SEEN through a frame. She watches a white cat walking in the snow below her, a ripple in the whiteness, already corrupted by the grey stones of the courtyard. She thinks of the cat that was left behind in Sharabka while Gittel was forced, screaming and coughing, into the wagon. "She can't breathe. She can't breathe. Let her take the cat," Mama cried. But Papa was whipping the horse and they had already left the house, while Gittel choked on the floor of the wagon with Mama beating her on the back, and they all stared into the night. They cannot look behind them – the house is a shell, inhabited by a cat still sleeping in its basket and the cow with swelling udders in the shed. Please let Wlad take it away and milk it before the villagers break down the door and loot whatever is left. The cat will survive, turn wild and kill fieldmice and birds. The chickens! Who will save the chickens that Gittel warmed in her apron pocket when they were still forming in their shells, and crowded around her feet when they were hatched? And Mama was beating Gittel on her back: "We'll buy a new cat in Warsaw exactly the same. Don't cry. It's stopping your breath." And the horse could have trotted blindfold on the known pathway to Lodz. Then Lodz was behind them and Gittel's breath was rasping as she leaned her head on Mama's shoulder, and the way to Warsaw was unknown as the horse galloped, frothing and stumbling in the dark. It was a long night, and the only reality was the cart on the road and her family around her. Everything else was in doubt. Sharabka was already a tissue of memories receding into oblivion like the furthest star. Please let Wlad take the cow and milk her. Please let him take all the things they left behind. "What happened to my candlesticks?" Mama suddenly remembered. "I've forgotten my candlesticks. My candlesticks! How could I have forgotten my candlesticks?" And Mama and Gittel were both bent over and crying on the road to Warsaw. "My candlesticks. My candlesticks."

Chava watches the cat picking up its paw and shaking off the snow, stepping forward again. It digs a little depression and sits over it with an outstretched tail. A puff of steam rises and the cat covers the place carefully with snow, walks on. Fastidious cat, in this courtyard that smells of rotting debris and the oozing obscenity in the corner, swarming with flies in summer and stinking a little less in winter. She queues, gagging, to use it in the early morning. This is now her landscape, the view framed by her window, and shared by all the other families around her. Everything is shared and too close. She can hear the shouting and smell the food. There is no space or separation between lives. They are all woven together into a shabby fabric. A ragged community of watchers and listeners. Every conversation is heard, and repeated as a whisper. She has told Mama not to speak to anyone, but Papa is the talker. Everyone is his friend as the men huddle together smoking or playing cards. He has become quite a storyteller. He likes this place, he is a city man after all, and flees from Mama's silence. Late at night he comes home and they talk about money again. "I'm sick of this constant worry," she cries. "I'm sorry. I'm sorry," he cringes. Mama does washing for a wealthy Jewish family. Chava watches their children. They are lucky to be given work without having any papers. Gittel sits at home. Her breathing is worse in Warsaw. Perhaps she can learn to sew.

Outside the courtyard the street snarls like a wild animal until it exhausts its strength late in the night. In Sharabka each sound was single, distinct and cushioned by quietness around it: the mice rustling in a cupboard – you had to stand very still, hardly breathing, to hear them. Or Mama and Papa talking in their room – a murmur. And the luminosity of the candle, spending its energy in silence. Or Wlad whistling his sad whistle. "Why is it always the same sad tune?" she would ask him, and then he would cup his hands together and blow into them, making the crooning song of doves in the pine trees. Here it is the continuous rage of the city with only the harsh laughter of women heard in relief against it, or their screams over the balcony into the street, or the call of the eiernik or the milkman and the market outside where everything must be paid for with money that must be earned, somehow. Or the screeching of the crows circling the sky and picking through the garbage. Horses on cobbled stones and wagons with iron-rimmed wheels. It would be a mercy to be deaf. Let God not hear and curse her.

She watches through the window as the cat leaves its paw-prints in the snow, a delicate tracery left by its padded walk. It jumps through a window, sits completely still and looks out – a porcelain cat. The slowness fills her mind. She has lost her energy. Why not watch the cat all day?

The enclosure of the courtyard is choking her. She must run outside to save her life. The stench of the city rises from the gutters like belching breath. Rats and alley-cats run along the gutters and disappear into the drains. But entering the streets is like opening a window into a wide world where she can regain her strength again, swaggering, skirts swinging around her ankles. No one knows her or cares. They look at her impassively without recognition, a peasant girl useful for her labour. Sometimes men notice her in passing. Good hips. She is only of interest to the police who walk the streets looking for illegal Jews. Her status traps her in the frame. She has learnt to be subversive, to look into the reflecting glass of windows, to disappear into doorways and alleys, never to appear guilty or attract attention by running. The Warsaw women do not run. Their shoes are narrow and tight with pointed heels as they tip-tap on the pavements.

She enjoys the freedom of the street and the risks that make her blood course again, slowly recovering her strength. In the cold afternoons she looks into the cafes and restaurants, looking through windows at the warmth and comfort inside. A woman with red hair sits at a table eating cake and sipping cognac with a gloved hand. It stings her memory suddenly. In summer these people sit outside under umbrellas, drinking lemonade late into the night, with gypsy violins playing. Everything is being done for their distraction and delight. Why is she excluded from it? She wants it, she wants it. How can she break through the frame that separates her? She's had enough of watching. Wlad and the wheatfields are far away. This is Warsaw.

But she can only look through windows, dodge the police and walk quickly back to the courtyard where Mama and Papa sit up at night talking. Papa is making his lists and staring: five dozen eggs, ten chickens. "It's winter, the chickens aren't laying. How can I deliver the eggs?"

"There's always a reason. In summer you'll say it's too hot. Blame the chickens," says Mama.

Once a week they go to a student next door to learn a new language. The room is full of people, all in transit like themselves. Some, like Mama, cannot write their names in any language. Chava is also struggling. She feels awkward with the new sounds and her ear cannot communicate with her tongue. Has she also become stupid since she left Sharabka, one of a crowd who is clumsy and ignorant in its new location? She cannot call it home. They are always in a mass and they are all the same – poor. Poor people look old and tired. Hollow-eyed like Mama. Poverty has a look that she has learnt to recognise. Even on the Sabbath when they dress up for synagogue and promenade the streets, they are imitating the rich. A cheap copy of the aristocrats: sable-trimmed hats and gabardine, and women wearing fashionable perukes. The fur is rabbit. The gabardine is rough as goat's hair. When they come home they put on their old clothes and slop around the house again until the next Sabbath. She is learning things they never taught her at school. Things that make her mouth turn downwards when she laughs. A new kind of laughter. Sometimes she would like to cry, but they would be dry tears.

When she goes next door for her lessons a young man always sits next to her. A city man wearing a jacket and shirt with a stiff collar. Papa likes to talk business with him, and sometimes he comes to their room for lemon tea. She sits next to Papa and watches this young man, a spot on his skin just under his cheekbone that moves when he talks. He is not listening carefully to Papa because he says: "I beg your pardon? I'm sorry," and when he looks at her the skin on his cheeks changes colour, he spills his tea on his tie and apologises. "I'm sorry. I'm so sorry." He is sorry, like Papa. She feels older than him and braver even though she is a country girl. Is she immodest to sit with them at the table? She does not feel ashamed to examine him closely: his city cap in a tweedy material, his soft white hands with faint half-moons on his nails. He is also talking about eggs and chickens and bags of potatoes and sacks of flour. They make figures on a page and he and Papa shake hands.

Every week now he comes to talk to Papa and sometimes he comes for dinner on Friday night. He is named after his village where they grow apples; a place with apple blossoms and the sound of bees humming like violins through the village in spring. It is only apples and the picking of apples and the transport and selling of them; the sound of a good apple when you tap it with your finger, dense and tight; the smell when they are ripe that tingles the senses, and the taste when you pick it off the tree, dripping green blood as it spills its soul. "You can tell a good apple," he says. "You have to tear it off the tree because of its passionate attachment to life. And its skin is radiant like Moses' at Sinai when he came down from the mountain." And this young man's eyes shine like a prophet's when he talks about apples, and he is never boring.

He comes every Friday night now, his seat next to her at the table. She serves him after she serves Papa, quietly giving him the next best piece of chicken, breast basted slowly with onion and potatoes. He always says: "Mmm. Mmm. It's delicious." Poor young man with no family. He and Papa are doing good business. Soon they will have enough money to buy tickets for the boat. She will be glad to leave this place, and perhaps they will all travel together. She is beginning to like him, that small spot under his cheekbone. She wants to touch it softly with her finger. And the shine in his eyes. Green. Green as apples, even by candlelight.

She feels strangely restless after he has gone, and sleepless with thinking. Perhaps next Friday she will gently, accidentally, touch his hand under the table. No one will see but perhaps he will jump, knock over a glass and blush with fright. Every Friday night he spills the wine. "Good luck," they all say, as Mama covers the stain with salt, and Chava hides her smile with a napkin. "I'm so sorry." He is always sorry. She feels more sensible than him. Sometimes women are cleverer from the things they learn in the house and outside in the street from ordinary people. She feels stronger from all the things that have happened. Their lives have all been broken in some way, and she knows that broken things can always be fixed. She thinks of him the whole night, sleeping like someone who is floating just below the surface of water, seeing the rippling skin and the blue light above.

At last the darkness is lifting and the children next door are beginning to cry. There is the smell of burnt milk. She has hardly slept, still fixed on the same thought . . . to touch his hand under the table. She will have to wait for next Friday. It is a kind of agony.

She has waited a week. If not now, when? A woman must not be timid or frightened of change. This is Warsaw. Things happen quickly. She cannot wait for the slow progress of events, the meetings between families, the slow deliberation of formalities. Too many days between one Friday and the next. It is unbearable.

They are sitting at the table. A little covenant is made as the wine is blessed. The silver goblet is passed from mouth to mouth in mutual acceptance, the plaited bread is salted and broken. Then the noise of serving and eating breaks the silence. Papa always makes toasts on Fridays. Tonight he drinks to the continuing relationship with the young man, to the growing contentment of chickens and the increased production of eggs. They clink glasses to solemnise the wish with smiles and laughter. And again the young man spills and tonight he also breaks the glass. "I'm sorry. I'm sorry." He falls to his knees to pick up the pieces. If not now, when?

Chava immediately drops to the floor with him. They are under the table, with Mama's and Papa's feet around them and Gittel's legs swinging over the chair. The air is fragrant with the smell of cooking and the scent of wine. Chava looks at him and touches his hand, holds it and strokes the little moons. Immodest. Flagrant. His cheeks change colour with emotion. He stares at her for as long a time as between one Friday night and the next. They crouch, motionless, under the table. She is absorbed into the dark centres of his eyes. His face has gone white.

"I will marry you, if you want me to," he whispers between Mama's skirts, and the sweet wine is dripping onto his face like a sacrament. "I do want you to," she says. He stands up, wine-stained and recites:

> *For the sun*
> *He has set a tent in their midst.*
> *And it is like a groom*
> *Departing his bridal chamber.*

There is silence. The young man is still standing at the table. They all look at each other with amazement. What does this mean, "groom"? "bridal chamber"?

It is astonishing. Mama and Papa have not been consulted. This is Friday night and they have not even eaten the chicken. This is very rash and impudent to ignore the time-honoured protocol. They are bewildered. And then suddenly it is all laughter and celebration.

"I knew it was auspicious, I knew it when he broke the wineglass," Papa says, with the neighbours bursting in to shake him by the hand and to kiss Mama on the cheek.

"The chicken is getting dry in the oven. We haven't even eaten yet. How did this happen so quickly?" Mama shouts.

"Good luck. Good luck," they all scream and bring cakes and cherry brandy to congratulate them.

Tonight, she is calm. Everything is quiet around her in the little room she shares with Gittel. She thinks of Faiga's trousseau, how her sister sat at night embroidering little roses on those white sheets. Everything abandoned in Sharabka with Mama's candlesticks. A young woman should start her own home with her mother's candlesticks.

But she will begin with nothing, and she will not be afraid of change. She has learnt to write her new name, Eva, which she whispers like a secret, strange upon her lips. When she looks at herself in the mirror she repeats it. It doesn't match the way she sees herself or have any connection with what has happened to her in her other life. Eva is a woman. Chava was a child.

Perhaps it is right. Her life is changing quickly and her new name will be the vessel that carries her forward, like the ship which will soon be taking her to a new land. For the second time she will be leaving everything behind her and she is forbidden to look back.

Lying in the darkness, she sees Gittel's sleeping shape in the bed. She has become very quiet in this city life without the cat and the cow and the chickens; utterly deprived, while Chava has been favoured. Where is the justice of it? She is suddenly apologetic for her happiness. Ashamed, undeserving, as though she has no right to it. Disrespectful of the sad lives around her: Mama, also lying in the darkness, wondering how she will pay for the wedding. Even happy events become a struggle when they must be paid for. The burden will fall on Mama. Papa will come forward grandiosely with a large hat when it is time to make the speeches. He has become a performer with his jokes and stories. He is irresistible, while Mama who is doing all the work is wretched. She sits in a corner, silent, while he performs. And Faiga, also with a new name: Francis. And Wlad, her farm boy with the important name, Wladimir. Her happiness separates her from them like the rich are separated from the poor.

Sorry, for being happy. So sorry.

SIX
Jew's Market

FRIDAY AGAIN. EARLY MORNING, AND THE SUN BURNS LIKE A BRANDING-iron, searing cut flowers, blistering dewy English strawberries and the tender skins of tomatoes, prices dropping as the gaseous smudge rises to its meridian in the sky. Wentworth Street smokes with the heat, chokes with barrows, and bristles with black umbrellas that cover the fruit and vegetables.

"Sixpenceapaaawnd . . .!" Voices with special projection have been cultivated from childhoods spent clamouring in the streets: alto, soprano – as penetrating as screams in a jungle – pierce the air. Wealthy customers are buying fruit at high prices, rushing them home to stand in cool pantries until dinner-time. But others stand patiently on street corners: sly-eyed matrons, waiting for the fruit to sicken and weep until the call changes to, "Thruppenceapaaawnd . . .! Take. Take. I saw you waiting for the sun to ruin them. Take. I'm giving them away. You should worry what I'm losing every day."

Such is the justice of the Jew's market in Wentworth Street. For every commodity its fair price and for every price its quality and its customer. Is it not said, "You shall have perfect stone weights and just ones, a perfect measure and a just one. On this account your days shall long endure upon the soil"? Or if a person should falter – rearrange the strawberries a little, place the fresh ones on top – is it also not written that there is no man so wholly righteous on earth who doeth only good and sineth not?

Tailored suits hang on racks, like leaves on trees, outside workshops where buyers rub the fabric between thumb and index finger. The experienced thumb is an organ that can discriminate like the nose can smell, and eyebrows lift with respect or lips purse as though tasting something sour and the customer moves on. Apprentices continuously brush and press the jackets to remove the fine black soot which filters down from the chimneys onto the street below. A boy gets a cuff across the head: "Idiot. How many times must I tell you to press the shoulder on the ham and the sleeve on the board? Don't you know a straight line from a curve?"

Buyers of "slop" clothing stir the vats continuously like soup. Someone pulls out trousers by its leg or a shirt by its arm, still creased at the groin or smudged on the collar from the life of its last owner. The leg is measured for size or tested for strength. Sometimes the trousers are purchased and wrapped respectfully in brown paper, but usually the dismembered body is thrown back into the pot to merge with the soup again.

Next door the butcher-shop swings with freshly slaughtered chickens hanging from the ceilings by their feet and dripping blood through open beaks onto the sawdust, sharing mute company with chains of pink sausages plump as cherubim and pickled tongues turning blue from lying in trays of vinegar and saltpetre. Chickens are prodded for fat and smelt for freshness, a nose is not shy of entering the gaping carcass. Practised hands turn the sides of beef pirouetting on meathooks. The butchery is no place for dreamers. It requires fast thinking and an unsentimental calculation of goods for money, the size of stomachs and the number of mouths that must be fed. Considering it shrinks, a pound of brisket will be enough for five people: Papa will have a big slice, Mendel quite a big slice, after all he's a growing boy and must eat, Mama and Miriam don't have big appetites because they have been tasting all day while they cook, and Grandpa will have the remnants because without his teeth he can't eat the meat, and he can have an extra potato.

The crowds bulge and wrestle around the entrance to the fish shop like the teeming mackerel emptied out of canvas bags into large zinc buckets of ice. Carp, sea bass, soles, fillets of plaice, North Sea sturgeon, fresh sardines, Scotch salmon and pike (... pike? Whoever heard of pike? You mean butten. Ask any Jew ...) are glossy-eyed and still bleeding from the gills (who would buy a fish that wasn't?). They share a marble bier in the democracy of death, while whole codfish, split open and dried flat, hang from the beams like pages of parchment. The fishwives swathe their skirts in blood-smeared calico and stand behind the counter removing scales with steel brushes, their big red fingers always wet and swollen and sometimes bleeding with engorged fishbones. They detach a spine with delicate precision, rip out the gut and tear off the skin with the jerk of a forearm while the customer stands at the counter, watching with narrowing eyes every incision into the bought flesh on the slab.

"I want the skin, bones and head" – a call through the noise, and the surgeon acknowledges the command. Outside the shop fishmongers bend over barrels of salt herrings, groping for floating bodies in the milky brine. "Too small, haven't you got any bigger ones? By the time they're filleted there's nothing left. What am I paying for? Skin and bones?" They share the pavement with costermongers who line both sides of the narrow street, offering bargain prices in competition with the ground-floor shops. Awnings reach out like arms to embrace the writhing mass that seeks to consume a week's earnings in one night of celebration – "Spend! It's a blessing to feast on the Sabbath!" The only adequate meal of the week – Friday night's dinner.

Sometimes an outsider finds his way by accident into the crowded streets. The natives spot him immediately – pressed blue suit, starched shirt with the collar corners ironed into stiff right-angle folds. Only a stranger stands in the street looking up at the crumbling garrets or searches for street names to locate himself. He cannot understand the signs of the shops or the writing on shop windows, and only by reading the street markers can he confirm that he is still in England. Where are the squares and green gardens, wide-curved avenues fringed with Edwardian buildings, immaculate nannies pushing proud perambulators? Or, where are the recognizable slums of the labouring poor who attempt to imitate the established standards of the rich? The stranger stands on the corner confused at the sight of his city fluttering with gabardine-coated figures, bearded faces wearing black hats, all speaking a Germanic dialect salted with accented English. He hears the sounds of children's voices chanting Hebrew in school. Incomprehensible. Now he is the foreigner, lost in a city that lives in the fibrous womb of another city, like an unloved foetus: two square miles of density and dirt on the east side of London, attached to its parent by an umbilicus of bridges and twisting streets, constantly threatening to contaminate its host, and threatened by the septic fluid of the Thames.

On another street, trapped on a corner like flotsam, they are immediately observed. Friday, when the boats come in, confused, blinded by the sunlight, bending under the weight of broken baskets and sacks, a group of greeners, foul-smelling and squinting in the sun from three days and nights in the hold of a ship. Fair game to the natives, they are already sighted and approached by one. They negotiate: food and accommodation for work. Take it or leave it. The transaction is brief and binding, and they follow him into one of the smoking alleys where they are absorbed like effluent into the teeming stream.

They pause to rest inside a doorway, blinded again, everything green-black before their eyes, but cool. They continue up the stairs carrying their lives on their backs like a hunch. They stoop under the low ceiling of the stairs above them, trying not to slip on the trough in the centre of the steps, worn smooth and treacherous by other feet before them. Climbing one behind the other without thinking. They stopped thinking separately when they made the descent like Jonah into the deep bladder of the ship. When they ascended into the light they were merged into a single primitive mind, walking faithfully behind the man in front. As it is said, if you know not where to graze follow the footsteps of the sheep.

Surely one Jew will help another? If it were not for Mr Lipman they would still be stranded on a corner, prey to any trickster with false offers. He had a friendly face did you notice? A nice smile. They pause on the first landing to breathe. A smell of leather and boot polish comes through the door of a small room, heavy with the heat of bodies and the sweet odour leaking from a gas lamp. Shadowy piles of boots surround the slumped shapes of men like hills in a lunar landscape. They proceed up the stairwell, away from the receding slice of light at the ground floor doorway. Still looking down at their feet – a forced posture which is becoming an acquired attitude – to avoid broken boards and the weak railing. If one man falls they will all tumble like standing dominoes.

On the second landing they drop their sacks and enter a room directly above the boot workshop. The heat thickens like a barrier across the doorway. They wade into the atmosphere without revulsion. They are intimate with smells: unwashed bodies packed into a small space without air, the yellow smoke from the coke stove, coughing. They only see people cutting, stitching, steam-pressing, and the drum roll of sewing machines running wondrously across fabric.

Faces look up as they enter the room. Friday morning! A shipload of greeners again, stinking and penniless, prepared to work eighteen hours a day for a blanket in a rotting attic and black bread and a herring tail to eat. Back home they will not believe the stories or read the letters that reach them: loneliness, tuberculosis in the rooms and cholera in the streets. Things are still better there than they are at home where one Jew cannot make a rouble from all the other Jews around him, they think. Not a wretched soul to hire his labour, and the Czar kidnapping any boy over thirteen to serve in the army. Is tuberculosis new to us? In the knees, in the back? How did Herschel get his limp and Isador his hunch? We survived it. Lungs are nothing – a little cough. So they come! Believing in redemption and gold in the streets, undercutting wages, pushing up the rents, despised by every other Jew in London.

A buttonholer sitting near the window looks up from her work, tightening her eyes to change the focus. The workshop is already overcrowded and every week a new lot arrives. Where will they sit, what will they do, looking hopeful and ready to do any work for half the money? She puts her hand into her pocket to touch the letter like a lucky charm, to feel the safety of the money and the swell of her stomach. "Here is fifteen shillings to buy the baby a coat." She feels old and tired with thinking about money and sewing for Lipman. Every Friday morning at the same time he goes out into the street. She can watch him through the window, threading through the crowds to collect his catch – beached fish on a corner. The whole transaction takes three minutes and they arrive breathless in the workshop eight minutes later. She remembers her first awareness of commerce with her father. Money meant fun and sheer spoiling: sour milk and custard cake at the market, Napoleon kuchen, puffed and creamy with pleasure, or sesame cookies or roasted salted pumpkin seeds. Or else money was proof of your wits, a sign of daring – blood on a gypsy's arm. Put money in his hat. Blood money. The reason why her mother cried and her father counted with hypnotised eyes – two sheep, four cows, ten bags of potatoes, a bag of nails, four boxes of cabbages – and then ran out of the house not to hear her shouting. And Lipman has taught her that in Wentworth Street she is the lowest unit in the commerce of cash for labour. Now she knows why her father's choice cherries sold cheap and why the price of her work falls with every shipload of new arrivals. She is learning every day.

The buttonhole blurs and her thoughts swim like pictures in front of her eyes. A sing-song repeats continuously inside her head: "Here is fifteen shillings to buy the baby a coat. Here is . . ." The sadness has become remote from its cause but persists as a heaviness behind her eyes. She hardly knew him. A city man, softer than the rest, with a delicate frame and soft white hands. Half-moons on his nails. Once she saw someone in the street, an astonishing similarity: graceful, a man in a suit with a white shirt and a tweedy cap, like all the men who live in towns – paid weekly. But she cannot remember his face. A mole on the cusp of his beard. She was always looking at it, wanting to put the tip of her finger on it, to lick it with her tongue. The loneliness has forgotten its source and become behaviour.

She will not tell Lipman about the baby until the very end. Strength and deceit are her only assets; and darkness. The dark workshop will conceal the secret even from the other girls. She wants no friends.

"Come and talk to us, Eva. Why are you always sewing on your own?"

She still does not recognise her new name, awkward in her mouth, this language. And her clothes are also English: puffed sleeves and a pink satin sash around her waist; a parody of the rich women who sometimes come to Wentworth Street looking for bargains. And English money in her pocket – fifteen shillings. Right and fitting that her name should change. Chava was the young girl, left behind in the snowfields of Sharabka and separated from Mama and Papa in Warsaw. There was not enough money for the boat. The prettiest women and the strongest men always went first, and the family would follow. Mama could do washing here as anywhere, but Papa would never survive. The Jews like Lipman shave their faces, they don't cover their heads, they eat blood sausage, perhaps they even eat pig. Papa would be humbled and despised in the streets with the other greeners. At home he is known, he tells stories to an audience. He is Schneider!

She is married now and her direction has changed. She used to feel different to the others and haughty; mistress of the potato field, the prettiest, the fastest. Now she is the same as everyone around her. Language is locked in her mouth. Must she be a poet to make people understand? She is like a dog that does not know its name. And she sits here with the other women, seeing a picture of her life in their faces. They are all worthy of the slop clothing they produce.

Early afternoon. The girls are standing outside Lipman's office. They go in according to rank. He makes them wait for their money. The learners are last in line. Never mind, no one wants to go in first. Sara comes out wiping her mouth on her sleeve. She spits on the floor. And then Taubie comes out quickly, counting her money, and then Mira takes a long time in the room and comes out flushed and looking down, and Sylvie and Nora and then Tamar who is always losing money because Lipman makes her undo her work. "Do it again. And again," and then takes off money for lost time. And Eva. They are all the same and too ashamed to talk. She stands in line with a beating heart. How long will she be able to endure his closeness and the dead hand that pretends that it does not know where it is touching as he delivers her wages. His face shows no change in expression. Did she imagine it? How long will she be able to keep him away, smiling through clenched teeth and looking sideways? His voice is hoarse, dry as the sound Wlad made when he blew into a blade of grass.

"You know, Eva, how much I like your work and how sorry I would be to see you go. The workshop is getting crowded you know."

He comes nearer. She would know him in the dark by his smell.

"You're staid, eh?" he says fingering her yellow scarf. Please God let the little creature inside her not turn with shame.

She touches the letter in her pocket again. Fifteen shillings that have sailed the seas.

She returns to her place near the window again, straightening her yellow scarf, released from his office until payday next week. It is too soon to allow herself the stiffness in her back. Friday, and they must finish all their work. It must be late afternoon already because the children are out of school and playing in the street. She knows the time by watching other people's lives. Young girls skipping with a rope:

> O Mr Porter what shall I do?
> I want to go to Bendigo, send me back to Crewe.
> I want to go to London as quickly as I can
> O Mr Porter what a silly girl I am.

The sick sun lapses behind the buildings. The shops have closed behind metal blinds. Wentworth Street is suddenly empty except for a schoolboy kicking an orange in the gutter and the bakery selling its last few breads before the Sabbath. Its life is silent for a day. In the workshop the women are packing up, but Eva still sits, working slowly – tenpence a dozen shirts. She has learnt the value of her labour. No matter, she has nowhere to go. But her secret is with her everywhere – quite an active chappie. "Chappie", an English word.

She has seen a room in Cable Street along the river, fresh and wholesome and away from the sour alleys of the workshop. Every week she sends a little money home to Gittel who is coming to help her with the baby. There is no money for Mama and Papa and it would be a foreign life for them here. She and Gittel will walk the pavements with wind in their hair for miles down Cable Street and watch the water, alive and twirling in a thousand shiny whorls, carrying the slow barges downstream to sea. And at low tide at night, perhaps they will see the evening star and the river-bed glittering with moving lights as the children come out to dig for cockles in the silt, and sell steaming soup on street corners the next day. Then on Fridays as the sky darkens she and Gittel will wear their best clothes, lace jabots and velvet jackets. Eva will wear her yellow scarf, now frayed at the edges. They are the remnants of the family, but her prayers will travel with the speed of thought as she names them all: Mama and Papa and Faiga and Wlad, she will always remember them. And the young man, far away, whose child is growing inside her. She is also allowed to pray for herself and Gittel. They will cover their heads and kindle the lights.

> *Feel not ashamed, be not humiliated,*
> *Why are you downcast? Why are you disconsolate?*
> *Come my beloved to greet The Bride . . .*

At dinner they will bless the wine and the bread and say the whole prayer in the flickering room because there are no men to say it for them: "And it was evening and it was morning on the sixth day . . . "She will rest and sleep, only rousing herself the next day with the darkening sky. Sacred time. Take to the streets again to breathe the moving air over the cyclical waters. Waiting for three stars that bring in the return to ordinary time.

She forms even stitches into a chain around the edges, binding the cut fabric with a continuous thread to strengthen the small buttonhole against injury; the tearing and rending by rough hands throughout its lifetime. She thinks of the letter again and the man who will be sending for her. Fifteen shillings. The earth is full of diamonds there, little white stones lying in the rivers; walk in the waters barefoot like a child to collect them, scratch the untouched soil with your finger and they are there. She reads the writing printed on the stamp in heavy black lettering: THE CAPE OF GOOD HOPE.

SEVEN
World In A Cage

EVA TURNS HER BACK TO THE SEA AND LOOKS NORTH WHERE A BARBAROUS landmass rises vertically into a great mountain, a blockade to penetration, reducing human scale to stunted creatures that creep around its base. The precipice soars to its horizontal summit that scrapes a strident sky. She blinks as the light pierces her eyes.

In Africa, to look north is to face the tropics of a continent covered in flowering trees and thorn-bushes, or desert dunes that drift overnight into sheer valleys and rise the next day into peaks. Migrating herds roam jungle kingdoms watered by aboriginal rivers that fill volcanic lakes. She has been told that some tribes live naked and others wear animal skins and feathered headdresses, and further north, painted giants and tattooed pygmies with rings in their lips and needles in their tongues drink foaming blood from living cattle. She, the foreigner, thinks them strange. She stands still, holding her bags, looking upwards to the rock with awe. Must she fall to her knees and pray? She holds the baby tight as an anchor in a shifting universe.

Skin colour has blackened since she left the blond Poles and the sallow English. Dark men in short trousers walk barefoot on melting tar as they off-load cargo and balance crates and suitcases on their heads. Is it the sun that singed their hair and scorched their skins ten thousand years ago? The colour covers their armpits and deepens in the folds around their necks. Suddenly intrigued by skin, she is amazed how it covers their hands and turns pink on their palms and the soles of their feet. She shades her eyes from the glare, tilting the hat firmly over the baby's face. He throws it off and laughs.

But the men in uniform are white. Strict white that punishes her eyesight. Why is everything so harsh? They searched her bundles and emptied her bags onto the ground: the baby's jackets and caps, the bag with soiled napkins, dropping them with revulsion as her mouth turned downward in a sneer. The violation when their hands touched her possessions, feeling her combs and brushes, her shoes and stockings, the yellow scarf, her petticoat. They are indecent. The uniform gives them the right and the golden trimmings the authority. What are they looking for in a bundle of unwashed rags that still bear her smell? Then the struggle with language again. To say her name. How to write, how to understand their papers. The small black letters blur in front of her eyes. She cannot understand what "naturalisation" means. Can someone help? They are all dazed and sweating in this African heat. They do what they're told. Somehow they will get through it with a new name, shortened, without permission, for convenience: Wolfowitz changes to Wolf, Davidowich becomes David, Brittanitsky becomes Brittan. Useful, very English.

She should know what it is to be a stranger arriving in a new land without money, no friend or family to meet her. Is it ignorance or innocence that sustains her? She has been told to speak to no one and not to ask for favours or accept them. There are people here like Lipman who make promises and then take your money. She will have to stand for hours in lines, then stand again, always surrounded by others like her, swamped and mocked by their numbers. They have lost their shame as the men nudge roughly to get ahead, push and bump the women who push back and curse – "a black year on you" – and they spit to seal the oath. "May you grow like an onion with your head in the ground." "Why don't you go break a leg?" and someone gets an elbow in a rib. She learned to push on the boat, grab a potato or an egg when she could. Children standing breathless and crying at their parents' feet.

She waits meekly in front of a desk holding her paper – she is never asked to sit down – watching the eye's perusal. Brown hands bring him a cup of tea, put it down on the table, the body bending in subservience and then shuffling backwards toward the door. He stirs the sugar slowly and pauses to drink. Wipes his mouth, opens and closes a drawer. He reads her application, looks at her – should she smile? – and leaves the room. She waits. Everything stops like a clock wound down. Maybe he has gone forever. And then he returns buckling his belt and the world begins to tick again. They crowd outside his office, but he does not hurry, and stops to exchange a joke with someone else in uniform. The badge of bullies. Will they deport her or make her go to the end of the line and stand outside again? His hand is raised over the document with a stamp. She waits . . . then the gratitude

. . . a thud. The blunt fact of exile expressed in that sound. Now is she "naturalised"? She has not felt natural since she left Sharabka.

She lifts her bags and walks away quickly in case they change their minds, gripping the papers in her hand, her life, her legitimacy. She is laden like a donkey, carrying every possession on her back. She hates carrying.

Her legs feel unstable. The land is still tilting with the rhythm of the boat. She steps over ropes and chains and twisted cables. Everything seems abandoned and empty in the windowless warehouses. Keep walking until you find something to drink and somewhere to stay. She will avoid the large shops and offices of this small city at the base of a mountain. Quite English, she thinks. She has always lived on the margins with the poor. The rich are as foreign to her as tattooed pygmies and painted giants. She will feel safer somewhere small and dark where she can rest; a quiet place.

The city is suddenly upon her as she crosses the tramlines, walking away quickly from the noise. She acts on instinct, wandering up the steep streets toward the clustered communities built around the mountain, not looking at anyone or talking, now passing small houses that smell of spices with dark children playing in the street. A turbaned woman calls them inside. She passes men wearing robes and tasseled hats, and the air fills with the smell of decay as a wagon passes, carrying fish. The streets are becoming narrower as women sit on the pavements selling gourds and pumpkins, apples and figs. New kinds of fruit with thorny skins spliced open into red flesh. And the sweet scent of freshly slaughtered meat as she sees tables arranged with goats' heads, their shining eyes staring out of blue-veined faces.

She covers her mouth, nearly retching, and moves toward a shop, reading with difficulty: WINKEL. Another language? Isn't this an English colony? Her skirt beats against her heels, hot in this country in a woolen suit, hot in the hold of the boat next to the groaning engine. Her feet are beginning to swell in the leather boots. She puts the suitcase down and shifts the baby. Interesting how the little body fits around her hips, his legs riding her like a horse. Natural. She unbuttons the starched collar and takes off his heavy cap. The English dress babies like old men. Unnatural.

"Look at the mountain," she says pointing upwards.

"Mounty," says the baby pointing.

"Do you want some water to drink?"

"Dink," says the baby. English will be his language.

She looks at her image in the window, reflecting over the display of paraffin stoves, coloured blankets, snuff, cough syrup, soap, brightly printed material. She tries to flatten her hair and straighten her jacket, stained and smelling of damp and her unwashed body after three weeks at sea. The stench of fish and meat hangs about her and the memory of skinned heads fills her mind. She was always fastidious, "fussy," her sisters said, "always washing her hands and testing things for freshness," a useless scruple on the boat with all the filth around her.

The shop is cool inside, dark and smelling of timber and tobacco. Natural. A man stands behind the counter smoking a pipe; thin with veiny cheeks. They are usually bad-tempered or drinkers. She has learnt to assess people's faces before speaking to them, watching them first. She has not come to spend money and she pretends to ignore him. She picks up a handful of dry beans in a sack, feeling some fabric, looking at a hard vegetable – corn, she thinks – and a basket of green herbs – chillies?

"Mr Winkel, do you speak English? Please can I have some water for the baby to drink?"

"Dink," says the baby.

"'Dink' means 'think' in this country, my boy. But drinking is good in any language, eh?"

Eva thinks she can smell liquor as he opens his mouth to laugh, and she laughs back.

He scoops some water from a barrel with an empty gourd. She hopes the water is drinkable in this country. Is the ladle clean? She wipes the rim on the cuff of her jacket. Cool and sweet. She tries to hide her nails. Homeless and dirty in a new country for the second time, now with a baby on her hip.

... Here is fifteen shillings to buy the baby a coat ... It was spent in the boat buying water and food, and when it was finished she used the only resource she had left, allowing the man's groping in the night. First tentative to test her, and then when she offered no resistance, his weight on her, heavy, importunate from being so long at sea. Anything could happen on those dirty mattresses, men and women all crowded together without light or air. His hand clutched her skirts and they exchanged commodities cynically: food for favours, and she got some salted fish and dry biscuits. A woman needed a man's protection in that place. He found her a herring or an orange or some black bread and tea. They never spoke. He never asked her name. She wound her hair into a knot, and in the morning she ran with the baby, covering her mouth and fleeing the filth of the buckets. To be away from nagging children, sick women and men gambling and fighting over matchsticks, their only currency. She fled from the infected air, hiding high up on the deck. All day watching the rippling black skirts of the sea, split open and ruffling its lacy petticoats. Sometimes a young man came onto the deck and hid behind the small boats to pray. One had to hide away to be alone. She saved the crusts of black bread to feed the little birds resting on the railings – they had a long way to go. Once she saw a brown mouse – it also had a life. She brushed her hair in the stinging daylight, her yellow scarf flying like a pennant, and she opened the baby's skin to the sun, breathing the gusty air and watching flocks of migrating gulls, switching the pitch of their wings, squawking and scavenging into the wake. Only to sway to the sounds of mewling seabirds and shower in the salty spray, her face getting browner as they travelled south and the sunlight sanitising her imagination.

When the sun went down she descended into the pit again where she mingled her smells with the man in the dark, hearing intimate human sounds all around her and children crying in their dreams. Some passengers were sleeping fifteen to a cabin, and others in "open berth" were lying in passages or cupboards or even on unused tables. But on Fridays it was quieter. There were prayers and some of the women lit candles in the night.

Fifteen shillings was not enough. When they landed in Cape Town she picked up her bags and walked away. Please, let her never see him again. She did not turn around.

"Are you new here? You look like you've just got off the boat. Do you have any family or friends or anywhere to stay? Luister, my name is Jan. It's getting late. I'll call die vetvrou and tell her ons het gaste vanaand. We live in an old house behind the shop. This is a Malay area. You won't find anywhere else to stay. There are only bars for sailors or hotels in town for the English who come out for the summer. You can stay with us until you find somewhere else."

He beckons to a black man to watch the shop, and takes her through the back door. They walk through a passage that leads to a kitchen. Two dogs snarl and leap through the open door.

"Down Harry. Down Kabous. Where are your manners? Down my boys."

A cage stands on a table outside the kitchen door with two lovebirds hanging onto the bars, entangled like one body with two heads.

"I saved them twice. Trudy threw them away and I put them in the oven for warmth and she threw them away again and I rescued them. Eventually they survived, but they're slightly retarded ever since. They think they're in love. Shut up," he shouts, rattling the cage. "Is that the thanks I get for saving you? Kom. I want to show you my fish. I bought them from a sailor who caught them in the East Indies. How are my seuntjies?"

Tropical fish swim around a miniature submerged pagoda and under a porcelain bridge.

"They're used to Oriental furnishings, ey, my boys? Don't tell them they're in Africa or they'll want to emigrate. Kom," he slaps Eva on the back. "Die vetvrou will make us some tea. This is Trudy."

She comes toward them wearing a wide dress, her upper arms swinging as she shakes hands. Eva is not sure what "vetvrou" means but guesses it is some kind of joke – fat wife? Something that makes her want to laugh, and then cover her mouth with shame at her collusion with Jan and at the same time embarrassment for Trudy.

"Ag, Jan is always making jokes. Never mind," Trudy says with blushes blossoming around her neck. "Ag shame. I've got a spare room that overlooks the yard. The geese splash at night and wake up with the sun in the morning. I hope the smell won't upset you."

"It's like home. Natural," says Eva, feeling sympathy for the woman, missing two front teeth.

"Never mind. Gasvryheid. We can't leave you and the baby in the street. It's getting dark. I'll bring you something to eat."

Eva wakes in the darkness, quietly leaves the room and walks through the yard. She can see the backs of the surrounding houses: the muddled meeting of iron rooftops with roosting chickens, washing on lines, and the smell of refuse. The neighbourhood fits into a patchwork of flavours and scents. Harry and Kabous each sleep on a bed with a pillow in a disused wagon. The birdcage is covered with a cloth and nine grey geese are fenced into a small enclosure, paddling in a pool and eating gruel from a trough. She has not seen live geese since she left Sharabka, only dead ones on a butcher's hook. These nine geese would separate permanently into four mating pairs with one left over, and the choice would be binding for life. Which is the ninth goose? They wag fatty tails, eat slops and live committed to the bond undertaken there.

The gold band hangs loosely around her fourth finger. She has not seen him for two years. She cannot remember his face – only a spot below his cheek and faint half-moons on his nails. A slender build. He loved apples she recalls. He will send her a letter from a mining settlement called Kimberley and travel four days by mule wagon to see her. They will lie long nights together for a week, and then he will go back.

She looks up into the southern sky, dazzling as the desert diamond-fields. A new moon inhabits the blackness with Venus cradled in the crescent around it. It throbs like an amorous heart. Here on the edge of the earth, the great constellations slowly revolve beyond the mountain and out of sight. She is a mote in the vastness and the mountain gapes in the darkness like a crack. She cowers under it and walks quickly back, needing human scale and a roof above her head.

Inside the house she hears Jan and Trudy talking softly in their room. Despite his jokes they make promises, whisper secrets, share the same dreamspace.

She wonders how it feels to be a wife; the mysterious orbit that pulls her to a stranger in a desert town in Africa. She has crossed an ocean but cannot remember his face.

She walks quietly to her room and looks out of the window. Which is the ninth goose in the farmyard?

The animals are quiet. The ringing insects fill the night with the clamour of procreation. She thinks about the affections of the two birds, brain-damaged and crippled, joined as one flesh in a world the size of a cage.

EIGHT
Casualties Of The Dust

HE WAS A FOOL. HE WAS A FAILURE. THE STREETS ARE EMPTY, THE SHOPS are closing down. He was a fool. His mouth was soft. His hands too gentle. There are no offices, there are no jobs. He was a fool.

May His great name be exalted and sanctified.

The sand clings to her boots and powders the hem of her black skirt. Little eddies spin around the gravestones, blowing dust onto the inscriptions. Eva stands next to a loose mound of red soil, the wind beginning to erode its surface. Small stones roll down the sides and soon the ground will have hardened.

He had already been buried five days when she received the letter, and ten Jews taken off the street recited the prayer for the dead. His wife was not needed to make up the quorum.

May His great name be exalted and sanctified in the world that He created as He willed.

They could not wait for her because of the heat and the rot and disease carried by the wind. "We put 'em in the same day, if we can," they told her.

He was a fool. He was a failure. The heyday is over and the fortunes have been made. The struggle is past and decided. The rich have meetings in paneled boardrooms and the diggers have all gone north to find gold in Johannesburg. He was a fool. Now the women have come. Flowers are planted and gardens are beginning to give shade. The sport is over and the madness is done.

He was a dreamer. His body was smooth and his hair was springy against his skin like the long grass that grows through sand near the sea. She always wanted to touch it. His skin was cool, fresh even on the hottest day. But she cannot remember his face; only the spot on the curve of his cheek that she would touch softly with the tip of her finger. He had half-moons on his nails.

She hardly knew him. A city man scheming of ways to make money. Fifteen shillings to buy a coat. He had only seen the child, Max, once and had never seen the baby. They were together for a week and then he had gone. A baby a year when the men come home, and letters every month with small amounts of money. He would not allow her to come to Kimberley. "People drop like flies. The women miscarry and the children grow up pale and puny," he argued "The cemetery is full of small graves. And where will you live? In a tent?"

"Yes!" she cried. "I'll sew. I'll work."

And now she is standing here, looking at a mound of sand. She waited for him in London and she waited in Cape Town. Waiting for the waiting to be easy; a stranger to the matrimonial bed.

He was a fool surrounded by thieves. She has been standing for an hour in a waiting-room, looking down at her shoes. The widow on show. What can they see in her face? Tomorrow will be their turn – please God let her not make a curse.

"Oh yes. Please come inside for a moment. Your name again? Yes. Very unfortunate and terribly quick. That's the way it happens to them here. One day they are sitting in the office with everyone else, the next day they're coughing and three days later they're dead. Nothing to stop it. It's the climate, you know. Unfit for anyone but Boers and Blacks. We make the risks quite clear in the terms of the contract. Poor fellow. He was quite frail, if I remember. This is Africa, you know. Unfortunately we had to use his money for the burial: the coffin and other miscellaneous expenses. Perhaps you ought to know that if this hadn't happened to him, we would have had to let him go anyway. A nice enough fellow. We all liked him, if I can recall. But there are no jobs, you see. There's only one company and they own it all. It's over. The men are working in road-gangs and eat in soup-kitchens, and with all the trouble in the Transvaal the soldiers are beginning to garrison the town. I'm sending my own wife back to Cape Town. I'm afraid that's all I can tell you. They sent this bag of clothes from the hospital. That's all that's left. Perhaps Matron can tell you more. Most unfortunate. I can't quite remember his face."

They never asked her to sit down.

Eva looks down at the grave. This is a place where the soil is sovereign. Everyone is grubbing in it. They dig and carry and sift and steal the little white stones, dull stones, from the red sand. They stand with their feet in it. They sit and eat in it. They carve it up and put their names on it, erect cable lines and swing buckets in and out of it. Then in another place, this place, they dig other holes in it, more long than wide, and they return bodies to it in exchange for the white stones they take out of it.

This cemetery is new and shallow as the town it serves; no more than a large circle of thorny cacti. Yet it is old with affliction. Beyond it lies the open scrub, clean of human suffering, touched only by the wind. But this little corner has been reserved by universal consent for bones and tears and horror. It was officially opened by aldermen in silk hats. There will be a place for them too.

Even here the Jews lie separate, and on the other side, far away, are some graves with no names. They are the thieves and beggars dumped quickly into the soil because there is nowhere else to put them before they stink.

> *Blessed, praised, glorified, exalted, extolled, mighty, upraised and lauded be the name of the Holy One, blessed is He.*

It is the sand she hates and the wind. It is in her hair and her eyes and its grains grind between her teeth. As a child she kicked clods of earth in the potato-field, but it was wholesome soil that left her skin feeling clean. This grit insinuates into her shoes, inside her stockings and grinds against her feet, eroding everything soft and human. Only the squat bushes can control it with their fibrous roots.

Will I stand here staring at a heap of earth until I'm blind? What is it that I'm staring at? She cannot lift her feet; they will never return to this place.

At last she moves away without looking back. Some of the graves are nameless again, uneven hollows in the soil with a few stones to mark the place. Unmourned victims of the dust. Some have only their names scratched on a piece of slate. The arrangement is crudely deliberate – all toes pointing in the same direction.

"Is it east or west? Which way points to Jerusalem in this empty land?"
Everything is quiet except for the wind and the dust.

She walks past the graves trying to read the words carved in stone: husband and three sons chained together as though it will hold them beyond the grave.

> IN MEMORY OF
> MY DEAR HUSBAND
> MORGAN DAVIES
> DIED 1/10/1873
> AGED 37 YEARS
>
> ALSO MY DEARLY BELOVED SON
> GLYNDWR WINSLADE DAVIES
> WHO PASSED AWAY
> OCTOBER 8 1880
> AGED 18 YEARS
>
> IN LOVING MEMORY OF
> MY BELOVED SON
> KENNETH ELSOON DAVIES
> WHO DIED ON
> JANUARY 12 1895
> WE CANNOT LORD THY PURPOSE SEE
> ALL IS WELL THAT IS DONE BY THEE
>
> IN LOVING MEMORY OF MY DEAR SON
> CYRIL WASHINGTON DAVIES
> WHO PASSED AWAY
> SEPTEMBER 28 1895
> THY WILL BE DONE

Where is Mrs Davies now, six years later? The inscriptions tell lies. They are furnished phrases produced by a cleric or a friend while they stood her up, fainting at the place of death, to be witness for the fourth time on September twenty-eighth, eighteen ninety-five. Or did she stand there tamed and quiet, listening to the sods of earth drop six feet onto the hollow box? A thud like the sound of exile.

On the other side of the path lies WILLIAM THOMAS JONES next to GRACE ROBERTS JONES. Her life was WELL SPENT and he LIVED TO SERVE. Eva turns away, envious of Grace Roberts Jones and her bones lying for all time next to William Thomas in their "matrimonial bed".

She walks away from the graves, stepping over the circle of stones which separates this place from the living world. Her fingers clutch into a fist around the bag of clothes – her legacy. The shirt is limp from the heat and sweat, smelling stale from the empty room where it lay in the bag. She cannot remember his face. The collar is smudged where it touched his skin and curls in a circle where it closed around his neck. Slender. The trousers still carry his scent. She looks furtively into the bag as though it is indecent. It's him! She wants to breathe it like smelling flowers, an intimacy she has never known.

In the street again. Everyone has somewhere to go. But for everyone the cemetery is at the end of the road. The rows of iron houses match the tidy lines of the graves. One door, four windows facing the street and a eucalyptus tree on the pavement. All lies. Orderly patterns that hide the desire and the terror within.

She crosses into Dutoitspan Road and passes the hospital. Matron comes onto the wooden verandah. Starched midwife to all the dead in Kimberley – quite pretty with bobbed brown hair curling around her face and a lace cap balancing on top of her head. He was fed, scrubbed and dispatched by her red hands. Was she gentle with him or harsh as he lay helpless, his life leaking out of him onto the sheets? There is no information except the clothing in the bag: a crumpled handkerchief in the trouser pocket, his soiled shirt and tie, his shoes, moulded to the shape of his feet, quite small for a man and wearing down more on the left heel than the right. He leaned to one side, she remembers. Must she read his clothing like a book and keep them as relics? An inheritance for his children?

Iron houses have given way to brick. Eva walks past homes with tended gardens and ornamental balconies that decorate the buildings like lace trimmings on a dress. The hateful red sand is buried under tar, covered by smooth pavements and edged with firmly stacked curbing stones. No other white women are walking in the street, only black ones with babies strapped to their backs. The ladies ride to the shops in hooded carriages, driven by servants. Her footsteps tap the pavement like a mechanical beat and her fingers grip the bag that contains the living smells of a dead man. She cannot remember his face. She keeps getting a picture of her father. But he liked apples, she remembers. She is a widow before she was a wife.

The houses are closer together now, interspersed with shops and canopied pavements. She turns the corner and Dutoitspan Road fans out into the central shopping area, suddenly crowded with carts and people. Double-storey buildings are flanked by fluted columns and rise into ornamental gables. Africa imitating England. This is where the ladies shop, ABRAHAMS AND CO – HIGH CLASS IMPORTERS OF NORWEGIAN DELICACIES AND FRENCH AND ENGLISH CONFECTIONARY. That is what the gentlemen eat. Her mouth is dry and her stomach is flat. She has hardly eaten since she left Cape Town.

A carriage crosses the corner in front of her, pulling up outside the Theatre Royal. VERY LAST NIGHT OF WHEELER AS PADDY. LAST NIGHT OF THE SKIPPING ROPE DANCE AND LAST NIGHT OF WHEELER'S SKETCH "ROOMS TO LET". Two women unpack their skirts, holding their hats and veils with gloved hands, gliding into the building. Eva smells cologne and horse-sweat as she passes the carriage. The scent of hay and worn leather surrounds the animal. She strokes its flanks, feels the twitch of muscles under the skin, warm and damp on her hands. How comforting to touch a living thing. She is remote from all the events that have brought her here to this desert town. Her reflection in shop windows is unfamiliar. Who is she? The widow with a dry mouth and a dead man's clothes in a bag. Give them to any beggar in the street.

She crosses into Market Square, passing the new Town Hall and the produce market, strangely vacant. Sheets of corrugated iron, wooden planks, rusty pipes, sieves, iron bed-heads, soiled mattresses, picks, shovels, coils of rope, twenty mules in a pen, numbered and marked, wait for inspection – everything needed for a man's work in a mining town. The only food is a pile of dried salted meat. She picks up a piece of sun-bleached wood, pale and pitted, but intact and resilient after all. Still useful and too weathered to warp; an essential support, a pillar in someone's life, mellow and seasoned. Functional because of its age and endurance.

She leaves the market behind, and all its rusted, damaged materials that are discarded but bought back to serve a further cycle in mining life.

The buildings are spaced further apart again, and the red sand shifts and slides under her feet as she moves across unoccupied space, back to the railway station that is no more than two sheds and the station master's box. Her legs have a rhythm of their own, a vigorous full stride now. Her skirt beats against her boots as she steps out, wanting to run, remembering where she is going and feeling hungry again, needing to eat and walking faster. She has strong eyes and careful fingers. Shirts will always have buttons and buttons must be closed. Her little stitches are incomparable. Gittel has come to South Africa to help her, and there will be a living for them all.

The railway tracks gleam in the red sand, join, divide, join, curve past the platform and then travel far south in a straight line out of sight like the screeching guinea-fowl that fly across the veld. The station is empty except for a rag-tag clump of soldiers smoking and singing a song:

> *First comes night and then comes day*
> *So we pass our time away*
> *First come young ones then come old ones*
> *Over the hills and far away.*

She is going back to little Max and baby Theo with his infant smell of warm flannel and bubbling spittle. Back to the retarded birds in their cage and the nine geese and Harry and Kabous and the room overlooking the yard on the cold side of Jan and Trudie's house.

NINE
Incurable And Damned

FRIDAY AFTER SCHOOL IS WHEN IT HAPPENS. EARLY CLOSING. THEY BURST out of classrooms like thrashing trout, breaching the doors as they come bounding down the stairs. Then sun-dazed they struggle through the gate, stroll three blocks hands-in-pockets and squat in the field behind the Jew shop, waiting for the others to arrive. The Jew never interferes, locks up for the Sabbath and walks home. Today is a big one. Notes and letters have been changing hands all day. Max, the new boy from Cape Town, doesn't play or talk, won't make way for the old boys in the passage, won't yield up his best marbles. Proud bastard, they'll teach him. Bad-tempered too. It's going to be a fight to the finish. As they all arrive, they separate into two groups: one older, stronger, crouching down in the long grass, stretched out sucking dry straws, legs lolling outwards; Max's supporters on the other side.

"I wonder where his father is?" it comes sky-stunned and school-spent.

"Yes, I wonder," an answer, heard and not seen. A fart in the long grass. High-pitched laughter.

"Perhaps he never had one, like Taffy Edelman and Murray Cooper. My mother has a special name for them."

"We know where your father is, Stubbs, and your mother has to fetch him home every morning." They fall about silly in the sun, rolling and sneezing in a field of dandelions.

"At least I have one. Where's your father, then, Maxie?" A challenge from the older boys.

The two groups are standing now, facing each other with a narrow corridor between them, neutral ground. Two adversaries come forward. Gladiators in school socks, face to face across the battle lines.

"My father's dead. What of it?"

"Where's your mother then?" He kicks sand onto Max's shoes.

"Nunnaya business, Stubbs. Wanna make something of it?"

They all recognise the moment. Max jerks off his jacket and unbuttons his shirt, starched and clean this morning. He must wear it two days before it is washed again and he dare not tear it in a fight as he did last week and the week before or his mother will look at him silently. He knows her eyes, reads them quickly and shrewdly after school. He can measure the merest contraction of muscles, the slightest shadow. He calculates his behaviour accordingly.

Both sides close round into an arena. They know and respect the rules.

"Put up ya dooks," Max challenges and they poise their fists in front of their faces, knickerbocker pugilists dancing lightly from foot to foot, thumbing noses and making threatening circles with their fists. Butterflies flicker on the dandelions.

"Get 'im Maxie!" Max sends out mock jabs to Stubbs's face, weaving and prancing on his toes like the Welsh miners at Ferreira's. He strikes out with his right arm and Stubbs dodges out of reach.

"Ask me again about my mother." Still dancing, he drops his arms and bumps the boy with his chest. He would like to close the distance and tear him with his hands.

"Wha' did ya say?"

He grabs the boy's collar and trips him with his foot. The crowd screams, yaaaiiihooorayiii.

"Say it again I dare ya." He falls onto Stubbs and they strain against each other on the ground, legs and arms entangled. Stubbs forces himself over on top of Max.

"She's a yid and so are you. She stinks and she can't read or write."

Max claws the ground with his feet, scrapes and scuffs his shoes, groans and forces the boy over.

"Say it again say it again." Saliva and sand stick to the corners of his mouth. Grit between his teeth. "Wha'didyacall'er?" Max sits on his stomach and pins down his arms while his legs thrash and jerk. He forces the words over the boy's face, holding his neck and beating his head against the ground.

"I'll kill ya I'll kill ya say it again!"

"Ikeykikeyyid."

"Hold 'im down Maxie you got 'im. Apologise nicely Stubbs. Ya got 'im for sure Maxie. Let 'im go let 'im go Maxie. Enough. Let 'im go."

Max cannot loosen his fingers from Stubbs' shirt or stop himself from beating the head on the ground. A thin red thread trickles from Stubbs' nostril and Max's eyes shine.

"I'll kill ya, I swear."

The show of blood determines the winner. "Jeez, he's got a bad temper." The marshals drag them apart, still struggling, one on each arm, and lift them onto their feet, dusting them off and separating into two groups again. Stubbs turns away to vomit.

"You got 'im Maxie, now shake hands."

"I'll kill 'im next time, I swear, I'll kill 'im with my bare hands. Anybody else for a fight?"

His back is pitted with pebbles, his front tooth sore, a bit loose, he wiggles it with his tongue, sweet taste of blood. His body is still shaking, and the grazes on his back burn as he puts on his shirt – clean on the hot skin, covering the bruises with white-cool calico. His shirts and Theo's are his mother's pride. Scrubbed with bare knuckles and seared with an iron. They must sting the eyes with brightness and the collars must crackle with starch, lift their chins with stiffness. She will not be shamed by poverty and she is sickened by the children in the street with clotted noses and the smell of urine.

"Sewer rats and pischwasser, their mothers don't care, do you want to be like them? Wipe your nose, you should be ashamed!" she says to Theo who stands vacantly for a long time with a finger in his nose.

Max turns his back on the boys in the street, puts on his cap and walks away, kicking a stone. "I'll kill 'im I swear." The clash is settled for the week, but by Wednesday he will be refusing to give way in the passage again. She will never know that he has been fighting but he sees that his black shoes are scuffed white and his trousers torn at the knee. Maybe he can fix them with glue. He walks down the street, towards the last wooden houses and the sheds with iron roofs – scrapyards storing rotting wagon-wheels, old carriages and bicycles – until he reaches the very last house in the street. He always looks inside to see the crumbling brick with broken windows, a rusty billycan, some burnt newspapers and a crusted turd in the corner. Someone sleeps there at night. "Next time I'll kill 'im. I'll kill that Stubbs I swear."

And now no houses in front of him and he can see the trees and koppies of the open veld. His feet are on grass. He wriggles under the prickly wire surrounding Ferreira's mine, careful not to catch his shirt, still walking until he passes the grey iron factory, square and strict against the blue sky, with large turning wheels and twisted steel cables that carry the rocks in buckets out of the ground. The miners let him pass in his schoolboy's jacket. He takes off his cap, stuffs it in his pocket, crossing in the direction of the dam where the native boys swim kaalgat in the afternoon, their buttocks shining dark like the inky mine water in the sun. The acid water will compress the swellings and flush out the small stones buried in the grazes on his back. And jumping from high up down into the dam, like hitting a solid surface with his feet, the blood will be beaten into his skin and the lacerations will seal.

He throws off his clothes and together with the other boys he crawls on his hands and knees along a narrow pipe high over the water. If they fall now they will break their legs because here the water is rippling and shallow with a muddy bottom full of reeds. But when Max sees it getting deep underneath him, smooth and still on the surface, he looks down into the black depths feeling a great wallowing inside him. He looks back to the shore yearning for the safety of the miners who sit quietly on the bank catching fish and the small children wading in the shallows collecting tadpoles in bottles. There is no going back now because he cannot turn around on the narrow swaying pipe and the others are crawling close behind him. He promises himself that he will never ever climb the pipe again. When he comes to the end with no other way to go but over the edge and the children saying hurry up or they'll push him over. He holds his nose and hesitates again with a last paralyzing terror. It is the end of the wooooorld . . . and he jumps, screaming as he falls, his feet smacking the solid skin of the water and filling up his ears . . . sinking . . . sinking . . . deaf and blind sinking without end into a cold dark place, horrified that he will fall forever, or worse, that his feet will touch the slimy underwater weeds that will entangle him like prey – frantically wriggling like a frog, he begins to see the green light of the surface like a high ceiling above him. He scrambles shivering out of the dam, runs along the side and crawls back onto the pipe with the native boys to jump again.

Afterwards they sit on a grassy bank, teeth chattering and goose-skinned to warm in the sun. He swops his jujubes for small pieces of sugar-cane, and they lie there sucking on the sweetness and spitting the chewed-out fibres.

Then they collect flat stones and skip them one-two-three crikey, did you see, four times across the water. The trick is the way you swing your arm. Swinging and swinging, did you see that one? Until the sun goes down behind the hills.

Crikey! He has forgotten again. Friday and he is supposed to be home early, long before his mother lights the candles at sunset so that he can help her to pluck and singe the chicken and make a fire in the stove. Theo doesn't help because he is allergic to the fluff and is allowed to lie and draw his pictures on paper. But Max loves the smell of burning feathers in the bag. Then making the fire, the sudden ignition with a flash and the slow spread of flames if he has balanced everything right, the wood delicately poised with enough space for the hungry red tongues to lick the draught. He is the eldest child, it is his job. No one can make a fire like he can.

He and his mother work together silently. She no longer asks him where he goes on Friday afternoon to make the skin on his body red, especially his nose, or why he should always be late, and whether the two things are related. But her quietness tells him that she suspects him. He also suspects her. He works without speaking because he knows that the special preparation for dinner – soup and fish and chicken and compote – is to entertain Elias Zalman and his three daughters again. Every week she warns him to behave.

"He always brings meat from his shop," she says. "Smoked beef and sausages and eggs and food for the whole week. Don't be ungrateful. You can see how hard I have to work. One day I'll go blind from those buttonholes. And last week he brought you a whipping top and licorice for Theo. He always brings something nice. And why shouldn't he eat with us on Friday night? My mother always had a stranger eating with us on the Sabbath; it's a blessing. Selfish thing."

"I hate him, he's fat and smells of blood and his fingers are always red with bits of meat stuck under the nails. And I hate his daughters, they're stupid and they waddle their bums like ducks. I don't care if he doesn't bring us food. I'd rather eat bread and jam and chicken once a week the way we used to.

"I'll thrash you if you use rude words," she says.

Then they work in silence again, thinking of what they've said.

"Just behave," she says.

That night the lace tablecloth is on the table and the candlesticks shine bright. Eva has wiped and buffed each knife and spoon. She inspects them carefully before laying them on the table and the white plates glisten in the candlelight. She has a way with tables, folds the napkins into fancy frills, finds flowers in the streets, steals roses through fences: "There are so many they'll never notice." Elias Zalman makes the prayer before dinner; practised and fluent: "And it was morning and it was evening on the seventh day . . ." – versed and unceremonious. Then they all drink Sabbath wine. Tonight there is chicken baked with honeyed carrots and prunes, Max's favourite. He likes to eat with his hands and lick his fingers, leaving all the small bones in a neat pile on his empty plate, sucked dry and then sucked again.

But tonight he has no taste for its sweetness. He watches the candlelight reflecting on the pink dome of Zalman's head. He notices the moist folds around his nostrils and under his chin. Zalman dabs the folds with a handkerchief that was clean white and becoming clammy as he wipes his eyes and then his nose and pushes it with a sticky gravied hand into his pocket. Max watches the opening of the mouth, the puffypink tongue thrusting forward to receive the food and the steady grind of teeth, clockwise, while he prepares the next mouthful; then the swallowing with a loaded fork waiting in front of his lips. Max is always placed directly across the table from him. It rivets his eyes. The sticky hand pinches his mother's neck and he wants to kick the fat feet under the table and rise up overturning the plates and upsetting his chair and . . . then he sees his mother put the last-scraped spoon of rice pudding and compote into Theo's plate. He eats it to the last grain like a good boy.

After dinner the sisters play with Theo, combing his hair with scented pomade, their stumpy fingers making shiny waves and slick sideburns, laughing and kissing him and laughing again when his cheeks burn red with blotches and he hides behind the curtain.

"Little mannikin," they call him, and tickle him through the curtain. They feed him sugared jellies, "What's your favourite colour? Black's the best. My turn, my turn. Who do you like best? Choose me! Choose me!" they scream and stamp their legs, spinning him around until he falls breathless on the floor and they tickle his tortured armpits until he shrieks.

Eva is still sitting at the table with Elias Zalman, talking softly, their chairs pushed together and their heads touching. Zalman says something in her ear, nuzzling his nose into her hair and absentmindedly stroking the ruffle on her sleeve. She smiles, looks down and watches Theo playing with the three girls. Zalman is still looking at her, waiting, now his finger is stroking her hand. Max can see their feet touching under the table, her bootlaces pulled tight across the studs and up the fine ankle, and his shoe, the laces stretched wide to accommodate the fleshy instep, the sole tilting upwards at the toes.

Max gets up and leaves them all in the airless sitting-room and goes out into the cool night to stand in the light of the comet. The street is empty. People are losing their excitement with it. But he watches it every night, a plume of light suspended high over the houses and illuminating the rows of rooftops and chimneys in a glowing outline. Everyone is saying that the earth has passed right through it, and Max is waiting for a shudder or a shower of stars or fragments of glittering flint to fall from the sky. But each night it becomes fainter as it moves away from the sun, and he wonders about the frozen mists that drift with its tail and its vast pathway through the silent spaces, unknown and terrifying like the black water of the dam. Sometimes he thinks it is a blessing, and everyone who has stood under its holy light will be saved: all the stray dogs and feral cats and mice and rats that live in the drains, and the vagrants who sleep in the alleys, and the painted ladies who come out at night and stand alone in doorways talking softly to men who pass in the street. They will all be redeemed. But other times, as he lies in bed, the comet points at him through the open window and casts tangled shadows through the trees onto the white walls of his room. Then he closes the curtains against its leprous light, hiding himself under the blanket without moving and unable to breathe, wet with sweat and itchy and nearly choking, until it passes across the sky and he is safe again.

He stands across the street watching them through the window. All the children are sitting on the floor in a small circle, talking and laughing. Maybe they are telling funny stories or singing. His mother and Elias Zalman go out of the room for a long time. Max walks up the street and down again. They are not back. He walks around the block, peeping into the Chinese gambling-room through the gap in the swing-doors, men sitting at long tables under bright lights, and into the bar where Stubbs's father is standing at an empty counter drinking. Slowly back to his mother's house, slowly, slowly, looking down, kicking a stone . . . two sheep, four cows, ten bags of potatoes, a bag of nails, four boxes of cabbages . . . they must be back in the sitting-room by this time. Zalman is holding her hand and Theo is slouched over the table leaning against her. Will they never go? He walks up the street and down again. If it is true that he is less than a spot of dust in the universe, then why does he feel as fiery as an exploding star? Now the front room is in darkness except for the Sabbath candles magnified through the glass into golden crowns. They have left the front door unlatched for him. He goes back into the house and locks the door behind him.

It is Saturday morning. Max leaves the house dressed in his tweed suit and cap, walking up Commissioner Street towards the synagogue in Mooi Street. The curtains of the houses are all closed, everyone sleeping except a child still wearing his slippers, walking on the pavement carrying a bottle of milk. Eva sleeps late on Saturday, keeps her bedroom door closed, and Theo lies quietly in bed looking at the ceiling. Max likes to be the first to open the front door and leave – the first surprise of light and air and space outside the dark house with its smell of sleep and Theo yawning and turning over to dream again.

So perhaps, only because it is still too early, he will cross the road and just walk past Market Square on his way – absolutely 'struewasgod without stopping. The streets become busier as he leaves the still-asleep houses behind him, women already on their way back from shopping, carrying live chickens upside down by their feet, nearly dead with eyes staring, and bundles of fresh greens to cook them in. Too early for the trams and only a few bicycles on the street. So he walks hands in pockets in the middle of the road with the black men wrapped in patterned blankets. Some of the shopkeepers are unwinding their awnings and sweeping the pavements. He passes office buildings rising up two storeys and then three storeys and – there it is – now he can see the rickshaws: fifty in a line making a perfect right angle with the long row of horse-drawn cabs standing in profile like an ornamental wall along the side of Market Square.

It is still too early for synagogue, so perhaps . . . and suddenly he feels hungry, he will just step into the Market to buy some milk and bread and only for a moment watch the teams of spanned oxen. Twenty-four identical upturned horns harnessed in pairs into a solid wooden shaft. He passes his hands over the fatty hump that falls into the silky folds around the neck and between its front legs like a skirt, and he slaps the rounded rump, stinging his hand on the buttock, stretched tight as a drum. His hand is hypnotised by the touch, stroking and stroking, but he must mind their horns as they could skewer a hole right through him as they suddenly toss their heads sideways to scatter the flies.

He takes off his jacket and helps the farmer's children carry bales of fodder and sweep up the manure into a bag. He does not speak their language except to say "Ja" and "Nee" and "Kom" and "Wag 'n bietjie" but they play together by imitation, picking up discarded carrots and apples to feed the cab horses and carrying buckets of water for them to drink. He loves the light touch of the muzzle as they lift the carrots with their lips and the hot draught of breath against his hand. He stands listening to the grind of their teeth and gives them more.

Then he submerges himself under the moving crowd, rises up to pinch a peach and submerges again, allowing the crowd to carry him. He can only understand things with his hands. He works the hinges and measures the dead weight of tools – nothing as solid as a heavy hammer. He runs his thumb over the knives, pulls out piles of rusted chains and twisted bits of metal. He is alone and unobserved in the buying, breathing mass. He knows that Mr Abrahams will tell his mother that he did not arrive for the choir again and, crickey! he has lost his jacket! She will look at him without speaking, that special look, thin-lipped, narrow-eyed, and this time he will get a bad punishment for the jacket, something he hates like washing the dishes every night, or worse, emptying and cleaning the dustbins. And she will spoil Theo even more. Perhaps he can find her a little silver thimble and her face will soften and smile. But he has gone too far this morning and he has the cheerfulness of the incurable and the indifference of the damned.

It must be nearly lunchtime. There are only a few cabs left in the street and the remaining stall-owners are packing their remnants into boxes and crates. He stays until the farmers have loaded their wagons and begun to lead the slow-moving teams out of sight, down the narrow streets where the tar ends and the green grass begins.

He walks home down Commissioner Street, past the brown stone buildings with high-carved doors and marble columns. A clock on a high tower says half-past twelve. "Too shameless to care," that is what she'll say, so he stops for an ice-cream in the Arcade and stands licking the cone outside the barbershop window watching a man being shaved; a drop of blood spreads through the shaving-cream like a blossoming rose. He defies the Sabbath irredeemably by jumping onto the bumper of a passing tram, hanging onto the side with the wind in his face and crouching out of sight for a free ride home.

The buildings are getting smaller – single-storey shops, sun-dried brick homes, and then rows of semis in Ferreirastown where he jumps off before they reach the terminus. Strange to think that the comet and all the stars are still in the sky, invisible in the bright light. He walks down the pavement and up two steps onto the verandah of the iron cottage. At least he is still wearing his cap. He tries to look just ordinary and unperturbed, tucking in his shirt and smiling nicely. Perhaps his mother won't notice the jacket.

She is sitting on the stoep watching him. His eyes are not dull from reading mildewed manuscripts nor do his clothes smell of damp walls and old carpets. His mouth is stained with chocolate ice-cream and his tweed trousers are stuck with straw and as he passes there is an unmistakable scent of fodder and manure.

TEN

Everything Clean And Pure

TOMORROW IS THE EVE OF THE NEW YEAR: THE YEAR FIVE THOUSAND SIX hundred and seventy-nine, corresponding in the secular calendar to one thousand nine hundred and nineteen.

Eva has worked for a week in preparation, she and the black woman moving everything in the house; dragging the sitting-room carpet into the yard, thrashing it with a stick to remove the dust, and again and again and another whack until there is no more harvest of dust. Her energy grows like an appetite and she looks about with hungry eyes, sees recalcitrance everywhere: the wooden furniture, dull from standing in one place. She must scourge it to bring out its light. Push it about, whip its slack spirit and then placate its anger. One spot of wax – not too much spoiling – then smooth the fiery surface with softest fleece. They strip the stagnant walls with carbolic soap, scourging all the scars and smears of its previous history. Scrape the floors with bleach down to raw skin – pale and delicate after the ordeal but displaying its indelible genetic patterning and the rings of its growth, hardened into lines. Then the kitchen. She sees corruption everywhere. The stove – a sanctuary of vice and vermin. Each crack and corner a nest of defilement. All surfaces must be purged of the year's acquired taint until the room stands spotless as a bridal chamber before a wedding feast.

Eva wears a long white apron over her skirt and wraps a rough blue cloth around her head to cover every strand of hair. Her hands are coarse and red from the cleaning powders and the veins stand out darkly knotted under the skin. She won't wear gloves, she must pursue the dirt with her naked fingers, for it is cunningly disguised everywhere in a different cast: here slippery, there grainy or resinous, and most sinister of all when it parasitically imitates the skin of its captive, the chameleon filth must be eliminated down to its residual scabs with bare nails.

She and the black woman work together on their knees. First the cupboards. The woman holds the brush in both hands, pushing forward with the whole weight of her body and then scraping backwards, while Eva pours fresh water across the boards wiping away the dirt until the grain comes out tight and ropy against the pulp. All the cupboard doors stand open to let in the light and flush out the tiny spiders that spin webs in the cracks. Then they crouch down to scour the floor together, scratching with a brush and smoothing with a sponge. Both bodies merge like a beast with four arms, four legs and two heads, but grafted into a single mind with one sustaining vision of perfection.

When they have finished they sit separately, the black woman in the yard eating white bread and drinking sweet tea – Eva has watched her, counted four heaped teaspoons of sugar and not even stirring them properly – and Eva resting on a stiff kitchen chair, weak, shaking, but satisfied. The house is clean. She recognises each twist and curl in the wood as when she looks in the mirror, feels the lines between her eyebrows hewn by the moods that cleave her face. She remembers how she used to run as a child, mud-soaked and filthy, through the potato-field, careless of anything but playing and laughing. Her days were as unperturbed as her face, the skin smooth over her cheekbones like a Kirghiz. She cannot change the events of her life, marked now like a map on her face. She accepts her circumstances as they are. But her house will be clean! In all the world that is one thing she can and will control.

That night she feeds the child, Miriam, early and puts her to bed, and she covers the kitchen table with newspaper and calls her three stepdaughters to eat. They always have to eat!

"Can we have something to eat? What's for supper? We haven't eaten since lunch. Our dad doesn't want us to go hungry."

"You don't look hungry," she mutters. "Must you always be eating?"

The kitchen can never be at rest to recover from its distress, not even for one night! She makes supper of bread and jam and tea the way she used to when the boys were small in the rented house in Fordsburg. Before all the goodness and fatness of Zalman, when the house was still skinny and spare. She will not use the stove, because tomorrow the big cooking begins. She brushes the crumbs off the table with her hands and sweeps the floor again. She hates crumbs. There will be no peace for anyone until she sweeps the floor.

The house is a different place when Elias is away. Then it is her house.

The child plays alone with her toys and the three girls, big girls, sit in their room working for school. Max goes out at night, he does what he likes. He is too big, she cannot control him any more, and he leaves the house to avoid Elias. She doesn't know where he goes and it's better that he should be away. He disturbs the surface. But in the morning, on his table, there will be drawings of houses – all the rooms inside and the decorations, pillars and columns and moulded sculptures drawn in fine lines. Theo is in his room, drafting his light pencil pictures, or reading, always reading when he should be doing homework. He will eat when he's hungry, take a piece of bread and butter late at night and leave the crumbs. Never mind, Theo has to eat something. She always goes back into the kitchen to sweep anyway and check that the stove is off before she goes to bed. It would wake her in her sleep if she didn't.

It is quiet in the house. She keeps the lights low. Slatted shadows fall on the walls, with the lights flickering through the swaying fringes of the lampshade and the beads making soft clicking noises as they touch. The leaves of the fern fill the dim corners of the lounge, luxuriant as they unfold out of the fecund centre. But the kitchen is spare. Bread and cheese and fruit to eat. There is no smell of meat in the house when he is not there. She walks from room to room quiet as a cat, looking at the shadows, and the children at work. And at last there are no more lights under their doors. Sometimes she pours a small glass of sweet wine and sits alone, absolute quiet except for the twitch of creaking wood, alive and readjusting its tension like an old ship at sea; the house at rest. It is her own house. Hers.

When Elias comes home from his room over the butcher-shop on Friday nights the house is different again. He comes with parcels, the cupboards are packed with sweets and nuts and dried fruit. He brings bagels and smoked sausages, pickled tongue, herrings and sour cucumbers, as when they were courting. He kisses her and feels her arms, presses his fingers around them, squeezing, and says: "Yes, she's a little heavier than last week." Then they all sit eating for a long time.

The fat is everywhere. It splashes onto the walls around the stove, it hardens like candle wax on the bottom of the pots and the smell sticks to her hair as the steam rises from the stove. He likes a mixed grill: chops, liver, kidneys and two fried eggs. She salts the meat as she cooks and he adds salt again at the table and squirts spicy brown sauce from a bottle over the eggs.

The girls come out of their room to be with their father and the house is full of gossip and screams. He kisses them and pinches their cheeks with the thumb that lost a joint in the butcher-shop, and he says: "Now tell me my chickens, what have you been learning at school? What am I working for? Learn! Learn!"

Then later he is with her in her bed. He is good. He is kind. He has been away from home for a week. He is her husband and it is a blessing to lie with him on the Sabbath, to merge and satiate with love like God for his people on a Friday night. But she cannot breathe with his weight on her, trussed, spliced, spread-eagled like a gutted chicken, and the springs of the bed groaning as he lies with her. "Shhh, the children . . ." He is kind, he is generous but her mouth twists and her eyes shut tight as he flounders over her. Let him not hear her whispers as he pants, or see her face. She tries to remember how she felt with Wlad long ago when his hand brushed over her breasts playing, and she wanted it again and again, the touch of his hands in the wheatfield. Hidden in the long grass and looking up at the sky with the workers far away and the farm horses wrenching out bunches of hay and the grind of their teeth and the sounds of fieldmice squealing in their nests. Only wanting to be with him. Dark and secret and a yawning inside her, low and deep, that makes her want to touch and do things with him she does not know – to rub him with her body and press her mouth close and the smell of straw in his hair and his sweet soft breath on her face. And as she lies in this bed, she thinks of the poor young man with green eyes, the father of her two sons. He was timid and shy. She had to have pity and help him, hold his hands, kiss the half-moons on his fingers and teach him. She always felt older and stronger as she stroked him, his skin unblemished, cool and sweet. Even in his pleasure he was shy, and she would turn her head away and smile. His eyebrows were soft as the wings of a bird.

Elias is kind. He is good. Let him not see that her eyes are wet and her face is twisted as he lies next to her, hot and already sleeping soundly in the matrimonial bed.

Eva sits alone on the wooden verandah. It is the eve of the New Year. The whole family will be together. Max is at home so there will be eight people for dinner. The dining-room table is covered with a white table-cloth, the special lace table-cloth from her mother's house; the cloth that her mother snatched from the drawer as they fled from home in the snow and she has hoarded and hidden it across two oceans. On either end of the table stand the silver candlesticks that Elias gave her on their wedding.

The waiting table is covered with all the auspicious foods. At the top is a fish-head for New Year, the "head" of all holidays, and they will pray that they be as the head and not as the tail, and then holding a leek they will pray that their enemies be decimated. Eva will try and find a pomegranate, she will go to all the greengrocers, it is important that they bless it and wish for their merits to increase like the multitude of its seeds. She has made two round poppy-seed breads, round for fullness and completion, and pastries knotted and stuffed with prunes and boiled in syrup for hours until they drip with sweetness. Max's favourite. He can eat four, one after the other, and then he will tell her that they are as good as last year but perhaps there should have been a bit more syrup. She will listen to him carefully. It is no trivial matter and she wants discerning eaters. But Elias will say: "No, they are as good if not better than last year," and lick his fingers. His "luscious hen" can do no wrong. And Max will look at him and say nothing.

Elias and his daughters have left the house before sunset to walk to the synagogue. When they return they will all eat slices of apple dipped in honey and ask inwardly for a time of happiness and joy. They have been lucky. Elias's business has grown, he has paid for the house and put it in Eva's name. Perhaps he will be able to open a branch in the suburbs and next year another. But he works hard, sleeping over the shop in Fox Street so he can go to the stockyards early to choose his animals for slaughter in the ritual way and open his doors at six in the morning.

Eva sits waiting for them. The work is done and she is rubbing cream into her hands, sliding one hand over the other in a circular motion until the balm is taken into the rough skin. Eve of the New Year, but she brings with her the gnarled rings of her history: red hands and Matron Gordon standing upright and starched, quite pretty, they're always pretty except for their red hands and bony knuckles. Eva never spoke to her. She just stood still on the pavement outside the hospital looking in; thin men in striped pajamas waiting for something to heal inside their bodies, to get well, to get fat, to go home. New Year! When will the memory sweeten? She hardly knew him, cannot remember his face. She dips her fingers into the cream-pot and begins again, rubbing her thumbs along the black veins until they begin to rise under the skin. She can see the pulse. She presses it to make it throb and glides one hand over the other until the cream is absorbed. She presses the swelling around the joints; acid in the bone. She presses hard to feel the point of pain.

She is wearing white for the New Year, a white lace jabot around her neck, and her ankles look small in the studded boots. The kitchen is in perfect order even though she has been cooking all day, and the festive smell of roast turkey and sweet-potatoes gives her pleasure. It is already dark but she will watch them come down the street, walk under the lights, appearing and disappearing as they pass the bluegum trees that line the pavement. Elias will be hard to distinguish at night in his blue suit and black hat, but she will recognise his white face rocking from side to side as the weight of his body falls onto one leg and then the other, surrounded by his daughters like puffed white cushions. The flesh dimples around their elbows and swells into folds around their wrists despite the thrift of her home.

She wants the mood to change, to feel a release from the silence and a loosening of the tightness around her eyes. She wants to atone for feelings she has never understood and secrets that only her body knows are true when she is alone with Elias. He is good, he is kind. He is her husband. The next ten days are a period of trial when she will be watched and judged for the New Year, and then The Book will be closed.

> *May the expressions of my mouth and thoughts of my heart find favour before you my God . . .*

She wants to be whipped into remorse and peeled down to new skin.

> *And for the sin that we have sinned before you through hardness of the heart . . .*

To immerse her naked body in icy water and bleach it white in the sun; to cut through the cuticle of her life like blossoms through black bark and green grass through the crust of the earth.

> *And for the sin that we have sinned before you with the evil inclination . . .*

A dark figure is walking down Kimberley Road with three young girls in white dresses. She wants to run down to meet them returning from synagogue and embrace them and kiss them as a blessing for the New Year. They are her family now, she coupled her body with his, grew his seed inside her, Miriam, swarthy like he is but with square eyebrows and small bones like her own; he puts money in her bag and food in her house.

But she does not move. She sits in her chair watching the figures approach the house and cross the road. They walk past the Joselowitzes in eighteen A who have just come back from synagogue, past the Sanidas brothers and their wives in the cottage that smells of incense and spice, past the coloured people in number fourteen who always have washing on the line. She wants to join him and walk together. Now they are passing the Nathans who sit on the verandah and quarrel, past the Bolds who never greet her, and the Mackays who live quietly next door. She is the one to whom he comes home. She wants to open the gate and meet him, kiss him full on the mouth and take his hand and feel the sweetness of his coming . . .

They walk up the steps to the verandah. He stoops down to her and she smells the dampness of his body inside the blue suit, the indigo dye turning black with sweat. She tightens her lips and moves her mouth away from his face, rolling into folds with its own liberality. The three girls stand at a distance.

Max and Miriam and Theo bring out the apples steeped in honey, for happiness, for the New Year. Elias dips his fingers into the plate. Eva sees the stump jerking without its knuckle. He licks it for its richness and says the prayer, rote, rapid, unceremonious: "May it be your will, our God and God of our forefathers that you renew for us a good and a sweet year."

They stand on the verandah and eat.

ELEVEN

The City

MAX STRIDES THROUGH THE STREETS OF THE CITY, EXHILARATED. LATE, always late. Skips over the tramlines, pushes through the crowds, energy and aggression all around him. Shop-fronts thrust forward onto narrow pavements, buildings grow side by side like living organisms. Businesses are announced, advertised, flourishing, famous and then bankrupt in a city that still has the manners of a mining camp: scratch and grovel for your fortune. A proper city with its centre reluctant to spread, preferring density to space and only expanding under pressure like the ore in its veins of gold. It pitches upward out of its core. Violate, with mountains of toxic sediment, the stretched blue highveld sky!

But it is also an intimate place. Town! Max knows the feel of the streets under his feet – how many steps across Eloff Street at a careless pace and how many wide strides when he rushes to reach the other side, escaping a predatory tram; he never looks down, his foot never misses the curb. How far back to tilt your head to see the malevolent black clock on Markhams' tower. Late again, very late. That clock persecutes him. He leaps onto the pavement holding his hat at Cuthbert's corner, looks up amused at the garlanded Graces that skip and frolic on the moulded frieze above the ground-floor shoe-shop. Town! Going to Town! Been to Town! Let's meet in Town! A place that shares its age with anyone born in its streets thirty-five years before. Too young to respect its own unformed silhouette and believing that antiquity can be bought cheap with plaster pediments, Doric columns and Georgian doors. Too rash to wait for time to shape its face, and presumptuous enough to achieve, in one generation, a parodied profile of spires, copper turrets, arches, vaults, finials, sky-lighted arcades and Victorian domes. A boisterous schoolboy, noisy braggart, strutting in his father's shoes. Scratch the surface and a puff of gold-flecked dust appears; turn the corner and you see its hidden face, botched into being with bricks and stones and broken windows and scraps of tin. In fifty years "town" will be a metropolis.

Max wants to be part of its growth. Why copy colonial Edwardian style when the great cities of America offer vigorous models of modernity constructed from new mutated metals: chrome and aluminium; new materials, veneers, inlays and ornamental motifs displaying the progress of man. Now is the time to leave your mark.

He walks with all the rudeness of the crowds around him. Uptown streets where he hid away from synagogue and Hebrew classes; downtown where he kicked soccer balls, played whipping top, fought and wrestled his way through school and stood, amazed, in the white light of the comet to escape the airless rooms of his mother's iron house, her invasive eyes and the pulpy presence of his stepfather. The crowded streets are a place where he could always be alone, a watcher, where anyone can walk and anything can happen. He knows and follows the rules – cripples and beggars to one side, natives off the pavements and into the road, keep the stream going fast, push the man ahead to accelerate the flow, do not stop and never never obstruct anyone's forward advance.

When he visits his mother in the suburbs he feels separated from people's lives; unnaturally quiet in the domestic avenues where whites are unseen and remote behind the safety of fenced gardens. A pebbled driveway encircles a palm, a rose garden encloses a birdbath, a cat sleeps on a cushion and a dog barks at the gate. The sign next to the postbox reads in three languages: BEWARE OF THE DOG. PASOP VIR DIE HOND. PASOBHA IZINJA.

Max sits with the family, drinking tea on linen embroidered with daisychains, the houseboy serving at the table in white gloves that cover his calloused hands. Max must repeat everything twice in a loud voice into his mother's ear and Elias sits in his chair moving his lips and sucking his teeth. The tea makes him perspire and he dabs his dome with a starched napkin and then spreads it over his head for shade, a lacy daisied corner hanging over each eye. When they have finished Eva rings a little silver bell twice and the Zulu boy – everyone agrees they are the best servants and she is jolly lucky to have a good one – removes the tray. She tells the girl not to forget to wipe the window-sills and to polish the door handles with Brasso – she has to watch her and tell her the same thing every day! – and she walks around the flower-beds digging with a small stick around a pansy that has been snapped by a cutworm or removing snails from lilies. "Little blighters" she calls them and gives them to the garden boy – who has removed his white gloves for the purpose – to kill. Then they sit on the verandah, not speaking very much, and wait for lunch.

"The house is too big for two people," Elias complains, leaning back to accommodate his equator. "I lose your mother in it. I call her and she calls back: 'I'm here, I'm here,' and I say: 'Where's here?' and I go from room to room looking. Sometimes she doesn't hear and I have to wait for her to find me."

One of his daughters is married to a hardware merchant, another to a dentist and the third to a Free State farmer. Theo, like Max, has a room in town, and only Miriam lives at home, still at school and playing tennis with her friends in the afternoons. But Eva will not sell the house. She loves the vacant rooms, clean and tidy and airy with all the windows open. Empty cupboards! She tries to persuade Elias to get out more, to play bowls or rummy with his friends, to join a club.

"Why don't you become a city councillor?"

After lunch Elias puts his feet up on a chair and opens the top button of his trousers. Eva sweeps the floor under the lunch-table.

"I've told the girl a hundred times," and she begins to arrange the table for tea.

Max sits with them until he cannot sit any more.

In the evenings he returns to his room in Rissik Street over the tailor's shop where he and Theo work carefully on their drawings, assembling their instruments and leaning over a large table with a bright light. Max sharpens the points on his pencils and they continue drafting a block of flats in Loveday Street, their first big job. They work late, etching with fine lines and delicate shadings. It is a successful collaboration. Max has an instinct for values and property and Theo has a sensitive hand. Late at night Max pages through the newspapers and listens to the noisy meetings in the Trades Hall downstairs and the arguments in the party offices.

Late! He walks half-running along Pritchard Street threading through the Saturday morning crowds and turns in at a doorway. Something about the urgency of being breathless and late that rouses the blood, rather than the boredom of being early and patiently waiting for other people to arrive who look at you with pity for coming first – "nothing better to do with your time, eh?" He jumps the stairs two at a time in the dark stairwell and rushes onto the terrace, dazed by the sudden light, looking for a man with a tweed cap. Perhaps he's left. Yes, there he is.

"Sorry, Lelio. So sorry." Embarrassing to arrive with an apology, especially with Lelio who is always consulting his watch. "Just had to get a message down to the party office!" Damnable lies and it shows on his face.

Lelio looks at his watch: "Never mind this time, old chap. I was enjoying myself. Let's sit here like the master class contemplating the enduring face of the multitudes below."

He snaps his fingers twice at a waiter.

"They deliberately look the other way when you want them. The worker's revenge. Two teas, one chelsea bun and one anchovy toast. And we're in a hurry. No soft liberal talk on an empty stomach, eh Maxie?"

He leans back with one arm over the back of the chair and crosses his legs. His left leg rises and falls with the pulse-beat.

"Just look at them, Max. The slumbering masses; every one a torch-carrier for the system. When you look down there you can read it as a book. Perfect products of the bourgeois institutions of society. To me it's obvious."

He looks at his watch, snaps his fingers at the waiter, lifting himself off the chair to attract his attention.

"Hey, waiter! Hurry up. One bun, one anchovy toast and two teas." He crosses his legs again. "Organised social control must harness unrestrained individualism and rampant greed. Here's our tea. How many lumps of sugar, two or three?"

He stirs the tea, lifts the teaspoon to his mouth and tests the sweetness; adds half a lump.

"It's a typical imperialist pyramid: a thousand captains of commerce perched on the apex and cheap black labour crawling at the base. Look at them in the streets, poor sods: labourers and consumers, while up here at the top sit the owners of capital and hoarders of profits. How's your bun?"

Max opens his mouth pouched with fullness, tries to swallow in time to answer. Impossible to be significant with a bun in your mouth. He has to be vigilant with Lelio.

"Dip it in your tea this time, Max. Be a hedonist while you can."

A corner of Max's bun falls into his cup and floats in the tea. He tries to capture it with a spoon. Why is he always so clumsy while Lelio delicately brushes a few crumbs off his fingers.

"In the usual anarchic manner of capitalist societies – hey, waiter," he snaps a finger, "one more buttered toast – some people have more than is good for them and others, not enough."

"I don't know, Lelio," Max says wiping tea off his chin. "Large theories are all very well but it is a complex creature down there in the streets. There is the Republican issue raised by Afrikaners, the Coolie question in Natal, the Coloureds in the Cape and most important the Native problem, or as they call it the 'white problem'. Then there's drought, locusts, soil-erosion, plague, east-coast fever." He flicks a crumb off the table for emphasis – a successful gesture, in the main. "Your theories emerged out of the cold cities of Europe. How can you just graft solutions onto the hot racial conflicts of South Africa?" He pokes at a buried raisin in a hollow tooth – must remember to see a dentist.

"Wait a minute, Maxie. You're seeing it all as race, whereas it's the same old class war dressed up in colour as a South African variation. The theory still holds. Drought, locusts, plague and fever will be conquered in a society that values social effort above private wealth."

Lelio looks at his watch, waves at the waiter.

"And no tips for a proletarian who is only doing what he's paid for."

He hands Max the bill.

"Your turn, old chap. You see, Max, it's obvious. The same old struggle between those who exploit and those who are exploited."

Max puts his hand in his pocket. He must remember that it will be Lelio's turn to pay next time. Dear fellow, but he's got to be watched. They get up and walk down the stairs into Pritchard Street. Max anticipates the mirror outside Cuthbert's window. Wipes the butter off his moustache and corrects the angle of his hat. Slightly to the left, slightly over his eyebrow, yes.

"The remedy is obvious, Lelio. It means an awakening of the masses."

Lelio stops to have his shoes buffed and lifts his trouser cuffs. A decadent practice, Max thinks, as the cleaner, on his knees, spits onto the rag to bring the leather into a shine. But Lelio gives it a panache and respectability which defies reproach. Max must study to acquire that air of conviction, useful in the cut and thrust of street politics.

"Obviously," Lelio replies, jingling the money in his pocket. "And a development of the economic struggle. But in the meantime let's keep our powder dry."

He throws down some silver as payment and steps over a legless beggar with a collection cup in his hand, "Go and make a revolution man!"

They walk along Pritchard Street under the awnings and balconies of ground-floor shops.

"The fight, Maxie, for free primary education . . ." they are separated by the crowds but continue to shout over the heads of obstructing pedestrians, "is one which involves the entire . . ." they meet again behind a large woman carrying parcels, "working class, black and white. Unless the native standard . . ." they cross the street dodging a canvas-topped convertible, "rises, the white level will eventually . . ." they miss a bicycle by inches, ". . . crash."

Lunch-time congestion burgeons around the City Hall, swelling like a gelatinous sea. Pedestrians are trapped trying to cross the road, some jumping onto overflowing trams ringing their bells at other tramcars landlocked in front of them. A traffic officer flutters white-gloved hands at motorists spilling across the intersection and blocking all movement in the street. He changes his arabesques into thrashing gestures, shouts insults at bicycles, horse-drawn wagons and rickshaws as the pressure increases from surrounding roadways. Three trams in a row ring their bells incessantly at a cyclist with his tyre stuck in a tramline. Two natives help him to wrench his wheel free and slowly the traffic begins to move.

The City Hall straddles Rissik Street like a buxom matron corseted with eight stone columns around her. Her imperious spine rises portentously into two tiers of colonnades, a pediment, a dome, a cupola and a pinnacle. Crowds argue and scramble around the steps, hang over the balconies, perch on platforms, climb columns like unruly offspring thrashing around the fringes of the matron's petticoats, all straining to reach the speaker standing on a rostrum. Cyclists push their bicycles between bodies, and newspaper vendors whistle for attention. Gallagher's Cafe De Move On stands immovable on a corner of the square erupting steam that smells of coffee and fried viennas from its vaporous kitchen. Spectators stand in groups or singly, stretching necks to find friends or food or fights in the engorged mass.

"It's obvious . . ." says Lelio over the head of a doomsday prophet threatening the crowd with a raised Bible. "Here are the multitudes, and the theory fits like a glove onto the sweaty African hand . . ."

Not a good metaphor, Max thinks.

The two men are driven further apart by the Salvation Army band on the march and its soldiers rattling coins in collection-boxes.

". . . It's obvious Maxie. For those who are unwilling to work . . ." Max drops a tickey surreptitiously into a vagrant's coffers, ". . . there will be nothing to eat."

People are straining towards a woman on a platform raising her voice over the noise of tramcars and hooters. Max is too far away to hear but he can see she is challenging someone in the crowd and waving a newspaper over her head. He squeezes himself between bodies, stepping on feet, apologizing, wriggling forward through spaces with his right shoulder and holding his hat.

"What's she saying? Wat sê sy?" he asks the man standing next to him.

"Kannie hoor nie. Something about a factory in Vrededorp."

Max shifts sideways, slips into a gap, sorry, a little closer, sorry again, and he is near the speaker's platform, where he looks around for Lelio. He sees the hat bobbing steadily forward like a small boat in a storm. The woman on the platform is lifting up the arm of a young girl standing next to her.

". . . Twelve shillings a week to Afrikaans girls working in a sweet factory . . ."

Max stands on his toes to hear the voice straining against an ice-cream vendor's cowbell.

"This girl would starve to death if she didn't live at home. What native would work for two pounds a month without board and lodging besides?"

"Bloody right," shouts the man next to Max. "And what about apprentices who earn ten shillings a week for three years and lose their jobs when they ask for a rise?"

"And apprentices of the gold mines," Max turns to see a red-faced young man in a tweed jacket behind him, ". . . earning two shillings a day?"

"And the unemployed and the poor whites?" The woman on the platform bangs the table and shouts over voices coming in all directions. "And the natives at the bottom of the scale?"

"Ask your friends in Moscow." Laughter from the spectators. "Vra jou vriende in Moskou."

"No, you ask your friends who own the mines."

Heads jerk sharply and Max holds his hat. Shock-waves ripple through the crowd as people stumble to clear a space around two men clutching at each other's jackets. A woman falls, bringing down the man next to her. She is helped to her feet and dusted off, crying. The Salvation Army band strikes up with a rousing boombang! on the drums and an apocalyptic blast of the trumpets. The doomsday prophet arrives, screaming incoherently holding the Bible over his head, and the two entangled men are wrenched apart and threatened by a policeman.

Max signals to Lelio, and they push through the crowd toward Gallagher's, passing a blind violinist and a child shaking a cup. They meet and sidestep, Lelio's head disappearing and re-emerging downstream, and Max holds onto his hat like a raft keeping him afloat.

"It's obvious," Lelio shouts. "All economics. Look around you . . . look at that."

A man in a faded brown suit asks Max for a penny for coffee.

"He's a pawn of the system and he believes that the enemy is black."

Max has lost his hat. He presses forward to Gallagher's, pushing his way past other consumers, floundering, and finally reaching the counter. He can still see the woman banging on the platform and shouting at someone in the crowd. Lelio is already there trying to redefine the crease in his hat. Smoky exhalations rise from the open kitchen.

"I'm starving," says Lelio. "Russians for me and my friend, Mr Gallagher, fried for him and boiled for me. I never eat anything else, for obvious reasons."

The chef wipes his face and hands with his apron, "With or without?"

"With!"

He slaps mustard onto the sausages and writes out the bill. Lelio looks at it raising his eyebrows.

"You see, it's obvious, Maxie. A capitalist system corrupts all natural relationships." He passes the bill to Max. "You've sold out to the Captains of Industry, designing palaces of profit for the rich. Your turn, old chap."

Max puts his hand in his pocket to pay. Lelio is already eating. A bad metaphor, he thinks. I wonder why they call them "Russians"?

TWELVE
Russian

HANNAH MAKES SMALL DENTS IN THE CHOCOLATE ICE-CREAM WITH A SPOON and takes little nibbles out of the vanilla wafer. She must not let her little finger stick out when she holds a spoon, her aunt has told her – looking up quickly at her escort across the table and then looking down as he opens his mouth wide to admit a fork impaling a Danish pastry. And it is not good manners to watch people when they are eating, her aunt says. It is a private activity even though people do it in public. But at least this one is an improvement on the last – thirty years younger and he has his own teeth. Pity about the gold filling in the front. Somehow she always looks at it when he speaks. And don't look too closely at people, it's rude. Disregard the body behind the shirt that overlaps his belt. Nobody is perfect and it is not his fault and it has nothing whatsoever to do with his character. She smiles at him with an open mouth – "show your teeth", her aunt has told her, "your best feature" – rather than trying to make herself heard over the music. She taps her foot in sprightly three-four time so he can see that she is enjoying it and recognises "The Vienna Woods". La laaa, la laaa, lalaaa, la la. "Strauss," she says nonchalantly – she comes from such a musical family.

She looks around the room at the cafe scene. Streamers ripple in the draught of a large revolving fan on the ceiling, and bunches of balloons, blown up to bursting, tug against their strings like restless puppies on a lead. Patrons and special guests laugh and wave, communicate in sign language, lip-reading – "How are you?", "Phone me", "See you soon" – across the room tangled with twisted tinsel and paper flowers, while patrons waiting for tables surge around the door and collect in corners.

She does not understand the humour of the city's night-life or feel the excitement of the opening of a new social venue, which her aunt told her is as eventful as the launching of a ship. Strange to see all the men dressed identically in dark-blue suits, stiff white shirts and striped ties – strange to tie a knot around your neck when you think about it – and women in shiny long dresses with a flower pinned to a breast. And the angry man in a black suit with a red sash, waving his hands furiously to control the traffic.

She sees the young man again, twisting sideways to squeeze between chairs and around the corners of closely-packed tables, pulling the corner of a tablecloth as he brushes his leg against it, then knocking down a fork and a napkin folded into a cone. He bends down to pick up the fork and stands up, narrowly missing a waiter carrying a silver salver of sandwiches and a pot of tea. Something about the straightness of his back, and yet not stiff. Erect. Unusual. She can see it even with his jacket on. Then she sees the young woman following him, drawing up the hem of her satin dress with a cord attached to her finger as she moves closer to the table to make a passage for the waiter. Her handbag catches a woman's hair and she apologises with her hand over her mouth, trying to keep up with the young man in front of her. They stop to speak to friends, laughing and shaking hands, obstructing a waiter balancing a tray of dirty plates. They move forward between tables to allow the waiter to continue and to make room for a woman with blond bobbed hair and a painted rosebud mouth.

Hannah looks back at her partner and smiles, showing her teeth. She moves her finger in waltz time, inclining her head to the music. "La laaa la laaa . . . Very nice," smiling. Something about the way that young man tilts his chin. Slightly upward. He must be very proud to hold his neck like that. And his chest, lifted, but not forced like a soldier or strained like the men who carried barrels of herrings over their heads at home. She wishes he could see the two empty places at their table, but people here don't like to share. He continues to shift forward, turning sideways between chairs and moving toward the annex next door.

She looks across the table. Should she smile again or will he think she's forcing herself or simple-minded with nothing to say?

"Would you like another ice-cream?" He exaggerates the formation of each word and points to the plate.

"No thank you."

She would love another ice-cream. The people at the next table have it with hot chocolate sauce, a cherry and a finger-biscuit. But her mother told her that when she goes out she must never appear greedy and never finish everything on her plate as though she is eating because she is hungry – rather as if for fun or to be friendly. Like the time when she was invited to the rich girl's house to play and she said "no, thank you" to the chocolates and "no, thank you" to the cake. And when she went home the girl's mother said to her, "What a polite child. You hardly eat a thing."

Taffeta crackles as it passes her chair, leaving a scent of cologne. Too strong. She looks around to see a long black dress fashioned over one shoulder and a flaccid furry body with dangling paws arranged over the other. Two glass eyes stare and a snout is hooked onto its own bushy tail. Just like the little red foxes that live in the forests at home. She would never wear one of those around her neck.

She looks down at the dress her aunty in Nigel has given her – a blue and white sailor suit that her cousin has discarded. It is loose in the waist and across the chest because her stomach is flatter than her cousin's and her breasts are not overgrown like two heavy melons. She wears the dress nearly every day, washing it at night and pressing it stiff and fresh in the morning. Next time she goes out at night she must pin a flower onto her breast. But her hair is shiny and red like that little fox and her teeth are perfect, not one hole, unlike her cousin's that are filled with silver because she eats too many sweets.

She is grateful that the music saves her from trying to speak. The conductor ignores the noise of rattling teacups and strident conversation, straightens his coat-tails and smooths his hair. He looks over his shoulder at the audience, still making patterns in the air with his baton. Smiling exuberantly, he defies an outburst of laughter and the thump of the service doors opening and closing, giving blinking glimpses of a steaming kitchen with smoking cauldrons of food. He turns back to the orchestra, eliciting "feeling" with an expression of suffering, and "legato" with a desperate appeal of his outstretched left hand, while beating out a steady rhythm with his right. His gestures become more excitable as a waiter drops a plate and he summons three trumpet players to stand and deliver a single blast followed by a solo performance of the drums, and the music is brought to an exhilarating finale.

There is a sudden quiet as the music stops and the orchestra bows, leaving the room to a patronising patter of applause. She claps her hands noiselessly like the lady at the next table. Her partner is looking at her, she can sense it, while she holds a pleasing profile. Her nose is her best feature. She must try and speak to him or he will think that she is stupid or unfriendly and he will not ask her out again and her aunt will force her to see the old man. What can she say that is witty or amusing? The English like to talk about the weather, she was told. "It is a hot night, no?" Everything she says sounds stilted. She cannot go on smiling. Her friends always said that she had a lively nature, and the boys at home spoiled her with baskets of wild mushrooms and bunches of lilac. But now she is dull, an object of ridicule in her cousin's dress that is too long and with a button that doesn't match in the front. And her nails are not lacquered like the woman in the satin dress or the lady at the next table stirring her tea with an elegant hand. Better to keep them under the table. What are they saying that is so funny? She feels clumsy and simple amongst all the glitter, unable to laugh and ashamed to speak English.

Auntie Sasha says that she is stubborn and ungrateful to reject the old man, and a poor girl in no position to be choosy. Every time they are together she makes a speech.

"He is rich and you'll inherit his money. Make sure the house is in your name, although you don't want him to die, God forbid. Let him live to eighty in good health. But can a man live forever? And in the meantime, is it such a terrible thing to have comfort and servants? Do you think you are a princess that you should be so fussy? Do you know what you are? A girl with no money, no family, alone in a strange country. A girl with no advantages. Ask the marriage-broker. And you refuse a wealthy man who wants to marry you? Just now you'll be too old: 'on the shelf' they call it, and nobody will look at you. You think your looks will last forever? You know nothing about life, my girl. A woman needs a man. Your mother spoilt you, chased you out of the kitchen. A little princess and a snob who never learnt to cook or sew. Now you listen to me. Forget about that boy at home, a revolutionary, he'll come to a bad end. No one had money where we come from. God knows how we lived. Someone had a cow, someone planted potatoes, we got fish from the boats. But in South Africa you need a man with a bank account and a business."

Auntie Sasha has married well here. That is what they call it when you drink tea with your friends at eleven in the morning and rest in the afternoon, play tennis in short white dresses and belong to a country club. Sasha has forgotten how the family at home cared for her two daughters for years when she went to Africa as a widow looking for a husband. And Uncle

Abram, in the Cape, has also forgotten how his older sister carried him around on her hip, wiped his nose, fed him and sang him to sleep. And he doesn't send her sixpence now that he is a rich farmer in De Aar with a wife who can slaughter sheep single-handedly and make soap and candles from the fat.

The orchestra returns to the room to take their seats, tuning their instruments. So untidy, why don't they do it before they come in? The conductor enters and they rise to their feet. His hair is slicked close to his head and he carefully blots his face with a folded white handkerchief and puts it back into his pocket still folded. That way it still looks unused, she thinks. Auntie Sasha has told her to only use a clean handkerchief once, flick it open and dab her nostrils, and never to blow her nose in public. No one is dancing, they only sit and talk. This is called "social life" in South Africa. She would like to be alone with someone in a quiet place where she could learn to speak again; tell little stories that make people laugh the way she used to at home. Not sneers or mocking laughter because of her English or hidden smiles because of her clothes. Or else to dance smoothly around the floor with her partner, their steps perfectly matched and circling around and around until the whole room whirls in front of her eyes and she falls into a chair breathless and giddy. Fun! Can't he see how she is tapping her foot and nodding in time to the music? Are they dead, an empty floor with the music playing? Why does everyone just sit and talk? "Conversation," they call it.

"And don't keep thinking of home. You'll never get used to it here." Auntie Sasha's voice is in her head like a continuous commentary on her behaviour.

The heat and noise bring colour to her face. She takes out her cotton handkerchief embroidered with violets and smelling of talcum, flicks it open casually, dabs her upper lip and puts it back in her bag. Has he noticed?

Every day her mother and sister are waiting to receive money from her or two tickets for a ship to South Africa. And one day soon Auntie Sasha will tell her either to marry or to get out of the house. She looks sideways at her escort across the table. Perhaps he is a kind man, but he does not even try to talk to her.

"So what do you do with yourself?" he asks and looks away when she tries to answer. Has he been observing her and calculating her value on the marriage market? Perhaps she should go back to the shoe-shop, trying shoes on people's feet, or go to work in an orphanage with poor children or stow away in a ship returning home. She always believed that it was a good thing to be clever and pretty; special gifts for a girl in a poor family. "Improve your life," her mother warned. "Do you want to be like me?" But now she wants to scar and scratch her face, hide away from the responsibility of beauty, the price of prettiness on her head: to marry rich and bring her mother and sister to Africa.

Then she sees the young man again coming back into the main salon, unable to find a place in the annex, with the lady still behind him. A waiter has noticed the two empty chairs and ushers them across the room to their table. She looks up, embarrassed that she has been watching him and now he is standing next to her. There is an arrogance in the straightness of his back and the tilt of his chin. But she is not ashamed as he looks at her for the first time. He likes her straight away. She can see it in the fullness of his eyes.

Her partner gets up immediately, smiles and slaps his back.

"Max, I didn't see you. These chairs must have been waiting for you. Didn't they reserve you a special table or are you incognito tonight? Hello Hilda." He places his cheek next to hers and makes a sucking noise with his lips.

"This is Hannah."

She stands up offering her cheek and pouting her mouth.

"It's all right, my dear, just shake hands. She's only been here a few months. Still learning," winking at Max. Hannah saw him. "And her manners are rather amusing. These daughters of the Russian Revolution are charming but primitive. We'll teach her won't we? You'll never guess how we met." He whispers in Max's ear, laughing and slapping his knees. "Quite amusing, but don't tell a soul or I'm finished socially. You sit next to her, Max, lovely girl, but I'm a bit tired of struggling."

"I'd love to struggle a little," Max says sitting down. "Is your English improving?"

"What is 'improving'?" she asks.

"Hannah, you are sitting next to the architect of Johannesburg's newest cafe. Architect, my dear." He looks at the ceiling, appealing for help. "This place . . ." he says in a loud voice and making large circles with his hands and then shaking his head. "Quite useless, Max. I'm exhausted, you try. I'm going to talk to Hilda. Just ordinary conversation for a change, not this serious stuff about the pine forests and wild strawberries at home. Don't be alarmed, Hilda, she's quite harmless and straight out of school. Living with 'auntie' in Nigel and she doesn't open her mouth. Quite fetching, but not clever enough for our Maxie. Can I get you a strawberry parfait? Do you know that Russians are the largest consumers of ice-cream in the world?"

Suddenly the lights go out. Women scream and drums roll. The sound of shattering glass somewhere in the dark. Someone lights a match and the hot centres of cigarettes pulsate. Two rows of white-coated waiters enter the room carrying a layered cake shimmering with small candles. Little shrieks rise above the low hum of voices and a squeal of laughter from the lady with lacquered nails. Hannah sits quietly and still, very still, only aware of the young man's closeness to her in the trembling candlelight. The lady in black taffeta is called up to blow out the candles and . . . blackout! There is an instant of complete silence as the room vanishes into the dark. Hannah waits with her eyes wide open in the blackness, hardly breathing and alert to every sound and movement of the stranger sitting near her. Their feet are nearly touching under the table, she dare not move, and his hand is resting on the back of her chair, she can feel it. Silence in the darkness and a sense of all the excitement about to happen. A balloon bursts and women scream. The lights go on, whitebright, and the audience rises to its feet, breaking into laughter and applause with the clash of cymbals and the flowing of champagne. Balloons are drifting slowly from the ceiling and streamers criss-cross the air with trailing tails like an exploding universe. Men scramble on the floor for garlands of paper flowers and chinese lanterns and golden moons, and waiters step over them carrying slices of cake on silver platters and glasses of champagne. Hannah laughs and claps her hands as a red balloon bumps Max on the head and bursts into fragments of glitter falling about his feet. Her partner has found a whistle which he blows at Hilda and they pull a cracker, staggering back and falling, screaming against chairs as the cracker pops.

Hannah stands back in her own circle of quietness, absorbed in images: the young boy who used to write poems, delicate love lyrics in Russian, far away now; she will never see him again. And her uncle in De Aar, on his vast dry sheep farm with iron windmills and shallow dams and the slaghuis and shop, who cannot spare a sixpence for her mother. She thinks of her father – runaway crippled vagabond. Go to the theatre if you want to find him – limping and penniless mother's-boy whom she has not seen since she was a small child at home.

Then she looks at Max, entangled in streamers and wearing a paper crown. The proud young man, spangled with tinsel and surrounded by laughter and noise.

THIRTEEN
Wedding Breakfast

EVA HAS PREPARED HER HOUSE AT FIFTY HILLBROW STREET FOR THE RECEPtion, filling the wedding table with platters of small triangular sandwiches resting on beds of lettuce, and scattering raisins and nuts on the white tablecloth between plates of sugared cakes. A long plaited loaf glazed with egg and spotted with poppy-seeds lies in the middle of the table. The bread and wine have been blessed and the bread broken. The marriage has been sanctified with seven blessings and Max stands with his hand raised, proposing a toast to his bride: "Nazdorovye," he says, swallowing his vodka, and smashing the glass on the wall behind him, as all the guests repeat "Nazdorovye," drinking and laughing. They are tearing the floury centre out of the loaf, dipping it into bowls of chopped herring and liver pate, licking their fingers. They swill it down with small glasses of pure schnapps. It is nine o'clock in the morning. A wedding breakfast.

Eva is bewildered by the speed of events and the sudden change in circumstances, but she does not question them. Every decision has its implications. Max has not consulted her, never did, not even as a child. She watches, and knows things without being told. The consequences of every choice will unfold. It is as it is.

Hannah is standing to one side on her own. Photographs always show the bride as sun of her universe, encircled by orbiting satellites of smiling bridesmaids, fussing matrons and laughing relatives, everyone reflected in her light. A friend is correcting a curl, fluffing a fold, tweaking a satin sleeve. Always in a frame of flowers, cakes, candles and wedding presents; the centre of adoration, everyone wants to see the bride. "Isn't she lovely?" linking arms with the admiring groom. But Hannah is standing alone. She remembers seeing a picture of an Indian bride with sequins patterning her face and her hair twisted with tassels. She stood alone and radiant. Behind her rolled an ocean of waves mysteriously in the night.

Hannah is wearing a pink wedding dress, all fancy, and she is sure her face looks pretty. She washed her hair very early in the morning with chamomile and rainwater and her skin is clear and natural with the softest blush warming her cheeks. But she is standing alone.

Auntie Sasha cannot forgive her for the dress.

"A bride must wear white. That's all there is to it."

Plain white. Dead white. But Hannah will not have a white wedding without her mother. Bold white. Blinding white, and arrogant with a mystical white veil.

"I want the pink dress, Auntie Sasha."

Softest chiffon like flamingo-down, and a petticoat of palest grey.

Auntie Sasha hates her for the dress and she is sour with jealousy. She pretends not to look when Hannah is standing with Max and Theo, tall South African men, big-boned, untainted by the ghetto and the dark wet alleys of Europe. Sasha coughs as her throat tightens around the champagne, and she looks away or down at her feet, but Hannah can see a twitch in her eye. They bought the trousseau together with one hundred pounds given to her by Uncle Abram in the Cape: the wedding dress and some cotton frocks from Foschini, pillow-slips, sheets, a few towels and a pair of small scissors and some sewing cotton.

"Let's save money on the dress and you can buy two good kitchen pots as well. Do you want to go into a marriage empty-handed like a pauper? You need things like a toaster and a roaster and a kettle and an egg-timer and a meat-pounder and a meat-grinder and a cleaver and a whisk for soufflés and sauces and a rolling pin for pastry and a grater and wooden spoons and a garlic-press. What will you do when your husband comes home with fifteen friends unexpectedly for dinner? And as your aunt there are other things that I ought to tell you about married life because your mother is not here and you come from a family of women. I've had two husbands, don't forget, and there are things that every young girl has to know about men."

"But Auntie Sasha, Max and I have known each other for three months and he likes me and I'm sure we'll learn to understand each other. And there was also Volodya at home and he was my boyfriend for a long time."

"Now listen to me carefully, my girl," and Sasha puts her into a chair. "You're a green girl from a fishing village on the Baltic. You only know about fish and forests and flowers. I've had two daughters of my own and I'm telling you this for your mother's sake. Every woman is obliged to satisfy a man whether she wants to or not. Usually not. And especially a successful man who is used to getting his way with women will be extremely demanding. Do you know what that means? I'm not talking about your little poet at home with his head in Pushkin and Lermontov who couldn't earn a sixpence if he tried. I'm talking about a robust South African man, who lives in a world with other men. He'll probably want a lot of children. And do you think your mother-in-law will be easy?"

Hannah listened while Sasha spoke, but she was only thinking about the Indian bride with tasseled hair and eyes outlined with black pigment and the dark rolling ocean behind her; and of lying close to her boy at home, long and late with the midnight sun balanced on the horizon under a violet sky.

Hannah needed the pink dress with the little velvet jacket and matching hat. She knew that Max would have her without the dowry, and even though her mother was not there and she was alone in a strange country, she would marry with pride; not like a poor girl on her wedding day. She had to beg Sasha, her only relation, to be there.

"Please Auntie Sasha. For Mama's sake."

And now Sasha stands there, not talking to anyone nor eating, and looking down at the floor. Her husband stands next to her eating from a full plate of food which he finishes and fills a second time.

Hannah looks at her mother-in-law, Eva, sitting in a chair across the room. Her sister-in-law, Miriam, is leaning on an arm of the chair, and Max and Theo are standing on either side. Eva is a widow for the second time, silent and solitary, nearly deaf, but her eyes, framed with square eyebrows, range wide and deep, although no one notices that an old woman is watching. Eva looks at Hannah, a young girl who is marrying into security and comfort. Hannah nods at her, a slow nod with a slight inclination of the body. Not a bow! Eva hates obsequiousness. And not a smile or a wink, she hates coyness and complicity. Hannah acknowledges Eva as a handsome woman, once beautiful, a fierce Polish Jewess, hard and clean. A desert woman with short steely hair and narrow lips, a woman who does not adopt outsiders into a family, but initiates them slowly into it through her silent watching way. She has never said that Hannah is not good enough, not dark and tall like her son. Never said it. But Hannah can read her eyes. Eyes that make no allowance. It is as it is. And Eva judges her softness as a flaw, a defect like weak bones, and her green eyes as colourless and watery. Eva has buried two husbands and never spoken about them. She has never pretended to love her stepdaughters. That is as it is. Her knuckles are knotted and her joints twist like old wood. Her eyes are cloudy from making buttonholes. How will she respect a young girl who can only dance and sing; exhibitionistic and trivial, "superficial" she will call it, even though Hannah finished school in ten subjects and could have done much better.

How can she speak for herself, humbled without a proper dowry or a white wedding, and no father to argue for her or "give her away"? No friends to stand for her, no family to give her rank. This is South Africa, a strange country where she has no known background or history. Must she stand on a box and make a speech? And there is always the comparison with Miriam, their half-sister, dark and selfish and laughing, with a pretty black spot on her upper lip; prized and queened by the family. She can do what she likes, buy another dress that she doesn't need and throw out the old ones, and Eva approves. Some days she parades them for Hannah, throwing the rejects on the floor for "the girl".

But Hannah makes a vow as she stands there: to love her mother-in-law, to accept her sternness, slowly breaking down her resistance with gentleness and tenacity like grass growing through mountain rock. She will be her acolyte and earn her respect with service and devotion through her marriage.

Max moves away from Eva, his hand stroking Miriam's hair as he walks past her. Hannah hopes he is coming to stand next to her, but he goes to speak to Mr Broderick the builder. Mr Broderick likes her and always tells her she has lovely teeth.

"Like the best white Italian ceramic. I wish I could get some for the bathroom of my next job."

Hannah walks up to them, and Broderick puts his arm around her.

"You just tell me if he misbehaves. I'll put him in a concrete-mixer, shake him up until he begs for mercy. We builders have our punishments."

She smiles to show her teeth. Theo joins them and kisses her on the forehead. They are always together, the three of them: Max, Theo and Hannah. She walks so proudly between them, tall and flourishing. She will love Theo like the brother she always wanted in her family at home, dominated by women, sisters, aunts, weak and sickly from cousins marrying cousins. No one to knock in a nail or turn a screw or open a tight bottle. Only women.

The men went to Africa looking for work and for wives outside of the family to strengthen the blood. Theo is quiet and distant. She has never seen him forget himself and laugh. Sometimes he smiles and a low chuckle vibrates in his throat. She will press his clothes and darn his socks and tend him like a sister.

Then Lelio joins them. "Congratulations on entering domestic life. I should have warned you that wives are the magistrates of this bourgeous regime. Soon she will be telling you to put away your shoes and to take your feet off the furniture. But he must be in love if he managed to be on time for his wedding, eh?"

Max has told her that he loves her, but he does not speak it easily, and she must be careful not to stare at him with her eyes, searching for confirmation. She delights him with her clear skin and full mouth and when she plays the piano and sings Russian songs. Then he sits quietly watching her with one leg crossed over the other, his back upright against the chair, saying nothing. But his face is still and his eyes are round and dark as she sings of meadows and slow-moving rivers and legendary heroes in fur pelts who ride through deep snow. He always asks her to sing about the Cossack who loves his Persian bride but sacrifices her to the river because of the mockery of his friends. Max speaks the words very softly as she sings:

> *With a sudden mighty movement*
> *Raizen lifts the beauty high*
> *And he cast her where the waters*
> *Of the Volga move and sigh.*
>
> *Dance you fool and men make merry*
> *What has got into your eyes?*
> *Let us thunder out a chanty*
> *Of a place where beauty lies.*

Then he stands up to sing his German drinking-songs, his back straight and his chin lifted while she plays the piano:

> *Warum ist es am Rhine so schön?*
> *Warum ist es am Rhine so schön?*
> *Am Rhiiiine soooo schoöoon?*

She would like to touch him and be familiar while he is laughing and off-guard; take his hand blatantly in front of the family to flaunt her position – wife – kiss his cheek, unashamed. Is it a South African custom to be so formal and reserved? She misses the naturalness of the boys at home who would climb trees in spring to break full clusters of lilac to put in her hair; then they would fill their pockets with wild berries, take off their shirts and shoes and lie in the summer sun.

She is still a stranger to the glance of his eyes and the touch of his hand but tonight she will be left alone with him in a hotel room, having to behave in a different and unknown way: flagrantly unashamed with one another, voluptuous and rude, and yet delicate and discreet. She must be receptive, but he must not think her skilled and expert. Husbands must teach their wives. Mr Broderick was smirking and making jokes that she could not understand, and it will not be enough tonight to smile and show her teeth. She will be expected to "succeed" with him in some way, to excel, to pass a test set by "a demanding man who must be satisfied" – remembering Auntie Sasha's warning but forgetting her advice about how to please a husband. Must she surrender, acquiesce? Supposing she should fail? It was so easy to lie with Volodya, long and tender under a luminous sky.

Tonight she and Max will be alone in a dark room with the door locked from the inside and performing tricks and duties and struggling towards some kind of goal, she knows not what, and they will not unlock the door until morning and they will be changed, she knows not how. Will he be kind with her in this new way of being together as husband and wife? He has gentle hands, she has watched him, but she has also seen his temper, and she looked at him with trepidation. Auntie Sasha is right. She hardly knows this man. Whatever the initiation, will it be gentle or will it be harsh?

She has a secret inside her which she must disclose; a guilty thing that she has hidden all the months of their engagement because she was too afraid that he would leave her. He is standing next to her, innocent, talking and laughing with Mr Broderick but she is full of sin. When she tells him he will call her a plotter and schemer with Auntie Sasha, a glittering emissary sent from a murky world to take money from the unsuspecting to send back to her crippled relatives at home. What will he say when he sees her sister Dora, withered with illness and poverty from the Revolution and scarred in every organ from the epidemics that swept through the country. Will he be disgusted and refuse to have children for fear of having a monster or a dwarf? He will always doubt her love and never trust her again. And what will he say when she asks him for money on her wedding night or the next morning and after that every month to support a family of women at home?

She is suddenly afraid to look at him with her fraudulent eyes, or to smile with her lying mouth. She hears Miriam laugh on the other side of the room and Eva is still watching her carefully. Perhaps she should have married the old man. He would have been grateful and indulgent like a father, accommodating every request with a pinch and a giggle. She had no right to aspire to the tall young man, envied and admired; his whole life transparent and nothing to hide.

Perhaps she should have worn white. Cheap white, chalk white, like a poor immigrant with a heavy veil over her face to hide her shame.

The guests have all gone. Auntie Sasha has left without saying goodbye, and for Mr Broderick it is an ordinary Monday morning and he is expected at work. Lelio takes a last sandwich and another schnapps: "Will there be a place for old bachelors in this new dispensation?" he asks, and leaves. The chairs are still in groupings where people were sitting with glasses next to them on the floor. Littered ashtrays are left on the table with the plaited bread and the plates smeared in herring and crumbled cake. Miriam is picking nuts off the table. Theo sits in a corner, smoking.

Hannah leaves the room to change out of her wedding dress and prepare for the honeymoon. She takes off the velvet jacket and hat and wraps it carefully in tissue-paper. Then she packs her dress into a box, covering it in camphor crystals to show her mother when there is enough money to send for her. She dresses in a spotted frock from her trousseau and carries her suitcase into the sitting-room.

Max is waiting for her, and Eva is already sitting in the car. Her mother-in-law is deaf and cannot take a holiday alone. So the three of them will be together. Hannah will read the menu to her and help her up the stairs to her room. She will take her to the beach early in the morning before the sun is too hot and the wind too strong and then take her to the cubicle to dress before she catches cold. She will sit with her on the beach until the wind begins to sting her legs with sand, and walk her slowly back to the hotel where she can leave her for a few hours before lunch. In the afternoon there will be long drives in the mountains and drinking tea in the little cafes along the coast. Hannah will not lose her patience when they are sitting in the dining-room and Eva takes her napkin to wipe every fork and spoon before she uses them. And she will restrain Max's irritation when Eva smells the meat for freshness in front of the waiter.

Hannah will be dutiful as she was with her grandfather at home when he called her to help him with his breathing. She was the one, with her gentle hands, who rubbed his back as he coughed and spat, breathing in the burning herbs to open his lungs.

She will convince them of her love until they lose their doubts, this distrusting family. She has time; a lifetime.

But how will she live through this night?

They drive off waving to Theo and Miriam standing at the door. Eva sits in the front seat next to Max. Hannah sits at the back next to the suitcases – she doesn't mind, she told them so.

Max is singing as he points the car to the south:

Warum ist es am Rhine so schön?
Am Rhiiiine sooooo schoöoon?

FOURTEEN
The Brown-Eyed Baby

IT IS A NICE LITTLE HOUSE, CORNER OF WEST STREET AND RIVIERA ROAD. Her own house. In Max's name of course, but her house. Always open to their friends. His friends really. And every weekend full of people and food. "Open House" they call it, especially on Sundays when everyone comes for tea and stays on for drinks – very English – and then supper: a finger supper when you are allowed to eat with your fingers.

They all sit and talk about things she does not understand. "What is the Gold Standard, Max?" and the Depression is something like the loss of value and the sadness a person can feel in their lives, but it refers to banks and money and upsets the whole country. She can remember her father's suitcases filled with promissory notes and money as worthless as the Sunday newspapers Max is reading. Here everyone reads the papers for information, but at home everyone knew things because events changed their lives. Max and his friends always argue about the government, and she asks him for his opinions: "Do you like General Smuts, Max?" Lelio brings his own bottle of whisky, drinks it slowly. "Gold and diamonds are the biggest fraud ever perpetrated by man," he says, finishes the bottle and calls everyone "bloody fools," laughing. They all know him and laugh. Hannah is not sure of the joke but she laughs too.

A nice little house with a room waiting for the baby and a small room next to the kitchen for her sister, Dora, who has come to live with her in South Africa. Painted white with shutters on the windows and an enclosed garden at the back with fruit-trees. She still feels strange having to close the shutters every night and bolt them tight, the whole world locked out and she and Max and Dora shut in. And then Max walks around the house double-checking every outside door and turning the key in every inside one. He tests each window and switches off the lights.

"You forgot to close the latch on the kitchen door," he says, or "You didn't take the key out of the front door and put it on the table. Every night it's the same."

"But Max, we didn't have to lock where I come from," she says.

"You didn't have to lock because there was nothing to steal and your neighbours were as poor as you. But this is South Africa."

"But I'm not used to it. And what about the people who work inside? You can't shut them out, and how do you stop them from stealing?"

He shakes his head helplessly and takes a deep breath.

"It's always the same. She refuses to understand," he says, looking upwards, appealing to some cosmic force.

He cuts half an orange, puts it on his side-table and they go to bed. He sleeps on his left side and she sleeps on her right, their buttocks touching. If he turns over he begins to make strangling noises in his throat and she must touch him very softly and whisper "Dear, would you mind turning over?" and he turns like a rolling log, rocking the mattress, and goes to sleep again. In the morning he tells her that she was snoring again.

When she wakes up the house is dark except for cracks of light coming through the closed shutters. She is always dressed before him, lifting her feet carefully so as not to wake him, but the bathroom tap whines and whinges when she turns it. She has tried three ways of opening it: slow, fast and squeezing, but still it shudders and bangs through all the pipes in the house.

"Every morning it's the same," he mutters lying in bed. He lifts himself up and sucks the half orange on the table.

Then she opens the back door for Lena and throws open the shutters to let the sharp light in, feeling pricks of pain as her pupils contract; early in the morning but already hot and she must tilt the blinds.

Max gets up slowly in crumpled pajamas and stays in the bathroom for a long time. She is like a sleuth, beginning to understand all the sounds and signals in her husband's house: vigorous slapping, accompanied by "aaaaah" and "ooooo" which means he is standing naked on the floor after his bath, stimulating his muscles in front of the mirror. The sequence of sounds is always the same. She hears a rhythmic scraping and snapping sound, he is sharpening his razor on the leather strop that hangs on the door-handle, and then the silence which means he is shaving. The daily encounter with his face: whipping up the soap with a shaving-brush, masking his skin with the thick lather like a white beard, scraping the exposed blade with steady strokes across the known contours, confident and sweeping, until he comes to his moustache, carefully touching the corners, and then he bites his lower lip to stretch the skin on his chin. The razor knows all the angles, sculpting smooth tracks over the curves of his cheeks and jawbone drawn tight until his whole face is unmasked again, baby-smooth except for a little web of red veins on his cheeks, and smelling astringent. He opens the door and leaves his footprints in talcum powder from the bathroom across the passage into the bedroom. She always acknowledges the arch between the ball and the heel of his foot, with a narrow spine down one side, delicate in a tall man – a dancer's feet, except for the hammer-toe, crooked and callused, which needs a little cushion of lambswool in his left shoe. After he uses the bathroom it smells of brilliantine, and steam condenses on the mirrors and drips down the wall. His pajamas are on the floor. She hears the sliding of the cupboard drawers as he chooses a shirt and socks, then the drawer closing and the dull thump of the cupboard door that never shuts properly. He slams it again.

The sun is bright on the breakfast-table, melting the butter, as he studies the newspaper. He sits with a straight back and one leg crossed over the other, turning the pages. And then the bang of the front door because he is rushing and late, "bye-bye" . . . and the starting of his car. The sound fades away after he has changed gears a second time and turned the corner up the hill. The empty eggshell of one boiled egg still stands on the breakfast-table and the remaining cold tea discolours the porcelain cup. She feels strange about the debris of a man's life. The disarranged pages of the newspaper. A grown man, a working man. She always puts her own litter away.

Then she is alone with Lena and there is silence in the house except for the whisk of the grass broom against the kitchen floor and the creak of the ironing-board as Lena presses his suits.

He comes home when long shadows have fallen across the grass.

Once he invited her to the office for tea. She put on her gloves and bag and the leather beret tilted over her right eye, and matching leather jacket. She wore the shirt that buttoned up to her neck with a green spotted tie – appropriately formal for visiting a man in his office. She polished her pointed shoes dark and shiny; the silk stockings, kept up with a tight elastic above her knees, made her legs look smooth.

Every month she puts away bits of the money that Max gives her for food, and after a few months she can buy a dress or new shoes. She has to be very clever and hide the new things away for a while and bring them out slowly. If he asks her, she says, surprised: "Oh no, Max, I've had this dress for months, don't you remember? I can't go out in this country without my hat, bag and gloves." It's not really cheating, and that way she does not have to ask him directly for money and plead and account for herself.

At the office Max introduced her to Hettie, the lady at the typewriter with whom she has often spoken on the telephone – she thought she was older from her voice – quite pretty. Hettie shook hands with long red nails and smudges of blue carbon on her fingers. They had tea and cake – very English. Max was sitting behind his desk, pouring the tea, and Hannah was sitting with her hands on her lap like a visitor. She looked around at the place where he lives a second life, perhaps a first life, a life away from home; there Hettie does his housekeeping, tidies his shelves, makes him lunch and serves his friends and clients with tea. She fills his diary, asks "Who is speaking?" before connecting his telephone calls, knows all his movements and the contents of his cupboards and drawers. Hannah wonders why some of them are locked, there is only paper inside. Hettie even opens his letters. Hannah has never been allowed to do that. While they were drinking tea, Mr Broderick arrived and Theo came into the room and they were all laughing and teasing Max about the two women in his life. Then Max asked her to go out while they spoke business and she had to leave, her face feeling puffy and hot under the beret tilted down over one eye. Is she a stranger in his life or a child? She waited outside the closed door while Hettie sat inside taking notes. Then Hettie made her another cup of tea and Hannah sat listening to her answering the telephone and watching the long red nails tapping on the typewriter. She paged through a trade journal, reading about stone-crushing and advanced methods of baking bricks and new models of town-planning in South America and a glut of office space in Durban. Until they opened the door and she was allowed to go back into the room.

All day she is alone in the house with Dora. She can feel her stomach stretching and twitching every day with the little creature floating inside her like a fish, breathing through its skin and feeding through the ropy arteries that connect them. Was that an elbow or a knee or a small fist pressing the elastic walls of its swampy sac, its whole self-sustaining world where each can feel the throb of the other's heart?

She sits outside on the lawn with Dora, sucking the sweet white centres of grass. South African women wear gardening gloves and hats, digging and planting with the garden boy, calling the flowers by botanical names. But a gazania is just a daisy. She likes to lie on the grass watching the sky. High summer with the peaches ripe on the trees. In the afternoons when she begins to feel that she is drugged with heat and the heavy ceiling above the earth has swollen to bursting, the black rain-clouds come rumbling in from the south. Once she saw three white birds fly deep into the dark electric folds.

The heavy clouds roll in covering the whole sky, cracking violently overhead and the great udders hang low and then burst. She and Dora run through the house closing the windows and bringing in the washing, and they stand watching the peachtrees bend and the drains and gutters flood. Then the blue breaks through like a gateway and the black clouds sail northwards carrying water to the dry interior, twitching with friction. Already the rain is falling in the distance, hanging like grey veils from the sky and all around hot vapour rises from the roads and rooftops.

But sometimes the sky becomes yellow all over and suddenly cold. Ice falls from the sky, slashing everything down to the ground, not a leaf left on the trees and the peaches gashed and dripping their juices and the grass covered white like snow in midsummer. Later the garden boy rakes up piles of debris, all the green stripped from the trees with grass flies swarming and the world looks stricken. A few weeks later the flowers grow again and bloom late a second time. Sometimes after steamy showers in the early evening the air begins to flutter with little creatures. They fly into the night with silky wings, obeying a mysterious commandment to leave their underground nests, and they rise like earth spirits released into the sky.

It is a nice little house with a small room for Dora: a bed, a table and chair, a rug on the floor and curtains to soften the afternoon sun. What more does she need? During the day they sit outside.

"Come and lie on the grass," says Hannah. "It's so cool and soft."

"Please Hannah, you ask me every day. The ants bite me and the grass makes my skin itch. Liebergott, you can't sit without something stinging you in this country. Mosquitoes breeding in the drains and crabs crawling out of the sewers. Please, Hannah. Please."

So she sits on the chair with her little hands resting on her puffy belly.

"It's the salt. Why does Lena put so much salt in the food? Liebergott look how blown up I am. Have you noticed how she only listens to Max? And how she eats all the bread and sugar? Have you seen how many teaspoons she puts in her tea and how thick she smears the butter and jam? Liebergott does she think you're millionaires? And I'm sure she's stealing the peaches off the trees. Where are they? I've only had one."

When Theo and Eva come to visit, Dora runs to her room, shutting the door against the tall dark people who stoop down when they look at her. She sits in her room on the edge of the bed, her feet not touching the floor. Her body sweats with the afternoon sun reflecting on white walls, and she waits, listening to the murmur of voices through the door and the buzz of a fly on the window hurling itself against the glass. Very quiet here in South Africa, still and static in the afternoons as when a clock stops. No one ever walks in the streets. A big Zulu with rings in his ears could come and hit you over the head with his stick. Liebergott will those people never leave? A person can suffocate in this country all alone in a hot room and the burnt smell of the servant's stew coming from the stove in the scullery.

Then when she hears the front door close she runs out looking for Hannah again.

It was always the same – Hannah's fault because she was prettier, with curly chestnut hair and green eyes and younger and cleverer than Dora.

"Come Dora, we're all going for a walk on the beach. I'll help you with your mathematics. And you just tell me which girls won't sit next to you and I'll pull their plaits at school. And if its Volodya's sister he'll put stones in her shoes. Come for a walk, Dora. Come, we'll look for shells on the beach."

But Dora always had her piano. She learnt to stretch her fingers an octave easily and reach down with her feet to touch the pedals near the floor. She could not concentrate at school. Hannah always had to help her, but who needs to memorise dates in history? The textbooks give causes and results of war but she knows the spicy scent of gunsmoke in the streets and the fecal smell of soldiers. Why should she care about the rainfall in Brazil or the largest river in China? She understands the language of music, its grammar, its arithmetic: sixths, sevenths, octaves. She can calculate dominants, tonics, harmonics, overtones. She can anticipate pauses too subtle for notations on the page and sense the structure of variations like a clairvoyant. She can sight-read at any speed, all the flats and all the sharps, arpeggios and chords, her fingers leaping when she cannot reach, straight-backed, raising her elbows like wings and lifting her wrists high, then pressing down, crescendo! nearly standing with the full weight of her body over the keys. Her arms are as strong as any man's and she can break open apples with her hands. On Sundays she would make concerts for Grossmama and Grosspapa and all the cousins and aunts, accompanying Hannah in the Russian songs. And the family would clap and stamp their feet. "Encore," they would scream, as she and Hannah curtseyed deep and slow with ostrich feathers in their hair and fringed shawls over their shoulders. She loved Spanish music, playing their Gypsy rhythms while Hannah made grand poses. And she taught Hannah to sing: "Say aaaah. Say aaaah as though a doctor is pressing down your tongue . . . aaaah . . . aaaah." Why can't she learn Spanish at school or Italian? She can nearly speak them from knowing the songs?

> *Sul mare luccica*
> *L'astro d'argento,*
> *Placida è l'onda,*
> *Prospero è vento.*
> *Venite all'agile*
> *Barchetta mia*
> *Santa Lucia,*
> *Santa Lucia!*

Even with her runny ear that drove all the girls away with its stink, she had perfect pitch. The children would stand outside in the street listening to her play, sometimes creeping into the house and sitting quietly in a corner.

And yet behind her back they would still whisper "Phui!" and hold their noses when she passed, exploding with laughter.

At night she sits between Max and Hannah at the dining-room table. Sometimes Theo is there but he never talks to her. She cuts her meat into small squares, placing it neatly and slowly on the fork with the peas and potatoes, and swallowing them as though they are stones while everyone waits for her to finish. Theo taps his fingers. After supper she sits on a chair in the living room, her hands folded over her belly – she has swollen up from the salt again – and her feet swinging off the floor. Then she excuses herself and goes to bed.

Hannah cannot protect Dora from Max and his family. Cannot shield her from her husband who never looks at her. Even when he is sitting next to her he looks straight ahead. Why can't she tell them? "Dora has clever hands at the piano and she can teach you to sing in three languages."

But small, small. Never noticed in a room with other people, wearing small dresses with big hems made by Mama from fragments at home. Even Grosspapa called her: "Dwarf".

Every night Hannah lies in bed and cries because soon she will have to tell Dora to leave the house. Dora must learn to look after herself in South Africa, work and earn money. It is not like "home" where there was no rent and no accounts and always enough food. Everyone lived, God knows how. There were always boiled potatoes and sour cream and onions and dense black bread which Grosspapa gripped under his armpit, cutting thick slices with a curved knife. There were herring and mackerel from the fishing boats in the harbour and Grosspapa salted large sides of hake that hung from the ceiling in summer. A bit of this a bit of that – milk soup with noodles when you were sick, egg yolk frothed into a nog with sugar and relished a teaspoon at a time, chicken on Friday nights, goose on holidays. Everyone lived.

Hannah has found a job for Dora as a nurse-girl and companion. She will sleep in a small room near the kitchen and wear a white overall and a starched cap on her head.

It is three months now since Dora has left the house. In the mornings Hannah opens the shutters early to catch the first sun; a few minutes of pure glory as the ether ignites, intensifies into pure gold and then lights up the whole sky.

She is alone all day waiting for Max to come home. Fig-leaves hang on frail stems like yellowing handprints; maroon bulrushes grow in a bog near the leaky tap, getting ready to burst open into silky filaments; orange berries hang full from spiky bushes, plucked by crested birds and swallowed whole; pure light and colour and crackle underfoot. She holds a tortoise-shell kitten on her lap, looks into the black lens growing wide and then narrow like snakes' eyes. The fur shines where her hand smooths it over and over and she puts a drop of cologne on each paw. It has green eyes like her own. She prays that the baby will be dark, brown hair and brown eyes like Max, with strong straight bones.

Now that Dora is not in the house she does not want to think about her. Sometimes she could not bear to look at her with her child's body, little hands and feet – she can never find shoes to fit – but a woman's buttocks and a woman's breasts. And the baby moving inside her own stomach, and Eva watching every day, the swelling under her dress. Even Lena has asked her how many months, touching her and asking why she is so small? At night she lies awake with Max sleeping next to her, waiting for the movements under her skin. Does it sleep at night also? Frightened of her body's secrets and the inherited codes in her blood and the unknown creature that feeds and floats inside her.

The nursery is empty. There are no small clothes in the house. Hannah is forbidden to buy even one knitted cap until the infant is wriggling in her hands. She makes herself strong by walking and drinking milk, and only thinks of the brown-eyed baby she will bring into the house.

Every week letters come from her mother, Rosa. Max picks them up to examine the foreign stamps and scratchy writing. Sometimes he laughs and asks how the post office can decipher the address, and other times he looks at her with suspicion as though he will never really understand her mind which is as inaccessible to him as her mother's scribbles.

Soon Rosa will arrive carrying old suitcases tied with leather straps and wearing long faded dresses with drooping hems. The last of the family to come to Africa. She will occupy Dora's room and sit on Dora's chair at the dining-room table. Eva will examine her closely when she first sees her, the way she looked at Dora, silently, and then not look at her again after that. Theo will not be here as he is going to live in America. And Max will say – has already said – can he never be finished with the women in her family and now that Theo has gone are there never any men? Hannah will have to save more money every week to buy her mother shoes and stockings, and also to keep in the bank in her own name, just in case. She is not devious. Is she not allowed one place in this world where her name, her own signature, has value? Then on Sundays there will be two old women in the garden. But Hannah will sit with Eva, talking loudly into her ear and kissing her softly on the cheek, spoiling her especially because Theo has gone to live in America. Perhaps Eva knows, but has never said anything, that Max will also leave. Theo's letters arrive and she examines the American stamps with shrewd eyes, Max reading to her in a loud voice, and a second time because she has not heard.

Rosa will have to sit alone, knitting and humming her monotonous little songs.

And then the brown-eyed baby will come. Hannnah's secret is to call him Paul. She'll argue with Max about it later. There are ways of speaking to a man. And then there will be Amy and then . . .

"We'll have two children and no more," says Max.

It's a nice little house. His house really.

FIFTEEN
King Of The Castle

HE'S KING OF THE CASTLE, SURVEYING HIS POSSESSIONS: HIS TRICYCLE, ALL the coloured blocks lying on the steps, his kite, the swing, his red and blue striped ball and one shoe lying on the driveway. And then he inspects his entire estate: the prickly bush that scratches his skin, the tree with large leaves like a fan, the flowerbed, the mulberry bush and all the grass as far away as the fence around the garden. A king crowned with curls. Mother brushes them softly, twirling them around her finger and away from his eyes; a brown-eyed baby, she calls him. She lifts him high up over her shoulder, making a comfy seat with her arm, holding him firm with her hands so he can see the distant borders of his province.

"You see, Paul, all around you, all the flowers, all the trees, all the birds in the trees, the sun high in the sky, and the stars far away at night. It's all yours." She walks him through his territory, and he leaves a stone, a ball, a shell, a feather to demarcate his ground. Smell the flower," she says, and he buries his nose in pollen. "Can you hear the cricket?"

"Ccrrrk ccrrrk," he says.

"And look," says Mother, "see the daytime moon high in the sky."

"Kye," he says pointing a fat finger.

"Clever boy," says Mother rocking him and singing a Russian ditty dedicated to his genius.

"Put him down," says Pa. "You're spoiling him. Put up yer dukes," says Pa making a jab under his chin. "There's my boy, keep up yer defences, don't let 'em get through. Hit back, hit back. Don't cry. Now let's kick a ball. Enough of women's company. Let's cut off these curls."

He cries when Mother sings "Who killed Cock Robin?" – he closes the door and climbs into the new baby's cot, lying next to the rubbery little body, too close, perhaps. He raises an arm high and brings his fist down on her small smooth head. "I" said the fly. "With my little eye. I saw him die."

In the beginning there is nothing, nothing. A deep night of hunger and sleep and crying in the void with the sweet faraway sound of a voice. Crying. Warm warm in that darkness and soft. Darkness fades slowly into light and song. All flat and bright and smiling faces hover happy. A heavy hand upon her head and pain again and crying in the night. "I" said the fly. "With my little eye." Crying. Slowly coming into the light again, then wide awake. The world is bright and upright to touch and reach. "She's on her feet. Don't push her, Paul," says Pa. A giddy place, on spongy legs and pulpy ground. High up and fall down and up and down and sit on Pa's lap quietly sucking a finger. Softness and song. Say: "Mama". Again and again a sound called Amy. Aaammmyyy . . . Laughing.

Laughing on the beach in Durban, the wind on her face, rolling over and over, dizzy in the sand and stamping her feet in the runaway waves. Then she's sitting on Pa's lap; white trousers creased with sand and a sticky salty wind blowing in from the blue-green openness. White towels and white sand and soft sun screened with gauzy mesh, and big boys selling mangoes and bananas in baskets. Pa wears his white suit, tie and shoes, his hat pulled down over one eye. He crosses his legs and she can see the garter holding up his socks. Pa's white suit smells of powder and cologne and it makes her feel quiet and sleepy on a blanket with the tickle of the tide on her feet. She holds Mother's hand and plays with the shiny stone around her neck, the same colour as the sea-water, the same colour as her eyes. Mother draws the outline of her face with the tip of her finger: along the snub of her nose, along the line of her eyebrows, feather-light, around the eyes, brown eyes creasing with a smile. Her hair is ruffled into corkscrews by the wind, sea-fresh against her face. Durban beach with its barnacled pier going far out to sea and boys sitting along the edge of it with cans of wriggling bait. Two grandmothers sit on beach chairs wearing gloves and hats and bags. Granny Eva wears a yellow scarf, and Mother always tries to please her. Pa's fat tummy in his swimming costume; he dives under the bubbles like dead weight, and floats up like driftwood. Her brother is shouting and thumping a ball. He kicks her sandcastle.

Then they are packing suitcases. Amy pats the cat and tells it to listen to Granny, and gives a final piece of lettuce to the tortoise. She looks at the house for the last time.

"Wave goodbye to both your grandmothers," says Pa. Mother kisses them both, crying. Two old ladies dressed in hats and gloves stand on the pier. A yellow scarf flutters. Passengers throw coloured streamers to their friends and relations waving from the dockside, connecting them like veins in a womb, stretching as the ship slides away, and becoming torn and limp in the churning water. Mother is crying as the coastline fades.

Paul already knows all the lounges and all the stairs and runs round and round the deck. He plays games with other boys throwing a ball over a net or a dart onto a board or knocking on cabin doors and running away laughing. Amy stays next to Mother, with the air getting colder and ice beginning to form on the decks. Paul will not come inside and slides up and down the slippery decks, coughing and running round and round with the other boys, throwing ice-balls against the windows. Then he is too sick to get out of bed and his face is red and sweating even though ice is floating in the sea.

A new land appears out of the mist as the ship passes a tall statue with a crown.

"We're in America."

They walk down the gangplank following Paul who is carried to an ambulance on a stretcher.

"It's a bad beginning," says Pa.

Now Amy knows the camera. She faces it straight with a smile, standing with Mother in a leopardskin swimming costume, hair brushed shiny and tamed into two plaits ending in a curl. Her skin is child-smooth, and plump fingers reach up to the sky. Mother wears a turban. Fine shadows outline her luminous face. Amy tipples into the water, slips silently into the blue, slim as a snake in the deep-down blue, blowing bubbles, easy and no need to breathe. True blue, happy blue, bluey blue. Mother is looking fearfully in the water to find her as she bursts through the surface laughing. She climbs the ladder high up to the board. Twenty feet high. Step, step, jump, and the board flips her up and over, slicing the water keen as a knife and gliding wide-eyed and earless along the deep with the verge far away, satin-smooth and silent with rainbow ripples on her skin.

"She won a blue ribbon for swimming against children twice her age," says Pa, lifting his chin. Night lights shine on wet cement as she crouches on the edge, taut as a whistle, and cuts into the water, sharp as steel. The strong black line leads her. She sees her arms splice slow-motion and heavy bubbles rise, still as a lake and soundless beneath the brim, stretched eel-sleek in its element. One breath takes her and she's there, bursting through the silence into bright lights. The timekeepers clock her home.

Brother watches from the side.

They live in a large house surrounded by trees. The back door has black mosquito netting across the frame and whines when it opens and bangs when it shuts; a flat sound, rude as a slap. There are still mosquitoes in every room. She plays under the dense bushes with her cousin, bushes higher than her head in the dark garden; slow games through the twisted roots smelling of damp and rotting undergrowth. Do they talk or do they play mutely under the large leaves? The same game every day; lose and find and lose again without words or laughter. Her brother kicks a ball all afternoon. At night Mother takes her up the wide staircase onto a landing and into a room with a high ceiling. She wants the blanket folded down smoothly, precise at the corners, no pleats or creases and exactly equal on both sides where it folds over with the sheet. Tuck it in firmly under her arms. She pulls the fluff from the woolly blanket and slowly rubs it into a ball. Mother holds her hand. At night she dreams of roots and leaves that twist and tangle.

Sometimes they swim in straight narrow canals with crabs and catfish living in the mud. She's scared to put down her feet in the slushy bottom with creatures that hide under stones or little fish that nibble her toes. She screams when Paul takes black bloodsucking worms and puts them on her skin, laughing. They walk to the sea, wide open and breathing, curving far away in a misty arc under the mother-of-pearl sky. The air is heavy with salt and hangs low as a ceiling. They coast the rollers from far out at sea, catch it before it crashes, ride the crest like kings and wash in with the waves.

This is a hot place, so Pa still wears his white linen suit. On very hot days he wears white trousers and a white shirt, open at the throat, and sleeves rolled up to his elbows. His handkerchief smells of lavender when he takes it out of his pocket to wipe his face.

One day they go to a wild place with islands surrounded by water and trees twisted with vines. They cross the water on low-lying slatted bridges that skim the surface, swinging and bending under their feet. There is no one living in this place.

"Be careful of crabs and alligators and look for the snakes wriggling in the water," says Pa. "Lean the gun on this tree and aim for the head."

Amy closes one eye and squints through the sights, pointing the rod at the squirming thing. The gun is heavy in her hands, slim and dense. Black metal invites the twitchy finger. The curve of the trigger fits. She can feel its leaden soul when she points and squeezes.

"Fix your eye and shoot," says Pa.

She fires into the water and misses. Pa seems disappointed and Paul is pleased. A boil is growing on her elbow. They have to prick it with a needle and thick yellow blood bursts out.

One day Pa says something about a war and not having enough money to live near the sea where it is always warm and nobody works, where people swim and sleep in the sun. So they travel to a cold city where Pa finds an apartment in a building that casts a long shadow over the street. Now Amy plays on the pavement with her friends, bouncing a ball and lifting their legs in wide circles over the bouncing ball, over and over again, skirts fluttering. Or skipping rope or hopping on one leg. If you step on the lines you're out. Paul jokes and talks to girls, leaning against the building and smoking where Pa and Mother can't see. She has seen him put a knife in his pocket, and all the boys are hiding razor-blades in the tips of their shoes. She listens to the radio at night about men who murder and steal. The police describe them with scarred faces and tattooed arms. "This man is dangerous," says the radio. "Last seen in the streets of the city." Then she dreams about tangled trees and roots and dark forests and she is standing blinking in a lighted room when she wakes up, and Mother wide-eyed walks her slowly back to bed.

But they go away for long summer holidays. They leave the littered streets and go to the lakes further north; small seas with green hills where rich men have their farms. All the city people sit crowded on the edge of the wide water looking at the roofs of large white houses on the other side and sailing boats they keep tied up on the edge. Amy digs for worms, fat wriggling night-crawlers to use for bait. "That's your job," Paul commands. "Aye aye sir," she replies obediently, and rips them from their resting-place in the warm manure, as the darkness sparks with fireflies. She sits with Mother who looks up at the glowing night sky and asks if it is true that there is still a life on the hot city streets and whether there is a terrible war in this same world far away?

One summer they take rooms in a farmhouse.

"Amy, Amy, come out and play."

The farmer's children stand outside her window and call. She puts on rubber boots and opens the door with her hair flying behind her. They follow the cows to a faraway place, beyond the barns and the fences and the potato-fields, where the grass grows blue with greenness. There they watch tree spiders build gauzy webs and hairy caterpillars weave cocoons. They poke sticks into a snake's hole and leave warm milk in a scooped-out stone. Georgiy and Trushia sing songs in their mother's language and make an altar of stones. Georgiy nearly steps on the snake coiled tightly in the sand and tries to catch it with string. It opens its mouth wide, pink and puffy inside with two curved teeth, and slithers away into the grass. And once they found its dried-out skin lying on a rock with the pale patterns of its diamond scales. Then they count the rings in a sawn-off tree. "If you read the rings you'll know the inside secrets of the tree's life," says Georgiy. Some rings are wide and smooth when the roots drank deep and some grew tough and horny when the ground was dry. You can count the seasons. All afternoon they watch the cows chew green-blue grass and flick gadflies with tufted tails and blink quiet eyes. Thirty-two chews before the cows swallow and bring up the foamy cud to chew again. Slow time, smoking long stalks until the sun goes down. Then the cows make a tardy line, walking to the dull sound of cowbells and swinging dripping udders, back to the barn to be milked. When they come home Amy goes to Georgiy and Trushia's room to eat Post Toasties and they come to her room to eat real food.

Paul spends all day in the hayloft with Trushia's sister Bibi. "Paul, come down immediately," Mother calls. "Paul, come down at once!" She stands with a broomstick and threatens to tell Pa, but he won't come down. And Amy is crying because the farmer chopped off a chicken's head, and she saw it flap its headless wings and she swears she will never eat meat again. Then mother says that perhaps country holidays are not so good for city children after all and they go back to the apartment building and to running in the streets and drawing chalk squares on the pavements.

If they stand in the street and look up they can see everybody's lives through the windows. When Amy plays with her friend Joan, they both look up to the apartment window where Mother sits at the piano singing. All the children look up and pull faces at her, a thumb on their nose and wiggling fingers, then they sing up and down and laugh. There is no sound of the radio or gramophone music as from other windows, but only Mother singing loudly in languages they cannot understand. She sits in the steamy bathroom with the hot tap running, singing up and down and up and down and then she doesn't speak for weeks because her teacher, who she calls Professor, has told her to rest her voice. This is very important because she has lost it and must recover it. Lost and found and lost and found and Mother cries a lot in case she can't find it.

The war is something that Amy hears Pa talk about but he is not allowed to be a soldier because he comes from another country and can't be trusted. At night they black out the windows, and strong beams of light make arcs across the sky and when they hear the siren in the night they must all stand outside in the passage looking at one another in pajamas.

Once Joan's father came home from the war in his khaki uniform bringing presents and there was singing and dancing in their home. Soon after he went away again they got a special letter and now there is a gold star in the window to show that he will never come back. Amy doesn't understand why they are fighting but many windows have gold stars and when she visits Joan in her apartment she has seen her mother sitting in a chair crying.

When Amy comes off the streets to go upstairs she sees Mother at the piano with her foot down loud on the pedal, her left hand working feverishly on the bass keys and her voice soaring high above them. Perhaps she has found her voice again. Amy stands behind her reading the words about walled castles and men on horseback and spirits of the night.

> *Who rides there so late through night so wild*
> *A loving father with his young child*
> *He clasp'd his boy close with his fond arm*
> *And closer closer to keep him warm.*
> *"Dear Son what makes thy sweet face grow so white?"*
> *"See Father 'tis the Erl King in sight!*
> *Erl King stands there with crown and shroud."*
> *"Dear Son, it is some misty cloud."*
> *"Dear Father, my father, and can'st thou not trace*
> *The Erl King's daughter in yon dark place?"*

> "Dear Son, dear Son, the form you there see
> Is only the hollow grey willow tree."
> "My father! My father, thy child closer clasp
> Erl King seiz'd me with icy grasp!"
> His father shudder'd. His pace grew more wild,
> He held to his bosom his poor swooning child.
> He reach'd that house with toil and dread,
> But in his arms, lo! his child lay dead!

Those stories seem very far away from their life in the apartment building with gold stars on the windows and children playing ball in the street, but they catch something inside her like the horny rings in a tree and she listens with a quiet kind of fear.

Amy feels very different to Joan, her clothes and her food. Mother must learn to make hamburgers. They are not the same as klops. Joan's school is also different. There nuns stick chewing-gum in her hair if she is naughty and she memorises things about God from a catechism book. Amy's mother and father are very different to Joan's, and inside of herself, like the soft rings in a growing tree, she feels different to the other children at school. She is not sure why.

But in the apartment building, when she stands behind her mother sitting at the piano with hands rumbling on the bass keys and her voice is soaring above them like the wind in that dark forest, they are both reading the words of that song and crying.

SIXTEEN
Hannah To Rosa

OCTOBER 1943

My dearest Mama,
I am writing to you from far away still, never knowing if the letter will reach you or even if you received the last.

I have not had a letter for a long time and I feel very separated from you and estranged, my family so dispersed and scattered. A memory without any reality. But I continue to write because it brings me nearer in thought and records all my deepest experiences and feelings.

So far there is no danger of an invasion to this country. Instead, shiploads of men are packed and sent to Europe and the East to fight over there. We buy food with rationing stamps, the children wear identification tags and at night strong beams of light criss-cross the sky until morning. The children know all the war songs which are broadcast over the radio continuously. Some are proud and rousing: "Over there . . . over there . . . the Yanks are coming . . . the Yanks are coming . . ." And some are sad and the children sing them softly: "Coming in on a wing and a prayer . . . Coming in on a wing and a prayer . . ." Sometimes I sing them also. Everyone does. And the children march and sing: "When Johnny comes marching home again hooray, hooray . . ."

This is a different kind of war to the one I remember as a child, where we were surrounded by filth and lived in constant terror. Wartime here is like living in a proud culture that surrounds you with its art and icons: flags, films, military music, parades and pictures of a smiling president. The city streets are full of young "Johnnies" wearing crisp khaki shirts, their ties furled into the front opening, and trousers pressed into perfect creases. They walk in an indolent way, smiling slowly, lopsidedly, strolling with tilting hips and shoulders. They are carefully groomed athletes, their identity disks hanging on chains around smooth necks and the brass-buckled belts lying flat, slick, on slim stomachs. The uniforms are identical except for trimmings of gold braid for rank, and yet each young man is different, smart and free 'n' easy. They make the war look sporty – gilded gladiators at play.

But then we see the footsoldiers on newsreels, wading through mud or abandoned and bloated next to a ditch or crawling across open beaches gutted with mines, mutilated, screaming. The survivors still stroll free 'n' easy, loose-limbed on the long walk through the roads of Europe, but like the rag-and-bone man, carrying everything they need: guns and bayonets, water-bottles and a knife and fork and a metal plate strapped to their backs. Standing against a gutted house smoking a cigarette, leaning against a wall, asleep on their feet, unwashed and stinking inside the khaki. Others walk on crutches or limp with a dirty bandaged foot, only the best men chosen to crawl in all the horror. And then they come back to us clean and smiling again, parading on the city streets where wealthy American women shop on Fifth Avenue wearing mink coats even though food is rationed and it is wartime.

Imagine, Mama, the apartment building where we live: yellow face-brick like all the others in the street, and a canvas awning outside the front entrance with the name WASHINGTON ARMS; a square, squat building with children playing outside in the street and windows dotted with blue satin flags and gold stars. These flags show the number of dead soldiers in the family. I have seen three gold stars on a flag in someone's window. A gold star in exchange for a life and lace curtains that never open. A lady in our building has a flag with two stars in her window. When I see her in the street I search her face for something, as though her eyes will tell me the secrets of her life.

Does suffering always give you understanding? Do you remember uncle Isadore? How his face changed when he lost his wife? He looked like a tired animal and never recovered. Food lost its flavour for him and he could only taste salt. And yet when he opened his mouth he spoke inanities and laughed his silly laugh. "I don't know, I really don't know," was all he could say. And there was Rachel, vain and haughty, bleaching her hair blonde, and marrying five different husbands, one after the other. Then, when she had a stroke she couldn't walk or talk. She could only say: "Dish, dish, dish, dish, dish," wanting to kiss people on their hands and faces, clutching them and holding them close with her crooked fingers. She wouldn't let them go. I used to be pretty but it surprised me when people said: "She's so pretty." I was Hannah and that was all. Now I feel the same but I also feel different and I don't know how my life has changed me. When you lose your beauty people judge you: "She's lost her looks," they say accusingly as though you should hide your face. I watch very plain people or fat or even old people in the street holding hands, looking at each other and seeing something extraordinary. They have a privileged view that is only seen with love. The rest of the world sees the surface.

But when I see how some of the soldiers have come back from the war, then I think that it is enough that a face has eyes and a nose and a mouth, and a body has two arms and two legs.

Women knit khaki socks and children buy war bonds to save their money. We pay for food with rationing books, collecting our coupons to buy something special like butter. Otherwise Amy just takes the ordinary slab of white fat and mixes it with yellow dye. We play tricks with food like cooking sausage-meat and apples with sage and calling it Mock Goose. And to make eggs: mix one level tablespoon of yellow powder with two tablespoons of water. This paste equals one fresh egg. I have nearly forgotten that food is grown, and not made in a factory.

But the fighting is "over there". The American people don't know what it is to have battlefields in the streets and bodies infected with lice like we had. I will never forget how you stole flour to feed us and how you got horse sugar – that is what we called it – yellow and watery, from a soldier; how we ate it in handfuls with sticky fingers and pouched cheeks and my teeth aching from the sweetness.

Now I know how you persuaded him to part with his sugar and how you got candles and pieces of soap and bits of firewood. There were things that I saw as a child that I could not understand – soldiers coming to visit you – and how I found you, once, in a cellar. Forgive me Mama, but children see things without understanding or making judgments, and now it is too long ago for you to be ashamed. He did not have time to take the cap off his head or the gun off his hip while he was with you. And you were ugly with your hair matted and your eyes wild. You came out of the cellar with a few coins jingling in your pocket, without any false sense of remorse. You sold the only thing you had to keep us alive, and you went back to sweeping the floor.

Our life here is so different. We have no real friends. We just invite people to eat in our apartment – our food which they do not really like, stuffed cabbage or klops and potatoes – and six months later they ask us, and we eat hamburgers with ketchup. But I am grateful, because otherwise we would be completely alone. Of course there is Theo, but he has married an American woman and we never see him. The last time I saw him he sat smoking all night, never speaking once. He is living with his wife in a house in Brooklyn together with their boy and the stepchildren. It is unfortunate how his life has changed but there is nothing that we can do because the two brothers have become estranged like two enemies in a war.

Max and I have shared many experiences, bringing us very close. It is a strange closeness with many differences between us, especially his anger which I will never understand. But I can truly say we are a family. And now that we have been demoted to immigrant status, we are both the same: foreigners in a country without friends and relations. "Aliens," they call us. People in our building mistrust us. They suspect that Max is a spy because he has a moustache and speaks with a foreign accent, and I behave very differently from the American housewives. Perhaps it is the way I wrap a scarf around my head like a turban in cold weather or my pointy shoes or the spotted veil I wear on my hair in summer. I am very conspicuous in an ordinary suburban street. When we pass on the pavements I see them look at my shoes or my scarf, and when I turn around, they have also turned to look at me behind my back. I have learnt to push and use foul language in the laundry queue waiting for washing machines and trying to find a place to dry the clothes. But often I am last in the line, and then I have to wash by hand and hang the wet clothes from a rack in the bathroom. Then the family complains about the dripping landscape for days. I wash and cook and iron and the strong chemicals infect my hands until my nails ooze with pus. It is not like at home where we scrubbed the pots with mud and it made our skin soft and clean.

Amy was a small child when we left South Africa. We were frightened. I still remember having those fears that grip your mind at night. Amy wore the same little dresses and embroidered aprons for many seasons until she cried that she was too old for aprons and embroidery and she wanted to wear the same clothes as everyone else, dresses and short socks and rubber-soled sneakers, because the children at school were laughing.

Max often stands her against the wall barefoot to make a line over her head with a ruler. He tells her to stretch her back and lift her chin, then he writes the date. The lines were obstinate from month to month despite everything we did: feeding her butter and cheese and meat and fruit with all our coupons. But then, like a miracle, the lines began climbing like a ladder. The dates on the wall tell the whole story.

Max doesn't measure Paul any more and they are always arguing because Paul takes his shirts and socks. Even their feet are the same size. Everyone wants to be tall here and nothing small has any value. All the children drink milk like a special potion to make them grow, and everything is oversized: the potatoes are as large as ostrich eggs, the people grow long limbs like giants and the office buildings tower like Babel, trying to touch God in the sky.

Rich people try to live out of town but we have very little money because it is wartime and Max cannot find a job. Once he sold diamonds for a big company in the city. Can you imagine, Mama, diamonds in wartime? Another time he took an office job in a different town, living there during the week in one small room and coming home to us for the weekend with presents of sharp pencils for the children. Amy hoarded her pencils in a special box like a collection, examining the points and sharpening them as fine as needles. Then Paul found them and broke the points, and there was terrible crying.

I did not like Max to be away while I was alone with them in this large city with dark streets and Paul out late with his bad friends and Amy pale and small. I sat sleepless in a chair every night in the blacked-out apartment, waiting for the daylight to show between the slits of the curtains.

Often we talk to the children about South Africa and their family. They listen as though it is an imaginary land that has private houses and gardens and wild animals that live without interference in large herds. They ask whether it is safe to walk in the streets with elephants and lions, and they cannot understand that some South Africans speak English and others speak a language called Afrikaans and that the black people speak many other languages and that there are Indians and Chinese also, all in the same country, living separate lives. Our kind of Babel. They listen quietly, wondering about the place where they were born, and ask how anyone can understand anyone else if they all speak different languages. Then they go back to playing in the streets as though all the stories are fiction. They can only understand a life on city pavements where Amy skips on cement and Paul walks up and down with his friends.

As I write to you I feel so strange describing them and giving you information, instead of your knowing them closely and sharing their lives.

When Max is not working he stays at home unwashed and not dressed, making bread or repairing torn sheets with an old sewing machine. He sits in his pajamas, painting all morning. He will not take lessons because he wants to develop his own individual style; "primitive" he calls it. Teachers make you all the same, he says. All of his pictures have one incurable flaw. So he paints over and over the same place, trying to correct his mistakes, not dressing or washing and smelling of turps.

I have taken a job teaching singing at a tap-dancing studio, and I come back to the apartment at night with my ears still ringing from the sound of tapping feet. This is how people live in America, everyone trying to earn something extra whichever way they can. They have given me a room with a piano, and I teach scales and songs with loud jazz music all around me. This is special American music, slangy, quite catchy, and sometimes I wake up in the morning already singing:

> *Ole man Johnson's jazzin' around.*
> *Don' push 'im, don' touch 'im,*
> *Or he'll fall to de ground.*
> *He's sure to be late*
> *Cos he can't walk straight –*
> *Cos he's jus' jazzin' around.*

How my life has changed since I left you and all the familiar things of my childhood: the concerts that we made for Grosspapa and Grossmama and the cousins and aunts – Dora playing so grandly with a velvet ribbon around her head, and I, singing next to the small upright piano with a long lace tablecloth tied around my waist, draped on the floor behind me.

Perhaps childhood games are not so innocent at all. They should fall away painlessly like milk-teeth, or else they will have to be extracted later when they are rotten and deformed with age.

I still sit at the piano, singing, in this shabby apartment with paint peeling off the walls and wet washing hanging in the bathroom over everyone's heads. I go to a teacher in one of the glass buildings in the city. He says that my voice is as fresh as willow-wood, and he will not take money for my lessons. He plays the piano and has the power to make my voice ring. I open my mouth and it soars. I can feel my lips tremble and the bones in my head vibrate. You have always been so practical, Mama, honest and simple even when you dragged us, sick and filthy, through the war. Can you imagine? I am in a state of exhilaration. I feel as though I'm racing a wild horse or swimming through the colours of a rainbow.

My teacher tells me to speak very little to save my voice, not even to the children or Max. And I carry my music everywhere, waiting for a bus, sitting in a train, studying, studying. I hum the songs as I walk in the street and I sit in a steamy bathroom for hours to open my throat. When I go out children walk behind me pulling faces because they hear me singing in the street and they think I am mad. Max is insisting that I stop and Amy and Paul tease me and imitate my gestures. I have to admit that it is all that I think about and even in my sleep I hear the music continuously.

When I have my lessons my head spins with sound. My teacher comes very close to me and kisses my hand. There are times when he looks at me in a way that makes me worry about my marriage and the children, and I am becoming nervous to be alone with him in the studio. I am not clever enough to know what to do or how to behave. I am afraid to smile or encourage him and I am frightened to reject him. He understands my voice and he believes more intensely in my singing than I do. His genius works mysteriously. When I open my mouth, the sound flows like liquid silver. I know that if I left him I would lose my voice. I have never known the effort of trying to force it. It comes out of its own nature like crystal. But if I left my teacher it would fall like lead.

It is a curse to possess something rare like love or beauty because every day you live in fear of losing it. Loss is the worst kind of suffering. I have lost my country. I know what it is to live without any sense of belonging or my own esteem. I have lived with the loss of my father when I was a child. I remember seeing him with a suitcase full of worthless money. And do you remember how I travelled to Poland alone to find him in his hairdressing shop? I sat secretly like a client for a haircut. I waited in the chair without speaking; only wanting to feel his gentle hands, watching his smart scissors click-click as he trimmed my hair, looking in the mirror at his long thin face, loving the feel of his fingers. I looked from his image to mine, seeing myself in his green eyes and cheekbones and recognised Dora's clever fingers in the way he touched my curls. I didn't want it to end. And when he was finished and I had the money in my hand to pay him, I said: "You don't even know your own child," throwing the money down on the floor and running away in the street, not looking back at that thin man standing at the door. I never saw him again.

I don't blame you that you left him. Your life was better without him. But I loved my father and I have lived with a place that was always empty. And now, if I lose my voice, I will never recover. It will be like a death. Life will be a suitcase full of worthless money.

It is night-time and I am sitting here alone in a sleeping apartment. A quiet time to sit and think. It is snowing again and the searchlights circle endlessly like beams of light behind layers of muslin. I think of you in the south and remember how the sun is directly overhead this time of the year, shooting spears of white light, bull's eye, into the centre of the dark fireplace at midday. Soon your sun will be here, dimmed behind the snow, weak and far away, saving all its strength for you in the south.

Dearest Mama, you have lost everything and endured so cheerfully, singing in your cracked little voice, while I claw selfishly to life like a crab with its quarry. I am only absorbed with the sudden miracle of my life here, the treasure I have found, beyond diamonds and rubies. While the whole world sinks deeper into the horror of war. It is unbearable.

Always your daughter,
Hannah

SEVENTEEN
Dora To Hannah

20TH JANUARY 1945

My dearest sister,

It is such a long time since I have written or since I have heard from you. Sometimes I feel as though our family is merely Mama and me, and you are the sister that I only dreamed about. But I don't apologise, because Schicklgruber prefers dropping bombs to dropping letters, and we have to live with his preferences for a little while longer. The postbox in the street is like a fat goose which swallows and swallows through an open mouth but will not lay an egg.

These days only the postbox gets fatter and the world is like a starved goat that eats paper and wood shavings to stay alive. You should see the state of some of the soldiers who have returned. They come to rest and recover, sit in the sun, eat good plain food.

Not that we do not have our little sacrifices like one meatless day a week. The bakeries are only permitted to make brown bread mixed with soya flour and the sugar we get in the shops is dirty, and that's all there is to it. The natives must eat yellow mealie meal and they are used to white. But there is plenty of food for everyone even though some people are born dissatisfied and won't accept any deprivations. So they buy their quota of flour from the shops and they sift out the bran so they can make fancy cakes on Sundays and fluffy white bread. I have to confess that on Mama's birthday I secretly made her a chiffon cake, and we ate it with a feeling of sheer luxury and contemptible crime, expecting at any time to be caught and punished with our mouths full of this manna and still salivating with the taste.

Bread has become quite a scandal here. Some of the bakers want us to eat like rats. They supplement the flour with sawdust and put the profits in their pockets. Some people are losing their sons, their husbands, their jobs, their lives, and others are becoming millionaires in wartime.

Things are not nice, and that's all there is to it. I sit next to my little wireless every day listening to the news of fighting in France, as we once used to hear terrible things that were happening on this very continent – "up North" – as they called it, and that meant past the equator and getting hotter. We heard the names of Monty and Rommel over and over, and a little town on the edge of the desert called Tobruk. We saw pictures of endless sand and a bleached wooden board pointing with an arrow into the wilderness, and whole armies that disappeared over the dunes. Where were they going? Can you imagine tank battles in an inferno of smoke and twisted steel, only for a speck of wasteland called *Tobruk*?

Then they released the names of the war dead and the next of kin: Walters or Goldberg, Bezuidenhout or Odendaal, and they have worn red ribbons in their lapels to show that they would fight on any front to support the allies. There were also Buthelezis and Shabalalas "up North", but they were not allowed to carry guns. They only cooked and cleaned and carried stretchers. Not permitted to arm themselves, and yet allowed to endure sandstorms and plagues of flies for their country and die with a cooking-spoon in their hands.

Dearest sister, I have delayed telling you, but many things are starting to come out now through information published in Swiss newspapers and the reports of a few survivors. There are terrible stories that poison my mouth when I speak them and reports of the crimes against our people, friends and relatives who were left behind. Can you imagine that our forests, where we played and picnicked, were turned into mass graveyards and the pure water of our lakes was polluted with blood? Forget all the pretty pictures of our childhood. There were public executions in the main square, and our little town became a charnel-house. I have heard stories that haunt my sleep.

No one at home has escaped this slaughter and I have to tell you, with deep sorrow, that I heard that our father perished in Poland, utterly alone. He died the day before the German invasion. Everyone ran away to save themselves, with nothing but the clothes they were wearing; his sisters and cousins fled, and he was abandoned in bed, crippled with one leg off, too weak to move. The storosh of the building gave him a glass of water to drink, and then he deserted him too. After that, nothing more is known. When I heard the news, I burnt a candle every night for a month and read the prayer for the dead. I prayed for Papa and the millions who died with him. I thought of Grosspapa covering his head, saying the words softly and weaving forward and back:

> *May God remember the soul of my father, my teacher, and may he be bound in the Bond of Life together with the souls of Abraham, Isaac and Jacob and together with the other righteous men and women in the Garden of Eden.*

What else could I do? I have found an old photograph of our father. You know that his leg was diseased in the bone. He is lying careless on an unmade bed, all the sheets creased, and he is supported on a pillow, his long pale face expressionless. There are two women on the one side and two men on the other. The room looks so dark with a weak light coming in from one side and the walls are covered in faded wallpaper. The old country seems so foreign to me now, so cold and cheerless. Five people came together to record an instant in their lives and the photographer was there to witness it, quite normal before the horror overtook them. Everyone so vivid in that picture, devoured by the predator that is stalking Europe. I could not stop crying. This small photograph is all we've got.

Then one day I had a magnificent dream. I saw the face that I knew as a child. Papa was young and healthy, wearing a blue sash across his chest. He was standing on both legs and laughing out loud. When I woke up I was enveloped by the radiance of that dream the whole day and since then I have never cried for him again.

With the turbulence of the war that has turned the world upside down, something has also taken hold of my life, given me a good shaking-out, and it has all changed. I am no longer the little greener from Europe, and I am no longer the nursemaid with a white cap and apron. But it all served a purpose, and I slowly saved up my pocket money and bought a piano. From that moment my life changed. I am where I always wanted to be – behind a piano again, teaching singing. People come to me for instruction, paying me for something that gives me the greatest pleasure.

Do you remember, Hannah, in summer when everyone was out running on the beach or picking flowers in the forest, how I remained at home with my music? And in winter when you were all reading next to the stove or studying for school I was at the piano again? That was where I wanted to be because it was the only thing that I could do better than anyone else. And my tutor who made me play Mozart and Bach until I was sick and tired of it – I tell you, sick and tired – three hours in the morning, three hours at night. And now I have a piano again and it is the second time that it has saved me. Can you imagine, Hannah? In wartime, not a gun has saved me, but a piano.

I know you will laugh, but all I tell my pupils to do is stand with their two feet on the floor, drop their chin and say "aaaaaaaaaaah". I tell them to imagine a doctor is pressing down their tongue with his flat stick to look at their tonsils, and to say "aaaaaaaaaaah". You can't "put" your voice the way a dancer "puts" his feet. And that is my method. You must hear what comes out! A sound like silk. And my ear – my bad ear that oozed and stank as a child so no one would come near me – I listen with my ear and it never deceives me. I can listen with my eyes closed, and my ear tells me if the mouth is stretched or the tongue is too high or the throat is closed. Who needs eyes if you have an ear?

Believe me, Hannah (and I know that there were many times when you cried for my sake), believe me when I say to you that now my life is good. And it is good for Mama also. We have a little flat in Troye Street, in the middle of town, near the OK Bazaars. That is where she wants to be – town. First thing in the morning she puts on her spotted suit and hat with the veil, and she is standing, humming, outside the OK waiting for the doors to open. No more dreams about forests and wild strawberries. Then she goes to the fishmonger demanding to see the gills and the heads before buying – the eyes must be bright and lively, and inside she looks for fresh red blood. Then she comes home and cooks and sews. When my pupils arrive she makes them tea. The water is always boiling, and she keeps a special sausage for my Russian pupil Ivanoff. He bangs the table with his fists and says: "Bring the kolbassa!" And she hurries, laughing, into the kitchen to fetch it.

Once she came home from the OK breathless from running. She said that some young men wearing grey shirts were fighting with soldiers wearing the red ribbon in their lapels. Sometimes the streets are like a battlefield, especially after one of the rallies at the City Hall. But that is war. Some people in this country want Schicklgruber to win, and they march through the streets imitating him with flags and loud music. And we sit next to the radio, waiting for the news – always the news.

We all do what we can. There is so much intrigue and spying, and sometimes a pupil gives me pamphlets or letters to hide in my flat. They know that I will never ask what is inside them. But I trust my pupils and I put the papers in a drawer inside Mama's old winter broekies. I put the documents deep inside the left leg and fold the right leg over. Cosy as can be. Who would think of searching there?

Mama goes to the hospital every day to visit the sick. There she found a Polish Jew called Boris Peskanoff, who miraculously escaped from France and arrived here with TB. Mama used to bring him milk and butter from her fridge every day until the colour came back into his face. And that is how she cured him.

And now I will tell you the end of the story. I have kept it for last, the same as you keep the best food on your plate for last. Boris Peskanoff got better, and when he left the hospital he used to come to the flat to visit. I enjoyed speaking Russian to him, and this poor, thin creature had a way with stories that made Mama laugh. Then, as he got stronger, we went with him to bioscope on Saturdays and for drives into the country on Sundays. Once we all went to Warmbaths for the weekend. You can imagine how much he enjoyed those sulphur baths, and how he just sat in the steamy water, breathing deeply with his poor lungs.

In wintertime we worried that he would get sick. And then he began to cough again, and also to sweat. Can you imagine that on our coldest days he would be wet with perspiration? We went to his flat, took his mattress and blankets, and left everything else. We put a curtain in the middle of our bedroom, and that is how we lived: Mama and I on one side, and Peskanoff on the other. At least I could make him milk in the middle of the night, and sponge him and wrap him up when he was sweating.

One morning I got up early. I put on the water for porridge, I put on the water for tea, and he came into the kitchen and he asked me: "If not you, who will look after me?" And I said: "Well as long as my eyes are open I will look after you." He took my hand and he told Mama what I had said. The next week we got married. This is his photograph. Still thin, and if you look at his eyes for a long time you can see the sadness deep inside them. Can you believe it, Hannah? It was the most natural thing in the world. The night we got married, I just crossed the room and went to sleep with Boris on the other side of the curtain. And now we are the same as before: the three of us in the flat, with our lives separated at night by a curtain.

I could not believe that my little body could contain such happiness. I am immensely attached to him, and he is immensely attached to me. Is that love? I don't know, I really don't know. I have had friends in my life. I have even had men-friends like Ivanoff. But only Boris married me. I call him "Zolotko" because he is my piece of gold. And now everyone calls me Mrs P.

And so, Hannah, another letter is fed into the fat goose of a postbox. But even if this letter does not reach you, what is written is written. In between us is the terrible calamity of war. But here on this side, in a small flat with a sagging curtain hanging on a string, three people have found peace.

Your sister,
Dora

EIGHTEEN
Death By Drowning

AMY LOVES THE WAY PA EATS FRIED EGGS ON TOAST.

Mother goes out in the morning, importantly busy, carrying her music and singing – can't be late. Paul is already in the street with his friends. So they are both left at home together. Early-morning hungry. Pa stands in the kitchen wearing his food-stained, paint-stained dressing-gown, sleeves rolled up and a dishcloth in his pocket. Both ready, they also have their work.

It is a grave process, never hurried, with solemn pauses at every stage. Pa lifts his eyebrow: One egg or two? Amy wants one. Pa wants two. Turned over? No, runny sunnyside up. Ordinary toast, or bread fried brown in butter?

Amy is also in her dressing-gown, her hair falling in two long plaits ending in a coil, and fluffed around her head in a bird's nest of strands and knots where it was ruffled during the night. She and Pa are unwashed. That's when you do your best work: straight out of bed, grains in the corners of your eyes and bed-warm pajamas next to your skin.

She stands with him at the stove. His left hand cradles three eggs. She can only hold one. His hands can unscrew the tightest jar, and he has chalky fingernails that grow horny ridges from when he was sick. Blue veins twist under the flaky skin and furrow out into the fingers like a delta. Now, a critical moment, a pause, then one sharp tap which could change the entire outcome, accurate and firm, against the rim of the pan to make a single crack.

She loves to see the whites blister as they fall into the fat and the slime turn into a firm skin, frying into frills around the edges, exploding like Chinese fireworks. Bubbles of butter splatter the cupboard and the wall, and Pa smears fatty droplets into the floor with his feet and wipes them off the lapels of his dressing-gown with the back of his hand.

He bastes and bathes the creatures, not vegetable, not animal: birds flapping wild white wings and yellow eyes deepening into gold.

The whole kitchen is yellow. Last year's paint bought at the hardware shop on the corner, going cheap. Sulphur yellow. Yellow walls, yellow cupboard, yellow table and chairs. And a yellow toilet seat in the bathroom with the last paint in the bottom of the tin. "Why waste it?" Pa had said. Only the stove is black and white in hard baked enamel. Chipped. And the kettle is always ready to whistle.

They both eat out of the same plate. Amy does not really like fried eggs, will never eat them on her own. But Pa has a way with them that makes her hungry just to watch. First he cuts the toast into small squares, then makes a tidy pyramid of the white and yellow by piercing with the fork and smoothing with his knife. He sprinkles salt like a pope.

"Put it on the fork for me, Pa." And he follows her instructions, cutting neatly as though he is preparing to eat the food himself. That's the way she likes it. One for me, and one for you. They work down to the last crust of bread, wiping the final smears of butter off the plate. Then she licks it shiny-clean.

There is always one terrible risk: "Mind the slippery-white, Pa." That sinewy slick of albumen that never cooks and constantly threatens to infiltrate the yolk or slide onto the toast no matter how watchful the preparation. An insidious enemy against which one must be constantly vigilant and examine every forkful before one puts it into one's mouth. But Pa doesn't mind. He's fearless, and also full of trust. Sometimes he doesn't look at all, even closing his eyes with pleasure as the fork enters his mouth. And one day when one is grown-up one will also not mind the slippery white, but one will not be properly grown-up until one reaches that time of one's life.

Then on other days he makes porridge for her.

"Make it with lumps, Pa. Not the big ones that break into chalky powder in your mouth. I want the little ones that are tight and gluey so I can chew them."

And then she orders the consistency to be made firm so that it sticks to the spoon, and not too many lumps either or else they become ordinary and common. Just enough so that she never knows when a lump will find its way into the spoon and each spoonful will be a surprise. You never know. Perhaps some spoons will carry two lumps, and then she may have to wait three spoonfuls before she gets another. Sometimes she will have to eat the whole plate just for one lovely lump, and sometimes it is the very last spoonful which contains the best lump of all.

Pa listens carefully to the instructions and begins to make the mixture to order – he knows exactly how to do it – while she sits at the yellow table, waiting. The mixing is the most dangerous time, because once it is in the pot the texture is final, you can never add lumps or successfully take them away.

And then there is the special delicacy of allowing the porridge to cool until a smooth skin forms on the top. She must lift it off carefully in one piece not to break it, and then chew through its tender resistance. The final pleasure is to go straight to the pot and eat all the burnt pieces that stick to the bottom and sides. This can take quite a lot of scraping with a spoon, and each pot is different; sometimes the gleanings peel off easily in a single crispy crust that tastes like popcorn, and other times she has to work hard for small shreds. But every yield has its own beauty.

If Mother is still out, Pa will have to do her hair – two long plaits, thick and matted. She stands while he sits on a chair next to her. The comb will not pass through the knots and he tries with small gentle movements to disentangle them. But he never has the nerve to tear through them, breaking the teeth of the comb, rough and confident, the way mother does. He always leaves the snarls when Amy cries: "Ouwwwch." He just ignores them and ties off the ends with a piece of white sewing-cotton. He starts the plaits above her ears, pulling the hair firmly and weaving tightly and unevenly so that they stand away from her head at stiff right-angles, bouncing when she walks. She can feel them moving like limbs.

And after that there is a slow quiet time. Just sitting at the kitchen window, leaning her elbows on the yellow window-sill and her chin on her hand, watching people in the street or throwing breadcrumbs to the squirrels. Pa sits at an old sewing-machine repairing the linen. His hand moves the wheel round and round in rhythmic circles, his eyes fixed on the small steel foot walking stitch by stitch across the crumpled sheet. Pa and Mother had a terrible fight about that old machine. Antique, he calls it. She was crying because he bought it with money that was supposed to pay for the rent. They often fight and shout, and the people next door can hear and also the children playing in the street.

One morning Pa and Amy decide to make lemon meringue pie from his own made-up recipe: beaten eggs, lemon juice and sugar with a crust of fried breadcrumbs. Pa never cooks from books. "That's for beginners. If you can eat, you can cook," he says. And . . . out of the oven it comes . . . with a deflated meringue and tasting like sweet and sour scrambled eggs on toast. They eat enthusiastically and devoutly loyal, "Mmmmm." But decide not to be greedy and leave most of it for Mother and Paul to enjoy. "Next time we'll just add a pinch of bicarb to the egg whites. That's all it needs, eh, my girly?" says Pa walking out of the kitchen that is dusted finely with flour. He makes large floury footprints and she makes smaller ones next to his, patterning the floor with their feet. They leave all the pans in the basin for Mother to wash when she comes home from work. She likes to be included in the fun.

Pa is still in his dressing-gown. He never gets dressed until the middle of the morning. He has to read the newspaper first. He hunches forward over a low table with the paper spread out in front of him, reading the left-hand page slowly, his eyes moving along the lines from the top to the bottom, and then his head moves slightly to read the right-hand side. He turns the wide page, making a slight rustling noise, and slow and graceful and completely final as o-v-e-r-i-t-g-o-e-s . . . like the pages of history. Once they are turned he never goes back and leaves the record of world events abandoned and out of order on the floor for someone else to read.

Sometimes he sits in front of the radio, trying to find overseas stations. He searches carefully for the beam in-between long fields of scratchy interference, turning the little dial forward and back, forward and back with his ear to the speaker of the wooden box and a staring look in his eyes. He persists with the dials and the wooden box, ignoring Amy's cries that the grating noise is terrible and she has to stick her fingers in her ears or run out of the room. He does not look up until he finds a weak voice in Hungarian or Chinese. And then he searches again for a pinpoint of focus which will render the rare sounds more clearly.

After a long time he gets up and potters with a piece of furry green cheese, kept on a high shelf in the kitchen in a cracked saucer where he is breeding his own penicillin.

Events are slowly leading up to his bath. But first he must cut away his corns. Again there is the slow preparation of the tools, the bathing of the feet, and sitting in front of the same low table: bending forward stiffly, right leg bent over the left knee and the right foot twisting awkwardly at the ankle to face him.

He takes the scalpel off a sterile napkin in front of him and works with surgical precision. Pa never feels the pain as he slices finely through layers of skin, his eyes fixed on the bulging nodule. He collects the cuttings of old skin in a neat pile on the table, and examines each piece closely, then returns them one by one to the pile. He is completely absorbed in his attention to his toes, especially the hammer-toe on his left foot, which is bent into a fiery right-angle with a crusty callous on the bottom. But he always goes too far, giving himself raw cuts and lacerations which require immediate first aid from Mother. She has had to save him twice from near septicaemia, and he had to sit for long hours with his feet in the sun to dry the weeping wounds.

Pa is always bothering about his bowels and his sinuses. He calls them "pockets of evil," and so he must use witchcraft to sanitise them. Once a month he purges his sinuses.

It is Sunday morning, some kind of a Sabbath, with Beethoven's Ninth playing full volume on the radio. Amy assists him.

"Fetch the box," he commands, and she runs to the special cupboard. They unpack all the bottles and rubber pipes, fuse them together with nozzles into a tortured network of tubes and siphons running along shelves and over hangers and curtain rods in the bathroom delicately balanced to maintain a gravitational pull. She sits on the yellow toilet seat holding an empty bottle in her hand, while Pa chants: "Kaykaykaykaykaykaykaykay," continuously while the contraption pumps water through a nipple into one nostril and sucks all the wicked wastes in a stream out of the other. She watches the spoils drain out of his nose and collect in the bottle carrying finny flotsam like fish in a bowl, while he stands in his paint-stained egg-stained dressing-gown, alone and triumphant on a watery floor, his head thrown back, receiving and discharging water through a blowhole, like a floundering whale just managing to survive drowning.

Once a month – sometimes once in six weeks, and by that time the grey is already growing out in a silvery fringe around his hairline – he hennas his hair. Amy is allowed to mix it in a chipped cup, and as she adds water and tea to make a thick brown paste, an acrid smell of dried herbs rises. Pa stands in front of the mirror. He delves down to the roots of his hair, examines them carefully, shaking his head sadly, and applies the mixture with an old stained toothbrush. If she has added too much water the paste will be runny and will seep like rusty water down his forehead. He goes back to the radio or cleans his paintbrushes with turps, waiting for the colour to take, while streams of dye leak down his neck like mud, and clot on his dressing-gown.

Only then is the penitential body ready for immersion, and after thrashing and slapping and deep breathing behind the bathroom door, Pa comes out a young brunette again, and his skin is pink as a newborn mouse.

The morning of the lemon meringue pie, Mother comes home early from work. She stands silently in the kitchen for a long time. Her eyes are shining as they move slowly from the footprints on the floor, to the pools of grease on the stove, to the spattered wall, to the pots and plates and knives and forks balanced into a precarious ziggurat in the basin, to the remains of the meringue pie on the table. Then, when she sees Amy's knotted plaits standing away from her head at right-angles, she breathes deeply and there is a rising wateriness in her eyes.

She stands at the basin banging noisily and scraping the pots with exaggerated energy. Then she knocks the table to attract Amy's attention. She is still resting her voice, mouthing her words voicelessly through pursed lips, gesticulating violently and distending her eyes.

There is no reaction from the adjoining room. Now in a sibilant whisper she says slowly:

"No matter, Amy, how educated the man is, or how cultured and refined he may think he is," and her voice breaks through the whisper, "he does not have the same standards of cleanliness or the consideration," and now her voice is a scream, "or the sensitivity of a woman," and the water spills in great gouts out of the corners of her eyes, then rests and glistens on her cheeks.

Mother has spoken, nay shouted, for the first time in a month, straining and wrenching her vocal cords against her singing teacher's instruction. She is standing in the kitchen stroking her throat, and a tear is balancing on an eyelash. Still silence in the next room.

Even though Amy is moved by Mother's tears, she is not moved enough to help with the pots, and definitely not moved enough to mop the floor. But she is very quiet because her mother is unpredictable in this mood. She is too dangerous to speak to or even to try to placate. And she has not yet noticed the bathroom.

Amy can see Pa next door, sitting in front of the radio, deaf to everything except the scratchy voice in Chinese coming through the static. He is dressed in a blue suit and shiny shoes, his nails are clipped and his moustache is trimmed. He is ready, impatient for the larger world of events and action. Mother is back and in her place, and the memories of the kitchen are lost in the labyrinths of his mind like the forgotten experiences of a past incarnation.

NINETEEN
Rags And Fragments

WAITING . . .

"When will they lift the gangplank, Pa? I'm tired of waiting."

The patient accumulation of cargo proceeds at its own pace. One hundred and fifty pockets of Idaho potatoes and two hundred bags of oranges labeled CALIFORNIA disappear into the kitchen hatch.

"Are we going to eat all of that, Pa?" Amy asks.

A uniformed officer carries a letter up the gangplank followed by a sailor balancing two crates of cabbages and a nest of pots. A passenger with a briefcase embarks with a steward wheeling two metal trunks behind him. Some of the crew stand on the deck smoking. And waiting . . . Amy and Hannah are in one cabin, Paul and Max in another. Single people walk up and down the gangplank and then, at last, no one.

"When, Pa?" Waiting for the world to move.

Amy can feel the listing of the ship; everything is solid and unstable at the same time and a constant hum fills her ears. There is no movement and the world is in abeyance, waiting for the signal to unhinge.

"The gangplank's lifting, Pa! Where's the brass band? And no one to see us off?"

A sailor casts a great rope into the water casually, as though untethering an old horse, lazy from too long in a stable, and unyielding as dead weight while two tugs churn against the towlines. Slowly, obstinately, the hulk begins to separate from shore, and the whole world is sliding.

And now the ship glides smoothly past the copper statue – a giant figure swathed in sculptured folds, and wearing a coronet, a spiked helmet, turned green by the poisonous mists that rise from the river. Its arm stretches skyward, a torch in its hand. Amy's teacher, Miss B.B. Curry, told them that the right arm is forty-two feet long and twelve feet in diameter, and the forefinger clasping the torch is eight feet long. The passengers hunch their shoulders into their ears and stamp their feet with cold, crowding onto the top deck and looking up to its flat blind eyes staring out to sea.

Amy stands on a lower deck enclosed in glass. The rolling motion passes through her body from one leg slowly to the other and the engine vibrates under her feet. Water condenses and trickles down the glass. A clammy heat clings where the woolen clothing touches her skin.

"You'll be a good sailor, just like me," Max had said.

But everything is rising inside her like a tide, and the metallic smell of rust and damp from the floorboards makes her hot and weak. She has an unpleasant and persistent memory of lunch, vegetable soup – why did Mother force her to eat? – wallowing and waning like the swells of the grey-green sea.

She looks back at the city, tightly packed onto an island in the river, blurred by the cold fog and misted behind the beads of moisture on the glass. Max and Hannah never even asked her if she wanted to leave. They made all the decisions, whispering and talking in the night. Yesterday she was at school with Miss B.B. Curry, and skipping rope with her friends. And today she has left the empty apartment like an abandoned box, cluttered with rags and fragments, her fingerprints and food-stains and her growth measured on the walls. She feels fraudulent leaving the mess behind, all the outgrown clothes, torn and stained with their life in the apartment, she and Paul buying new things at Macy's sale, and Hannah fainting on the ground from the crowds. And Paul cross because some of his clothes are rejects, at half-price. "A few flaws? What's so terrible?" Pa had said.

A life abandoned on an island, like litter in the city streets.

Amy holds onto the railings as she reels along the deck and through the doors into the passage, looking for the lounge. Hot again and giddy in the yellow light and residual odour of interior corridors that never breathe. She sways sideways with the yawing motion of the ship.

Everyone is in the lounge, seated four to a table, playing bridge. "Let me teach you how to play," says Max. "You and me and Paul, and Ma will be dummy. I wonder who's sitting at the captain's table?"

Amy stumbles to the window for air; round peepholes bolted closed with a single large screw and misted on the outside. She watches the city recede; no longer a teeming island but the undulating coastline of a continent. The tugs are returning to shore and the bilious ship, turned loose, lurches and heaves in the open sea.

Almost out of sight, nearly gone now, a life faded into blurred shapes, tracings, shadows.

Rags in a box and shop-soiled objects on a shelf of the five and dime . . .

the first-floor apartment facing the street. The kitchen, jaundiced with last year's cheap yellow paint. The bathroom, wet with washing that drips onto the head of the person sitting on the yellow toilet seat. The upholstered chair with the broken spring and the small white dog waiting at the window for the children to return from school. "It's cruel to keep Smoky in an apartment," says Mother. "Why is it cruel if we love him?" Crying . . . Lurching arcs of light search through the opaque night sky, sirens and alarmbells in a midnight drill, and staring, sleepless, in the corridor. The tall wooden radio with a purple cloth covering the speaker and white globes inside. A place called Hiroshima. "This is the end of the world," says Pa, tuning the dials. "WhatsgoingtohappenPa?" The end of the world. And then celebration, shouting and laughing and cars hooting and bandy-legged sailors in white starched uniforms kissing girls full on the mouth and everyone kissing in the street and happy like candyland. Suddenly Pa is fighting with a stranger outside Emet's Ice-Cream Parlour. Pa puts up his dukes and Mother is crying tears into her chocolate peppermint ice-cream. A lump rises on Pa's head. "Why is he fighting? Whatsgoingtohappen?" Blond children carry carefully wrapped sandwiches to school and one chocolate-covered marshmallow cookie every day, only one, and wearing springy cotton dresses and black patent shoes, and mothers standing outside school with umbrellas when it rains and hot soup for lunch. Vito Ciccolello's mother drags him out of Music Appreciation Class and throws him squealing against the wall while Fritz Kreisler plays "Humouresque" on the gramophone. Vito's blood spatters the wall. Miss B.B. Curry covers her sand-coloured hair with a net and trusses her body like a sandbag. Fat folds make bracelets around her wrists and her hands are like trotters. Jeannie's fine gold necklace rests on her buttercup skin and a single link glints in the sun. Jeannie's mother packs lunch with a cake of yeast a day. The man at the corner shop wears a diamond ring on a hairy finger, and cigar ash falls into the strawberry ice-cream. Roseanne plays alone because she has big breasts and menstruates at eleven; she leapfrogs over a bush with her legs apart. What is happening between Roseanne's legs? "Don't tell. Meet you in the alley. Let's watch the naked man in front of his window. Run, he's coming down to catch us." The tree outside the dark house with long-legged birds in its branches. Waking in the night . . . the hollow room and echoing emptiness and square walls that bend and wobble. Large birds flap membranous wings. Swimming in wide lakes. "Can I come too, Paul?"

"Race you to the shore."

The lake turns black and angry: "Follow us in a boat, a storm's coming," says Paul. Digging for bait in the manure pit, fat and wriggling; fish gulp hot air on concrete and slowly die. Dreams in the hollow room and the walls that stretch and wobble. Mother, fat and with her hair dyed red, locked into the steamy bathroom singing, not talking, to save her voice. Crying at the piano, "I've lost my voice. I've lost my voice. I'm not well, Max." Crying... The policeman's daughter recites catechism by heart: "Why can the Jews never go to heaven? The Jews can never go to heaven because they killed our Lord." "Is it true, Pa?" Hiding the fine gold necklace just like Jeannie's. "Where did you get that necklace?" asks Mother. And the great wind blows in from the sea. Pa's radio says: "Hurricane warning." Its ferocious eye looks down from the sky. The second-hand maroon Packard covered with snow turns grey and then yellow and drips black into the gutter. Pop's small dark shop has Canada Dry and penny sweets that colour your tongue red, and Christmas trees and newspapers and comics and candles and chewing-gum and string. On Sundays: Canada Dry and roast chicken with potatoes, and Beethoven's Ninth on Pa's radio and Eisenstein with subtitles and Janochek hangs on a meat hook, dancing. The Russian ballet-master hits legs with a stick, walking around high mirrored walls: "Y one! Y two! Y three! Y four!" "President Roosevelt is dead," says Pa's radio. The brownstone house near the river: Auntie Mary sleeps in the attic; and hiding in the butler's room in the damp basement, and hauling the dumbwaiter from the kitchen like drawing water from a well; sleeping buttock to buttock with Auntie Mary in the attic. And Mother crying at the piano. "It sounds like lead." Crying... Seeing Smoky in his new home... crying...

Her life closes behind her like water. And now the whole world turns liquid as the coastline dissolves. Forms melt and shift like memories, and the only constancy is the swaying of the ship and the immeasurable distance to the horizon. They are moving through the open sea, to a life that functions and breathes on the other side. A ready-made family that she does not know or remember. Born into it a second time wearing her new clothes and immediately loved and accepted by two grannies, two aunts, three cousins and some uncles waiting to embrace her with kisses and smiles. A home, already standing, waits to house her, and a chair in a classroom, and a place on a bus. While she rolls and drifts toward the Southern Cross in a featureless world whose only attribute is space. Looking and looking at the fine line of the horizon and the immense embrace of sea and sky. The eye never stops looking.

"Let me teach you the new money," says Max: "Twelve pence in a shilling, twenty shillings in a pound. Now, suppose I want to subtract three pounds nineteen shillings and sixpence from four pounds seventeen shillings and three? Starting from the right: I have to take sixpence from a tickey, so I have to borrow a shilling."

"What's a tickey, Pa?"

"A tickey is three pence."

"But who are you borrowing from, Pa?"

"I'm borrowing a shilling from the nineteen on the bottom line. So I add twelve to the three pence on the top line giving me fifteen pence, and then I can take away six from fifteen leaving a remainder of nine."

"I don't understand, Pa."

"Never mind, you'll understand as we go on. I have to return the shilling from where I borrowed it and subtract from the seventeen in the middle column. Now I must subtract in the middle column. Remember I have borrowed a shilling. So I must subtract nineteen plus one from seventeen. I cannot subtract twenty from seventeen, so I borrow a pound – twenty shillings – from the first column. Twenty from thirty-seven leaves seventeen. Then I give back the pound that I have borrowed and subtract three plus one from four. Leaving nothing. The answer, therefore, is seventeen shillings and nine."

"Never mind. We've done enough for today. We'll have another lesson tomorrow."

Three weeks of dreaming in sleepy suspension, crossing boundaries that only exist as marks on a map, passing in and out of tropical squalls as through gauzy gateways and under triple rainbows that cast auspicious crescents.

One day she sees the boy on the deck, standing in the sun with his shirt off, polishing the railings. The next day she sees him again and the next. Then she waits every day to see him and she follows him around the ship, moving from window to window, hiding behind the curtains to watch until he drops down the hatch below. Every day now she walks around the deck to find him, first hiding but now showing herself to the smooth-skinned boy with his shirt off, his chest lifting softly towards his nipples and a fine curve down his back. When it rains he doesn't appear, and then she walks restlessly around and around the enclosed deck. How did she pass the days before? She plays quoits and then goes into the lounge to play bridge with Paul and Max. The next day she sees him talking to someone with his hands in his pockets, resting his foot on a rail and leaning over his knee. His trousers balance just below his navel. She is quiet again, at peace just to watch him walk. His legs bend outwards slightly, like a cowboy, and his belt tilts as he moves with a hint of his hips. Sometimes he props his elbows on the rail and just looks out to sea, chewing a matchstick, the warm wind lifting his hair. His skin is getting darker and his hair is turning fair from the salt. Has he seen her as she leans on the railings? One day she discovers him on the bridge covered in thick grease. She watches him lying on his back fixing a machine. Looking and looking at him, without mind, not knowing why. She becomes bolder, he must see her. She stands forward and he moves toward her. She is struck with terror and a palpitating heart. Then he disappears down below the hatch where he eats in the steaming kitchens and sleeps in narrow bunks near the noise of the turbines, low, low and dense where there are no windows looking out to sea, drinking and swearing and gambling with tattooed men in overalls. Coarse and dirty. No women in that place.

The days are getting longer and the time is getting shorter to watch the boy on the deck. One day a shadow appears on the horizon; tracings, shapes that do not go away, getting darker and nearer. Then all the passengers come forward to the deck to look at the shadow. They spend the whole day looking as it comes nearer and then they start packing clothes into suitcases. The shadow hardens into a mass, a stony mass, an end to water. A mountain rising out of the sea, flat on top like a table; a green mountain, washed clean by the sea and widening out into green hills, fresh green, green everywhere, and little houses on the slopes. The sun shines full and bright on the houses and the windows flash like marcasite. Looking and looking at the mountain. And then it slowly fades, vanishes again into blackness, leaving behind a fringe of lights. They stand at the front of the ship watching the lights and wondering about the mountain and its people who have dissolved into darkness.

And that night her bunk does not rock her like a cradle.

The next day the ship is tied and fettered, and machines with jointed arms dig and prod in its hidden places. People walk up and down with bags and suitcases. Men she has never seen before, crawling from the dark places into the light, with their heads sticking out of the round windows, wearing limp sweatshirts damp under their arms. She goes from window to window searching for the boy. She finds him on the deck standing in a line with other men, pulling a thick rope. He doesn't look at her, doesn't see her in her new clothes. He has covered his body with a shirt and his trousers are torn and smeared with oil. She tries to recall the curve of his back.

Now the ship is taken apart. Whole sides which were decent and solid are now exposed, with ropes and ladders hanging out of holes like entrails. It loses its secrets and dumps its filth. Sailors empty rotting garbage from a hatch, and a stream of brown water drips from a gap in its side, corroded with rust. She uses last night's serviette for breakfast and the tablecloth is stained with yesterday's soup.

"Eat a big breakfast and then we don't have to buy lunch," says Max.

And air no longer blows through the windows.

Black men are offloading the cargo, and passengers are walking up and down the gangplank with more black men carrying their luggage. She hesitates. She is forbidden to turn around and look back. Irreversible. And then she steps onto the land. It is solid yet feels as though it is rocking. She sways slightly and the sky swings, but the concrete is hard under her feet.

SLEGS VIR BLANKES is stenciled onto a wooden bench, and MOENIE ROOK NIE says the sign outside Customs and NO SMOKING next to it.

"Moenie rook nie," she says to Paul.

"Ag voetsek," says Paul and laughs, nudging a boy standing next to him who looks at Amy and smirks.

"What does 'voetsek' mean, Pa?"

"Don't take any notice," says Max.

"What is going to happen, Max, if Malan is prime minister?" asks Hannah.

"I don't know what's going to happen," says Max.

"Who is Malan, Pa? Whatsgoingtohappen?"

"Ag voetsek," says Paul.

She looks down at the sea and it slides with slicks of blue. Her eyes reach for the horizon but buildings hide the sky. The world is soiled and sensible, with firm outlines and stinging light as she stands with suitcases on the southern tip of Africa.

TWENTY

Houses

AMY DID NOT KNOW WHAT FAMILY WAS EXCEPT FOR HANNAH AND MAX AND Paul. There were just the four of them in the apartment, the core of her life. It was complete, it was enough. Enough space for Hannah and Max in one bedroom and Paul and Amy and the little turtle on the windowsill in the other. In-between was the sitting-room with the piano and the radio. Their lives were lived in those rooms. Large enough for Mother's crying and nearly large enough for Pa's temper and for Paul to split the door with his fist in a rage, "I hate him, I hate him." And small enough for his whispers with Amy, and the little turtle that was encased in ice on the windowsill, one cold night. It was space enough.

"Don't tell you saw me smoking in the street," he says.

"I won't tell if you let me come with you and your friends and play. Otherwise I'll tell," she says.

"Okay. You can come if you walk six steps behind us and you don't talk. Okay?"

"Okay."

And she follows Paul and his friends wherever they go.

And now as they step off the boat, who are these strangers who embrace her with smothering arms and kiss her mouth with emotion, stare at her face and search it for resemblances? "I think she's got Max's eyebrows and his mother's nose. But she's definitely got Hannah's smile. I don't know who Paul looks like. The postman, eh, Hannah?" "Take your hands out of your pockets, Paul," says Max.

First there is Cape Town. She meets cousins Fay and Fanya and Auntie Frieda who everyone says is a very capable woman and an excellent cook. Auntie Frieda had run the sheep farm for Uncle Aaron in De Aar like a sergeant-major and had made everything herself, from soap to sausages. If they were short of a hand she would stand alongside the labourers, her sleeves rolled up and skirt hitched up around her thighs, dipping the sheep and then squatting down to shear the wool with a sheep's head locked between her knees. She stands tall with high breasts extending in front of her like a shelf. When she settles down into a chair they swell up under her chin like a rising tide, her head floating on top as though she is in deep water. She smokes continuously, her lips gripping the receding cigarette as she inhales audibly through the sides of her mouth. The ash breaks off in segments falling into the breach of her breasts below. She has a scabby rash on her elbows that everyone says is from nerves.

Their house is on the hot foothills of a mountain that looks like a baboon's head and the afternoon sun fills the rooms with an airless heat and a blinding flash reflected off the sea. The house belongs to the family. Owned, not rented. Amy never believed that a house could be owned.

Auntie Frieda's kitchen is lined with bottles of pickling cucumbers and onions and trays of soaking herrings. When Amy opens the fridge she sees racks of food: joints of fried chicken, slices of roast beef and jars of potato salad. The cupboards are packed with sweets and nuts and dried fruit. Amy is not used to food that is at hand and ready to eat. A constant supply. It is there all the time, and she wants to eat continuously. Hannah's fridge in the apartment had only the raw materials: raw meat, raw eggs, raw fish. You had to wait hours for a meal, and there was nothing to eat if you were hungry. "Eat a lovely carrot," Hannah would say. "Very healthy."

For lunch they eat smoked sausage with chicken-fat and mustard and pickled cucumbers on rye bread. And at four o'clock they all sit down to tea, like another meal. There are always biscuits but Fay and Fanya are indifferent to the everyday custom and never eat more than one. Auntie Frieda just sits and smokes. Amy admires their detachment. She feels coarse and greedy and puts her hand into the dish five or six times when they are not looking until she is embarrassed to take more. She cannot understand how you can have as many as you want and only eat one.

It is interesting to meet relations. Kissing and embracing complete strangers; the unreasonable affection which can turn to unreasonable hate, and a continuous connection despite it all because you are linked to the same dead or unknown ancestors. "Every Bernitz in the world is related," Auntie Frieda says, "all blond and blue-eyed. Do you know that we had family who were physicians to the Spanish kings?" Hannah had told Amy that Auntie Frieda was large and beautiful as a young woman and had had a love-affair with a German officer while Uncle Aaron was away in Africa looking for work. They had all lived together with Grossmama and Grosspapa, Hannah carrying Frieda's babies on her hip while she was constantly "absent".

For the first time Amy is aware of a traditional life. Insiders recognise all the signs without curiosity or surprise. Is a fish surprised to be living in water? Amy hears for the first time a language, jokes and gestures, terrible curses like wishing cholera on people, music you have never heard before that makes you cry, other music that makes you want to dance and clap your hands and throw yourself around the room. A kind of inheritance rooted in a buried memory.

This is not Pa's family, so he just sits and reads the paper without talking.

In Cape Town everyone packs blankets and umbrellas and folding chairs and towels and cameras and a change of clothing and money for ice-cream and baskets of food and flasks of tea to go down to the beach to eat. Amy sees a notice that says NET BLANKES – WHITES ONLY, stuck into the soft sand. Then she sees the same words displayed over the door of the Post Office and stencilled onto a bench at the bus-stop and again at the entrance of a hotel. While high in the sky above them the Twelve Apostles, bearded with white cloud, rise into the sky as a barricade against the interior.

And then there is Johannesburg. She meets more cousins and aunts and two grandmothers, Eva and Rosa, one for each side of the family. It is Passover and they all sit around the ritual table. She is the youngest and must ask the prescribed question: "Why is this night different from all other nights?" They eat the unleavened bread and the bitter herbs of affliction, and they dip hard-boiled eggs in the salt water of tears. Max twirls his finger around a strand of Auntie Miriam's hair and kisses her head. Amy watches Hannah watching Max. He has never fondled Hannah's hair. Paul is saying "Voetsek Amy" and "Voetsek" again, to the sniggers and applause of his audience of new cousins. She has learnt what it means. Why is this night different from all other nights . . .? And they put drops of salt water on a saucer for all the plagues of Egypt.

There is something about the nights in Johannesburg. Closed windows and doors, and thick darkness filling the spaces between streetlights. Stone walls surround the rented house and the night air flattens the sound of the growly voice on the radio. The houseboy stands alone in the kitchen, dressed in a white waiter's suit and tennis shoes, watching the vegetables boil on the stove and then waiting in the servery to hear the little brass dinner bell announce that they are ready to eat. Dull light filters through yellowing lampshades, too weak to keep the darkness out of the corners of rooms, and when Amy sits at her desk doing her homework a shadow covers her books. The window is made of pieces of diamond-shaped glass all framed in lead. When she looks out there are black bars in front of her eyes as she watches the headlights of cars swinging in an arc around Observatory Curve. On the other side of the road, pools of electric light hang heavily around the large brick orphanage building. The diamond-shaped glass makes the orphanage wobble in front of her eyes. Everything is sealed up for the night against a world turned dangerous after dark.

Amy has never lived in a house with a garden. She is used to living in the brick honeycomb of families clustered together in one building; the long L-shaped corridor with eleven doors and a hive of life behind each one. She could smell the Schultzes' dinner which hung like a fog around their door, and hear the Robinsons' shouting as they played cards, and meet Mrs Webster when she dumped the refuse into the incinerator, or pass Allan Appelman as he ran up the stairs two at a time. There was a nearness to other lives as she crossed the Michaeloviches' doormat with the front-door key and money for milk and bread hidden underneath for Zika when he came home from school. Everyone knew about the key and the money but it was safe under the mat. She could hear the sound of the Murphys' quarreling through her bedroom wall which was their bedroom on the other side, and everyone could hear Hannah sing and Max shout.

Before supper she used to walk along the passage to the Weinsteins' and sit on Sandra's bed reading magazines or stand with her in the kitchen talking to her sisters, while a voice droned continuously on the radio. Sometimes she and Sandra would page through a photo album or Sandra would clean her cupboards. Sandra wanted to be a ballet dancer but her legs were too fat. Once she took out her little jewellery box and Amy played with the silver charms on a bracelet – tinkling bells and silver hearts and a twirling ballerina, and she knotted some coloured beads around her neck. And then she saw a fine gold chain like Jeannie's at the bottom of the box.

She held it up to see it shine in the light. She wanted it, wanted it, and it made her think that if she took it, it would make her neck look milky-white like Jeannie's, and sparkle on one single link and it would not matter that she was not given a cake of yeast and a marshmallow biscuit every day for lunch and hot soup when it rained. If she had that chain, she would never want anything again.

And now, in Observatory, when she looks through the bars at the neighbours' lights far away over the wall, she has that same feeling inside her as when Hannah told her to return the necklace to Sandra's box. The L-shaped passage was long and empty and dark in front of her and the walls bent and wobbled like the hollow corridors in her dreams.

In Observatory Max closes up carefully for the night, all the outside doors and also the inside doors along the passage. They sleep in separate rooms far away from each other and there is a different room for every activity. Amy feels surrounded by unused space, especially at the back of the house which narrows into a warren of cubicles, each one progressively darker and shabbier: the servery, the scullery, the laundry, the servant's room, the shed, the kennel. She has been told not to walk in the street after the sun goes down and not to be alone at home with Daniel, the house boy, when he drinks. Sometimes, at night, he comes to her if no one else is at home, asking her to write him a "special", which allows him to be on the street after nine o'clock at night. She writes in her best handwriting, in stiff English, "To Whom it May Concern", and "I authorise that", and "Yours faithfully" and her fancy signature with an extra loop at the end. She knows when Daniel has been drinking because he comes out of the kitchen and leans against the back of her chair, talking to her for a long time about his family and his home and his cattle in the mountains of Basutoland. He also asks to have her watch. When he has not been drinking he stands in Paul's room laughing and joking, showing the empty gums in the front of his mouth with two rotten teeth on the sides. He shakes Paul's hand three times over in a special grip and says, "Goodnight. Aaiiya daoo," and he goes out to his room through the cubicles at the back of the house.

One night Max calls the police because Hannah's diamond ring has disappeared. A police car arrives with a siren and a flashing light, and they ask Daniel questions and ask to see his pass. He just shakes his head saying, "Ek weet nie. Ek weet nie." And they go and look in his room. After that time he only stays in the kitchen at night and never comes into Amy's or Paul's room to talk.

Slowly Amy begins to like living in the house in Observatory. She takes a tram to school with the girl who lives around the corner. She visits her house in the afternoon so they can do their homework together. They get tea and biscuits at four o'clock and Amy takes five or six. Paul has made friends with the boy across the road and they also go to school together. Paul hates the compulsory black and white striped jacket with grey trousers that he must wear to school and carries it in a paper bag until he stands outside the gates. He puts it on and then takes it off again when he comes out. On her thirteenth birthday Amy's friends come from school to her house. They play hide-'n-seek in the scullery and the laundry and the kennel and under all the prickly bushes and weeds of the unused tennis court, and the "prisoners" are locked up and punished in the dark shed. Amy likes the feeling of having friends to visit. It makes her feel as if she is the same as everyone else – giving them cake and biscuits and walking them halfway home.

That night she sits at her desk again, under the yellow lampshade with a shadow on her books, looking at the orphanage through the window faceted with lead-framed glass that ripples, protected by black bars.

One day Max says that they must leave the house because the owners are coming back to live there. They couldn't find another house quickly enough, so now there are the hotels.

She walks through the lobby of the Sheraton in Berea wearing black stockings and a gym and a black felt hat after school. She carries her canvas school-bag in one hand, her tennis shoes and racket over her shoulder and lunch-box under her arm. She has been told to collect the big key on a ring with a piece of wood from the lady at the desk and she walks through large rooms with carpets smelling of dust. Men and women smoke and drink beer at glass-topped tables. Her black felt hat and canvas bag look shapeless and flabby next to the hard furniture built to survive injury in a hotel room.

Max says that she must stay in her room until he and Hannah come back from work because it is wrong for a schoolgirl to sit alone in a hotel lounge or wait around in the street. She lies on her bed or sits on the hard chair looking out of the window into the street until it is dark. At night they all walk into the dining-room lit with a sharp white light. Max always walks with his chin lifted and smiling when they enter, to show that he doesn't care if people have heard him fighting with Hannah or shouting at Paul. It is the only time that they are all together. There are the same hard tables with white tablecloths under the glass and pointy napkins on top. The waiter puts a menu in front of her eyes and Max says: "Order." She orders four courses, each one coming out of the kitchen as a small square of food on a white plate. But she always gets three scoops of ice-cream with a dry wafer on each side as dessert.

After one month Max says that the place is unsuitable for children, so they go to a residential hotel around the corner. He is tired of packing suitcases especially as they are only moving over the road, so he says they must put all their clothes into sheets, tying the four corners closed with a knot. Paul says, "I'm ashamed to walk through a hotel lounge with a sack on my back." Then he has to walk through the lounge a third and fourth time to help Amy carry hers, with the lady at the desk making clicking noises between her teeth and shaking her head as Paul bumps tables and knocks over chairs. Then she threatens to call the manager because Max is standing with his chin lifted and arguing about the account.

In the new hotel Amy has a small room on the second floor overlooking an inside alley. A bright square of sunlight shines hot onto the floor every morning between nine and ten, slowly shrinking into a thin rectangle and then a matchstick of light as the sun passes over the alley. The room is in a green gloom for the rest of the day. Crates of bottles arrive in a large truck and a sour smell of "empties" rises up from the delivery hatch in the alley below. The fabric on the chair has worn down to threads from all the people who sat in it before her. There is a cigarette burn on the blanket and cracked glass on the bedside table which must always be shifted into place like the pieces of a puzzle. She is woken every morning by the sound of a man polishing the passage on his hands and knees. If she puts out her shoes he polishes them also. His kneecaps pop out like golf balls when he stands up and the skin is thick and wrinkled and dark black, the same as on his elbows. She lies in bed listening to him talk in a loud voice to the flat-boy upstairs, until the sunlight shines a square on the floor. Then she gets dressed.

Amy does not know why they left the other hotel because she still gets little squares of food in the dining room and is never sure what they will bring out of the kitchen: toad in the hole, bubble 'n' squeak, kedgeree and ragout. Max teaches her to say, "ragooo," and not "rag-out," and she has learnt to be very careful of things like black pudding and tripe. In this hotel ice-cream is called "coupe". They only see Paul at mealtimes because his room is in the east wing on the first floor and Max never knows if he is in or out. Amy lies on her bed all afternoon. Sometimes she watches the old ladies playing rummy on the verandah or listens to the lady answering the telephone at the desk, always the same sing-song voice as though she is asking a question: "Good afternoo-oon? Casa Mia Residential Hoteh-el?" There is nowhere to bring her friends and their parents don't like them going to hotels.

Always waiting and waiting for Max and Hannah to return. She knows that they will be there when the clerk arrives at the desk for nightshift.

When they walk into the dining-room Max lifts his chin again, especially as people are staring at them. He smooths his moustache as he stops to talk to the blond lady with bright red lipstick leaking into the cracks around her mouth. Amy and Paul look at each other and pull faces. They hate her, and Hannah looks down and walks away quickly when she sees Max smoothing his moustache.

One night the waiter brings Amy mock turtle soup which she leaves in her plate, and then pickled ox-tongue in black pepper sauce which she leaves on her plate, and then blanc-mange with jelly and custard which she leaves in her bowl. The waiter wags his finger and says: "This piccanin don't eat." Then he brings her three different flavours of "coupe".

Max finds a furnished house in Yeoville and they move again. It is right next to the pavement and faces the street on two sides. Amy can almost touch the walls of the house next door if she stretches her arm out of the bedroom window. Again the light only comes in when the sun passes over the alley. The backyard is a cold square of cement with a servant's room for Daniel and a kennel. Late in the afternoon Amy can smell ox-lung boiling in a pot for the mangy dog that howls all night in the yard.

Uncle Theo has come back from America and visits for supper. He eats with them every night, smoking and leaving half his food, and then sits in a chair in the lounge until late, without speaking. He is tall like Max but veins in his eyes and nose stand out red and twisted. His fingers are brown where he holds his cigarette.

"Why doesn't he ever talk to anyone?" Amy asks. "He's been here every night this week but he never looks at me or laughs at Paul's stories about the teachers at school. He just sits in a corner all night."

After supper Amy stands in the dining-room on the parakeet-green carpet, looking through the window with her head between the curtains. She watches Paul and his friends push Max's car silently out of the garage and start it without a key. The car judders down the street and disappears around the corner. Max and Hannah are still sitting quietly with Uncle Theo in the sitting-room next door. Hannah says that she is exhausted from being with him late every night, but they have to let him sit quietly until he is ready to go home because he has left his American wife and lost his child.

In the mornings Amy walks down the hill to school in scuffed shoes. Her gym dress barely covers her school bloomers. She sits outside school waiting for the bell, doing last night's homework; a few paragraphs of English composition – AUTUMN RHAPSODY – and a few sums petering out on the page and ruled off without an answer, but just to show the teacher that she "tried" and to get some points for "method". She never learns for tests, but gets good marks because she copies from a book on her lap. Everything seems dull and incomprehensible as Miss Paterson's mouth opens and closes unintelligibly. The other girls seem to understand. She prefers to watch the pigeons on the grass, but was quite excited when Miss Paterson said she was going to teach "reproduction" at the next class. She is always hungry and has mastered the trick of eating fruity sweets without moving her lips and taking bites out of her sandwiches behind the lid of her desk, chewing and swallowing while she drops her head to tie her shoelace. But she is very good at conjugating French verbs by rote, raising her voice for Miss Longbottom to notice: je suis, tu est, il est, nous sommes, vous êtes, ils sont. She will always remember the verb "to be".

She never invites Hannah to school on Parents' Day. Hannah is not plain like the other mothers. Her hair is blond now and her nails are long and painted red. She is too vivid, too brilliant and conspicuous when she wears the black suit with the long skirt and wide-brimmed black hat clustered with red poppies. Everybody turns and notices. Amy does not like to be seen, and she wants to be alone on Open Day, free 'n' easy as she walks around the school unattached, lying on the grass, watching the girls introduce their parents to the teacher, smiling and displaying their work pinned on the walls, talking about their progress. "Very satisfactory," says Miss Longbottom. Amy never tries to make her books look pretty with drawings or coloured pictures from magazines. There are blank pages where there should be illustrations and writing, just blots and smudges and oil-marks from touching her cheese sandwiches.

She is ashamed of her mother's beauty. She feels small and grubby when she stands next to Hannah in her wide-brimmed hat clustered with red poppies. Empty and unfinished like one of the pages of her book.

In the afternoons Amy goes down the hill to the baths with Ivan and Alf. All the girls sit in a circle on the grass, talking and laughing and eating peanuts and chips from the kiosk and watching Alf walk slowly up and down in front of them. He knows that they are talking about him, the way he looks straight ahead at nothing in particular with one eyebrow raised. Suddenly he keels over sideways into the water, his skin turning dark and shiny like a black eel. He swims up and down freestyle, turning his head and pulling his mouth sideways just enough to catch a breath, somersaulting underwater in a tight ball when he gets to the end and pushing off in a blur of bubbles. He never swims more than five or six lengths and he is never breathless. Careless and lazy in the water, he hoists himself out of the pool and lies on the paving-stones to dry, velvety and oily like a seal with glistening drops of water on his back. He never dries himself off with his towel. Only old men do that. Amy sees them carefully wiping the water under their arms and between their legs and each toe and then their ears. Louis also walks up and down in front of the girls but they never watch him, and Arthur dives in after Alf with his legs bent. Ivan is swimming breaststroke up and down, up and down a hundred times, a slave to his swimming. Alf picks up his towel, wraps it around himself in a sarong, and walks out. Arthur follows him. Suddenly the baths look empty and lifeless. Alf goes home on his bicycle, leaning forward over the handlebars, sometimes pedaling with his hands in his pockets, controlling the bicycle with his knees. His green school blazer looks torrid against his skin with powdery pigment patches on his cheeks. Everyone leaves when Alf goes except Ivan who is still swimming up and down.

Amy walks home slowly up the hill. Ox lung is boiling in the scullery, and the late-afternoon sun shines on the dining-room carpet, submerging the room in green.

Then they move again to a rented house in Dunkeld.

"You'll like it," says Max, "double-storey with sliding glass windows and a big garden with flowers and high trees. We're lucky to have found it."

Amy is crying now because she must catch two buses to visit her friends and then two buses to come home and those buses only run every two hours on Sundays, and all the houses in the street are double-storeys with old rich people living in them.

Again the darkness surrounds the house at night, and the lights of the neighbours' front door are behind the hedge. The silence covers the house like a black hood. She goes alone upstairs to her bedroom and stands looking in the mirror at her breasts.

Saturday morning she meets her friends in town, waiting under the clock at the OK Bazaars next to the sick man holding a cup and a dirty sign that says "elephantiasis". Sometimes he closes his eyes and groans. Joyce and Greta and Jane come together in a bus and they meet Amy at eleven. She has been waiting for an hour. They want to buy the latest record by the Andrew Sisters or Nat King Cole. Amy never buys records. She listens to other people's.

"So what are you wearing tonight?" asks Greta.

"I don't know but can I borrow your jersey, Joyce?"

"I think Jane has got it," says Joyce.

"I don't have it," says Jane. "Didn't Daniella wear it last Saturday night?"

Joyce's jersey goes from body to body changing shapes and smells – a grey pullover with a dog chained to a sign that fits over the left breast saying "keep off". They walk and talk in a pack, tripping over each other's feet. After lunch they go to a matinee. Alf and Louis and Arthur are riding bikes or playing soccer.

After bioscope Amy goes home with Joyce. They wash their hair and make a big curl on their foreheads. Everyone is coming to Joyce's house to dance and play records.

Aaron and Barry have joined the group and everyone says it is because Aaron likes Amy. She doesn't know if she likes him back, but she gets hot and shivery when he walks into Joyce's house and looks at her for a long time without looking away. She pretends not to look back. They dance together all night, spinning and twirling when the music is fast, her skirt flaring out over her thighs and then flaring out the other way when she spins in the opposite direction. Aaron moves smoothly. His head remains level like water even though he bends his knees and steps out with his feet, pulling her towards him and pulling away, turning a full circle and coming back to catch her in time to the music. When the pace is not so fast they dance face to face, with one arm around each other's waist and the other stretched out sideways, clasping hands, while their feet do three steps and a double step, three steps and a double step. He holds her firmly as they turn, doing a little skip on the double step, and then spinning and spinning with their legs interlocking as they spin to the end. In-between records they stand together breathless and laughing. Someone puts out the light and plays slow music; songs that tell of blue moons and loneliness and broken hearts. Aaron pulls her body very close, his head next to hers and her face folded into the softness of his neck. His hand presses low into her back. Low. Low. There is something dangerous about Aaron – he gatecrashes parties and he doesn't care what people think and his arm is strong when he holds her, certain and not afraid. But never forcing. His red hair falls naturally into a thick curl on his forehead, just like the curl that she and Joyce make with a pin. He takes her into the darkness outside and they kiss for a long time, deep and slow, with Aaron's arm holding her strong and the Andrew Sisters singing "If I knew you were coming I'd have baked a cake." Daniella is standing against a tree with Gideon, and Betty is lying on the grass with Dave. Amy can feel the dampness inside Aaron's shirt when she presses close against him and the prickles of his hair when she strokes the back of his neck. Her body is getting hot, and now she is ashamed because Greta's smell rises from the armpits of Joyce's jersey.

Then Max arrives at the party with Hannah sitting in the car next to him, and they fetch her home, still hot from kissing Aaron.

On Sundays Amy's two grandmothers come to Dunkeld and sit in the garden – under different trees. Eva is deaf and only Hannah tries to talk to her, shouting into her ear. She wears brown shoes laced up tightly over brown cotton stockings, and she sits all day in her chair without speaking. She always wears a yellow scarf. Amy thinks she looks like an American Indian with her square eyebrows and narrow eyes. Once or twice her sister Gittel comes to the house. The cat always jumps onto her lap, and Gittel sits stroking it with her dry little hands. Max has told Amy about the third sister, Faiga, who had red hair and ran away from home to be in a convent. But Eva never speaks about her.

Granny Rosa wears a black and white spotted two-piece costume and a small black straw hat with a veil twisted over the brim. She sits under a tree humming tunelessly all day and knitting with small fast fingers in the German way – left to right with the wool wound around her left index finger, darting over and across the needles. Amy has never heard Max speak directly to Rosa. At lunch he says to Hannah, "Would your mother like another piece of meat?" or "Has your mother had enough to eat?" And at the end of the day, "Would your mother like to go home?"

After lunch Amy phones Joyce to ask, "What's happening this afternoon?" Once when she phoned, Joyce said, "I don't know. Phone Greta." And when she phoned Greta, Greta said, "I don't know. Phone Jane." And when she phoned Jane, Jane said, "I don't know. Phone Joyce." And when she phoned Joyce a second time, Joyce said, "Phone me back in fifteen minutes." But no one phones Amy. Then she catches two buses to Cyrildene and she sits with the other girls in Joyce's room and they are all saying that Betty has no respect because she lets the boys go too far. They all walk to the shop for sweets. Amy hopes that no one saw her going too far with Aaron.

Some Sundays they go into town for a radio show: ANYTHING GOES, performed in person on the stage. They laugh when a man appears with a board saying LAUGH, and they clap when the board says CLAP. Joyce's jersey appears again with a chocolate ice-cream stain under the dog on the chain. Anna Maria is wearing it together with Daniella's suede shoes. And on stage Artemis is singing, "Anything gooeees . . ."

After the show they stand talking and laughing until everyone has gone and the street is empty. The others catch a bus home to Yeoville and Cyrildene, and Amy returns to the borrowed house in Dunkeld, waiting an hour for the bus, running home through the scary streets in the dark.

Night again. Echoing rooms and the large glass windows turned black. Voices that sound different in the house at night, always the hollowness spiraling in her ears; a particular stillness on a Sunday night that feels wide and gaping. A memory lost to the brain and remembered only as a feeling of emptiness.

Max is sitting in the lounge listening to the news on the radio. The growly voice is flattened by the hollowness of the rooms.

She goes upstairs and looks in the mirror at her breasts.

TWENTY-ONE
Respite

THEN THERE ARE NO MORE HOUSES OR HOTELS, BUT LIVING IN FURNISHED flats and looking after them and their pets while the owners are away. Amy doesn't understand why all their own furniture, all the tables and chairs and the piano are packed away in boxes and kept in a warehouse, and they must always live with other people's possessions. Max calls it "freedom" to be able to give a month's notice, pack up their clothes, and live somewhere else.

First the corner flat on the second floor of a building facing the curve on a wide road. This is where all the buses and lorries grind down into low gear. There is a bus stop outside the entrance where the brakes of buses screech as they stop and the electrical overhead cables whine. Amy's room fits into an odd corner of the building, making it triangular with sharp corners, overlooking a grove of bluegums. This is where she meets her boyfriends in the afternoons, especially Harold, whom she sees secretly because Max and Hannah think that, at twenty, he is too old for her at sixteen. It is true that he is working and has money in his pocket, drives a car and buys her little gifts. She loves sitting next to him on the front seat, going wherever they like, to all the faraway places without having to catch a bus. Sometimes they drive to Zoo Lake at night and watch the fountains change from red to blue to green to white. And while they are lying close together on the back seat of the car, the skin on Harold's body changes from red to blue to green to white. When she goes home she tells Max and Hannah that she has been doing her homework with a friend, which she thinks is not altogether a lie.

Hannah leaves early in the morning for work, and Max walks around the flat until late in his pajamas that have no buttons on the pants, hiding the gap with the folded morning newspaper. Paul goes to university, where he sits every day in the canteen smoking and playing cards with his friends.

This flat is covered in pulpy carpeting that completely hides the floors. If you drop a button or a coin it falls into the woolly thickness and you'll never find it again. Everything is soft. There is no wood anywhere. Amy sinks deep into a spongy armchair upholstered with red, blue and yellow geometric patterns. She looks at the large chrome-framed painting on the wall; wondering and wondering what is the meaning of the large black shadow in one corner slowly moving across the canvas with prodding fingers to infiltrate the white.

She has to feed the parrot and talk to him. Call him by name and say, "Henry, there's a good boy," and tickle his neck, so he doesn't get lonely while his owners are away. He makes the sound of liquid pouring out of a bottle and into a glass, "Glugluglug," and he coughs, says "bugger off Nancy", coughs again and "cheers ole girl, let's have another". Amy wonders about Nancy's life and the hidden meaning of the painting showing the black cloud moving into the white. Pa also paints, but mainly pictures of people, and even one of himself standing in his dressing-gown in front of a mirror. He called it "Self-Portrait" and painted away all the jowls and lines and creases on his face.

Amy also has to feed the fish in a bowl. They rise up to the surface to meet her, and when the sun comes through the window they float and bask weightlessly in its warmth, glinting on a single golden link.

Then they move to an unfurnished flat in a building facing a circle with five streets feeding into it and a palm-tree growing in the centre. There is a little shelter outside the building with a Greek column in each corner. Hannah stands on the verandah of the flat watching streams of cars negotiating the circle like ants crawling around a breadcrumb – coming down one street, turning around the circle, and going out another. Sometimes they collide in the middle and the streams coagulate like a clot. From the balcony on the seventh floor she can look over the asphalt rooftops with washing, over the grassy parks to the green suburbs and shops of the north. Beyond is the blue outline of the Magaliesberg. A sooty pigeon nests in a flower-box in the corner.

For the first time Max takes their furniture out of storage. Hannah has her piano and her music again, and she calls the flat their home.

Every morning the alarm-clock slashes the silence of the sleeping flat. Hannah's fingers search in the dark for the shrieking instrument. Hurry. Mind the lamp and the glass of water on the table. Feel for the button. Quickly switch it off before Max wakes up. He must not be disturbed, roused from the warmth of his bed and the heavy weight of his sleep as he lies on his left side with one hand under his head. He must not be woken suddenly or he will complain that he has not slept all night and he will switch on the light, demand tea, perhaps buttered toast and then slip his feet along the floor to the toilet. Then he will get back into bed, prop up his head with a pillow folded in half, suck noisily on the orange left on the table next to his bed from the night before. He will pick up last night's paper from the floor and beat it as he turns the pages. Then demand tea again.

He must be left to sleep away his anger until it is light. Another two hours until the world begins to move again and his anger is muted by the noise of people and cars in the street seven floors below them. Another two hours and Sophie will let herself into the flat bringing the milk and the morning newspaper and he will be carried along by the sounds of teacups rattling and the whistling of the kettle. If left to wake up slowly he will say that he slept so well and that he had visions in his sleep, and perhaps describe his extraordinary dream.

Hannah has never understood his rage; its cause, its cure. A random thing. Immanent as a continuing possibility. Something physical, like a greed that grows out of him and wolfs and gorges until its hunger is slaked. She cannot understand or appease it. It is only to be endured. She runs away from it, but she cannot run far. Another two hours.

She wraps a blanket around her body and leaves him deep in the sound of his own breathing. She goes quietly into the room next door. The striking match rasps the silence and releases the smell of sulphur in the flickering room. She hears the jangle of metal springs as he turns over next door. She lights a stick of incense from the candle and the smoke gives off little puffs of scent as it coils around a photograph. Is that his breathing or her own in the heavy air? She sits on a cushion with her legs crossed under her, holding a string of sandalwood beads. She can hardly recognise her face in the small mirror behind the photograph, the skin sallow with sleep, creased on one cheek where her head lay on the pillow. The cropped hair is flattened on the same side of her head. She pushes away a streak of white that bends into a wave and falls across her forehead.

It has been years since she started leaving her hair grey and gave away her jewellery and clothes. She lost her voice, and the rest was easy. Easier not to grieve for what is gone or desire what she cannot have. Max loves her in an unspoken and unknown way. Perhaps beyond the display or articulation of it. She has never understood it. And she still has the old shame of asking him for money and wanting affection – a simple expression of it. She has had a lifetime of asking. Easier to leave her skin pale and her lips colourless. Eat plain food. Much easier to wear white blouses and spun cotton skirts. White for mourning, for surrender.

Her body weaves forward and back, facing the photograph, making small movements with her lips and slipping her fingers along the beads at regular intervals. The nails, once oozing with pus from the strong soap-powders, and then sleek with red varnish when she toyed with glamour, are now cut back to the skin. White for renunciation.

Tired. Exhausted from the struggle, the continual assaults, the trembling rage that does not understand itself and seeks to punish the nearest object. She knows the lick of his temper the way other women know the stroke of love. He has never touched her in anger, he has never touched her with love. But in his fury she feels closest to him, near to something active inside him like a virus. What did she do to detonate the rage? A look? A gesture? She must lie low and try not to be seen, look down and take cover, until slowly the anger subsides and he is mild again. Then she can come out of hiding. Read to him from the books and he will sit with his eyes closed, musing on universal things. She is tired. She sits quietly against the wall without speaking. But beware not to appear injured or accusing or the illness flares again.

Even Paul has been scorched.

"You can't make a fire or tie a parcel or pack suitcases into a car. Only lie around and crack jokes. Ho, ho. Go on, laugh, crack jokes. Play cards with your friends and smoke. Look how much butter you put on your bread. Where are the callouses on your fingers and the grease under your nails? Go out and wash the car and run around the block. Take your hands out of your pockets and work. Unclench your fists and don't answer me back."

There is nothing that Hannah can do but cower. "I am not well, Max, I am not well." Wiping her eyes, always wiping her eyes. They beg to be forgiven without understanding what they have done. Sorry. Sorry. But he looks away. They know that Amy is the only one who can approach him.

"Talk to him, Amy."

She calls him "Pa" and speaks softly without fearing him. She asks him why he is upset and tells him not to worry because it will be all right. "Please Pa, please, forgive them."

They wait to see him soften. And then something breaks and Hannah is at his feet. The fury passes, leaving them empty and broken, but true, as when fire consumes dry grass and then green shoots can grow. He can be gentle again and he will forgive them. But they do not know for what. No matter. The old lesion begins to heal.

Max turns over as the alarm tears the silence of the early morning, his heart beating. So fast asleep. He hears Hannah searching for the clock, bumping the lamp. Yesterday she dropped the glass. She doesn't care, she'll wake the dead.

"I was having an extraordinary dream," he says. "I was walking on a vast chequerboard, slippery as ice, and I had to put my feet on the white squares and step over the black. Each white square was a glacier and the black an abyss. Then in the distance I saw a house. I walked toward it sliding and falling on the white squares and balancing on the edge of the black. When I arrived at the house I rang the bell and I said: "This is where I want to live. I opened the door and as I entered, I woke up. I was on the edge of life and death."

He sits on the side of the bed. "I'd love a cup of tea. Perhaps some toast." He drags his feet along the passage to the toilet. She'll wake the dead. She doesn't care. He knows her face – sallow with sleep, but her eyes are glazed with her own affairs, even at the very moment when she wakes. Later she will make herself tea and talk of her intuitions, her realizations. Talk of universal things. Talk, while he must always listen. Her clothes are laid out presumptuously for the day – her skirt, her blouse, her stockings and shoes, her glasses next to the book left open with the gold-tooled marker – everything laid out and waiting, even while she sits in front of the photograph and prays, eyebrows lifted in ecstasy. "I've been graced. I've left you far behind," she once said. She can never know his rage.

He gets back into bed and props up his head with a pillow folded double, sucking on the orange left on the table next to his bed. When will she sew the buttons onto his pajamas? Photographs of the holy man everywhere, in every room, in her bag, in the bedroom next to her bed, garlands of flowers around his neck, smiling for the camera. Max picks up last night's newspaper and beats it flat with his hand. Reads and turns the page. He hates the smell of incense.

The sky is luminous with first light and single cars grate their gears in the circle below. Sophie opens the front door, bringing in the newspaper and the milk.

Every morning when she comes upstairs from her room it is the same: the air inside is stale with breathing and heavy with sleep – deep sleep that comes in the morning after a bad night. She opens a window, sees Max's closed door and Hannah in her special room, a room for praying but she is always curled on the floor, her head on a cushion and the blanket wrapped around her body. Every morning when Sophie comes up it is the same. The perfumed stick makes little heaps of ash on the carpet and the candle has melted down into pools of wax.

TWENTY-TWO

Sabbath

"SOPHIE, YOU'RE LATE," SAYS HANNAH. "WHY DO YOU ALWAYS DO THIS ON Friday?" Already dragging her feet as she walks down the passageway. Works slowly, talks to her friends through the window and on the phone: "Sophie, your cousin's on the phone. Sophie, your sister's on the phone. Sophie, Sophie." And comes back late after lunch dragging her feet again. "You know my legs will be cramping and I'll be standing until late tonight."

"I'm coming. I'm coming," says Sophie. Friday again and she's waiting for the sound of my footsteps down the passage. No lunch, no rest and I'll be on my feet until late tonight.

Hannah always wakes up with the first light. The moon is still high over the buildings. Sometimes the moon, the stars and the sun are all visible in the early morning sky. An old habit. Mama always said: "Don't be late." She must already be working by the time it is light. No time for tea in the kitchen or sitting with Max and reading out loud from the books. Let him read the paper. She has taken the white tablecloth out of the drawer and pressed it a second time to take out the creases. Hot steel shocks it into stiffness and the skirt falls around the table in crisp folds. White on Friday like dressing a bride. She takes the special silver out of the wooden canteen – one shaky leg must fix it. Counts the knives and forks – one knife still missing – must find it. She sets the table for six: Max at the top in the carver. He assumes it like a throne – something about the way he lowers himself into it, ruling from the head of the table as he calls it, leaning back slowly, lifting his chin, waiting for the start of events initiated by his presence. Paul and Margaret sit on his left side, Amy and Josh on the right. Hannnah is in attendance, Max's lieutenant, perching at the end nearest to the kitchen, reflexes poised, so she can run up and down and Sophie can respond when she calls. Each person knows his or her place in the hierarchy, voluntarily chosen, but fixed by an unspoken understanding of family rank. Amy always sits next to Max and Hannah must be near Paul so she can nudge his foot under the table. Every Friday night it is the same.

Hannah thinks of each person as she places knives and forks and spoons in a square, closing off the fourth side with the chair against the edge of the table. She must leave space around Max's place so he can carve the meat, or he will complain that he has no room to move with all the clutter of candles and glasses and the breadboard and the knives that are never sharp. How can he carve with an instrument as blunt as an old man's gums? A man must have his tools! Then Amy will take the knife into the kitchen and slash steel against flint like an executioner. "Look Pa, razor-sharp," pressing the cushion of her thumb against the edge. "You'll cut yourself," says Hannah, "with all that showing off," as Amy returns with the blade on a white napkin.

Hannah will watch Max very carefully as he carves the best piece of meat for Amy. It's true that now she needs it, but Margaret, Paul's wife, must also get a good slice. There will be no favouritism at the Sabbath table! She knows Max's tricks with the carving knife, his sleight of hand, and saying, "she can always come back for more." Paul must get a good plate of food, he's been looking thin lately, and Amy's husband, Josh, must eat well after a long week – a businessman, a man of affairs, he must keep up his strength. Max always saves a good nugget for himself and she has been tasting all day so it doesn't matter. Anyway she likes eating in the kitchen afterwards, slicing off pieces of gristle and burnt fat.

Hannah takes the glass goblets from the cabinet, gives them a whisk with her apron before putting them on the table. There are only five left. She will have to take a kitchen glass for herself. She gathers the white napkins into peaks, flicking up the corners like a petticoat. White for the Sabbath, for the nuptial night.

She walks around the table shining away a fingerprint on a knife, nudging the table straight and passing her eyes over the blend of silver and glass. It's true what Sophie says, that she's never satisfied. She loves the first shock as people walk in through the door. An intake of breath: "Ah!" And there it stands! Chaste. Voluptuous. The senses tingle. They encircle the table with respect.

The candlesticks stand on the sideboard behind the table, wicks erect and waiting for the flame that ushers in the night. Hannah will cover her head and make wide circles with her arms to embrace the light. And in the kitchen the roast sizzles with flavours of crackling fat.

She passes the table, and straightens a chair, shifts a glass again, too much, shifts it back a little. Quiet. Nice to be vacantly alone; remembering the long table with eighteen people sitting down to eat – all the uncles and aunts and some cousins who do not have the money for meat on a Friday night. And pinecones snapping in the fire. Grossmama wears her black lace pelerine and puts food and money on the windowsill for beggars. Hannah has the privileged position. Her place! Important, sitting next to Grosspapa, trusted to be his "eyes" and to take the bones out of his fish. Only she is allowed to touch his food with her fingers and then feed him. She tucks the napkin into his collar to protect his shirt. She knows when he is ready. How obediently he opens his mouth for the food, then closes it and chews. She watches him swallow, and waits. Never rushes him . . . the mouth that could utter abuse on any other night of the week. "Dwarf!" he called Dora, and Mama would cradle her and take her out of the room. Suffer or learn to ignore him. Everyone has a turn with Grosspapa. That is the way he is. But this is Friday night. Never mind that he eats slowly, has hiccups and breaks wind. She waits for the food to settle and he opens his mouth for the spoon. Don't dare pull a face or drum your fingers at his table! And through the glitter of glass and flickering candles she glares at them: the cousins, the friends, the schoolboys with skullcaps, the children, the feeding mothers. They talk and eat until the candles burn down into molten shapes, watching the waxy globules solidify a trickle at a time into a delicate filigree. Then the children lean over and fall into an insensible sleep next to the ancestral stove.

Now she regrets that she and Max never kept the Sabbath when the children were small. "Why was it acceptable to read the books of Helena Petrovna Blavatsky, gold-tooled and illustrated in colour? Why was it valid to go to Sunday meetings, chant little jingles in a monotone: "Children of light . . . as ye go forth into the world . . . seek to render . . . gentle service . . . to all . . . that lives . . ." accompanied by gongs and cymbals? H.P.B. for short, her gilded portrait – a picture of a large woman with woolly gray hair – hanging portentously at meetings like the chairman of a company. Why was it acceptable to kneel to plaster idols and kiss the feet of pigtailed men in saffron robes? Burn acrid resins for purification, garland their necks and serve them rose-scented water from jeweled goblets? Kiss their skirts and genuflect, whispering, "Master, Your Grace, Your Obedient Servant, I humbly prostrate myself at your sacred feet and beg to satisfy your merest command," while they travelled the world collecting money for castles in France? And what about the worship of Karl Marx? Studying *Das Kapital* like holy writ, not one word could be amended or changed? And worshipping the remains of Lenin embalmed in a glass coffin like a saint? And memorizing Mao's aphorisms like chapter and verse? And drawing sticks and reading cards and drawing blood and counting stones and throwing bones? Why was that better than studying the words of Abraham and Isaac and the sages and prophets of the Kabbalah? Was it too ordinary? Were we ashamed of the bearded men in black coats and hats? Ashamed of something in ourselves: our past, our history, our memory of exile, our humiliation in the ghettos of Europe, poor, stinking, degraded? We turned away from them in the street. Stood apart, stared at them with distaste or curiosity, even disgust. Did we become too proud? Too enlightened? Too sophisticated in our concepts of justice to consider the laws of Moses? Or sing the psalms of David and relish the poetry of Solomon, lavish with voluptuous life on the Judean hills? What more did we want? What, the immemorial stubbornness? Five thousand years of obstinacy. Stiff-neckedness! Too intellectual to circumcise our hearts? What harm to burn candles on a Friday night? Was it too plain? Was the beauty not enough?"

And Max's answer: "Why separate meat dishes from milk in a modern kitchen? Or receive instruction from an unshaven man, aping his medieval masters by wearing black coats with tasseled sashes and fur hats? Do you want to wear a wig and cover your arms and legs as though any man who sees your elbows would want to indecently assault you? Do you want to speak a dead language and affect the culture of an Eastern European village that you left behind in childhood, pretending that history never happened? Didn't we flee the isolation of the ghettos? Didn't we have enough of separation and strict old men wagging fingers and frowning, muttering in a dialect we couldn't understand? Those stern old men! Where was the philosophy, the understanding? As if it were enough to mutter rote verse in darkened temples. Did they know what they were saying? Is it unleavened bread or sacramental food that opens the gates of the world to come? Isn't our God a Universal God? A God of all men and of all living things? Can we be done with cringing and stooping? Beating our breasts and suffering for the evils of our oppressors? Was our sin so great? Can there be enough of trying to appease our unnamable, unknowable God of the desert? We have doctors, we have teachers, we have judges. Can we leave the wilderness and cross the Jordan at last? We brought up our children as decent people. There was music in the house and books on the shelves and pictures on the walls. What was wrong with that? Why wasn't it enough?"

It was enough. Until Paul married Margaret with an exchange of signatures in a magistrate's office, followed by a small reception in her parents' house. Very small. Were they ashamed of us? "Why waste the money?" they said. A few sandwiches, a few snacks, some drinks. Just close family and a few old friends. And soon Amy was also married – a big affair in a hotel with cameras and speeches and a band and his friends from the golf club and the poker school and his business associates and their wives. Did we need them all? We never saw them again. But the catering was good.

And now with Amy there will be another generation. Don't the generations matter? She began to think of Grossmama's house and the long table and everyone eating together, the old people and all the children; Grosspapa's piety, even to the animals that were fed before anyone sat down at the table to eat. Don't the holy books tell us that Rebecca watered Isaac's camels at the well and gave them food and straw and made room for them in her father's house? Wasn't it a heavenly portent that she emptied water from her own pitcher into the camels' trough and went back to the well a second time for more? People lived in the shadow of God, heard his voice in their dreams, wrestled with angels and woke up bruised.

And one Friday night Hannah simply lit the candles at sunset. It was right. That was what she wanted. The golden crowns of light and the connection with something, who could know? The mysterious soul of the universe burning in a little flame? One day of the week different from all others and the division between the sacred and the profane. The beauty of it brought into her own home. And she could see candles through the windows of the flats around her. So there were other people too? A hallowed time on a Friday night.

She needed the candles that night, standing there in doubt, her head covered and a burning match in her hand. She, the apostate, who had prayed to blue-faced deities with bared teeth and distended eyes, who kept a house replete with profanities – porcelain dolls with sequined faces, and cloths embroidered with swastikas, and elephants with human faces, and spitting snakes, and bells, and chimes, and incense, and pictures of saronged men sitting on satin cushions in ecstasy. And when the time came, where would they bury her? Outside of consecrated ground with assassins and prisoners and wizards and witches and aborted monsters with no family name? Adrift with all the unholy ones in limbo?

And then she asked Max to cover his head and say the prayer,

> *And it was evening and it was morning. The sixth day.*
> *So it was completed. The heaven and the earth*
> *With their whole host . . .*

A celebration.

Tonight with the whole family, and the candles reflecting in the silver and glass, she feels expansive. The rich smell of food roasting in the oven, butter and cream and fresh bread fills the flat. And soon there will be a baby sleeping in the room next door when they all sit down to eat. She feels satisfied as they all gather around the table.

And perhaps mischievous, as Paul faces the tradition he has disowned; watching Margaret's face as the men cover their heads and read the sacred letters, searching her features for impatience or envy or even contempt. Watching, maybe enjoying, her separateness when the silver chalice is passed from mouth to mouth around the table. They savour the sweetness and the fruity flavour of Sabbath wine and break off little pieces of salted bread.

It is always the same on Friday nights. The table is rich with food as they sit down to eat and Max has Amy on his right side. Hannah's chair is empty because she is running up and down the passage for a serving-spoon or to mix the mustard. Hannah asks Amy to make the gravy. Max is carving the meat and discoursing on dialectical materialism. The juice oozes into the platter. Hannah interrupts him to ask Josh, "Do you want potatoes and peas?" Josh looks at the plate and says he wants both, and then Max begins again. Paul asks for the salad. Margaret passes him the salad and then takes it back. Serving-platters travel up and down the table and hands reach out to break large coils off the bread. Paul pours the wine. "Not a very good year," he says looking at the label. Hannah serves the men first and then the women, in-laws first and then the others. Josh is already eating. Is it

Hannah's imagination or does she notice a slight hesitation, an imperceptible stiffness in the arm when Max carves for Margaret? The slice is perfectly achieved; transparently thin, but intact. "She can always come back for more . . ." He always saves the big bone for Amy, putting it on a plate with the crusty outside cuts. Hannah asks continuously, "How is the meat?" and "Is the gravy all right?" Amy takes the bone in her hands, elbows on the table and droplets of fat running down her arm. She gnaws at the sinews noisily. Josh eats with concentration and asks for another potato.

Max closes his eyes and lifts his eyebrows while he eats, and then he says in a deliberately controlled voice, "It is a funny thing how she will always interrupt a conversation. She does not know what dialogue is. She and her mother and her sister, they only talk, they do not know what it is to listen. I've had it all my life."

"I must interrupt because I am serving. How are people going to eat? Would anyone like some juice?"

Paul says, "Carry on Dad, we're all listening. This is not the Fourth Internationale. Only a family dinner-table."

"I know that you will always disagree with me, no matter who is right," Max says looking deep into his plate. Hannah nudges Paul's foot under the table, mouthing silently that he must not argue with his father. And then she looks at Max with glaring eyes.

"Is this the way you treat my table? Have you seen me standing and cooking all day? You should all be ashamed. Sophie and I haven't sat down."

"This is the second Boer Republic, Dad, not the academic halls of the Kremlin. We have two proletarian groups here — one black and one white. And two Lenins, Verwoerd and Mandela, with different ideologies and conflicting interests. Ask a bus-driver what he feels about the dialectical contradictions inherent in the class struggle, and he'll say: 'White workers of the world unite.' Then ask Sophie to explain thesis, antithesis and synthesis. Ask her about labour and the means of production. She only knows what she earns for a month's work and how much it costs her to live. And then she sees us quarreling while we gorge on roast beef and potatoes."

"Leave Sophie alone," says Hannah. "She's just sitting in the kitchen waiting quietly for all the hungry intellectuals to finish eating so she can clean up and go to sleep. None of you know anything about revolutions. You got all your theories from books, and Sophie just talks to the other servants downstairs. But I lived through it. I have scars on my bones and holes in my lungs. We ate rats to stay alive. My mother stole and my sister starved. So now I eat when food is in front of me and I don't let it get cold while I talk politics."

Magaret says nothing. Only her eyes move, passing from face to face with no expression. Her hair is tightly knotted at the back of her head with one silver spike that stretches the skin over her cheekbones and across the corners of her eyes. What is she thinking as they bicker and argue? Picturesque how they behave on a Friday? Hannah looks sideways for Margaret's reaction. But the face says nothing; no curling of the mouth into a smile, no crinkling of the corners of her eyes. No opinions? And nothing to say while everyone chatters and shouts. Paul watches her, and Amy watches Paul. Josh is eating a second helping of meat and gravy.

"It is an interesting thing how your mother will always make herself the centre of attention; she and her mother and her sister and the whole family of women. Not one man to say 'Keep quiet while I'm talking.'"

Amy watches Margaret's hands on her lap. The fingers pick and scratch the skin around the nails, feeling for the rough edges and torn corners, pulling them away; working and scraping at the raw cuticle until it bleeds. Amy cannot look away from the hands – every finger maimed – or look away from the mouth, the tongue licking the corners as she eats. But the face shows no meaning. Whose side is she on? No one knows; the eyes have no expression.

"And you, Max," Josh stands up, scraping his chair against the floor. There is complete silence as the patriarch is challenged by the pretender: "You don't talk, you enunciate truths and expound theories as though they are divine pronouncements."

"I've always known you were a Trotskyite," says Max, pointing at him with his fork.

"Excuse me if I leave the table," Josh says looking at Hannah.

No one speaks.

Amy and Hannah pierce the vacuum with noise: clattering the plates as they clear them, stacking them together and keeping the knives and forks separate. They take them to the kitchen for Sophie to wash and come back to the dining-room for more. Amy brushes the crumbs and small pieces of food off the table with one hand and receives them into the palm of the other. She reaches across the table, making energetic movements around Margaret's place, cleaning with determination. But her sister-in-law does not look up or move. No little smile of recognition? Amy brings out the broom and sweeps the debris off the floor with busy gestures and noise, around and under the table. She is on her knees. "Be careful, Amy," says Hannah. Margaret lifts her feet to allow Amy to sweep underneath them, and Amy accidentally catches her toe with the broom – "Oh sorry" – the small fat strangled toe that peeps out, unwanted, from the straps of her sandal.

Paul and Margaret move to the sitting-room for coffee. Amy and Hannah stand in the kitchen arranging the cups and saucers on a tray, looking at each other without speaking; they still feel penetrated by the eyes, stretched sideways into a slant by the tightly twisted hair. The Hillbrow Tower stoops over the building with globed eyes like a Meccano mantis. "What's a Trotskyite?" asks Hannah. Lights surround them like fields of fallen stars and the moon is the thinnest crescent of light.

Hannah carries the tray into the sitting-room where Max is slumped in a chair with his eyes closed, listening to the radio. Paul is lying full length on a divan and Josh re-reads the newspaper. He unbuttons his collar and loosens his tie. "Relax, relax, that's nice," says Hannah. The windows are wide open and the slack movement of air on the seventh floor prods the curtains. The noise of traffic expands and rises off the hot street below, echoing along the valleys of cement and glass. Margaret is sitting in a chair, her head is slowly falling backward and her mouth drops open to show her tongue. Amy looks at her and then looks away, embarrassed to be watching her, as though the gaping mouth is an indecency. Max is stirring his coffee, hypnotised by his hand moving in continuous circles and grating the spoon rhythmically against the porcelain cup. Paul is looking in all the little cupboards and drawers for chocolates.

The lights of other windows pulse all around them. They used to be able to see the Magaliesberg.

Sophie calls "goodnight" and walks out carrying a plate of food which she eats in her small room downstairs with the other servants. Tomorrow. Too tired tonight.

Paul stands up and puts on his jacket. He and Margaret are always the first to leave. Amy helps to clear the cups and then she and Josh leave.

The cloth still lies on the table, spotted with gravy and red wine. Hannah counts the knives and forks – still one knife missing – and puts them back into the canteen until next week. Every Friday night it is the same.

"Why did you call him a Trotskyite?"

Max walks into the bedroom. With the heat he will disturb her two or three times in the night.

She leaves the candles to implode in their own flames.

TWENTY-THREE

Soup

MAX AND HANNAH WILL SURELY BE AT AMY'S HOUSE. BUT SHE, GRANNY Rosa, has her rights too. Her first great-grandchild. "Rights" is too strong; her pleasure. There is also the other great-grandmother, Eva. But she is old and ill and never leaves her flat. Rosa has been to see her once, taking a bus to Joubert Park. But Eva is deaf and unyielding in her silence, unable to make casual conversation, unwilling to talk. She prefers to stand on her balcony and watch the people in the street or the children in the park. So for one afternoon Rosa sat quietly with her reading the newspaper and trying to talk about the news, but never went back.

She looks down at her feet, counting four steps as she gets off the bus at stop sixty-five. Who knows how long she will be strong enough to take public transport. She stumbles as the man behind her pushes and the doors slam shut, the bus pulling away into the stream of traffic. "Gott im Himmel, do you want to kill me?" she says, shifting her hat and rearranging all her bundles: a parcel loosely wrapped in newspaper which she tucks under her arm, her black plastic handbag in one hand and a paper bag in the other. A nice big chicken. She can feel the dead weight hanging heavily and bumping against her knee as she walks. She hopes there is salt in the house. You can never be sure with a young married woman – a kitchen full of electrical appliances and an empty fridge. It's none of her business how they live, but now with the baby, there has to be something to eat in the house. She stops on the pavement to adjust the parcels. Funny how she cooks and sews with her right hand but carries babies and heavy bags from the grocer with her left.

She walks with small tight movements and a little quiver after each step like the rebound of a spring, looking down with faded grey eyes at the paving-stones, deliberately stepping on the cracks – why should she be superstitious? – and humming a tuneless song. Where did she hear it? Oh yes, the music they play every morning just before the news. The parcels drag her shoulders forward and she can see her shoes as she walks, the scuffed brown and white ones that press the flesh around her instep. She must try and remember to take her pills every day. The fluid is beginning to collect around her ankles and it is still only morning. She has been up and dressed since the seven o'clock news, leaving Dora in bed, and walking from her flat in Bree Street to be outside the OK Bazaars when the doors open. They still keep the best chickens in town.

She hears the sharp tap of her heels on the pavement, different here in the suburbs where she is the only person in the street and there is no noise of traffic. Each step sends a vibration through the black veil twisted around her hat and fastened through the crown with a long silver pin. It must be eleven o'clock. A lull in the morning before lunch. She never wears a watch. You can always tell the time by what other people are doing. The soup will take an hour to prepare and then she must catch a bus home to make supper for Dora.

She passes the tin-roofed houses in Orange Grove without looking up, only hearing her own humming and the tap of her heels on cement. Dogs sniff at her feet through wire fences or stand up on their back legs, barking and snarling. That is why she dislikes the suburbs. You have to live with an animal in your house and put a sign across the door BEWARE OF THE DOG. Dora could live for a week on what they eat every day. And the empty streets! Nobody walks. Even the postmen deliver the mail on scooter bikes. She does not look into the gardens as she passes; plants are for pots and flowers are for vases. She loves her little flat. Nature frightens her in this country – everything grows so fast. Weeds grow into trees with roots that crack pavements and even the birds have sharp beaks and claws and make wild noises. You can see them circling and swooping high over the city buildings and seagulls rooting in the garbage. Seagulls in Eloff Street, so far from the sea? She does not look through the windows into the houses. She has no curiosity about other people. Gott im Himmel why should she interfere with others' lives? She has Dora and Hannah, and now she must make soup and help Amy with the baby. Max and Hannah are making a fuss and commotion about the name. Their first grandchild. But will anyone else think of food? She only watches the gates for number nineteen.

She sees two cars parked outside the house. Visitors? She just woke up with the idea to visit, and Amy is not expecting her. Never mind, she has work to do and there is no time to sit and drink tea. The iron gate whines as she opens it. Thank goodness there isn't a dog. They can push you over and damage you for life with their love. She walks along the pathway – nine small paving-stones set into the grass, too far apart for her stride, and she must stretch out her legs or her heels will sink into the grass. Onto the red-polished front verandah and she knocks on the door. She listens for the responding footsteps on the other side and then the door opens.

"Hello Mama. I didn't know you were coming." Hannah kisses her on the cheek and puts her finger over her lips, "Sshhhh." Rosa steps softly into the house. The floorboards creak. "Sshhhh. The baby!" The last time she came to the house was for the engagement party – loud laughter, the smell of beer, men talking about golf and laughing about the nineteenth hole. What hole is that? Did she notice Josh sitting a little too close and talking too long to that plump lady with the bright lipstick? Already at the engagement party? And Amy watching them? Leave them alone. Why should she criticise other people's lives? Nobody's perfect. Today in the house there are whispers, hushed conversation and a scent of talcum and soap. The smell of baby.

"Have some tea." Hannah mouths the words soundlessly.

Rosa looks through to the sitting-room; Max is sinking deep into an upholstered armchair, drinking tea. His moustache tilts sideways as he chews a biscuit and his right elbow lifts as he draws the cup to his mouth. Swallowing audibly, he wipes his moustache with a handkerchief and burps. Let him enjoy his tea. Amy's sister-in-law, Myrtle, sits on the edge of a padded divan talking to Max, her feet placed side by side and she presses her knees tightly together. She always looks newly laundered and freshly baked. Rosa's shoes are scuffed, her skirt is creased and she still clutches the bus ticket in her hand. Once her fingers curl around an object she can hold it for hours. Just let Myrtle try public transport sometime, sit on those dusty seats and stumble, nearly fall, as someone pushes her from behind. Her husband, Aubrey, drives her around like a queen.

"Well, Selwyn weighed seven pounds four ounces at birth and Rodney weighed nine pounds three. Hey, Aubrey?" says Myrtle.

"Nine pounds three?" repeats Max with astonishment.

"He was so big my hips divided with the weight. I was in such agony I thought I was having twins." She smooths one hand over her hair and flicks the tips up into a curl as she speaks.

"What do you mean your hips divided?" Max sits up.

"The bones separate and the baby just hangs in the middle."

"Hangs in the middle where?" He leans forward in his chair.

"I don't know where. It's amazing it doesn't fall through. But I could hardly walk. I felt as though I had a stone between my legs. Do you remember, Aubrey?" She tightens the corners of her mouth and purses her lips over the rim of the teacup.

"Do I remember? I had to take two weeks off work and carry her around. She just sat all day in a chair propped up with cushions. It was mid-summer too. I had to wash her and sponge her down and all she did was eat: chocolates, biscuits, pickled cucumbers and herring. I nearly crippled myself carrying her." His laughter erupts through the quietness in short bursts.

"Sshhh," says Hannah. "The baby!" she mouths with alarm.

"And then in the labour room she just screamed for her mother: 'Mommeeeee . . .' The doctor kept coming out to tell me: 'Two fingers, three fingers.' I heard her right down the passage. I was sitting there with one of the other fathers, and he said to me, 'Is that your wife or mine?' And I said, 'Mine. I recognise her shouting.'" Aubrey expels three short cranks of laughter.

"His head was so big I tore wide open, and they pulled him out with forceps. Do you remember, Aubrey? When I saw that instrument before my eyes I just screamed, 'Mommy help meeee . . .' and they pulled him out like a waiter uncorking a bottle." She picks a hair off her skirt, making a pincer movement with her thumb and index finger. "Then they showed him to me, purple and water-logged with a dent in his head. Is this Aubrey Junior, I thought? You can send him right back! But not the way he came out." Eruptions of laughter again. "And then, Hannah, when the milk came, I blew up like a balloon. But hard as rock. Hey, Aubrey?"

"Her breasts were like canonballs, Max. God knows how they got milk out of them." Laughter again.

"Sshhh," says Hannah.

"And the pain! Only gums in his mouth but he was chewing me up alive! The oozing and dripping and chewing! My nipples were like raw meat, and all he got was wind. 'Go on trying,' they said to me, milking me like a cow every two hours. And the pulling and squeezing . . . I said, 'Dry me up, here and now.' Ask Aubrey."

Max leans back into his chair. "Well, we fed our children according to the method of Sir Truby King, the international authority on infant feeding. Very revolutionary for his time, of course." He clears his throat loudly.

"Max stood over me with a stopwatch," says Hannah. "Ten minutes on one breast and ten minutes on the other and four hours in-between, and he took the baby away, crying or not. I can tell you that it worked perfectly. Paul was as fat as a pig and I was skin and bone. I thought I had consumption. But today it's different. Amy just sits in the room all day. Every time the baby cries she picks her up and she only gains half an ounce. What kind of a name is Marina?"

"Why didn't they name her after my grandmother?" asks Max.

"Or mine?" asks Hannah. "I don't know what Amy's doing in there all the time. We would have done it all differently, eh Max? More tea, Myrtle?"

"Is there any more cake?" asks Max.

Rosa stands in the kitchen with a dishcloth tucked into her skirt. She has taken off her jacket and rolled up her sleeves. A chicken takes time to cook. She'll take off her hat at home this afternoon when she sits down next to the radio. She hasn't come here to drink tea.

She spreads a sheet of newspaper over the kitchen counter and takes the chicken out of the bag. She smells it for freshness. Instinctively. You never really know until the bird is open in front of you. She lays the body on the table and opens the legs wide. She knows the inside of a chicken blindfold. In her sleep she could do it and pushes her hand through the entrance and into the entrails up to her wrist, feeling the tubes and bladders, slippery with blood and mucous. Everything in its right place. Her fingers close and she rips out the liver, stomach and heart in one handful. She ferrets and tugs through the skin and fat, clearing a cavity and feeling with her fingers for the lungs. Her nails scrape the spongy tissue between the ribs, bright red, the way she likes it. Remember the second lung on the other side; sometimes she forgets. The fingers are inside again, searching. Something else. Gott im Himmel, its little secret. Tenderly she pulls out a round yellow sac, covered by a membrane and threaded with fine blood-vessels. Gently or it will break. A young hen. Had they waited a few days they would have had an egg as well. She cuts open the stomach, and its smell rises strong: decay and digestive juices mixed into a thick yellow paste.

She opens the pocket to wash out its last meal of grit and mash and a small piece of blue glass, made dull by the acids. Her fingers wash the organ clear and smooth, feeling for the ribbed muscles of its lining. She smells it again. The innards must be perfect, especially the liver. She scrapes off the bitter green skin. A little bile can spoil everything. It's a good bird with plenty of fat for melting. But she cannot get used to buying a fowl without the head and feet. Lieber Gott, they'll be breeding chickens without them soon. She peels off the fat with her fingers and it comes away from the flesh like the skin of an orange. She rinses the body under running water and smells it a last time – she's got a perfect nose, it's a gift, a talent. Ever since childhood people came to her to smell, "Rosa smell this, Rosa smell that." Her judgment is infallible. Satisfied with the carcass, fresh and pink, perfect inside and out, she drops it into a pot of cold water, always cold, slowly, to draw out the taste.

Now she unwraps the newspaper parcel and takes out three carrots, scraping away the sand and scars. Then three parsnips, two leeks, a bunch of parsley and two sticks of celery. She looks through the cupboards. Nothing on the shelves but a bottle of whisky? What do they eat in this house, Amy feeding a baby and Josh going to work every day? Just as well she brought the salt. She bangs closed the pot.

"Sshhh," says Hannah, running into the kitchen. "They want fresh tea. Max says he's hungry, and Amy hasn't even come out of the room to greet them."

A scent of herbs and soup-greens fills the house, together with the smell of chicken-fat and onions slowly rendering in a pan. At least they'll have food for two days.

Rosa looks down the passage at the closed door. A young girl is inside, feeding a small creature who has been torn out of a quiet place, only hearing the humming of blood and the beating of its mother's heart. Already it must prove its progress in spoonfuls and ounces to a house full of expectant relations. Its first proof is to get fat, the second is to sleep. The first judgment is on its behaviour. "Is she good?" they ask.

Rosa remembers the sound of Dora crying. Her first child. Her mother-in-law had to teach her everything. Where were her instincts? "Hold it like this, and don't let go." And the dryness in her breasts, little breasts, pert and tactful, never obtrusive under her dresses. Not like her sister Sasha who bound those udders flat with calico and slumped her shoulders forward to hide them. Her own breasts, neat and tidy, but stubborn as wood, refusing to respond to Dora's crying or her own prayers for the milk to come. She prayed with a pounding heart, please God, please God, don't withhold, rocking the baby on her breast. She thinks of the psalm: "I will favour who I will favour." Please don't withhold. She wants to feel the ache. The prickly pain. Little needles stabbing inside the gland before the rush of milk into the sacs. And then the wetness, the wetness like dew in a desert. She begged to hear the baby grunt and choke on the nipple as the white stuff filled its mouth, rushing and pouring down its chin. If only the legs would stop kicking. If only the toes would begin to wriggle with pleasure and the head fall sideways into sleep. She wants to see the skin plump and dimple, swell into pouches around the cheeks; milk fat from her own body. She wants to smile as it sucks, its lips glistening. She will tell her mother-in-law to leave the room immediately and close the door and wait outside. Can she have some privacy when she feeds her baby and can her husband come to her defence? But she was helpless. Watching Dora wither, with a large head and a small body. They all watched her turn yellow and shrink, and they closed their ears against the sound of crying in the night.

Rosa takes off the dishcloth from her skirt, unrolls her sleeves and puts on her jacket. She sits in the kitchen for some time, looking at the floor, blurred shapes wobble in front of her eyes.

She gets up and crosses the passage into the dining-room, walking with soft steps – she mustn't disturb the floorboards. She glances quickly into the sitting-room where they are still drinking tea and Hannah is looking at her watch. Rosa says goodbye and walks through the front door, over the nine small paving-stones set into the grass and out through the gate.

She feels light now, without the parcels. Everything seems clear and sharp as she walks past the houses and the dogs, and this time she looks into the windows as she passes. Has she been alone in her sadness? She wants to know. Who are the people in these houses? So quiet and orderly, except for the dogs eating refuse from a dustbin lying on its side. What has it been for them? What news in their letters? What sobs in their sleep?

Have they grown old in their houses? What has it been for them, their lives in this small street in the suburbs?

She sees a black woman sitting on the grass, smoking a cigarette as a baby tugs on her breast. Next to her a small child plays on the pavement, sucking a fizzy brown drink from a bottle. Taking a pause before they walk on.

Rosa stands at bus stop twenty-two on the other side of the street, going into town. She climbs the steps into the bus easily, only her handbag on her arm. Isn't this the same driver who dropped her this morning? Still going up and down? The bus is nearly empty. She sits next to the window, watching people walking in the street. Everyone has somewhere to go and a place to rest at the end. Trace their footsteps and you'll see the patterns of their lives.

Soon she will be in town. She must buy sausage for Ivanoff and meat for mincing. Dora wants klops and potatoes for dinner. She will make enough for two days.

TWENTY-FOUR
A Golden Star

MAX PUT UP A WHITE TOMBSTONE FOR EVA. CARRARA. WHITE WAS FOR PAIN and her silent endurance of it.

She had remained uncorrupted in her life; not polluted by the crowded courtyard of Warsaw, or the foul workshop of her youth. The filth of steerage and the groping of the man in the dark did not tarnish her mettle. Corruption was not her flaw. But white was for coldness. She could not arouse her affections in a loveless marriage or acquire a fondness for her stepdaughters. Her feelings were simple, uncomplicated by guilt. And the three girls had no love for her. There was a crude understanding between them. It was as it was. White was for silence.

The funeral was small. Max and Hannah, and Amy and Paul with their spouses walked behind the pine coffin, covered with a black velvet cloth that was embroidered with a gold star; two interpenetrating triangles. Miriam and Theo, and Miriam's husband and their three children walked in a separate group. The two brothers were still in enmity, but stood with rent garments over their mother's grave, reading the prayer for the dead. Her remaining sister, Gittel, was there, frail and walking with a stick. Eva had no friends. They had to ask a few strange men to make up the quorum for the prayers. That is how it is with old women.

Amy had never been to a funeral before and watched with some detachment. She had made no effort to know or understand Eva. She could not imagine the steely old woman as a young girl, but Eva called her "little nose". Eva never spoke about her youth. She never wanted admiration or sympathy. They discovered a faded photograph of her standing with her father Mordechai Schneider, taken in a photographer's studio. She wore a scarf around her neck, and there was a cardboard palm-tree next to her and a painted bird carrying a ribbon over her head. Once Amy had gone with Max to her flat in Joubert Park. They had sat there quietly for an hour and then left her, looking over the balcony at the people in the street. Her fridge had a bottle of milk, half a dozen eggs, a loaf of bread and a few apples. She had no need for more. The shelves of the refrigerator were lined with newspaper.

Hannah contended with her severity, and won. At last Eva called her "the sweet girl".

Max wrestled with her will from childhood, and in the end he behaved dutifully, visiting her once a week in her flat and bringing her to his garden on Sundays.

It is true that her feelings had always been soft and yielding to Theo. Who can say why?

When the struggles of her youth were over, she withdrew into the apathy of her second marriage, and then slowly into the silence which lasted the rest of her life. She made no attempt to explain herself. What more is there to say?

It is as it is.

TWENTY-FIVE

Land's End

THEY HAD STOLEN OUT OF THE HOUSE IN THE EARLY HOURS LIKE TWO thieves, turning the handle silently, closing the door stealthily behind them and disappearing down the street. Except they had left everything of value behind them and only taken a toothbrush, a cake of soap and some old clothes. They had locked the house and left a living thing behind, deeply asleep and unknowing in its trusted cot that it would wake up to capable caretakers. Amy always felt the betrayal of abandoning a sleeping life, soon to open clear eyes that would cloud over in seeing strange faces, the touch of unfamiliar hands.

Of course Hannah and Max were more than caretakers, they would look after the baby in the correct way. She would eat the right things and sleep at the right time. Routine was essential for babies. They should be dressed, eating and shiny-faced by seven in the morning. Slowly walked to sleep by the starched nanny and kept clean and jolly all day. And then bathed at five, fed at five-thirty and sleeping at seven right through the night. It was a case of capable management. Max would switch off the lights and Hannah would lock all the doors. There was a correct way to live in a house. You had to be responsible. And Amy was too young and Josh too careless to understand. They would see a smoothly running regime when they came back that would merely require maintenance and continuity.

So now they are just outside this foreign town. They do this periodically, "to get away". From what? she is thinking. What are they doing in this forsaken place, Josh, Amy and a stranger called Swanepoel, standing on a bridge over a river? Amy has not yet made the separation. She thinks of the child waking up and Hannah mixing the porridge, blowing on a spoonful to cool it down, persuading with tricks and games. One had to be patient and inventive. A child must learn to eat at regular hours. Max would be listening to the radio: the news, the weather, the religious program that he always turned down, and the morning concert which he turned up.

Josh looks at the water and looks away. Swanepoel is smoking a cigarette and Amy is not quite sure who she is talking to, or at least, who is listening; the centre of her life left behind, as she hunches herself over the railing, watching the water, its brown skin wrinkled into furrows and the banks spotted with bushes like peppercorn curls. Under the bridge the river twitches like a body flexing its muscles, bulging and contracting as the water catches a joint or nodule.

"So this is the Orange River?" Typically South African. It drags away half the earth every time it rains and dumps all the soil into the sea. Brown, brown, moving recklessly in one direction as though it has somewhere to go. Then it dries up, leaving the barbel bubbling in the mud like worms. Food for vultures.

"You should see it when it rains," says Swanepoel. "It covers the bridge and swallows those shacks on the lower slopes. They lose everything, and we have to put them into tents until they collect all the debris down river again: bits of tin and brick, a door, a window-frame, sheets of iron. Then they put the shack up in the same place again. When it rains up-country we get a wall of water down here four hours later. We just sit and wait for it, and they," he points to the shacks, "start moving everything to higher ground. You must see it at Aughrabies, how it bursts through the rock. They say the gorge has tons of diamonds trapped in the mud. This is diamond country, but you can't get them out because of the force of the water. Anyway, it all belongs to The Company, even the dirty water that trickles through the bush. And the beaches at the mouth sparkle in the light because the diamonds are all lying on the sand. You could pick them up and put them in your pocket, but you could never get through the electrified wire or the dogs. And the tractors run seven days a week moving tons of sand."

Swanepoel seems to be talking to the river. Or is he talking to her? The wind shivers across the water, quivering its skin. Amy contracts her neck into her collar.

It is the middle of September, a short spring, warm and wriggling with new shoots in Johannesburg. Jasmine flowering in sweet thick bunches and the wisteria forcing its purple flowers through the bark. Young girls are wearing the new season's dresses and caterpillars are eating the first leaves on the trees. The air is heavy with sweetness and the world looks edible. She had thought it would be pleasant to see spring in the country but the Northern Cape is still on the dark side of the earth with the land cold to the core. Winter rains fall to no visible effect and the land is locked in a leaden vault.

Somehow, within the three days of their holiday a relationship with Swanepoel would be formed. Amy cannot imagine him in his traffic officer's uniform. This same day she has seen him buy petrol illegally from a farmer, break the speed limit, and drive slightly "under the influence". He told her that he enjoyed these weekends, taking visitors around the Northern Cape and that he used the extra money to send his children to boarding-school.

"A proper school, man, where they learn Latin and English. Not one of those farm arrangements where the whole school sits in one classroom and everyone is called Van Rensburg, and cousin Ampie has six fingers on each hand and no forehead. Don't you agree, Mr Kruger?"

Josh is leaning with his back against the railings, his eyes stretched wide into a stare, looking at nothing in particular. Amy knows that stare – smoking or sitting at dinner or in a chair after work, his eyes slightly yellowing around the whites, beginning to water from the staring. She always hopes that being away it will be different. When Swanepoel speaks to him his eyes come back into focus. He laughs.

"Ja, man. Ses vingers is 'n aansteeklike siekte in 'n klaskamer."

The two men laugh in reciprocal appreciation. Amy cannot understand her husband's joke and she cannot keep asking him to explain: "What does 'aansteeklike' mean?" Josh enjoys speaking Afrikaans in the country and he is always saying that Swanepoel's special expressions are impossible to translate or that the jokes will lose their humour. And it is true that the explanations do not sound funny. She thinks of home again. Her place, where no interpretation is needed. Hannah must be sitting in the sun next to the pram with a net over the opening. She will not allow a fly or a mosquito to touch the child when she sleeps. Everything will be in order, with the washing dripping on the line. Max will still be listening to the radio – the ten o'clock news. When Amy returns it will take time to overturn their management, restore her influence, put the clock away and eat late, switch off the radio and have human voices or bird-sound. And who is this Swanepoel that she should care about his jokes or feel the exclusion, as they move further and further away from everything that really matters? Of course it was her holiday too. She would enjoy it in her own way. The way she did everything.

"Your husband says that six fingers is a highly contagious disease in a classroom," Swanepoel says. "And that's not to mention the contagious diseases that you get behind the classroom. Not so, Mr Kruger?"

The two men laugh.

"En jy hoef nie 'n Van Rensburg te wees om dit te kry nie." Josh is laughing and talking at the same time. "Jy kan sommer 'n Swanepoel wees of selfs 'n Kruger."

"I'm not translating for you this time, Mrs Kruger. Your husband has gone too far." And both men laugh again.

Amy is never sure what to do when people make "off-colour" jokes in front of her in Afrikaans and then look at her to see if she has understood. Just smile and look confused, she thinks. She is used to feeling like a foreigner when she goes into country towns. When she tries to speak Afrikaans she always gets a reply in English. She remembers being embarrassed only once when she was standing next to an Afrikaans Member of Parliament at an official occasion and she could not sing the anthem, either in English or Afrikaans, beyond the first line. It is strange how she can never remember the words after the first line of any song. True, she can sing "God save the Queen" in three parts, but refuses to stand up.

This time, with Swanepoel, she really wants to understand. She wants to laugh along with them but can only guess at what they are saying. Sometimes Josh gives her a partial translation but mostly not at all. If you speak Afrikaans in the country all doors are open to you, especially the door to the heart. You don't merely speak the language, you enter it, like kinship and brotherhood. Josh had forgiven them the abuse in Die Koshuis: "Kom ons speel met die Jood. Laat hom sukkel. Hang him by the feet out of the window. Make him clean the toilets, lick the floor." He had endured it for five years with the prefects winking and the housemaster looking away. But did the victim still seek approval? "Ons land" had a special meaning in Afrikaans. Possession. Election. Chosen race. And Josh still craved acceptance. She compromised him. He did not want to take her along and he did not want to share Swanepoel.

She envies their familiarity, their open fellowship and trust, using Afrikaans as a private code. And even though that morning she had been alone with Swanepoel buying provisions for their weekend – he had shown her the white fat of the Kalahari meat, saying that it is the same colour as the desert sand and tastes of the wild herbs that grow with the grass – and even though they had gone to buy bread and cheese and she had seen him stock up with, perhaps, too many beers and brandies from the bottle-store – she still felt a separateness and a stiffness; his suspicion of "die Engelssprekende vrou" from Johannesburg.

And then after the butcher and the bottle-store they had driven passed Babs's Unisex Hair Salon.

"You'll never get me into one of those. What kind of sex is 'unisex'? Blow-dry and hairspray, while my wife's friends are sitting next to me having a perm and highlights? Imagine. I'm standing next to the chief traffic officer and all you can smell is Ultimate Hold hairspray. Once we went to visit my wife's cousin in Jo'burg and all she wanted was a swimming-pool and a bathroom en-suite. Her husband wore pink shirts and drawstring trousers. *Ekskuus Mevrou*, but you know what I mean? No buttons. Think of the consequences."

"Doesn't your wife mind that you go away every weekend?" Amy asks the question from the back seat of the car, speaking into the gap between the two heads in the front. They are driving past the Grand Hotel and Kroeg where they had spent the night – just enough water for a shallow bath, candlewick bedspreads, built-in radio and light-panel next to the bed. For dinner they had ordered roast lamb and mint sauce, cooked according to a decree in country hotels to remove all taste and colour.

"Nee wat. Men must work and women must weep. Moer man, it's no good to spoil a woman, not so Mr Kruger? Anyway, my wife hates the Kalahari. She says the sand gets into her pantyhose. She visits her mother and goes to bioscope with her friends when I'm away. And when I come home it's just like Christmas. She's waiting for me at the door. It keeps her on her toes."

Swanepoel is smoking a cigarette in the driver's seat, his arm resting on the lip of the open window. Josh is reading the stock exchange prices in the newspaper that he had brought from Johannesburg. Amy knew that he would hold that newspaper, here in the country, like a lifeline; read and reread it until he was back in town and could buy the latest – the day's prices, the day's events.

"We don't go in for that sort of thing," Swanepoel says, looking at the financial page. "We leave it to die Jode en die Engelse. We just sit on the stoep of our farms drinking brandy, praying for rain and watching the gehoer van ons skape."

The two men laugh again, and Amy also laughs, without understanding. "Jood" always had a particular sting in Afrikaans.

They pass a single garage, a last row of houses and the town suddenly disappears like a line drawn across a page. They are immediately in the veld. Then after a distance of five kilometres they pass the smoky settlement of tin shacks and mud huts which service the town. The "locations" are always there and every one looks the same – makeshift in perpetuity; permanently improvised. Some cows grazing, some goats, some mules.

Swanepoel waves to the driver of a truck as they overtake it.

"That's Koekemoer. He farms sheep in the Kalahari. He drives the Ford and his wife drives the Mercedes. The women all come into town to buy dresses and do their hair. You must see their house on the inside – Queen Elizabeth wouldn't be ashamed."

They pass smallholdings with houses built close to the road: a wheelless car and a defunct tractor in the yard and an orchard of peach-trees. Close by there are always the mud huts that house the labourers, the naked children, three chickens and washing drying on the wire fence. The plots become larger, with plantations of fruit-trees and long tracts of open veld. Then the divisions consolidate into enormous squares of farmland, flat and enclosed in unending lines of barbed wire.

"The wine farms of the Northern Cape," says Swanepoel. "Small hard grapes too sour to eat. We only use them for blending or vinegar."

Each gnarled stump is cut back and twisted with wire over a pole like a little crucifixion. Amy's eyes move with the furrows, perfect lines that swing continuously in long arcs, from oblique to vertical to oblique to vertical as they speed past. She is looking for a vine that deviates from the geometrical regularity or a furrow that is crooked. Something to indicate that a man has ploughed a field, hands have planted a vine. But the stumps make uniform patterns with identical stunted trunks and swollen joints, forced into conformity. They look dead, untended in the winter months, left to endure the continuous erosion of the desert sand. The yellow-skinned people walk singly alongside the road, always carrying something in a plastic bag, their bodies wrapped in rags that tug and twitch in the wind.

She thinks of home again, where the first peach-blossoms have already pushed through winter wood. Everything she loves left behind while she sits in a car with two men, talking and joking in Afrikaans as they speed through arid landscape, constantly threatening to dissolve into desert, still untouched by spring.

Now they are driving along private farm tracks, opening and closing cattle gates behind them. Amy can feel the tires losing their grip on the sand, sliding from side to side without bearings and the hump in the middle of the road bumping the undercarriage of the car.

"That's Koekemoer's farm. Only sheep and karakul. He's fifth-generation Kalahari and probably the last. His children have all gone to live in town. They say it's too dangerous on the border here, even though the government has given some of the farmers guns and subsidies to stay on. If you sit with him for tea he'll tell you hunting stories, how a dying gemsbok will still hold its head up and if you throw it with stones it will knock every one off with the tip of its horns. Then he'll sit you down and his wife will give you roast lamb and sultana konfyt. Kyk die ou mal Hotnot prancing outside the shop. They give him a bag of mielie-meal every month. God knows where he sleeps."

The old man dances a spidery jig, kicking up the sand and waving his arms.

"He twitches like a dying Kalahari scorpion," Swanepoel says, throwing him some coins as they drive past. "He's been here for years. Even his own people won't have him. One night a leopard will get him and that will be that."

They drive on, penetrating deeper into the sand.

And then there are no more farms and they are standing directly on the border with South West Africa. On a map they would be standing right on the boundary line. Amy is intrigued by the "other side". There is no fence, no obvious separation. It seems the same and yet different. It withdraws into its own interior, mysterious, inaccessible. And yet people move across it every day and the sand shifts freely. But the border is not arbitrary. There are limits. Earth is not like air. It needs a name. It wants to belong.

Josh is staring again, without seeing. She can tell, even though she can only see the back of his head. She has learned to "read" him from behind – the backward turned shoulder, the figure walking away down the corridor at home as she watches him or speaks to him. A figure with his back turned. They were always passing in the passage. He was unable to come into a room and sit down. Unable to stay. You would find him in his study reading.

Home. A house, a child, one's own clothes in a cupboard? She never wants to be away from it again, not even for a holiday. She feels displaced on this sand road with two men talking to each other continuously, where all sound is absorbed into the emptiness of space.

The tyres of the car are skidding and Swanepoel has to avoid slipping into the deep drifts on either side of the track. Sand that continuously changes shape, as unstable as water.

Amy is still waiting to see the dunes.

"The Kalahari isn't like that," Swanepoel says. "It's sandy but there is always long grass and kameeldoring. Savannah, I think they call it."

The oblique afternoon light makes deep shadows on the grass and the wind moves it into bunches like sheaves of wheat. Sometimes the sand rises into smooth hills and elsewhere it lies in ripples like ribs under skin. The trees are taller now, making sculptured shapes against the grass, reaching inwards in retreating perspectives; the centre always receding away from them. Even when they reach a point that had seemed interior, when they get there the centre has escaped into the distance and they are on an infinite regress of peripheries again.

They are searching for a clearing and a tree where they can camp for the night. Josh and Swanepoel are talking and laughing. Occasionally Josh turns around and repeats the story in English.

"He says that he told his wife on their wedding-night that if she ever went home to her mother, even once, then he would never have her back. And if she ever divorced him, then he wouldn't give her a cent. He says that he is not going to give her his money so she can braai the best rumpsteak with her new husband while he must eat pilchards and pap."

Josh turns around and looks at her for a moment. Yes, it is true; he has always been generous.

"Ja man," Swanepoel says, "that rooinek in England had the right idea with his second-best bed."

It is night and they are cooking over an open fire.

"Man, braaivleis is like flying this new American spacecraft. You can't just let it burn and blister on one side and then freeze it on the other. I could have told them if they'd asked me."

The night is black as licorice except for the lamp on the table and the fire. Swanepoel shines his torch onto the meat as he turns it carefully and then rearranges the coals, glowing now without a flame. They sit looking at the rude raw sky and tearing the meat with their teeth.

"Kalahari lamb is the best meat in the world," says Swanepoel. "We keep them lean here. Only a little grass and the rest is wild sage. They grow with it in their flesh. Even the wool smells of it."

Amy is lying in her sleeping-bag fully dressed, gazing up at the black space. The sky is tight as a drum, stretching the stars into a piercing brilliance. Josh and Swanepoel are drinking straight out of a bottle of brandy that has been warming in the sand next to the fire. Their voices are barely audible and the outline of their bodies is dimming against the fading fire, backs hunched over their knees and heads retracted into their jackets. She has left them alone, murmuring in the darkness, their shapes disappearing as the fire dies down.

She can still hear them, softly now and not laughing. She feels only vaguely related to the events that have transplanted her to this place under a tree in the Kalahari. Its roots, cradling her head, tap deep through the sand to find water, and its branches are her only protection against the heavy dew that falls in the desert night. Her body begins to warm and a comfort surrounds her . . . surrendering to it . . . rippling brown with the water's skin closing over her head, sinking down below the verge, deep down and entering into the river's core – its secret life – now blue. Tumbling weightlessly in its violet light . . . true blue . . . bluey blue . . .

She opens her eyes to the sky in the morning, still dazzled with the memory. Sharp sensation is with her all day and the intensity of the bush surrounds her. Colour ignites as the lilac-breasted roller vanishes into a blue aura or the carmine bee-eater trembles in the tangled trees. A scorpion stands black as onyx against a stone, and a vygie erupts from the sand into purple petals. The grasses ripple pink and palomino in the breathing air.

They are walking through the bush now with dry sticks snapping under their feet. Josh is wearing his sloppy hat that he keeps for outdoor holidays. His face is rough with stubble and the skin on his legs is red from the sun.

He has forgotten to bring his special cream. He always suffers physically on these vacations like an animal in a changed habitat. When he sits on the beach he must swathe his body in towels. And now there are small scratches on his thighs from thorns and he is limping from the hiking-boots that blister the skin on his feet. But more than anything he resents being "out of touch". "Anything can happen while I'm away." Once on an island holiday the day's prices were brought to him every day by courier on bicycle, then ferry, then rowing-boat. This kind of holiday is a painful compromise and he gets back to the office "not a moment too soon".

Josh and Swanepoel are talking politics. Swanepoel's language is gnarled as the kameeldoring with its tough seed that must pass through an animal's gut before it can germinate. And Josh deliberately coarsens his "city" Afrikaans which he speaks mainly to government officials in Pretoria when he wants a favour.

"No man, in town it's different," says Swanepoel. "We're already, what do you call it? Progressief. But these old farmers in the Kalahari! 'I'll die today.' That's what they say and then they draw a line in the sand. One Afrikaner doesn't trust another any more. All the cracks are opening. And you Jews in Jo'burg can just pack up and leave and the ones who remain go on making money."

"Are you trying to tell me the Afrikaners are not interested in money? Your farmers with indoor swimming-pools tiled in marble? Greed nicely wrapped up in political ideology. I'm going nowhere. My grandfather was a pioneer who supplied horses to the Boers because he believed it was a just war of liberation, and Amy's father designed and built all the buildings in Johannesburg. We were developing and building the place while you were all quarreling over exclusive rights. And we'd all be building more and there'd be plenty for everyone including the blacks if only you chaps with your politics and your policemen would stop preventing it," says Josh. A vein is pulsing in his neck and his breathing is fast. He has gone beyond the safe limit of jokes into open ground, and waits for the reply. They are speaking English.

"Okay, Mr Kruger, my father was just a poor Dutchman who worked on the railways all his life and I'm a traffic cop trying to earn a bit of a extra money showing people the Kalahari. No one has ever consulted me for an opinion. Whichever way it goes, I'll go with it. We've made our bed, we'll sleep in it. Maar nie ons twee bymekaar nie."

Josh responds slowly and releases the muscles in his neck. They are within the safety zone of humour again but he has laid an old shame partially to rest.

"So shall we stop here and have something to drink?"

Swanepoel makes tea in a crusty billy-can, sweet with sugar and scented with wood smoke. Josh disappears into the bush, unbuttoning his trousers, and Amy sits on a stone drinking the tea and throwing little sticks into the fire. The air is quiet except for single birdcalls, starkly clear. All the sounds are sharply articulated: the crackle of twigs in the fire, the whirring of wings.

She is beginning to feel a slight discomfort being alone with Swanepoel, a sudden exposure to him with Josh not there. She wants to chatter to him easily, stand with her hands in her pockets and make a joke, see him laugh and joke back. Amy Kruger standing in the bush with Swanepoel laughing. She tries to think of something but cannot find anything amusing to say and her English sounds prim and mannered. He always looks at her vacantly when she speaks, as though he has not fully understood or it is not worthy of further comment. She watches him stamp out the fire with his thick-soled boots, making thudding sounds and releasing a spiral of smoke from the fire. She sees the light hairs on his legs and arms, gently curling, blond and soft as the Kalahari grass.

In the afternoon they drive to the northern border with South West. "Land's End, it's called," says Swanepoel. And yet the earth continues into its own deep hinterland unhampered by the name. They pass herds of gemsbok, each one identically patterned with black strokes along tawny underbellies and down the curved saddle of their backs, faces streaked with aboriginal lines and crowned with horns. Stripes, spots, zigzags, circles mingle in the stubbled grass. Camouflage and carnival in the bush. The zebra grazes with the masked springbok. A blue starling stares with topaz eyes. Yet all is still in Land's End.

Swanepoel brings the car to a careful halt, focusing on something in the distance. Beige on beige as they search for defining outlines hidden in the fawny mass, with only the tips of ears twitching above the grass-line. Suddenly a male lion rises up and squats over the body of the female, growling and biting her neck while she submits to his full body-weight beneath him, rumbling softly and showing her teeth. Ripe and sleek in their season and playing privately in their own world. Is it a violation to watch their snarling love rite? They are disturbed and stand up. The male looks at the car and charges, then stops suddenly, legs skidding in a cloud of sand. They turn and walk away through the long grass, retreating slowly into Land's End until the black mane and the tufts of their tails disappear into the stippled thicket.

That night Amy and Josh sit next to the fire drinking coffee and waiting for Swanepoel's toasted cheese.

"You'll never eat it any other way. Just leave it to me. The secret is thick filling and lots of butter on the outside. When it's ready molten cheese flows like lava."

"Do you ever cook at home?" Amy is trying to visualise him living in the last row of houses in the town, opening his front door, the children running up to meet him.

"No. My wife says that 'n man moet sy plek ken. And I know my place at home: sitting on a chair with my feet up."

Both men laugh.

A fine mist veils the air, hanging low around the fire and beginning to condense into droplets of moisture. Swanepoel puts all the sleeping-bags together, covering them with a plastic sheet. Amy is hot inside the bag. She looks up at the sky forming a warm haze around them. She feels the exposure to Swanepoel again, lying near her, enclosed under the same waterproof covering. His arms are resting over the outside of the sleeping-bag and his hands folded together. Hands that can make a fire and change a wheel on a car, and yet uncalloused. Can they touch a woman softly? She turns towards him, close enough to feel his breath on her face, light and warm. A halo of vapour surrounds the moon. She wants to put her hand on his arm, feel the silky hairs. She wants to touch his hands.

Both men are already asleep and breathing in different rhythms on either side of her. She looks at Josh. He is sleeping heavily from the long walk that morning. She hears him turn in his sleep to relieve the pain of his sunburn; skin that only comes into the light on these holidays. For him the outdoors is something to be looked at through windows. Even in their own garden he never knows if the figs are ripening or how the trees have been ravaged by drought. Only in the mulberry season he takes a slow walk across the grass and stands with his feet on fallen fruit, reaching up for the black berries, four or five, and then walks slowly back, leaving purple footprints in the house. He turns in his sleep again. There is a rasp gurgling in his chest. She is suddenly afraid that he has caught a chill, sleeping outside in the damp and the dew. He might choke in the night or stop breathing. It is selfish to impose these holidays on him; the infected insect bites that swell into painful blisters. He scratches his shoulder in his sleep. She looks away, sensing the intrusion of watching him, seeing all the imperfections of his face, the dense eyebrows, the wiry hairs of his moustache. Tomorrow night they will be sleeping in their bed in Johannesburg.

She lies awake for a long time, listening to the little explosions of gas coming from the fire, their only protection against the howling things, the hidden presences that stalk the camp. Deep into unbroken space they share the dark with creatures that graze or prowl or mate, green-eyed and growling in the night; with the echoing love song of crickets, muffled into a low rattle by the misty air.

The next day they make the journey back to town. They pass farms with day-old lambs' skins stretched across little wooden crosses hanging outside sheds to dry.

"You must see the ewes when the lambs are taken away from them. They run after the truck for miles with the milk pouring out of their udders."

Swanepoel is breaking the speed limit again on the small farm-tracks. The sand is gradually hardening under the tyres to become soil, and then it is the tar of the national road. He speaks very little and keeps his eyes on the road. He had said that he wanted to be home to make a braai for his family for lunch. What will he say about his weekend? The Jo'burg Jode come to the Kalahari? That they were different? Or onse mense? Had he looked at her or seen her once? Was Josh aware of her own experience? Did she have any shape or a form in other eyes? Did it matter? Tonight she will be home in Johannesburg.

Josh is clean-shaven, having removed three days' growth of beard. He is rearranging the papers in his briefcase and counting the money in his wallet as a tip. When he slips it into Swanepoel's hand, will he get a smile or a scowl? Swanepoel must be aware of him fingering the money. Does he tell the same stories on every trip? Are there bonuses for jokes in the Kalahari? How does one make the calculation?

She is looking again at the fences that enclose the vineyards. The wire is stuck with pieces of paper and plastic that were blown by the wind. She is still looking for green leaves on the knotted trunks, pruned and twisted for human cultivation. There must be one vine that anticipates the spring. The tattered people walk singly on either side of the road. An old man carries a live chicken hanging downwards by its feet.

Hannah and Max must be packing also: their own blankets and pillows and two small suitcases and Max's radio standing next to the front door. He is sitting on a chair with his hat on, tapping his stick, waiting impatiently to go home; his flat, his bed. It has only been three days. Will the child recognise her? Has the garden changed? Will there be any difference in their life or will it be the same?

In Johannesburg.

TWENTY-SIX

The Price Of Onions

SOMETIMES MAX IS MILD AND GENTLE WITH HIS AGE, AT LAST ENJOYING his dependence on Hannah. Not ashamed to be grateful for his tea, the cheerful steam curling off the surface and the sweet astringent liquor soothing his throat. Then he gets a biscuit and a pat on the head for waiting patiently. "Thank you, my sweetie. There's my treasure," and allowing himself to be stroked and petted when Hannah says, "Look how nice he looks. I bathed him and changed him early this morning and gave him a nice breakfast – boiled egg and toast and tea." Then he says, "She's a Trojan. You should see how she works. Busy since early this morning." Perhaps this is the petting he always wanted but was too commanding and too ashamed to accept. "You're spoiling him. Making him weak," he used to say to Hannah about Paul. Displays of affection could have a corrupting effect, making one tender and mild and trusting; unfit for rigour and for life. Max's mother did not love them. She saved them. Rescued them with struggle and endurance. Max stood alone: lonely captain of his leaky ship.

He has learned that dependency can have its pleasures. And when his pulse is irregular and he is so weak he can hardly stand, he asks for soft porridge with warm milk and sugar, or sago, or milk soup with noodles or even bread pudding with raisins like his mother made him to keep up his strength, allowing him to stay home from school. Now he asks Hannah to shut the windows and cover him with a blanket, tucking him in on all sides, his cheeks turning pink with warmth.

At other times he is angry with his weakness. "I'd throw myself off the building but I can't even put my leg over the side." And he sits silently for hours with his eyes closed and both hands folded over the knob of his walking-stick, refusing to eat or to open his eyes or even to listen to the radio. Then Hannah sits with him, coaxing him to eat a little bread and cheese, a cup of sweet tea, and brings out the books to read about "universal things".

So today Hannah and Amy will take him along to the market for the drive. It relieves the tedium of waiting for Hannah to come back, even though

Sophie is there to make him tea or a sandwich or to go to the shop for a newspaper and a slab of chocolate. "Not the milk chocolate, mind – too soft, too sweet, too easy. Bring me the dark one. The hard and bitter one. The pure one." He does not mind the little outings reserved for the elderly, just to give him some fresh air and relieve the monotony. "But park me in the shade! And don't leave me in the car too long," cries the travel-weary captain, chief engineer and lieutenant of the listing ship.

Amy fetches them from the bus stop outside the building. Max leans heavily on his stick to lift himself off the bench, walking with warped, swollen legs to the car. Hannah is singing F beyond high C into the exhausts of passing cars. Max gets in buttocks first, leaning forward to avoid bumping his hat on the doorframe, growling and pulling his legs like logs into the car with his hands. He straightens his hat and sits with the stick between his legs like a rudder, to navigate the limping ship.

He is wearing his brown suit with green checks and leather binding around the lapels and buttonholes.

"Do you know how long I've had this suit?" It's a game he plays with his clothes: the hand-loomed punjabi waistcoat lined with silk; the Harris tweed jacket with leather patches on the elbows; his blocked felt hat, perhaps brown, perhaps green, too old to tell, with sweat marks around the inside rim and an American label.

"Ten years?" He shakes his head.

"Fifteen years?"

Then he gives the answer: "T-w-e-n-t-y-t-w-o y-e-a-r-s."

"And do you see these buttonholes? Look how they've bound them with leather. Indestructible. Have you ever seen such work?"

"He hasn't bought a new suit in ten years," boasts Hannah.

"What's the matter with this one?"

"Why don't you buy one just for fun?" asks Amy.

"Fun? What's fun? I've never done anything for fun in my life."

They drive down Empire Road past the intersection with Jan Smuts to pick up the overhead highway. Names given to honour events and people; history outlived by other history and only remembered as a click of the tongue and a name-tag. They pass over the crematorium, the station network, the mosque and the old market at Newtown. Once arrogantly "new", now an old town with unused smokestacks and deserted warehouses.

"I used to buy a full bag of greens for ten shillings from the old Lebanese woman," Max says. "She had the contracts of every hotel in town but she always wore an old black dress and stockings. She used to scream from one end of the market to the other and all the young men were terrified. She died a multi-millionaire."

He covers his eyes as he gets the flash from the new glass building in the morning sun. The car is hemmed in by transport lorries that service the city on the overhead highway, casting a shadow over downtown clothing factories, abandoned hotels and garages. Amy looks away as they pass a doomed cattle truck headed for the new abattoirs. The air fills with the smell of manure. They sweep round the off-ramp at City Deep and onto the Heidelberg Road, the name – ah! Heidelberg redolent with nostalgia – now littered with plastic and paper.

They enter through the gate and decide that Max will wait for them at Dot's.

Amy drives to a block next to the public toilets and helps Max out of the car. A woman sleeps against the wall with a baby crawling on the curb next to her, sucking on a piece of bread.

"One tea, a chelsea and the *Daily Mail* for the old man at the table. Do you mind if we leave him here for a little while?" Amy pays at the counter, crowded in by labourers buying cartons of milk, white bread, cigarettes, and boerewors awash in gravy.

"Don't leave me for long," Max wails as they walk through the door.

Unburdened! Unencumbered! Light of foot and frivolous, Amy and Hannah drive to the produce halls, and park in-between a truck loading up with vegetables and a refrigerated pantechnicon marked TRANS-KAROO TRANSPORT. They find a discarded trolley and pass a security guard, balancing on two legs of a chair and asleep at the entrance. His shoes shine as brightly as Hannah's silver on a Friday night. Suddenly confused and blinded by the large dark shed, they pause . . . and then enter the war zone.

They dodge loaded wheelbarrows and forklift cars carrying two hundred boxes of tomatoes, driving and hooting along the narrow corridors. "They could crush a person to death," says Hannah backing up against a container with rotting vegetables. White-coated agents jackboot up and down the borders of their territory, screaming through the half-light for Amos or Lucas or Shorty or George or Johnny. The hall reverberates with the appeal to prophets: "Isiaaah, Jeremiaaah, Obediaaah." And Isiah, Jeremiah and Obediah corporealise out of the dismal deep.

Amy walks up to the carrot man: "Hello, Uncle Ronnie. What have you got today?"

He puts his arm around her, prodding the flesh on her back, "Hello, my darling. Something that will make your husband mad with envy."

"How much?"

"Anything for you. Three rand."

They pass the pineapple man whose wide-set eyes bulge and leer at them as they walk. He licks his lips and smooths back his hair. "Too high," Amy calls out in a small voice lost in the noise but she waves at him cheerfully for "next time". "Disgusting man," says Hannah under her breath, curling her lips into a wide smile. The tomato man's tomatoes are "plump and firm"; he cups each hand and wriggles his fingers to demonstrate the size. "Half green and just beginning to blush. Like you." The cucumber man's cucumbers are "long and hard" and he puts his hands in his pockets, lifting his eyebrows. "Something special for you, my lovey. Try one and see. You won't be disappointed."

Hannah stays in the background, a shadowy beneficiary of these transactions. She does not interfere with the banter, looking away and pretending not to hear. She leaves Amy to joke and laugh. It's worth it for the money they save.

They have reached the end of the hall, the section occupied by Portuguese women. Now Hannah does the buying because they ignore Amy. Hannah can appeal to them woman to woman – the shock! "Are you selling gold or green beans?" Then they give her a special price, "Only for you," one frugal wife to another.

"Do you know that one in six South Africans is Portuguese?" Amy asks Hannah. "And one in four working Afrikaners is in the civil service?"

"You don't say!" says Hannah. "And after that who's left?"

Amy pays at the cashier's block and Billie smiles at her from behind the glass, showing a gold filling in his front tooth. He grabs her hand as she puts the money on the counter.

"Hello, my darling, you make my day."

Hannah looks the other way. If it weren't for Amy they would give her rotten oranges and mouldy grapes.

They drag the trolley outside into the light and across the road to the onion and potato hall. The air smells of earth and damp in the high-ceilinged shed; cool and dark like an old farmhouse in the Karoo. They talk softly in the quiet place, silent as a vast sleeping dormitory for the onions and potatoes lying huddled in packs: First Grade Cape Large, Second Grade Free State Mediums, Smalls, Undergrade. Every bag is weighed, pedigreed, understood and loved. Not one bag unwanted or without value, they lie like grubs in a honeycomb, too heavy and contented to move. The labourers toil ceaselessly – pick them up, carry them, place them on trolleys, re-arranging the formations: head to tail, top to toe, held by two black arms across their bellies, embraced intimately, body to body and then placed carefully next to their silent sleeping partners.

Amy and Hannah walk through the channels, examining samples left next to the bags for inspection. Amy picks one up to feel its texture – a dusky smooth-skinned beauty, still powdered by the Cape soil; perfect when sliced into fingers for frying. And across the aisle, the label says Bethal – dark obstinate creatures, grown sullen from the drought and resistant to cooking until they succumb into puffs of carbohydrate confection. Perhaps this week they should take "smalls" – freckle-faced cherubs with paper-thin skins that curl back tenderly when steamed for a mere twenty minutes. Each flock lies clustered around its white-coated shepherd.

"That man looks like my father," Hannah says pointing to a thin man with a limp. "He was a bad husband and a bad father but I loved him. If you wanted to find him, you went to the theatre. I shall never forget him throwing suitcases of money away and my mother standing next to him crying. All worthless after the revolution."

They walk across the shed to the onions, stepping over one of the links in a chain of twenty trolleys. "Be careful. You'll lose a leg if the driver pulls off," Hannah says. "Once I saw a man lose his thumb. He just picked it up and walked out holding it in his hand."

"How are your babies today?" Amy asks Francois cheerfully. His head shines in the shadows like a white billiard ball on dark green felt. Today he is not smiling back. Her charm is not working. Does that mean they will have to pay more for onions?

"You know, my white customers never cheat. My black customers sometimes cheat. But my coloured customers always cheat. I'm losing money! I don't know why God saw fit to create them." He frowns over his brood like a god of retribution.

Amy watches his baleful eyes and the muscle in his jaw twitch as he grinds his teeth. His anger is absolute. How can she distract him from this mood? Happiness is good for the price of onions. Smile? Keep talking? Wait patiently? Her mind is in a vice. Everything hangs in the balance. It is a delicate situation and anything untoward could invoke a damaging decree.

When suddenly Hannah materialises out of the mystic darkness. She speaks! Words made flesh with piercing clarity: "God created them, but with a little help from ourselves! And you'd be surprised by what kind of people cheat."

There is a bewildered silence as they flounder with the recklessness of Hannah's remark. Amy turns to look at Hannah who is out-staring Francois with dilated eyes, and smiling innocently. Amy has been cultivating him for years and now Hannah has violated the relationship and endangered the price of onions. Perhaps he will forgive the remark because of her grey hair and wrinkles, sometimes an asset in the struggle for bargains. But today she looks rosy-cheeked and fresh, her eyes sparkling.

She walks away to look at the onions – "lying voluptuously", she always says, "and giving off their musky perfume in sheer love". She breathes deeply: "Good for the lungs," and looks for the one bag that shines out radiantly from the others; "wanting to be chosen".

Amy is left to appease Francois, sitting on his elevated chair like a magistrate about to deliver a sentence. Any interruption at this stage could finally prejudice the calculation. His onions cower in obeisance and she waits humbly for the judgement:

"Give them a bag at four rand."

Slightly up on last month, but she must accept the penalty. With all the risks it's still cheaper than the shops. The clerk writes out the order with a hand webbed with scar tissue. In bad times he can be a useful intercessor with the "magistrate", mitigating sentence. Today he writes two rand instead of four, and winks. Hannah winks back, carrying the trophy over her arms like a sleeping child and puts it tenderly on the trolley.

"Ta-ta Francois." They have the onions. What more is there to say?

They'll worry about him next time. They leave him glowering on his throne and stride past, waving victoriously.

Max is sitting in the cafe, his hat still on his head. The cafeteria is empty except for two men sitting at a table talking about soccer.

"What have you been doing all the time? They're about to close the shop. I've done everything for her but she doesn't give me a thought."

He gets into the car next to Amy, buttocks first and leaning forward to avoid bumping his hat on the doorframe. Hannah sits in the back seat with the vegetables. She doesn't mind, she says so. Little draughts of air release the green smell of parsley, celery, leeks and lettuce. They pass through the gates and back onto the highway. Max sits upright, holding his rudder as he navigates the limping vessel through dangerous seas. The black hearse of the Jewish Burial Society overtakes them and they spit three times.

"What was the price of onions?" Max asks.

"Too high," says Amy.

They turn off at Berea and pass the tennis courts at Barnato Park School, secured with barbed wire and spiked fencing. The girls in white dresses sit on the grass in small groups eating sandwiches.

"My old school," says Amy. "I wonder what has become of Greta and Joyce . . .?"

"I was married around the corner in my mother-in-law's house. It was a Monday morning. A wedding breakfast," Hannah says.

She is still travelling those streets, as known to her and carved onto her life as the network of lines on the palm of her hands.

"My country now."

TWENTY-SEVEN
A Dream Of Strawberries

HIGH IN THE SKY, A FLYING KITE, A BLAZING STAR IN A DAYTIME SKY. HOT-white and spreading like blindness; a voice calling . . . missus? . . . Yes? . . . Her name but not her face. A fracture in her face and a rubber tongue to fill it. Sweet taste of blood. She leans over the side of the bed and spits into a pan . . .

Perhaps now Max will be satisfied. Now that they are both toothless and she can also put her teeth in a glass next to her bed. Now they can kiss in the dark with gummy mouths and lips that shrink inwards into folds without their pearly wall; mutter thick goodnights with importunate tongues that wallow and roll in spaces too large to contain them. When they wake in the night they will both lisp through the large hole gaping, dribbling like babies learning to speak; all blunt gums and tongues flopping like fish out of water.

Then by day when she smiles she will show perfect teeth all in a row and pink plastic to cover the pitted meat underneath. There will be so many tricks – they can make clicking noises to each other when they chew and she will also become an expert at slipping the plates with her tongue to remove crumbs and fragments, discreetly, behind a napkin without anyone noticing. On long winter afternoons in the flat, just the two of them in a room watching TV or listening to the radio, they can jiggle them around and play or take them off and put them on a table, two disembodied jaws, smiling the deathly smile, with a fissure in their faces.

Now perhaps he will be satisfied. Now that they have been thrown into a bucket, the stubs that were hard as rhinoceros horn and nuggetted with eighteen carat; rooted deep in her cheekbones so she could crack nuts with them, uncork bottles and unscrew jars. But as fine as purest crystal and resonating with overtones when she sang. She could feel the vibrations against her lips. She used to irritate him when she crushed hard sweets noisily or chewed sticky toffees or gnawed on bones like a dog. But nothing could damage the enameled shell.

Even with the diseases of childhood that softened her bones and corrupted her lungs and the poverty that bent Dora's legs into brackets, Hannah's teeth grew strong and white. That was when she first learned the craft of displaying them. Smile, because there are lice in the seams of your dresses; smile when you beg the soldiers for food, and your eyes burn brightly. Smile. The poor girl, the Jewess in a Russian school. Don't be late, don't fail, and smile at the teacher. Only with her singing was there freedom and exhilaration. To lose her voice was like waking up toothless. Trying to find a prosthesis for her life. But the lost limb still aches.

Now perhaps, that she has lost her teeth and lost her womb and the skin of her scalp shows pink through sparse white hair, perhaps now, he will admit to his age. They have been married nearly fifty years but she has never seen his birth certificate or his passport. Even the children are not sure how old their father is. Once Amy came running with his passport in her hand but they were too frightened to look, and too ashamed to know his secret, like opening Bluebeard's chamber. They stood paralysed with it in their hands. So Amy put it back. They celebrate his birthday with presents the day after Christmas, with songs and speeches and kisses but no candles on the cake. He has left her to guess: "Is he seventy-nine, or eighty? If I was eighteen when we got married and he was fifteen years older than I, then he must be eighty by now. But he could be eighteen years older or twenty. Then that would make him eighty-three or eighty-four. Perhaps he is eighty-five."

She knows how proud he is of his body – the straight back and soft skin, despite his age. That he still smooths his moustache when he looks at other women; who knows what else he does with them or wants to do. He hates it that she is younger and will outlive him by years, inherit his money, spend it, lose it, everything he has saved. She has let her hair grow white, to pacify him, but every week he still brings out his little black bottle to touch up with a brush.

But soon he could begin to forget things: the day of the week, where he put his glasses, and what he had for breakfast. Forget everything that he'd said today or yesterday, and remember only what happened when he was a child. Or remember the only friend he ever had, Lelio – "Did I ever tell you that when we looked at each other we knew what we were thinking?" he would ask. "We never had to speak, walking through the early streets of town, me and Lelio, even though I knew nothing about him. He never spoke about himself."

She knows that Max sits with his memories as though he is hiding a crime, and nothing will open his lips as long as he has the grimness to seal them. Perhaps he will utter them as a last confession when he discloses the things that stoop his back and drop his chin. The hidden fault-line that lies quietly under the surface, and then moves into seizures until its rage is done and a new quiet is found. But the fault-line remains.

Then he will tell her the secrets that he has hidden for nearly fifty years, faltering and stuttering in his raving, woken by the dreams that make him sweat and twist in the night: how he saw himself as a heathen priest with scalding eyes, wearing a three-cornered mitre and an embroidered gown, and his hands were holding a silver mace that gave him the command of life or death. How he waved his mace and vassals cowered. Whose blood was on his hands? Who, entombed alive in his burial room – the wives, the slaves, the dogs? And how when he woke up he was frightened to see himself in a mirror, frightened of his own eyes. Of his power and his crimes. And frightened to look at her. Whose blood was on his gown, the executioner?

Perhaps then he will confess all – he will feel ridiculous, a man of his age – how he fought at school, murderous: "Where's your father?" and not knowing because his mother never spoke. No mention of a grave or a number or a piece of paper. No record of the death, no picture of a face, no stories, no name, no love. And then he will tell how he felt, clenching his nails into his bleeding hands, the day the fat man and his three daughters moved into his mother's house; their suitcases at the door, his clothes in her cupboard and lying in her bed, spread-out and snoring as though he was entitled. Or – preposterous in a grown man – how she always gave Theo the last spoon of rice pudding and a tickey in his hand, looking at Max and the three girls with cold eyes. Silly how he always wanted a dog. The strays followed him and licked his hand. But Eva was ungiving. Cold and silent. Was she never young? And laughing? And pretty? And now, when the fury takes him, when seismic shifts move him, or when his laughter breaks like a dike and he hiccups and sobs, he doesn't know if it's laughter or tears.

Amy was the only one who said to Hannah, "Don't do it. It will be like an amputation."

But the dentist said, "Take them out. Every time you eat hot things you'll feel it. Every time you eat cold things you'll feel it. Every time you eat a sweet it will travel through the nerve like a knife."

Max had said, "You'll never be finished with the dentists. Just think of the money. Take them out and you'll never sit in a dentist's chair again. Look at me. My plates are so tight sometimes I can't get them out. Why bother with it? Take them out."

That's what they said about her womb: "Why bother with the bleeding? Take it out."

So they took it out – and her appendix and anything else that was in the way while she was sleeping and they had their hands inside her. Her body is full of empty spaces and not enough organs to fill them; a sagging sack, a pig's bladder bloated with air and leaking urine. And now a hole in her face also. But they must leave her breasts. She will die first but they must not touch her breasts.

She wants to burn candles and wear black. To spend her days knitting in a doorway on a wooden chair, eating soft porridge and mince with a spoon, slowly sucking the taste out of pieces of meat and pouting her lips to tickle her nose.

She will not use those things, filling the emptiness with thick plastic right back to her tonsils. She wants to vomit. They force them over the torn stumps to make the gums fit the mould.

She will not wear them, cheap copy of the original, every tooth machine-matched and flawless. Her own teeth had a natural grain, faint lines and shadings mellowed with age into deep ivory, plumping out her mouth full and firm.

She will spit them out like garbage; dummy dentures from a toyshop. Let her cheeks cave in and her lips wither into folds. Let her whole face shrink until Max looks away with fright. And when she sneezes they'll fall and when she yawns they'll drop. Let him close his eyes and still see her face until it burns an image on his retina. Let him hear the sound of plastic clacking when she opens her mouth and her whole jaw slips.

She saw them that night in the dark, as old as he is. He and Sophie together, thinking she was asleep. Sophie was washing him with soap and a sponge, pinching and tickling, scented bubbles all over his skin, around all the tender folds and creases, and he was lying back and allowing. She saw him smiling, wanting it, as old as he is. Is that why he pays her? The servant? Takes the money out of his pocket and puts it into her hand? Is that why the others left? Julia and Melida and Georgina? And all the women in the building looking at her behind her back?

And this is her curse: let him see her face first thing in the morning and last thing at night and all through the day. And when he sleeps at night, let her teeth bubble in the water and smile at him through the glass.

She lifts herself up in bed and leans over to spit into the kidney-shaped pan on the table next to her. The taste of decay fills her head and the smell of bone-rot rises, mingling with the antiseptic smell of the ward. Her head pulsates with each heartbeat, travelling in thick throbs through the torn nerves in her jaw. Saliva fills her mouth. She closes her eyes and rests back on the pillow. Clean and crisp against the heat of her neck . . .

A cool hand rests on her face and rainwater heals her mouth . . . she is eating strawberries, large and fleshy and perfumed like powder sachets – violets and roses and lemon verbena. The scent rises while she is eating, like incense, fresh and wholesome inside her mouth. She puts her mouth to the fruit and breathes it, but there is something too sweet, overripe and clammy, losing the cleanness and the coolness of strawberry. As she closes her lips the flesh is warm, slimy and grey, with hollow chambers and fibrillating gills. A taste of putrefaction rises up her palate and into her head. She is eating offal, the living meat of hearts.

She reaches over to the side and spits into the metal pan on the table next to her bed.

TWENTY-EIGHT
An Old Goat Smelling Slaughter

MISTY PATTERNS SWIRL INSIDE THE HARDENING CUTICLE OF HIS CORNEA. Sometimes the shapes thicken into bars or spots or spinning nebulae or dead suns with luminous moons. White on white on white in his internal landscape.

Max sits in the bedroom on the edge of his bed, his shoulders slump and his head hangs forward onto his chest, both hands resting on his thighs.

Hannah is out again.

His eyes are closed as he listens to the radio and his glasses, like two closed windows, balance on the slippery sides of his nose. What is there to see that he hasn't seen a thousand times? He is beginning to prefer voices, hearing their nuances and moods, even listening to the women's program. He is not ashamed. Delightful poetry and household tips; very useful – you put your trousers in the deep-freeze to remove chewing-gum – you never know.

The door to the passage is open for ventilation and the front door is wedged back to let in air from the outside corridor. A security gate is locked across it and the key is on a hook. Now the whole flat whistles with draughts. He unbuttons his shirt to the waist for the wind to touch his skin and it bends the soft white hairs on his chest like winter grass. Always going out shopping with her friends. Shopping! Shopping! He takes a small brown pill bottle from the table next to the bed, shakes it, removes a cotton-wool stopper and empties the contents into his hand, feeling for three pills. He keeps them inside his cheek, reaching for the glass of water next to the bottle. Swallow them quickly or the bitter taste and the blue dye comes onto his tongue. Then he puts the remainder back into the bottle and closes it. Every movement is deliberate, dictated by habituated pathways in the brain. Everything must be in the place that corresponds with his mental map. Sophie knows that she must pick up the bottle, dust the table and put the bottle back in exactly the same place with the glass next to it.

He opens his eyes to focus on the picture of Amy on the wall. He closes one eye to test it and then the other. He shuts his eyes again and sits with his hands resting on his thighs.

It's going to be a long day.

He looks at the painting again, narrows each eye separately. Today the right is clearer than the left, and he looks down at his feet, tightens his eyes and tries to focus again.

The doctor has told him that he will never be completely blind but every day colour fades and outlines lose their firmness. Objects in front of him look spongy like spores and fungi, and his fingers are surprised by what they touch. When he eats, his mouth gets fish when he expects chicken. The watch on his wrist is out of time and he puts on his glasses every morning as an accessory to dressing like wearing a tie. What does he need them for? It is months since he could see the time or read the newspaper and he stands like an idiot in front of the bathroom mirror, shaving in the same way that he eats, by knowing where his mouth is on his map. But he must always have money in his pocket. Has he any control over his life? Is he an infant or a woman that his pockets should be empty? If Hannah wants bread or milk from the shops, he will put his hand in his pocket and give her the money. It does her good to ask.

He puts out his hand to feel for the radio and grasps the handle. He pushes down on the bed with his other hand to pry himself onto his feet and shuffles towards the entrance-hall; the coolest room, small and dark. He can hear people walking along the outside corridor and the whining of the pump as the lift rises up the shaft, thumping as it steadies before the sixth floor – Mrs Brightman carrying parcels from the shop. He hears her stop outside her front door and rustle the paper as she puts the packets down to find her keys. Then the crumpling of paper again as she moves inside and shuts the door behind her. There is something final in the shutting of a door and the grating of metal as she slips the security chain into the groove. Every day new sounds find a place on the map. He hears the flat-boy rubbing a cloth on the outside passage floor and the sound of a tin dragging against concrete. The radio gives a time-check for eleven o'clock, followed by the news.

"You're late with the floors eh, Petrus?"

He is usually outside the flat by ten. Max can hear his breathing, heavy this morning, and smell the lavender-scented floor polish through the open door. And there is a special place on the map for the cardboard box standing next to the lift with all Petrus's tools: the rags, the cloths, the brushes, the feather-duster, the rubber pads for his knees. That's all he needs to keep the building clean: rags and feathers. Everything else gets lost or broken.

Max looks towards the light. A haze covers his eyes and he can only see things when they move. Sometimes he cannot even distinguish between Hannah and Amy. He must teach himself to be satisfied with shapes and not grieve for the detail: the picture of Amy that he painted with the faint markings of an old painting of Paul underneath it. He enjoyed fusing one picture over another like the layers of memory. Now he can only use the frame to focus his eyes on and he has lost the slight smile on her face, her hair flying about with the dark purple hills behind her; a brooding background, primitive and mysterious he used to think. Leonardoesque, he was told.

He used to admire the detail in buildings: the frescoes, plaster reliefs, inlays, classical motifs. He loved the beauty of materials, the correct use of tools. Now he must try to find subtlety in sound, exploring the fine distinctions in voice and speech. He must use his hands as eyes, beginning to find meaning through touch, and just to remember, like pictures stored in an archive, always to remember how everything looked – the sculptured tendon on a woman's ankle, the blue vein under the right cheekbone on Hannah's face, her skin as delicate and transparent as tissue, the curve from the eyebrow to the nose and the outline of her lips to the little shadowy indent in the corners. It was her nose that he loved, with its patrician line from the forehead. Why could he never tell her? Why are things locked inside him as in a vault? Why can't he tell her even now? He would like to draw his fingers along her profile. He can remember drawing her sitting on the bed, nude, cutting her toenails. Where is that picture now?

Amy has told him to accept that age is natural and triumphant; three-score-and-ten is a blessing. Not a failure, not a humiliation. Not like the old dog in her house who has sugar rubbed into his eyes every day to grind back the membrane growing over them. He will school himself to live with his eyes growing milky. He will learn to move with his fingers in front of him like an insect with feelers; bumping into furniture and fumbling when he eats, his tie spotted with food stains and having to ask Hannah to read to him like a child. Spilling his tea on the floor when he misses his mouth and ranting with rage. He must learn not to protest.

He is sitting next to the large mahogany chest that is used as a telephone table, littered with open envelopes. The diary is open with a pen lying along the spine. He knows that the page is full of her writing: shopping in the morning, meetings in the afternoons and Sophie's messages for her – Clair phoned at nine and then again at ten and also Ursula.

"Sophie will make you tea. I'll be back for lunch. If you want anything, ask her."

He asked Hannah months ago to take him to buy new shoes but she always puts it off.

"Why don't men ever know whether their shoes fit? Too big, too small, too narrow?" she says.

And now he must slip-slop around the flat in slippers because his feet swell.

Sophie places a cup of tea next to him – he can hear the rattling of the teacup and feel the movement of the air, then the tinkle of the wind-chime as she passes, the opening and closing of doors by the changing air-pressure. The draught makes drumming noises through the slatted blinds in the sitting-room and flips scathingly through the pages of the diary.

In the old flat he used to enjoy being alone. He would go into the kitchen and make bread: dissolving the yeast in water and watching the spores rise into a brown, beery curd, mixing it with flour into dough and popping the yeast bubbles as they foamed in his fingers; stretching and kneading and slapping the dough with his hands until it was warm and elastic like a woman's breast. The feeling through his hands when the dough was ready. Is that how God made Adam? Pure instinct and touch. He couldn't take his hands away. "This is going to be a good one," and it would inflate into the perfect curve. He just knew it. Sometimes in the oven the shock would send it even higher. But never porous. Every loaf was different, sometimes with soya and sometimes with rye; no two were ever the same.

Hannah hated him in the kitchen.

"You're always interfering with the food. Always working without an apron. Look at your blue suit. Covered in flour! Have you washed your hands?"

He used to buy green chilies and fresh ginger from the Chinese man at the market to make curry, and pound six different spices by hand, the kitchen perfumed by the cardamom and cloves. But she never touched it. She left it on her plate and then ate bread and cheese in the kitchen.

"What have you put in it? Why don't you cook from a book?"

He used to make a salad with greens and radishes and spring onions and garlic. Sophie would stand next to him in privileged attendance, washing the lettuce – each leaf had to be perfect – and fresh coriander and basil, green sorrel and dill. He would roll up his sleeves, scrub his nails and then cut everything carefully into pieces. He would turn it only twice in the dressing with his hands so as not to bruise it. "Why don't you use vinegar? I hate lemon," she would say.

He never goes into the kitchen since they have moved to the new flat. It is too small and now he cannot see to make the bread.

How can he tell her gently that he needs her when it always comes out as a rage? Ask her nicely to take him for drives while he sits in the passenger seat and she stalls the car and grates the gears? He feels seasick when she stops and starts and brakes suddenly and starts again. How can he tell her that he is scared to be alone, frightened of the malignant darkness growing over his eyes? How can an old man talk about his childhood? Speak of the small boy lying alone in his room, stricken with the leprous light of the comet threatening him with an accusing finger in the night? Leprosy is coming? . . . leprosy is coming . . . And the terror in his sleep when he felt a presence in the blackness, lying with his eyes closed and sensing something shapeless and dark next to his bed, squatting, silent and foul . . . His fear to open his eyes and see its ugliness and its greed, wanting something in the darkness, its loathsome heart beating. "Shema Yisrael. Shema Yisrael." The only benediction he could think of. How he would hide away in his bed pulling in his feet and sweating under the blankets with his chest bursting, afraid to breathe.

And now, sometimes when he is sitting in the flat listening to the radio, everything suddenly goes black as in a box. Inside his head it is silent and a heavy weight crushes his chest. His throat tightens with fright. He stretches his eyes looking for light and turns to the window trying to breathe but it is black and airless. Waiting in terror and a ringing inside his head. He sees his own tombstone, his body numb, is he alive or dead? Then it is over and he is lying on the floor next to his overturned chair and he can breathe and see through the mist again.

He is afraid to be alone. An old coward with watery blood. How can he admit it to her or to Amy who calls him peevish, ungrateful for having reached a good age? Difficult! Unreasonable! She reprimands him like a child, giving him moral instruction. He needs help and he wants to tear his clothes with rage when Hannah leaves. Must he whimper and beg? Ask softly and appeal for pity? Must he grovel before she responds? And what if today the nightmare comes again and he is alone with the horror? What if there is no one to hear him choke or help him when he falls against the furniture, bleating like an old goat smelling slaughter? She's out and Sophie is standing at the window laughing with her friends while he lies on the floor gagging, rolling blind eyes and biting his tongue.

It was only comfort that he wanted from Sophie. His only indulgence is to feel cool hands on his creased forehead and on his blue swollen ankles. And his tortured legs that ache in his sleep. The skin on his body is still tender. Smooth for an old man. He wouldn't ask Hannah. He wants to be soothed and comforted like a child, like a boy, like a laughing schoolboy. It was only a little prank in the dark.

He gets up slowly from the chair, leaning forward to lift his back and straighten his legs. He grasps the handle of the radio, feeling his way into the sitting-room; careful not to slip on the rug or bump the corner of the chest. He asked Hannah months ago to clear the passage. He sits at the dining-room table listening to the one o'clock news, waiting for his lunch. He opens his eyes and focuses on the handle of the door. Then he slips the glasses down his nose and focuses again. He closes one eye to test it and then the other. He shuts his eyes and sits with his hands resting on his thighs.

She's late again.

TWENTY-NINE

Summer

IT WASN'T JUST THE HEAT. THE FULL-BLOWN HEAT THAT STARTS EARLY IN the morning from first light, spreading from inside the whole red core of the earth as it lies quietly to bake. Not just the heat, hanging full and turgid like an orchid's ooze or a musk-cat's stink. It wasn't just the heat. It was also the sound. Muffled sound – like the sound in fog or steam, or underwater sound that throbs, or goldfish sound pouting behind glass, or the sound of slow bubbles in a pot of porridge breaking in a puff. The sound that comes from far away and not quite arriving. The summer sound of one dove purring and the bark of one dog.

Amy knew the high summer green of dark shadows on the grass – nearly black – and the emerald highlights. Forever green, except for the mulberries crushed underfoot, and purple teeth, and the figs split open and bleeding. Jungle-green, with weeds suckering like tentacles. Juicy green spilling out all over, and the guinea-fowl grazing the grass like cows.

She also knew it was summer from the rain that fell at night like sweat, and the thunder like a drumming in her heart; and the sound from far away but only in the room next door. The sound of coughing, like the sawing of hard wood; metal teeth tearing through the flesh of wood, in the dark, in the room next door. His room.

Summer. She could feel it. Not on her skin, sticky as a stamen and slightly sweet; nor the way her thighs rubbed when she walked, the smell like tea from her armpits or the damp between her legs. It was that summer feeling like bees tumbling in jammy figs. There was something wriggling and gnawing in the unstable deep, wallowing like jelly, precariously inside her, and insidiously inside him.

In the room next door.

Summer, but cool in the house with stone floors and small windows. She sews in the coolness, looking up after every second stitch, sometimes after a third, looking up for a long time and then drawing the thread like a whisper. Pink silk in her fingers – a pink thing in silk like a wild bird on her lap.

Pink threads and fragments blow onto the grass and a small brown bird picks them up and flies away with streamers of silk to line a nest in a thorn-tree. The other fragments still lie on the grass, burning pink, too hot for a bird to touch.

Burning like fever in the room next door.

The black woman sits in the kitchen fanning herself with the corners of her apron, humming like summer bees, her heels slipped over the backs of her shoes. She has taken off her doek. She looks shy and small without the white starched cotton swathed around her head like a turban; and suddenly rude and nude with the hair erupting through the skin in little bushes. Amy has never seen her without her doek before. Is that how her hair grows in the other places too?

"Too hot for tea. Too hot to eat," the woman says, humming in the kitchen – a song learnt under thatch, sitting near her mother's feet, playing with sheep's knuckles on a cool dung floor.

Time is moving towards Christmas. She knows because they're all outside. The Apostolic Church. The Lutheran Church. The Methodist Church. The Church of Zion. Money, clothes, candles, food. "God bless you, madam. God bless." The man from the Catholic Church only asks for water.

Hot afternoons. Asleep in a chair and a book on the floor. Her leg kicks out suddenly and wakes her up. The green place outside waits with leaves beginning to curl. The willow, like an old elephant, with thick bark and shags of leaves waits for the rain with a twitch and a tremble.

Thursday afternoon. They all enter the house through the hot door; they stand there with the sun on their backs and she has the sun on her face as she opens, like opening the oven door. Marina stoops with the bag on her back, and the tennis racket, and shoes strapped to the bag, like a long-distance hiker. Knee-high socks rolled down into doughnuts around her ankles, and her earlobes transparent pink from the sun behind her head. She drops everything at the door and goes to lie down on her bed, "Too hot to eat." Little brown spots sprinkle her nose. Her midsummer nose and her fingers puff and prickle from the heat. "How can I play? Look at my fingers."

The piano teacher rings the bell and waits outside until he is rescued. He comes in through the hot door. The shiny skin on top of his head has brown spots turning into scabs. He has tea at every house. "Too hot for tea," he says. "Just water."

She takes her sewing into the bedroom. The pink silk creature is limp with smudge-marks where she holds it and the smell of her fingers is turning sour. She slides deep into a chair and looks out of the window, watching the trees – the way people at the seaside watch the sea. She tries to remember how it feels when it rains. The mercy when first drops fall onto hot stone, and steam and sizzle at the touch; the big drops that reach dry earth, and the powdery film that forms around them like a skin. The whole green world drinking, and water falling off the eaves like fringes; the secret place where birds go when it rains. She wonders how it feels when her neck is cool, and her hair twists into corkscrews like ferns curling through damp soil, and the clover is standing stiff.

She looks into the room. The room is also full of presences: a birthday card stuck on a wall – a little dancing man with a yellow face, wearing striped leggings and embroidered short pants. He waves a confetti umbrella over his head that bursts into a shower of sequins and stars: "To a year of smiling in Africa." Guinea fowl feathers stick out of a pepper pot moulded by a child's hands into the shape of a cat – crooked eyes, one broken ear and nearly no mouth. "Three Monkeys" in bronze on a table next to a small glazed duck without a nose; a framed picture of a girl in a red-checked dress, her knees loose with laughter; a nugget of fool's gold on a silver salver. The bedspread is embroidered with pink pelicans and peacocks. Another birthday card stands on a desk with pictures of fighting cocks. On the reverse side, some words:

> *There's no vocabulary*
> *For love within a family, love that's lived in*
> *But not looked at, love within the light of which*
> *All else is seen, the love within which*
> *All other love finds speech. This love is silent.*
> *Sorry. And sorry.*

"Für Elize" falls heavily on the air; hammers hit against thick felt without resonance. The child's swollen hands fall about the keys.

"'F'sharp! F'sharp!" The teacher takes the hot finger and hits it down on the note three times. "Für Elize" and a cup of tea in every house – today, a glass of water. She hears the scrape of the chair on the floor and intercepts the teacher in the passageway; opens the front door like opening the oven and lets him out.

On the other side of the house, the cold side where he sleeps and coughs, the side where storms come in from the south, dark clouds are forming.

She goes into the kitchen, the coolest room; sits down and watches the child eat her sandwiches. She loves watching people eat – putting the food in their mouths, chewing, swallowing. Is the child enjoying the sandwiches or has she noticed that the bread has formed a crust from the heat? Amy gets up and walks past the room that used to be the dining-room. The dog is eating an old bone. He always eats his bones in the room that used to be the dining-room. She lies on the carpet next to him; a privilege he allows her. She loves lying next to him when he is eating a bone – the dull knock of teeth, the slow grind through cartilage down to unbreakable core; an ancient sound: gnawing.

The rasp of coughing wakes her in the night; far away but only in the room next door. She sits on the edge of the bed in the dark. A summer feeling of something gnawing in the deep. Unstable deep that heaves and wallows like jelly and shudders like her heart; a feeling, for a moment – something shooting through her like lightning in a summer sky.

It has been raining, soft and slow like a night emission. She goes to the window – cool air against her skin. The green place is dark, unseen in its night-time life, with a white sky, like mutton-fat, hanging low. The green dark place, steaming like a hothouse and Guy Fawkes stars falling in a far-away sky. She goes back to bed, suddenly aware of her nakedness and the touch of her hands, a stranger's hands; cunning. Outside moths nuzzle in the cactus flower . . .

Outside in the dark place, with the strange silky creature . . . She holds it, and strokes its wings . . . a wild thing, pink and silky.

THIRTY
Mud

IT IS TIME TO TEND THE DEAD – THE TIME BETWEEN NEW YEAR AND THE DAY of Atonement. Time to think, to remember and to make peace. Time to give them pleasure, those unclad bones – our dead.

Max and Hannah are waiting at the bus stop for Amy. "It's a funny thing how you always have to be early. Looking at your watch even while I'm putting the food in my mouth and looking again as I swallow. You give me indigestion with your looking," Max says.

"If you had a childhood like mine, you would understand."

"What is five minutes in the universe?"

He sits on the bench talking to the people waiting for the bus. He doesn't really mind being early because he likes to be released from his isolation into the clamour of the street. Old people like bus stops.

Amy pulls up at the bench, obstructing three cars while Max approaches with mincing steps. His eyes are red from an operation. He holds his hat as he gets stiffly into the car, bottom first, hitting his head on the metal frame of the door and then dragging his legs inside after him. Hannah sits at the back humming.

They begin the journey through the living city, immediately absorbed into the stream of fast-moving cars. The hearse of the Jewish Burial Society overtakes, starkly functional – a plain black van with one large door at the back which opens wide at the hinge. They drive past the Hillbrow Police Station, flag flying, past the Transport Workers Hostel which used to be the Queen Victoria Maternity Hospital, past the clinic for disturbed children – on one wall is painted SNOW and on the other FREE MANDELA. They turn off at Helpmekaar Boys High and the Holiday Inn, speckled deep pink with the blossoms of a kapok tree.

They turn into Judith Road – the ordinary street with face-brick houses and standard rose-trees, that leads to the stone city: the city of the dead. A dreaded road, Judith, and yet just a suburban thoroughfare. Neat houses end abruptly in the wild bush of Melville Koppies where thorn-trees and long grass are enclosed by barbed wire, turned open to the public twice a month like a museum. The road rises and suddenly, like the click of a camera, the wide lawns of West Park spread across the horizon, studded with rows of tombstones, standing like fortifications. They cross D.F. Malan Street and stop at the flower-sellers sitting on either side of the gate to the cemetery.

"Cheap, Madam, cheap." They buy three bunches. "Quite enough for four graves," says Hannah. "Buy the yellow ones for Eva. She always loved yellow. And roses for my mother."

They drive around to the second entrance, passing a jogger in red satin running shorts and a man washing his car. A dog barks at the jogger.

"I wonder what it's like living next to a cemetery?" Hannah asks.

"Very quiet," says Amy.

The new graves have reached down to the entrance gate. Fresh mounds of soil lie in wait.

"Running out of space," says Max.

They drive up the road going backwards in time. Nineteen eighty-four, nineteen eighty-three, nineteen eighty-two; Robinson lies next to Graff who lies next to Miller who lies next to Lewis, with Kruger, Benjamin and Simon on all sides. Glossy rectangles of grey marble stand to attention – neighbours for all time.

"Not even enough room to stretch in," says Max.

They pass the central building called the House of Life which houses the mortuary.

"I always prefer the old part. Undisturbed and neglected, occupied by birds and lizards, absorbed back into nature," Hannah says.

The ground is soft underfoot from three days of rain and their feet sink as they step off the cement path. Mischa Alexander's tombstone is falling sideways toward Eva's grave and dandelions are growing out of the cracks. The stones are faded and dull like their grief. Hannah separates the yellow chrysanthemums and places them in the steel receptacle at the foot of the slab. Max stands behind the headstone, rocking forward and back: "May His great name be blessed . . . beyond any blessing and song, praise and consolation that are uttered in the world . . ."

It is thirty years since Eva died. She lived alone until the illness overwhelmed her, then she stayed with Max for the last six weeks of her life.

"She refused a bedpan and washed her own body and her teeth until she died. She was hard as a tattooed desert woman and unyielding as fate. She never spoke about her life and she never resisted her death. Life made her rugged as an old tree. I bruised myself against her for a long time when I was young, but I won her over in the end," says Hannah.

A gravedigger comes toward them with a watering-can and a cloth. He fills the flower container and wipes off the white granite, showing its fine pink veins. Next to Eva's grave lie Ellie and Solomon Kraft in a joint grave. He outlived her by four years, leaving his "grieving children and grandchildren," and returned to Ellie in the matrimonial bed.

Amy and Hannah walk back to the car and cross over to the adjoining block, looking for the other white tombstone. Damp clods cling to the soles of their shoes and they scrape off the mud on the grass. Max stands next to the grave with closed eyes . . . "Blessed, praised, glorified, exalted . . ."

"Poor Theo. He died a year after Eva, almost to the day. One floor down from us on the other side of the building. The cleaner found him in the morning, lying on his bed, fully clothed, with his collar open and his tie loosened around his neck. There was a glass of water next to the bed. He must have felt ill but he didn't even call us, one floor away. The two brothers remained estranged. His widow writes to us through the lawyer who manages the money," says Hannah.

Extolled, mighty, upraised, and lauded be the Name of the Holy One, Blessed is He. . .

Amy remembers the man sitting in the corner of the room, never smiling or speaking, with brown stains on his fingers. He never looked at her. He never looked at anyone but his eyes were dark and brooding. Every night he sat in the room without speaking until late and then he went home.

. . . Beyond any blessing and song, praise and consolation that are uttered in the world . . .

The gravedigger pours water into the vase and Max pays him. They watch him wipe the sand and sludge off the stone, dipping the rag into the bucket and squeezing out the muddy water with his hands. The white stone is weathered from thirty years of exposure.

> *. . . may there be abundant peace from Heaven, and life, upon us . . . He who makes peace in His heights, may He make peace upon us . . .*

They walk back to the car and scrape thick mud off the soles of their shoes again.

"Good soil," says Max. "Gets plenty of nourishment."

They reverse down the hill and drive along the road until it is blocked by a low wall. Max waits in the car while Hannah and Amy walk along the footpath looking for the nineteen sixty-nines – Fanya Goodman, Maurice Mendelsohn, nineteen sixty-seven. Amy is beginning to know her way, like visiting a friend who is always at home. Jackie Daniels, nineteen sixty-eight. They walk between the graves, their feet sinking into the soil. Some are only rough mounds of earth with a metal plate marked "reserved", and still waiting to be occupied by the wife or husband still alive, years later.

"There it is."

The stone is engraved across its belly with a remembrance from Rosa's two daughters and son-in-law; a heavy covering for the fragile woman underneath. Amy remembers how Granny Rosa arrived at her house with a raw chicken and vegetables to make soup, while she sat sleepless and unwashed in a closed room, helpless with a week-old baby and a house full of relatives demanding tea. A strong salty broth scented with herbs when she was too confused to shop or cook. She ate it with relish. Years later she remembers visiting Rosa at the old age home: the large square building with its sweet smell of sick bodies and stale air that hung like a barrier across the entrance. Rosa lay in a cot, tubes draining urine into a bottle, gentle in her dementia. If it was mealtime she would offer Amy a boiled potato or ice-cream and jelly. She laughed her witch-like cackle and hummed old Bolshevik songs, her girlish body sitting upright in bed, refusing to lie down until she died.

"She never got a bunch of flowers in her life," says Hannah.

"Yes, but she was happy in her flat with Dora."

"She loved her flat. 'My little flat,' she used to say, until that rotter Boris Peskanoff took all her savings and Dora's also and went to Australia where he married again."

They walk back to the car, leaving footprints in the wet earth behind them.

Max is waiting in the car, blinking and focusing on the nearest inscription to exercise his eyes. Hannah and Amy step over the graves and bump into tombstones, scrape the red mud off their shoes with a stick; thick clods that cling to their fingers. Amy wipes her hands on her skirt, leaving a smudge and rubs off the smudge with the cuff of her blouse.

They reverse back to the House of Life, compelled by religious law to wash their hands. Max puts money into the charity box. On the way out Amy acknowledges the section set aside for soldiers' graves.

"They fled Russia to avoid conscription into the Czar's army. They came here, and three generations later it's the same thing. Another Czar, another army and some have fled again."

Lichtenstein, Lewis, Miller, Graff – nineteen eighty-two, nineteen eighty-three, nineteen eighty-four . . . They drive out of the gate. The Indian flower-sellers are doing a brisk trade. Max sits in the front next to Amy with his hat on. He holds his walking-stick as a rudder to navigate the car. Hannah sits at the back humming. She leans forward between them: "Tell me Amy, are we going to the market tomorrow? And can we go to the Portuguese shop to buy fish and cheese and olives?"

"It's a funny thing how you are always leaving me. I used to take you everywhere and sometimes I waited in the car for hours. But now you just leave me." Max shakes his head appealing to a higher authority.

"If I don't shop for food, what are you going to eat? I don't know where all my tomatoes have gone. Sixty-two in a box, I counted them, and now there are only fifteen left. Sophie used ten to make soup and let's say we ate fifteen before that. But where are the rest? I'm missing twenty-two tomatoes," says Hannah.

Amy looks at her through the reverse mirror, and her face is smudged with mud.

THIRTY-ONE
Election

MAX IS A SPHINX. HE SITS IN HIS CHAIR WITH HIS EYES CLOSED, MYSTERIES and riddles behind them. His back is straight, always, even though a small sore is beginning to develop from his life of sitting. His shoulders balance squarely with his feet, sphinx-like on the floor. But he dresses in a suit, every day. Shoes without laces are indulgent, suspenders are vulgar, and underpants are effeminate. He has never learned to be casual. He wears a stiff white collar and tie, even when he goes to visit Amy on Sundays; usually the green-checked suit with leather-bound lapels and buttonholes.

"Look how they've repaired these buttonholes. A masterpiece. Do you know how old this suit is? Do you know how much we paid for these shoes?"

He clutches the round knob of his walking-stick, worn smooth and shiny from the oils of his hand and glowing yellow as an eagle's eye. He disdains a rubber cap on the tip. He is not lame! And it slides under his weight like a treacherous limb. It is not an invalid's stick! It is a mystic rod given to him by a holy man and when he holds it he feels the force in his fingers.

"Where's my stick? I was holding it in my hand and now it's gone."

Hannah comes into the room and picks it up from the floor. Sometimes he strikes the air with it in his rage and sometimes he opens his cloudy eyes and points with it like a holy staff.

Hannah says to him, "Come, Max. Don't be upset, eat your lunch quietly. Put down the stick."

"Send Sophie down for the newspaper," he orders, feeling for his back pocket where he keeps his wallet – Italian leather, finely engraved with gold, soft and dark from handling.

"Do you know how old this wallet is?"

He holds it with his left hand and feels for a note with his thumb and index finger. The same movement as when Amy and Paul were small and he would reach into his back pocket slowly, so slowly with his hand while they watched, not knowing whether they would get all, or a part, or none of their weekly money. They would stand in front of him and count. Then

Paul would beg for the remainder. And he would have to earn it piecemeal with good behaviour and improved marks at school. Amy would get it all and store it away in a box. Once Paul opened her locked metal box with a tin-opener. He ripped it open like a sardine tin, emptying all her shiny lucky pennies and silver coins that she had polished with a soft cloth every day. Then later he had stood in front of Max with the ravaged box in his hand, denying his responsibility. "Responsibility" was Max's word.

He still keeps his money in his wallet. He counts it and spends it, but his feet have not been into a shop for years. Hannah still asks, "Max, can I have some money for milk? I want to shop for supper. Can I have some money for meat and eggs and two lettuces and a bread for breakfast?" There is a kind of pleading in her voice. He lifts his chest and takes out his wallet with his right hand, feeling for the notes with his thumb and index finger. "Bring me the change."

When Amy comes to visit she stands in the kitchen listening to Hannah, while Sophie makes tea.

"He had a bad night again and I could hardly sleep. I was dreaming of Arab women swimming in a canopied pagoda. Then he woke me up and I made him warm milk and honey. What do you think it meant? The dream? And then he slept again. This morning I let him rest late until the sun was in the room and I washed him all over and combed his hair."

Hannah tells Amy not to forget Friday for dinner and she tells her not to be late and not to argue with Paul and Margaret. The table will be set with silver candlesticks and a lace cloth will cover the plaited bread. Hannah will have to chatter and laugh and tell jokes and repeat them again. She might have to kick Paul's foot under the table. "I've shopped and cooked and worked hard and there must be no arguments on a Friday night! We eat half a roast lamb and you all go home with indigestion."

"Do you know the cost of half a lamb?" Max asks.

Hannah carries tea into the room for him. She strokes his head and tells him to rest, covering his legs with a blanket and sitting down in a chair to knit. She switches on a light because a building obstructs the sun. They used to be able to see the Magaliesberg. Now they are surrounded by other people's windows and balconies with washing hanging out to dry. Some of the windows are empty and the curtains have come down because many people are leaving. Already the youngest and prettiest are going to Australia and Canada, leaving the old people behind. The same as when she left her country more than fifty years ago.

But Hannah is not leaving! "My mother and my grandmother are buried here and Max has made the buildings that still stand in the old part of town. And what country would take a man of ninety?"

When she reads the newspaper to him it tells of siege. People using ugly words like "bloodbath in the streets" and the experts say there is no money and few jobs. She reads carefully, asking first, "Do you want to hear about the price of petrol? Or shall I read to you about the drought and the new loans to farmers? Three black activists have disappeared in Grahamstown." Once when she read something to him he said, "Cut it out. I want to keep it in my pocket." Then when people come to the flat to visit, Max asks her to take the paper out of his pocket and read it to them: "Last year two whites became Malay, fourteen Malays became White, nine Indians became White, seven Chinese became White, forty Coloureds became Black, six hundred and sixty-six Blacks became Coloured, eighty-seven Coloureds became Indian, sixty-seven Indians became Coloured, fifty Malays became Indian, four Coloureds became Griquas, and two Griquas became Black. Eighteen Blacks became Griqua, twelve Coloureds became Chinese, ten Blacks became Indian, two Blacks became other Asian, two other Coloureds became Indian, and one Coloured became Black. One Griqua became White, twenty-six Coloureds became Malay, and sixty-one Indians became Malay. No Blacks applied to become White."

Then he takes his stick and pokes the air with it. Hannah says, "Don't be upset, Max." And the visitors say, "Thank you for tea, but we really must go." And they leave.

Hannah has seen many wars in her life but this one is different. When she walks in the street she does not know who is her enemy or who is her friend. It is everywhere. The little black children stand around the shops asking for money for bread and picking up cigarette stubs to smoke. There is a thin black woman, always in the same place; everyone knows her. Hannah thought she was a leper because her face looked as though it was peeling and her hands were covered with flaking skin. "Don't give her any money," someone said, "she's a glue-sniffer." But Hannah did not know how to say no. Then when she looked back at the woman she was already putting a small white bottle to her nose.

It is not like the war that Hannah knew as a child, when they filled themselves with garbage, aching with hunger. Here, she looks through doorways into restaurants and they are full of people, and women go to the hairdresser and paint their nails. And some black people are driving cars and moving into flats vacated by whites. While around the corner there might be a roadblock with white men in khaki searching cars. When she goes to a shop, even for a loaf of bread, a policeman looks into her bag for bombs.

"Why are you looking into my handbag? I'm old enough to be your grandmother. Every second man is walking around with a gun in his belt. Search them!" she says.

At home Sophie whispers in the kitchen in her own language and downstairs the flat-cleaners drink. Every night there are sirens in the street and the police station next door was blown up with a mine.

When Amy comes to the flat she asks Max, "What's going to happen, Pa?" And he says, "I don't know what's going to happen." And when Marina asks him, "What's going to happen, Grandpa?" he replies, "I don't know what's going to happen, my girlie."

Then they stand with Sophie in the kitchen and they ask her, "What's going to happen, Sophie?" And she lifts her shoulders and opens her palms upwards and says, "I don't know what's going to happen."

Next week there is going to be another white election. "For what? For what?" and Max tries to lift himself out of the chair. All the black leaders say it is irrelevant. But for the first time in her life, Hannah is voting. She bangs her fist on the table: "I want my paper to be counted! One revolution was enough!"

They are all coming up to the flat to try and get her vote: first the lady who says that she will guarantee white suburbs, and then the young man who says that some suburbs will be permitted to go grey. "What kind of a colour is grey?" Max asks him. And then the other man comes and asks why one suburb should be grey when all the others are either white or black? People must be allowed to live anywhere they can afford to.

Everyone in the building is asking whether the coloured people should be permitted to stay. But Hannah will not allow them to be moved! She wants her paper to be counted! They pay their rent and keep the flat clean.

Hannah has lived in the building for thirty years and she will not allow them to be moved!

"What kind of colour is 'coloured'?" Max wants to know.

He is sitting in his chair, waiting for lunch, a napkin tucked into his collar to cover his tie and shirt. Hannah is sweeping the breadcrumbs off the floor at his feet from breakfast. He begins to sing a song, tapping out the rhythm with his stick:

> O Mr Porter what shall I do?
> I want to go to Bendigo, send me back to Crewe
> I want to go to London as quickly as I can
> O Mr Proter what a silly boy I am.

"My mother used to sing me that song," he says. "To me and Theo when we lived in Jan and Trudie's house. Poor Theo." The muscles in his face suddenly twist as though something has broken.

Hannah gets up and strokes his head. He must not be upset.

The results of the election are out, and it has gone badly. It is no longer in her hands. Was it ever? Decisions are always made by other people who think differently. She must just sit and watch which way it goes.

It is autumn in Amy's garden. A long late autumn. The leaves have turned yellow but still hang on the trees because there is no wind to shake them off. Max and Hannah visit her on Sundays as an outing and to escape from the flat; the same chairs in the same place, and their angle always the same – to catch the morning sun or to watch TV in the afternoon. Max opens his shirt and rolls up his sleeves, holding his hands up to the sun like antennae, receiving its heat. So quiet on the grass, still green from the summer and only the crested barbets can be heard, screeching over a piece of paw-paw on the feeding-tray. Amy is somewhere in the garden trapping wild cats to protect the birds; one species sacrificed to save another.

And the trees remain very still, growing slowly inside into wider and wider rings.

THIRTY-TWO

Berth

AMY KNEW THAT JOSH WOULD DO HIS DYING AT HOME, THE SAME AS HE came home at night to do his sleeping. That is what home was for.

He did his living elsewhere.

Every night of his life he would prepare for the morning: put out a pair of socks, a vest, and a shirt. He would lay them out tenderly, freshly ironed, to wear the next day. The suit would be lying on the chair, ready to step into the shape and smell of the day before.

In the morning she would hear the click of the latch as he opened the front door and then the slam as the door closed behind him. She would be dead for him during the next twelve hours after which he would return with the newspaper and his briefcase. Tired.

After supper he would leave the table and prepare his clothes for the morning again.

And now he has come home for good. Unfit for anything else. He asks for ice-cream repeatedly; "Ice-cream. Ice-cream." He eats it delicately with a small spoon, leaving smears on his moustache. Sometimes he forgets to wear his trousers. Home for good. Sent home to do his dying.

Now she does the talking. She speaks for him. And dresses herself bright. She will be vivid for them both. He wears a hat to hide his head, slightly strange now with a bald patch. She will be funny. Make him laugh. They buy him pills for the pain, and when the chemist asks, "What for?" he says, "Just a little cancer." And they bend over laughing. Laughing down the street.

If he is to die, then let him die well. She will help him.

She walks him through the garden to show him the flowers, leading him by the hand.

"You're a good woman," he tells her.

That is not what she wanted to be!

She buys a gold wedding ring and puts it on his finger.

He never wore one.

THIRTY-THREE
Love

I KNOW I AM BEGINNING TO HATE PA BY THE WAY I AM LOOKING AT HIM.

"Amy, why don't you sit with me and talk to me?" he asks.

So I go into the room and sit down. I am wearing black leather boots that make knocking noises as I walk on the tiles. I walk with long strides when I wear those boots, long strides swinging forward from the hip. Heel-toe-stride. Knocking on the floor. "Today I look like a policeman," I say to the woman in the kitchen. "Blue trousers, blue shirt and long black boots." The woman looks at what I am wearing and we both laugh. I am a little surprised by my voice; strident as when I tell Pa that I am busy and not to call me so much. Not my old voice that wavered when I spoke to him. I like my new voice. I wonder whether I can find it in my throat even when I am not wearing my black boots. A voice that sounds as though it knows what it wants and will not be contradicted. My face feels good when I use that voice; no expression in it, and a kind of stare in my eyes that looks straight at him without my feeling ashamed. They all go together – eyes, voice and boots. And a straight back, but not stiff or forced. Just like the black boots, strong and straight when I take them off and they stand on the floor next to my bed – erect and to attention, with the shape of my foot inside. I always wear those blue trousers when I wear the boots and a black leather belt threaded through the loops, pulled tight into my waist, holding everything in place. It feels strong and good, being belted into place, and it makes my mouth turn up slightly in one corner. Not a smile. Not visible when I look in the mirror trying to find it. But I can feel it. And it goes with the stare in my eyes and the belt and boots.

I know I am beginning to hate Pa by the way I am looking at him.

"Why don't you sit with me and talk?" He doesn't just ask in an ordinary voice, an ordinary question. It is a voice that gets its way by begging.

"What do you want to talk about?" I am sitting across the room from him and I can see my black boots in the mirror and my legs crossed over. I know I am beginning to hate him by the way I don't try to speak to him and the way I swing my legs and the black boots swinging. I can see them in the mirror, in need of a buff and a polish. Black polish is best – it gives them a darkness and the brightest lights. And then the flannel: first gentle rubbing and then smart snapping with the cloth held tight; a little punishment to bring it all to life, hard and soft at the same time. "Never ask anyone to clean your shoes," he used to tell me. "That's something you do for yourself." And he taught me how: "Don't be in a hurry about it; take your time nicely, and spit on it to make it spread. Water's not the same, doesn't stick. Not too much polish either. Be mean and work it. Work it with your arm till the fat breaks down and delivers up the lights. Then work those lights till they flash like black eyes shining. And look after the heels. Keep them trim. And pick up your feet when you walk. Let them hear you coming by the click-click of your heels when you walk."

I can see my boots in the mirror, the sun warming the black polish and sending out the lights.

I know that I am beginning to hate him by the feel of my face. The slow blinking of my lids: not fast and in a flutter the way they sometimes do, not the way they did when I was a child. And the arch of my eyebrow. I can feel it. Just to look at him, sitting there with his eyes closed. Always with his eyes closed and his glasses on his nose, dirty, because he never looks through them except to see if I am still sitting there or to watch me walk past the room when he hears the click-clicking down the passage. "Why don't you come and talk to me?" when he hears the clicking.

"I'm coming," I say. I know I am beginning to hate him because I walk straight past without even looking in. Walking past, heel-toe-stride. Heel-toe-stride.

"Love is turning to hate," I hear him say as I walk past. "Do you remember the time with the tortoise? The day he disappeared? And you asked me, 'Pa, when is the tortoise coming back?' And I said, 'When the first rains come, then the tortoise will come back.' Do you remember?"

I know I am beginning to hate him because I don't answer. He always speaks about the tortoise. Tries to make me remember. That is another way of begging.

I don't want to remember the tortoise. Silly to be standing here in my boots, already with lines on my face, remembering the tortoise. Very far away, but close, the feeling inside me: the small house and a garden right next to the pavement; the feel of curls around my face. Silly to remember the curls around my face. And looking down the empty street for the tortoise. The street with other houses that were the same – small gardens near the pavement and every house with a big palm-tree near the gate. The street going far back, climbing higher, and if you went right back you could see the mountain. And the black scorpions that fell into the yard, pitch-black with large pincers like land crabs, but also with sharp stingers on their tails. If you went down the slanty hill, all the way, you came to the sea; feet stamping in the sea or standing still with the twirly waves tickling your toes. Strange to remember stamping feet and ticklish toes as I stand here in my black boots. Then, when it rained, the tortoise walked back – just as he had said. And a feeling like a bouncing ball as I stood in the empty street and saw the little creature coming back, walking up the pavement and under the gate. "I told you the tortoise would come home," Pa had said. He was right. How did he know those things? You could ask him anything. A ticklish feeling inside me to see the tortoise coming home. Pa was wearing white trousers and a white shirt and jacket that men wore in Durban.

But sometimes he was wrong. Another feeling, small and far away, but grown through me – like the dark rings in a tree. Pa's voice, not soft any more, but stiff as a stick, and loud when he told Paul that he was "a recalcitrant youth", and there was nothing sorry in Pa's voice. Silly to want him to be sorry for what he said, as I stand here in my boots. And a strict voice when he asked me, "Why don't you sit in the front of the class, near the teacher? You're always sitting at the back where no one can see you and you don't have to try. Hiding away at the back with the girls who stayed down." But that is where I wanted to be – at the back with Doris and Julie, leaning over my desk, with Evalina's head blocking out everything in front. Evalina, with her bushy hair; you could do what you liked behind it. Just to be quiet and alone at the back, looking at the bow pinned in Evalina's hair with everything springing out all around it. How hard it was to hide behind her head when her hair was held down with ribbons and clips, because then her head was half the size. Leaning over my desk, just letting my hand do what it wanted: sometimes patterns like a continuous wave circling over and over into peaks all around the margins of the page, or fine black lines drawn close together and other lines crossing through like a web, or circles starting wide and getting closer – very dark and inky in the middle – circles that turned into beads or bubbles or eggs, or circles that imploded into their own black centres. Some pages were filled with stars and shells and rivers of fish. And sometimes when the teacher's voice came through, my hand would write a word over and over on the page – any word, like "plateau" in geography. My hand would make boxes and squares and bars around it. Once my hand wrote "fire" all over the page and once "food", and I darkened the O's into small eyes staring.

That is where I wanted to sit. Quiet at the back with Julie and Doris, and the teacher fussing over the girls in the front. I did not want to sit in the front. And that is what I told them when Pa came to school to speak to the teacher. I did not believe that I deserved it. I had not earned it. You had to be entitled to sit with the girls who did their homework and cared about their marks. And if you sat in the middle, like Evalina, you were with the girls who were encouraged for "trying". But at the back it was quiet and you were left alone and no one cared if you passed or failed and you could see everyone in front of you and there was only the wall behind. In winter you were near the heaters and if you looked out of the window nobody would know, or if you put your head down to sleep no one could see, especially if Evalina's hair was bushed out.

At break I liked to walk around on my own, up and down the narrow cement pathways between the grass. I did not know how to saunter up to the girls standing together in noisy clusters, rowdy and laughing: Francine, near the tennis courts, sharing out her sandwiches and dividing up her cake; Joyce and Lola, sitting on the bench, talking about their penfriends in England; and Veronica and Geraldine and Cath, combing their hair and talking about clothes. I would have liked to share Francine's sandwiches and taste her cake but I didn't know how to hold out my hand. Asking was the trouble. Especially if you were not entitled or deserving.

There was no place at home that was like the back of the class. "You have deeply disappointed me," he had said with his stiff, straight voice, the same as when he spoke to Paul about school, or to the small dog that was big now and was not stroked and petted or allowed to sleep on your lap any more. "You're spoiling him. Making him soft," Pa had said. Even then there were times when I was beginning to hate him for being "disappointed" and for quarrelling with Paul and making Mother ask for money. There was no quiet place like under the chair where the dog hid away from his voice or like the dark place under the bed where the dog gnawed his bones.

And there was another voice that came from far away, or close as a key turning in a lock – a thin voice, like the dog's when he used to stand outside the door wanting to come in. That was the way to ask when you were not deserving or entitled and there was something you wanted. Just hold out your hand in front of you, and with that thin voice, ask. But at last when Pa opened the door for the dog, he no longer wanted to come in.

I know I am beginning to hate him because I do not care if I am late with his pills: half in the morning after breakfast and one after dinner at night. That was how Hannah told me to give them to him when she went into the hospital. And my husband dead and Pa living in my house now because Hannah is sick. Pa reading my husband's newspaper and using his shower as though no one else had ever used it; as though it is his right. I am old enough to be a widow but never old enough to be a wife. And here in my own house now, but still with my father and still a child.

"You'll bury us all," I tell him, "and then there will only be a nanny to look after you."

"He just lies back like a lord when Sophie washes him – everywhere," Hannah had said. "And then she sleeps next to him in my bed at night like a wife, while I sleep on a metal bed on the verandah. But he still wakes me up if he wants something. And Sophie just sleeps."

"It's not true," Pa said. "I call and call and nobody comes. Must I lie there and wet my pants like a baby before anyone hears? One day I'll die in my bed and they'll sleep through the night."

"I'm exhausted from him," Hannah said, "and in the morning he's up early calling me for tea. Sophie takes a nap in the afternoon and I give her more money for watching him at night, but she sits next door watching TV. No one washes him like I do: top to toe and then I clean his teeth. But he only praises Sophie."

"Lies. All lies. I've done everything for her, and now she just leaves me. I open my eyes as I'm talking to her and she's not even in the room. She leaves me talking to myself like an idiot."

"And then there's his money. I've saved all my life but he can keep it all. He's older than me but I'll die before him."

I know I am beginning to hate Pa because I don't care if I am late with his lunch. I hear him calling my name – calling and calling. And then I still wait until his voice is thin and reedy with calling, "Be a dear and bring me my lunch." I wait until he asks nicely. There are ways of asking when you are not entitled. I walk slowly towards his room. Slowly down the passage, stopping every now and then to look at the pictures on the wall. And eventually standing in his room with my hand on my hip – the hip tilted out sideways – giving him his lunch and waiting to walk out of the room. "Why don't you stay and talk to me?"

I know that I am beginning to hate him when I answer, 'What do you want me to say?' my voice strong and the slow fall of my lids and the boots shining back at me in the mirror; tapping my toe a little.

"Just like a policeman," says the woman in the kitchen.

"Not the ones in khaki," I say, "who drive those yellow and blue vans with bars on the windows like the dog-catcher, but catching people. 'Waar's jou pas?' And their nails all bitten down and dirty."

"Sies," says the woman.

"And their cheeks are pink and their noses turn upward into a snub. And their shoes! I could teach them how to keep their shoes." Both of us are laughing. "No, the other policemen," I say, "with dark glasses like compound eyes and long black boots, shiny and bright. And tight trousers that curve out around their hips, the holster on one side and the pink pad on the other. The police who walk slowly but smart inside their boots or ride sleek motorbikes and say: 'Pull over to the side.'"

"Haven't you got anything to say?" he asks. I know I hate him because I have nothing to say. When I go into his room I can see a metal bottle with a long neck standing in the corner for when he wakes up at night. Sometimes I can hear him and Sophie talking softly. What are they saying? And in the shower this morning I could see it on the soap! His pubic hair or mine in my dead husband's shower, on the soap. No respect for the dead. Nowhere for me to rest and recover. My own house now and still nowhere to be alone like the dog lying on the cushion in the corner where he sleeps at night.

"Turn the radio up and turn the music down," he says.

"Say please!" I say.

There are ways of talking when you are not entitled.

Every day the click-click of my boots as I walk past his room.

"Do you remember how I told you that the tortoise would come back?"

I look at him directly. I like the way my eyelids drop slowly and I like the sound of my voice.

It is remarkable how I found things to like in myself when I began to hate my father.

THIRTY-FOUR
Home

AMY IS WALKING PAST ME, STRUTTING DOWN THE PASSAGE. I HEAR HER steps on the stone floor coming closer. She knows I can hear the tap of her heels and the swish as she strides. Closer. She knows that I am sitting here with Sophie and I can't move, just waiting to hear her steps turn into the room. I feel a beat in my heart and I'm hardly breathing. She just calls out, "... Morning..." I know she hates me because she smiles at Sophie and she doesn't look at me as she walks down the passage. That emptiness when I hear her footsteps turn away and I can only wait for her to return. She walks up and down knowing that I'm waiting for her to come back. "I'm busy," she says, only reading the newspaper or standing at the window looking outside. But when she comes into my room she stands there with her hands on her hips. They think I can't see. But I hear like a bat as I sit with my eyes closed. I hear everything in the house, even when she laughs with the woman in the kitchen. What are they laughing at, those two? I can hear the tightening of the muscles between her eyes and the grinding of her teeth as she looks at me. She taps her foot as she looks in the mirror and her eyes glaze as she says: "What do you want me to say?"

Something has come into my life and changed it. No longer a mild ebbing towards death; no soft sleeping in the afternoons or going to bed early with hot chocolate on a tray, lying in my bed near the window, the curtain lapping softly while Hannah reads.

Home.

Since Hannah's illness, Amy and Paul surround me like wolves, snapping at my heels, and the only one who is quiet is Sophie. "Do you see how they treat me, Sophie?"

"Do you remember the time with the tortoise?" I can hear the whine in my voice. I'm even laughing a little, high-pitched and cracking, "... Heeeeeee..." I clown and hiccup to make her smile. She gets up and walks out. I know she hates me because she wants me to beg. An old man in a room, a father in my daughter's house. So now I beg: "It's not my fault,"

I say in a quivering voice. "I've gone white overnight." She doesn't care: "Only because you stopped painting your hair," she answers." She doesn't care what she says. I have to shout down the passage: "Your mother was always going out with her friends. I knew she would get sick. She was always arguing with Sophie about the phone and the tea and the sugar and speaking to people through the window. She put earplugs in her ears at night so she wouldn't hear me. I would call and call for help, and by then she would have to change my sheets and wash me. She left the bedroom of her own choice. Then she complained that Sophie slept next to me in her bed."

"She sleeps next to you like a wife. Let her service you like a wife," Hannah had said. "I've saved and hoarded like a miser and Sophie can have it all."

I have to shout it down the passage: "I've given her everything. I took her everywhere and waited in the car like a driver. I'm left with nothing. Small change in my pocket. Do you see this jacket? Twenty-five years old."

Love has turned to hate. Amy blames me for being alive and her husband is in his grave. I begged to die before him. I told her so. Please let me die first, I begged, I don't know of whom. I would have thrown myself off the balcony if I could have lifted my legs. Seeing him every week with that hat on his head, and getting thinner, and me eating Amy's food at Sunday lunch. I always wanted more and I spilt the food on my shirt and my tie with relish. It didn't help him if I didn't eat. But we were having a race to the finish, he and I. We both knew it. Who would die first? Amy said nothing, as though he had a toothache or a cold, and Hannah and I didn't say a word. But we watched him getting thinner. I begged to die first, I don't know of whom.

And now I'm living in his house, and I use his bathroom, and his toothbrush is still in the glass. I put my towel on his towel-rack, and I'm eating his food. She doesn't look at me as she struts up and down the passage in her boots. "I begged to die before him," I shout. "It's not my fault." She doesn't care. But soon, if they wait a little, there will be two widows in the family, not one.

Paul has asked me to stay with him. Then when I eat he tells me that I breathe too heavily and I slop my food. He runs into the room and he runs out. "Why don't you stay with me and talk?" I ask him. "What do you want me to say?" "Tell me about the world," I answer. "I can't see. I never go out. Tell me."

Two weeks with Amy and two weeks with Paul. I carry my blankets and my radio from house to house, and Sophie brings her blankets and the inflatable mattress so she can sleep next to me on the floor. I bring everything and Sophie does all my washing. Must I pay them for board and lodging?

I want to go home.

To my chair in the lounge – Chinese rosewood, dark as molasses – and the tray that Sophie wheels in with my food cut into pieces, and my spoon. I can switch on my radio and hear the news with my lunch and the women's program in the afternoon: a letter from a nun in Peking, or poetry, or cheap ways to feed a family of six. I can sleep in my chair with that low murmur in the room. Sophie will hear me when I call, and she can stand in the kitchen laughing and talking to her friends through the window. Then she'll wash me softly and put me to bed with hot chocolate and toast, tuck me in and shift the small table next to the bed so I don't fall out. She'll undress and get into the bed next to mine, wearing her cotton nightie and her little cotton cap, and sleep with one eye open all night. I'll hear her turn in the night and mumble something in a language I don't understand. Does she dream in that language? And if I wake I'll touch her arm next to mine. Smooth and black. So soft.

If I pay her she'll stay. That's why I need the money, must I shout and scream until they understand?

I want my chair in the corner, my stick against the wall and my hat on the table.

I want to go home.

THIRTY-FIVE
Sophie

I COME WHEN I'M CALLED. NOT WHEN HE CALLS FIRST TIME, BECAUSE SOMEtimes he forgets and falls asleep. But second time I come when I'm called. Amy always tells him not to shout. "Why do you always shout?" she asks. He doesn't shout the first time. Only the second: "Sophieeeeee." Modimo! But I never come first time. I stand in the kitchen and I can hear everything. The madam says she's tired, and it's true. But I'm the one who sleeps with him at night. I put him to bed after supper. Slowly we walk to the bedroom and he sits on the edge of the bed where I undress him and wash him softly. He lies back and allows me. He closes his eyes and I know where an old man gets his pleasure. Just a little comfort before he goes to bed with his blue feet and red eyes. No harm. Then I put a net around my hair and I undress myself near him and sleep on the bed next to his. Deep in the night he puts his hand on my arm. I can feel him looking at me but my eyes are closed and I don't move. Modimo waka! I put my hand on his and wait for him to turn over and soon he is asleep again. In the morning I make his bed and I make mine and we both drink sweet tea. I take him slowly to the toilet. Sometimes he leaves little drops on the floor if we take too long. Then I stand outside waiting for him to be finished. Sometimes I have to help him stand up. The madam always asks me how many times he woke up or if I made him a sandwich and some milk in the night, and I tell her. We look at each other like two wives and decide what we will make him for lunch. Then I make it.

I don't mind. I will look after him when his children have all gone home, or she has gone out or gone to sleep. I always come when I'm called. The second time. If I'm standing at the window with my friends or on the telephone, then I come the third time.

I need the job.

THIRTY-SIX
Two Widows

AMY KNOWS THAT MAX IS DEAD WHEN SHE SEES THE CHAIR. BEFORE THAT the knowledge was abstract: a piece of information, the use of the word "dead", a sound like a thud, a thump, empty of meaning. But when she goes to the flat she sees the chair and knows. It is just a chair standing in the corner of the room: wooden, with curved arms on which to lean his elbow or to rest his cup, straight-backed making right-angles to the seat, a scaffold to support his buttocks; firewood if necessary. And not what she always believed it to be: a throne. And the walking-stick, a whittled piece of wood, and not what she thought it was: a mace. It's knob that glowed like an owl's eye is going dull now, for want of the hand that warmed and oiled it. The room? Just a room, threadbare like his favourite jacket, and cluttered with too many ornaments and arrangements of dried flowers and too many candlesticks and photographs and a large spiky plant that is not doing too well and food-stains on the carpet under the chair where he ate his meals. Just a room with a vaporiser next to the chair: a yellowing plastic container that no longer emits the vapours that encircled him. Material objects have become inanimate and the bearded prophet does not inhabit his chair. The world is vacant and without rule.

Hannah comes into the room and sits on the chair. Amy waits for the transformation. But a chair is a chair with a white-haired woman of seventy-eight sitting on it in the ordinary way that people do.

"The old order changeth yielding place to new," he used to chant, occupying his chair, his eyes closed and his right hand on his staff, surrounded by steamy mists.

Amy would play Fool to his Lear and say: "You talk like a character in a Gothic novel. Why don't you just speak plain conversational English?" Then he would change his voice to a squeaky falsetto and sing:

O Mr Porter what shall I do?
I want to go to Bendigo, send me back to Crewe

I want to go to London as quickly as I can
O Mr Proter what a silly boy I am.

He would laugh a cracking falsetto laugh, ". . . hee hee heeeeeeeeeeee . . ." silly, with the Fool looking on. With everyone else he was stern.

"The flat looks nice and clean, doesn't it?" Hannah asks, passing her eyes over the chairs and tables, arranged in a pattern that matched the configuration of their lives: his chair in the corner with a small red cushion to comfort the ache in his spine. It was placed next to the door so he wouldn't have to walk far when he came into the room; and near the telephone so he could hear every conversation and orchestrate it; and near the passage so he could hear the front door; and just over the passage from the kitchen so he could call Sophie for a cup of tea or a small piece of bread and cheese because he was so weak he thought he was going to die, or to ask for a plate to be removed, or for the curtains to be opened, or closed. "You never leave Sophie alone," the Fool would say, and he would sit quietly for a while.

There is Hannah's chair directly across the room, facing him when they drank tea or when she read to him from the books or they spoke about money. He spoke about money, bitter talk: "You'll take it all, I know you, and leave me alone in the flat after I've sacrificed a lifetime," and Hannah crying and crying.

Against the window there is the couch for visitors with a little side-table for a cup of tea and a piece of cake, and a heater behind the vaporizor with one bar burning because his legs were blue and could never get warm, and the jar of red and green boiled sweets for when his mouth went sour. He could suck a boiled sweet slower than anyone, draining out its nectar, sitting in his chair with his eyes closed and his cracked tongue curling around the sweet red ball. One was enough and his freckled hands would screw the lid closed and tight. Hannah could never suck a sweet. She would grind it noisily until there was nothing left and look around for more. There is the mother-of-pearl candlestick from Marina on top of the small cupboards where he hid his peanut brittle, eating a little square at a time, wrapping it up carefully and putting it back in a dark corner where a few old prunes got harder. And then there is the small table in front of Hannah's chair with a pen and writing paper and the book of universal things.

"It was a good funeral. We sent him off well," says Hannah. "Except for the two sisters. I'll never forgive them. Miriam, his half-sister, said she couldn't afford to leave Port Elizabeth. I remember watching hungrily as he twirled his fingers through her hair. We travelled our lives together but he never touched me that way. And my sister Dora – she knew him for fifty years but said her legs were too swollen to come to the funeral. Fifty years is not time enough. It is two weeks today, then tomorrow is Wednesday and then Thursday makes it another week and a week after that it will be a month and then two months. I only want the time to pass. I want it to be three months and then four. If only I could forget, but I have to remember. I'm keeping his jacket with the leather buttonholes and one pair of shoes and his hat. They have to live somewhere. Sophie and I haven't stopped cleaning. Don't you think the flat looks nice and clean?"

Amy looks at her with awe. Only two weeks. Hannah is standing in the fire of deepest distress. The nights are bad. Next week will be better and the week after a little better. She remembers how Hannah would tuck a towel into his shirt collar when he was eating and how sometimes she would feed him with a spoon, cupping her hand under it to prevent spilling. Everything is a muddle and a mess, and a cushion in the back for pain, and a sour taste in the mouth, and food-stains on the carpet, and a smell of urine on the mattress. Only death is "nice and clean".

"I can't understand it," says Hannah. "It was the only time I left him in fifteen years and he leaves me. It wouldn't have happened had I been there. Perhaps he was embarrassed about his dying, or even ashamed of the ultimate weakness, and he only permitted Sophie to see it. She was the one to bath him and take him to the toilet and she cleaned it after him. Perhaps he thought it was one of the dirty things he had to do and she was the only one who could watch him without interfering, quietly allowing him. Or maybe it was his way of finally excluding me: to die when I wasn't there. The same as when he shut the door and I had to wait outside his office when he was talking business to Theo. I never had the courage to leave him but he slipped away forever when I wasn't here."

Amy thinks of the strange holiday they had had in Cape Town, she and Hannah staying in a friend's apartment with unfamiliar photographs on the tables and other people's clothes in the cupboards. Hannah had said that a hotel would have been better because you never knew who had been sleeping in the bed before you. Here, she was sleeping in Vera's place and

Amy was lying in the hollow made by Harry's chubby body and perhaps you could even have their dreams, lying next to each other in their matrimonial bed. During the day Hannah and Amy had sat at the window, watching the sea beat against the rocks, withdraw its wobbling mass to plunge itself on the rocks again. "It can never be still," Hannah had said. "I can't sleep at night with the sound of it."

They had gone for walks in the street, looking up at the villas suspended over the sea at wondrous angles, dense tropical gardens, and cars housed in marbled garages. And the dark, old building being demolished next door. Hannah shivered every time she passed it. "I don't know why that building frightens me – dark and empty – with the names of the last occupants still nailed to the doors." They passed games arcades and people with rotten teeth putting coins into machines, and corner shops selling milk and newspapers and spotted bananas, vagrants leaning against windows for a long time with nowhere else to go, seagulls standing one-legged against the wind on an empty beach, old men in white flannels and old ladies walking old dogs, balconied apartments looking far out to sea, and gracious villas there at the Cape of Storms. Inside the borrowed flat again, staring at the sea, not knowing why they had come to Cape Town except for a vague notion of holiday, and not knowing what to do. Hannah was always thinking of her uncle in Cape Town who had called her a greener and put her out to work in a shoe store as an assistant. Hannah shuddering every time she passed the dark, half-demolished building.

Then the morning phone call that rang like a scream through the sleeping flat: "There was no sign of a struggle and he had a quiet face. It was the gentlest thing he has ever done," Paul said. "He ate so well last night. He wanted another lamb chop and I said: 'No, I think you've had enough.' And we quarreled about it. He began ranting: 'O reason not the need. You heavens give me patience, that patience I need.' Later on I gave him a glass of port and he sat very quietly for a long time drinking it and went to bed. Then I fell asleep in my chair and it was too late to say goodnight to him. Sophie came running to call me in the morning. We had all slept right through."

"I can't understand it," Hannah says. "We went to Cape Town for a holiday and all we could do was walk the streets and watch the sea. And that mountain sticking up in the middle of everything so that you have to crawl around it. That rock that sits like a stone God. I never want to go to Cape Town again."

"I'll teach you how to be a widow," Amy says. "Now listen to me well. Sit in a corner on a low bench. Low for humility. Listen quietly with your head bowed while the bearded man in black chants from a book and mourners in black hats say 'Amen'. Then offer your cheek to be kissed and your hand to be shaken by people who wish you 'long life'. Comfort them as they shed a tear. Don't be confused by the table covered in cakes and biscuits and buns and sweets. Drink tea and eat. Meanwhile the men talk business and the women correct their lipstick. Soon everyone says goodbye and they all go home. Most of them you will never see again and you will be left alone. And there my teaching ends, because whatever you do now you will have to learn for yourself. But the learning will be hard."

"I can't believe that he asked for another lamb chop and I refused," Paul says.

In his house all the pictures are turned to face the wall and the mirrors are covered with cloth.

Amy and Hannah are living together in Amy's house now. But Hannah still keeps her flat with Sophie, going there early in the morning, so there is "one small place in the world which is my own".

"I don't know why you leave so early in the morning," Amy says. "It's so cold that you have to pour hot water on the windscreen to remove the ice. I hear you leave and the engine keeps stalling."

"I have to leave early in the morning or else there is too much traffic on the highway and I have to let Sophie into the flat."

"But it's too early for Sophie. It's still dark and Sophie is downstairs in her room."

"I don't know why I leave so early. I don't know. But this morning I was cleaning the flat and I found his spare set of teeth and an old hat and a piece of paper where he wrote some words:

First comes morning then comes evening
So we pass our time away
First come young ones then come old ones
Over the hills and far away.

From Amy's house they have found a short cut to the cemetery: up Jacaranda Drive to the corner, then up the hill past the grocer with all the imported cheeses and the smell of fresh coffee grains as you walk past the door and the rows of Italian salami, past the Indian shop and the Greek restaurant and all the dress shops of Rosebank. Then west all the way down Tyrwhitt Avenue, past the antique shops of Seventh Avenue and the cafe that sells fresh boerbrood on Sundays. Turn left into Emmarentia Drive and stop at the Portuguese fish and chip shop for vetkoek; try and be there at eleven in the morning when they are still frying in the fat. From there it is ten minutes away.

Very quiet at the cemetery during the week; only the gardeners weeding and trimming grass. Amy and Hannah walk down the pathway to the newest section. They look for the only pink tombstone: Jerusalem stone. "Flesh-coloured," Hannah had said when they stood in the stonemason's yard choosing it. Small white flowers have grown like lace over the mound. "So strange to see him crowded into a line with all the others. He always liked to be alone. He only had one friend in his life." Hannah reads the words on the stone: HE WAS A MAN. TAKE HIM FOR ALL IN ALL . . .

They put a small stone on the side of the grave for remembrance and walk away. Amy is looking for the tree that covers her husband's grave. Small bushes with fine white flowers grow over it. Amy takes a leaf and crushes it in her hand to release the scent. She stands there looking and looking at the inscription: I KNOW A BANK WHERE THE WILD THYME BLOWS . . . A smell of herbs rises from her fingers.

On the way home Amy says, "That time when you were sick and Pa was staying in the house with me, I was so angry with him that it felt like hate. My heart was a piece of meat with a knife in it. There was an ache in my chest as though my heart was bleeding. It was worse than when he died."

Hannah says, "I had a dream about him last night. He looked so dirty that I tried to wash him. I washed and washed but I couldn't make him clean."

The middle of winter; end of July. The Highveld is a bald plateau smothered in a sky-white blindfold. Air wheezes like an old man's breath and rasps like sharkskin. Warm words emerge, touch the cold and turn to smoke.

In the evenings they both sit together in Amy's house watching the sky slowly darken behind the bare willow branches until the delicate outlines, like an ink etching, fade and all definition disappears. Sometimes they argue because Amy likes to sit in the twilight listening to the cry of the birds, the last piercing wail before they take to their nests. Hannah wants bright lights so she can read.

"I hate the darkness," says Hannah.

"And I love it. To be quiet and watch the slow dissolving of day. Then how can we both sit in the same room?"

She goes outside to walk under the night sky, a wide winter sky, perforated with stars. Hannah stands at the door calling and calling: "Amy, where are you? Come back inside." Amy draws the curtains and brings in the dogs. There is only one room in the house that she closes and locks. But on Friday nights, with the candles burning and a white tablecloth on the table, she leaves it open and makes a prayer.

"I still cannot believe," Hannah says, " how I cried about the money. And after all that fighting he has left everything behind, unwatched, unguarded. So much has been left behind. So much has been abandoned – one's youth, one's faith, one's country. But this time I'm staying. And I'm still saving money every month. What am I saving for?"

"I must boil water to make the dogs' food," Amy says.

She goes into the kitchen to sweep. She can never be satisfied. She sweeps and sweeps until the last crumb is caught.

"Can't we leave it until tomorrow?" Hannah asks. "No one will see."

"But I'll see. No one can sweep a kitchen floor like me. The ordinary things go on."

A rhythm has settled into their lives and there is a kind of normality about it. On Friday nights they cover the table with a white cloth and candles and shining silver. A rich smell of baking food, of cream and butter and rising bread fills the house. The smell of Hannah's cooking. The rest of the week they eat a little bread and cheese. They talk of things: old dogs that shared their lives, a defunct washing machine standing in a corner. How old? Fifteen years? A good age for washing machines. Pajamas and vests that hang on a thread, their last winter, blankets that air in the sun. And so they count their days.

They sip whisky from small glasses and watch the dogs twitching in their dreams. All creatures take cover at night. Amy puts her head next to the small dog to feel the slow cycle of his breathing. A living thing. Hannah is beginning to fall asleep over her book – a Russian novel.

Outside, sticks lie scattered across the grass. Marina has been pruning the fruit trees and lopping off wood, but she has left some old stumps and logs, some hollow and rotten, some lined with abandoned beehives and birds' nests. A dry wind is blowing stiff branches against the window making light tapping sounds against the glass.

Sometimes Hannah walks through the garden, watching the ravages of the season. The brave land has suffered floods and famine. Her country now, after fifty years. It has taken a lifetime to understand it. The Highveld; the wide bright plateau enduring its winter drought, and the dew getting less and less in the morning air.

Deep in their centres the trees are expanding at the core. And under the crust they are beginning to swell at their nodes; incipient growth, rising under the husk that contains it; wanting to erupt . . . waiting for the mysterious signal.